FOR YOU, THE READER...
A SPECIAL INVITATION

Come journey with
wildest fro

Diamond
Wildflower
Romance

A breathtaking new line of
searing romance novels

...where destiny meets desire
in the untamed fury of the
American West.

...where passionate men
and women dare to embrace their
boldest dreams.

...where the heated rapture
of love runs free and wild
as the wind!

He brought a blush to her cheeks . . .

He couldn't look her in the eye. Instead, he stared down at his hat brim as if it held the answers to his problems. "I, uh . . . oh, hell." Ben forced his gaze up and noticed the rapid rise and fall of her chest before meeting her eyes. "I just wanted to say I'm sorry for the things I said yesterday. At the restaurant."

She cocked her head.

"You know, what I said about settin' fire to—"

"I remember," she interrupted hastily.

"I don't know why I went on like that, Kota. Never should have said something like that to a lady."

"Thank you."

"Oh, no need to thank me." He smiled his relief. "After all, what we did together didn't need talkin' about, we both know. And I don't think either one of us is likely to forget it. At least, I know *I'm* not gonna—"

"*Ben.*"

"Sorry. Doin' it again, aren't I?"

Dakota chuckled softly. She had the distinct feeling Ben Cable didn't apologize very often.

"It's just that," Ben whispered, "every time I see you, I remember. Just standing here with you, I want to touch you, kiss your—"

"Ben, please."

"But, Dakota, you have to understand what it's like for me. What goes through my mind every time I'm near you."

"I do understand." *Better than you know*, she thought . . .

FRONTIER BRIDE

ANN CARBERRY

DIAMOND BOOKS, NEW YORK

FRONTIER BRIDE

A Diamond Book / published by arrangement with
the author

PRINTING HISTORY
Diamond edition / August 1992

ISBN: 1-55773-753-3

Diamond Books are published by The Berkley Publishing
Group, 200 Madison Avenue, New York, New York 10016.
The name "DIAMOND" and its logo are trademarks
belonging to Charter Communications, Inc.

PRINTED IN THE UNITED STATES OF AMERICA

10 9 8 7 6 5 4 3 2 1

To Mary and Dan Child,
the Casaccio Family
and the Omaha Wild Bunch
with love

One

THE heavy downpour made it almost impossible to see. Dakota stared determinedly into the rain, sure she'd heard the faint drumming of horse's hooves. Finally the indistinct outline of a horse and rider came into view.

Instantly alert, she reached for her rifle just inside the front door. Then she stepped out of the open doorway's rectangle of light and moved into the shadows on the porch.

The horse pulled up short about twenty feet from the porch, and an unfamiliar voice called out, "Hello the house. Can I ride in?"

"Come ahead," she answered warily.

Advancing slowly the stranger fixed her with a dark stare, then climbed down from his big black horse, flipped the reins over the hitching post, and ran up the steps to the relative dryness of the open front porch.

In silence Dakota watched as he removed his hat and slapped it against his legs, shaking rainwater over the roughly planed boards. He ran a hand through his hair and commented as he unbuttoned his slicker, "A real gullywasher. And we sure can use it."

She held the rifle a little higher. Though the ranch hands were just across the yard in the bunkhouse, it paid to be careful.

He saw the movement and smiled. A slow, taunting smile that didn't reach his dark eyes. "Now, ma'am, there's no need for that."

She said nothing.

He studied her carefully, then shrugged and said, "I've got a message for you. That is," he added as his eyes roved over her impressive figure, "if you're Miss Dakota Lane."

"I am."

"Well, ma'am, I'm Mick Owens, from over to Red Creek? And Sheriff Cable sent me out here to let you know about your brother, Tenn."

"Well, what is it?" Dakota's voice faltered slightly. Her stomach tensed, and she could feel the pounding of her heart. It had to be bad news. There was no other explanation. She should have known something was wrong. Tenn had been gone too long with no word.

"Uh, ma'am? Suppose I could have a cup of coffee? It's been a mighty wet ride."

Dakota looked at him carefully, her sharp blue eyes assessing him. No stranger to the hazards of western life, she considered herself a good judge of character, and there was something about this man that made her reluctant to have him in her home. It was obvious, though, the man had no intention of telling her his news until he was good and ready . . . and if he caused any *real* trouble, she could always call her foreman, Jess, in from the bunkhouse.

Owens smirked at her, amused by her hesitation.

Finally Dakota showed him into the house. She kept her rifle with her, barrel down, and crossed the polished floor to the cast-iron stove in the far corner. Dakota leaned the rifle against the wall and quickly filled two cups with steaming black coffee from the always-ready blackened pot. She set both cups on the long handmade kitchen table, then sat down on one of the matching benches.

Owens set his hat on the table, then took off his rain slicker and tossed it carelessly on the floor beside him.

After a quick, disgusted glance at the wet slicker and the resulting puddle, Dakota turned her attention back to the man sitting opposite her. He appeared to be enjoying his control of the situation.

Patience gone, Dakota snapped, "You have your coffee. Now tell me about Tenn."

He took a long drink and began. "Your brother hit town about two weeks ago. Didn't have too much trouble arranging to sell his cows. Got a good price for 'em, too. Or so I hear. Some stranger in town. Paid top dollar." He took a few more sips of coffee, making a slurping sound that grated on Dakota's nerves.

"And—"

A door behind her flew open, and the round, worried face of Maria, housekeeper and surrogate mother to Dakota, poked out. "Qué pasa, niña?" she asked with her black eyes pinned on Owens.

Hurriedly Dakota soothed her. "It is nothing, Maria. Go back to bed." She stood and gently pushed the older woman back into her room. But Maria had no intention of going anywhere. The short, heavy woman stepped closer to the table, her black eyes suspiciously watching the intruder.

"I will stay," she said softly, her arms crossed over her ample bosom.

Dakota sighed and accepted defeat. There was no arguing with the woman once her mind was made up. Even at the ripe old age of twenty, Dakota knew she was still Maria's "child."

Turning back to face the man who silently watched her, she said, "Well, let's hear it."

The slovenly man, obviously irritated by the older woman's presence, took a deep breath and stared at the inky liquid in his cup. "He got himself a room at the hotel, and it looks like somebody broke into his room during the night, stole the money, and shot your brother."

"Shot!"

"Santa Maria," the older woman mumbled as she hurriedly crossed herself.

"Why didn't anyone tell me?" Dakota shouted. "How is he?"

"Hold on, ma'am," Owens said, completely unruffled by her anger. "Nobody said he was dead. In fact, Doc Burns says he's doin' real fine. As for not telling you, that was Sheriff Cable's doin'. He figured that if your brother died, you wouldn't have time to get there anyway, and if it looked like he was going to make it, well . . . then we ought to wait till he looked a sight better than he did."

At the thunderous look on her face, Owens continued quickly. "He said we shouldn't upset a woman unless we had to."

"Oh, he did, did he?" Dakota paced the room furiously. "How long ago was Tenn shot?"

"Three days." Owens glanced at Maria, whose mumbling had grown more fervent.

"Three days!" Dakota's hands balled into ineffectual fists at her sides. She glared at the messenger and challenged, "How dare that sheriff decide when and what I should be told? What gives him the right? Well, I'm leaving for town right now. Tonight."

A clap of thunder boomed and seemed to shake the house.

"In this storm, ma'am, I wouldn't if I was you. It wasn't raining when I left town. Rode right into it. And this here storm's a beaut."

Cold reason swamped her. He was right, of course. If she hadn't let her fear and anger get the best of her for a moment, she never would have suggested leaving during a storm. It wouldn't do Tenn any good if she got herself drowned in a flash flood!

"All right. I'll leave at first light. If you're ready then, you can ride back with me. Meanwhile, go out to the bunkhouse and tell the foreman you'll be staying the night. He'll show you where to bed down your horse."

Owens smiled at her as he left, but in her haste to make preparations for her trip, Dakota didn't see him. Her thoughts were for Tenn. And for what she would have to say to Sheriff Cable when she saw him.

Dakota was packed and waiting beside her horse by the time Owens entered the yard to saddle his own mount.

She stifled a yawn and thought about the previous night's arguments with Maria.

As soon as the door closed behind Owens, Maria had sailed through the house, shouting orders as she went.

"Get me your carpetbag, niña. Hurry. There is much to do."

Dakota carried the dilapidated old bag into her bedroom to find that Maria had already started sorting through her clothes.

"Maria . . ." Dakota crossed the room and picked up the dresses off the bed. She moved to hang them back up on their pegs, but Maria snatched them from her. "Maria. I won't be needing any dresses, for heaven's sake. I'm only going to town to see Tenn!"

"You should look like a lady when you are among strangers." The older woman carefully began folding the somewhat faded calico gowns.

Dakota flopped down onto the mattress. "Tenn won't even know me if I'm wearing one of those!"

"Hmmph!" Maria shook her finger at the young woman. "And you are *proud* of this?"

"What's wrong with how I look?" Dakota brushed at her shirt self-consciously.

The housekeeper reached out and grasped Dakota's chin firmly with a work-hardened hand. "You are a beautiful girl, niña. Why do you wish to hide that fact?"

"I'm not hiding anything."

"Ah. Sí. Well, then, you will be happy to have your dresses with you. Do you not remember the last time you went into town? All of the talk from the ladies? The whispers? The stares?"

Dakota remembered perfectly well. It was the main reason she hadn't been to town for months. But, she told herself . . . she wasn't hiding. She simply didn't care to make the long trip into Red Creek. And now that she *had* to go, she'd rather go as herself . . . no matter what anyone else thought.

"I'll be wearing my pants on the ride."

Maria considered this for a moment, then offered a compromise. "Sí. But you will take your dresses with you. You cannot always dress like a *vaquero*, little one." She smiled gently. "You are like my own child, and while you are in the company of strangers, I would be shamed to think my child was dressed as any trail hand."

Remembering that conversation now, Dakota smiled. Maria'd won, as usual. Though Dakota had no intention of actually wearing the gowns that were now carefully packed in the carpetbag tied down behind her saddle.

As she brushed at her long, black-clad legs, Dakota shook her head. It wasn't that she was deliberately trying to shock or outrage anyone by her choice of clothing. But Dakota refused to wear cumbersome dresses or to ride sidesaddle just to win the approval of the local gossips.

She was strapping her holstered pistol to her hip when Jess Turner, the foreman, came quietly up beside her and laid his callused hand gently on her shoulder. Dakota smiled at the only "father" she'd ever known.

Fifty years old, with a lined, weatherbeaten face and a gruff manner, he was also a man of unlimited patience and a kind heart. At the same time he demanded and received the loyalty and respect of the men who worked for him.

A tall woman, Dakota stood almost five feet eight inches in her boots. She looked directly into Jess's eyes and saw the worry written there.

"I'd feel a lot better about this," he growled, "if you'd stop bein' so damn stubborn and let me or one of the boys ride along with you." His gray eyes sought the man across the yard just swinging into his saddle. "I don't trust that young fella. I don't care *who* sent him."

She smiled at his concern, and though she would never admit it, she, too, was a little worried about going alone with Owens. There was something about him . . . maybe it was the fact that his eyes seemed to be constantly moving. Never staying still long enough to look at you directly. Shaking away her own uneasiness with a toss of her head, she said with more confidence than she felt, "You know you're needed right here on the ranch. It's all we have left, Jess. We *have* to make this place work."

He frowned. "This ain't Texas, you know. It won't happen again."

"We have to make sure of that. I'll be all right." Dakota laid her hand on his arm for a moment. "I'll keep an eye on him, don't you worry."

She gathered up her mass of fawn hair, twisted it into a knot on top of her head with one hand, and with the other situated her hat firmly on top. Then she slipped into a dark brown leather coat that Tenn had given her the Christmas before.

Stepping into the stirrup, she swung her other leg over the horse's back. "I'll be back as soon as I can." Her strong thighs hugged the body of the chestnut gelding as she pulled the collar of her white linen shirt out from under her coat, then picked up the reins. With a last look at Jess and Maria waving from the porch, she turned her horse toward the main gate.

Dawn streaked the clear Nevada sky with brilliant color as the two riders left the ranch behind. The huge white clouds were outlined in bright crimson that faded off into the palest lavender. And Dakota scarcely noticed. If it weren't for the muddy ground and the still-damp morning air, Dakota would have found it hard to believe that the previous night's storm had ever happened.

They'd been gone from the ranch more than an hour when Owens finally spoke.

"I surely do admire the way you fill out them clothes, Miss Dakota."

She snapped her head around and gave the man riding behind her a withering glare. It didn't stop him.

"Yes, sirree bob! You're a fine-lookin' woman."

Dakota swallowed back the anger rushing through her. She should have known better! Her own instincts had tried to warn her about the man. Now she was in the middle of nowhere with the fool!

"Mighty fine. Why, I reckon you're about the nicest-lookin' female in these parts. How come you never come to town? Don't you like folks?"

Dakota pulled up on the reins and the gelding came to a stop. Turning in the saddle, she met the grinning man's eyes before answering. "I can't tell you how little your opinion matters to me, *Mr.* Owens. So I would take it kindly if you would keep it to yourself. And as to why I don't go to town much, it is to avoid havin' to listen to fools tell me that I look 'mighty fine.' "

He stiffened at her tone, but before he could reply, she'd turned her horse away and was once more trotting toward Red Creek.

Several hours later Owens called a halt. Dakota would have been content to keep going, but the man insisted on giving the horses a break.

In a tight cluster of pines on the bank of a small stream, now swollen from the storm waters, they dismounted. While Owens tied the horses where they could reach both grass and water, Dakota sank to the damp ground, more tired than she'd thought. She took off her coat, then her hat, shaking her head to release her hair from its knot. The slight breeze felt delicious on her warmed skin. Leaning back against a tree, she settled herself comfortably, closed her eyes, and vowed to let herself rest only a moment.

Though her body was tired, her mind raced with thoughts of Tenn. Fifteen years older than herself, Tenn had always tried to be both mother and father to his younger sister. Their parents had died when Dakota was still an infant, and Tenn, already carrying the responsibilities of an adult, gladly took on the extra burden of raising his sister. Preferring to have her with him, Dakota grew up riding the range with Tenn and the other hands, and she'd learned to shoot almost before she learned to read.

She smiled softly as she remembered the terrible rows she'd had with Maria over the years. No matter how self-sufficient Dakota was on the ranch, the older woman had insisted that her charge be equally at home in the parlor. How Dakota'd hated those sewing lessons! And the time wasted learning to serve meals properly!

When Tenn left to fight in the War Between the States, Dakota, only ten years old, had worked beside Jess Turner day and night, struggling to keep their ranch in Texas together. And still, they'd failed.

She was roused from her woolgathering moments later by the touch of a hand at her throat. She opened her eyes slowly and found Mick Owens's face only inches from her own. Dakota pushed his hand away, and he obligingly moved back a bit. The smile on his face, though, told her he wasn't finished.

"What do you think you're doing?"

A cold smile touched his lips. He rubbed a hand across his stubbled jaw and said, "I figured you and me could get acquainted some." He reached out and touched her arm familiarly. "Have us a little party."

Dakota stood up, keeping her eyes locked with his. "You were wrong."

Owens rose lazily to his feet and shook his head. "That ain't no way to be." He took a step toward her and smiled as she moved back. "You and me . . . we could have a fine time together."

Dakota laughed shortly and let her gaze travel up and down his filthy body contemptuously. "You're out of your head."

"Think you're too good for me, do ya?"

She didn't answer, just turned her back on him.

Owens closed the space between them, grabbed her shoulders, and spun her around. "Don't you go playin' the high and mighty 'lady' with me, darlin'." He ran his hand over the line of her hip. "Why, soon's I seen you . . . I knew how it would be. No *lady* would wear a getup like this."

He lowered his head and planted his too-full lips against hers. Dakota gagged and gave him a hearty shove. What would *he* know about *ladies*? she fumed silently. She pushed past him and marched to her horse. Any other time his suggestion would have been funny. Almost. But now, in the middle of nowhere, all alone, Dakota's only thought was to be rid of him.

"What are you doin'?" he shouted.

"I'm going to town. To see my brother." She swung aboard her horse and grabbed for the reins, but Owens was faster and held them just out of her reach.

"*I* say when we leave. The sheriff sent *me* to get you. I'm in charge here."

A flicker of unease touched her, but she couldn't let him see it. Instead she stared down at him and said haughtily, "Any man who would put *you* in charge of anything isn't fit to be sheriff!"

He lunged for her, and Dakota drew her pistol, pointing it directly at him.

"Here, now! What's that for?"

"Whatever is necessary."

"You got no call to pull a gun on me," he whined nervously. "I only wanted a little fun."

"Mister, you drop the reins of my horse and you back off."

Eyes wide, he did as he was told.

Her pistol still aimed at him, Dakota reached down and grabbed the reins. While keeping her eye on him, she also gathered up the reins to his mount.

"Whatcha doin'?"

"I think you could use a walk, Mr. Owens. To think. Maybe next time you won't pester a lady so."

"Hold on! You can't leave me out here! I didn't do nothin' to you! Just wanted a little kiss is all." He took a step toward her, and she cocked the pistol. He stopped.

"A wise decision." She nodded approvingly. "It's about ten more miles to Red Creek. I suggest you start walking. When I get there, I will tell your precious sheriff where you are. But I don't plan on hurryin'. So if I were you, I wouldn't wait for help."

She backed the horses off a good distance before quickly turning them and urging them into a gallop.

Mick Owens stared after her until she was nothing more than an indistinct shape on the horizon. He couldn't believe she would leave him. Stranded. He took a long look around and sighed helplessly. Nothing. No one. He cursed loud and long and kicked at the dirt viciously before surrendering to the inevitable. Then he began his long walk to town.

Ben Cable leaned back against a porch railing and idly watched the goings-on on the wide, muddy street.

The shop owners of Red Creek were doing a brisk business after spending most of the day cleaning up the remnants of the previous night's storm. Farm wagons pulled by plodding horses lumbered past, and the shouting laughter of children filled the still air. Steam rose from the mudholes covering the thoroughfare as the afternoon sun beat unmercifully down on the small town and its inhabitants.

Ben pulled a bandanna from his back pocket and rubbed it slowly over the back of his neck. The sticky heat was uncomfortable and did nothing to improve his already sour mood.

The closed, forbidding look on his face spoke volumes and served to keep most of Red Creek's citizens at a distance. Men who passed Cable on the extended boardwalk nodded in greeting and moved quickly on.

The town's women, however, were not so easily intimidated. From beneath lowered lashes, they stole approving glances at the big man. More than a few of them nurtured secret dreams of being held and kissed by the taciturn yet fascinating sheriff.

As if unaware of the ladies' attentions, Ben ignored them with a studied indifference.

Clad almost entirely in black, save for his white shirt, he wore no star pinned to his black leather vest.

There was no need. Everyone in town knew who he was . . . and any newcomer with trouble in mind soon met Sheriff Ben Cable.

"How are ya, Ben?"

He turned quickly at the voice so close behind him and smiled at Ike Miller, the owner of the Mercantile. Ike's bald head caught the afternoon sun and reflected it like a mirror. Easygoing and good-natured, it was a wonder Ike was able to stay in business. More than half the ranches surrounding the town were run on lines of credit given by Ike Miller.

"Everything's quiet, Ike."

"Wasn't askin' about the town, Ben." Ike smiled knowingly. Ever since that damned holdup in the hotel, Ben Cable had been as touchy as a mountain lion with a sore paw. Ike, and everyone else in town, knew that Ben was blaming himself for what happened.

"Yeah, I know." Ben's answer was noncommittal, and he turned his eyes back to the street . . . hoping it would discourage any more conversation. It didn't.

"Now, Ben," Ike said firmly as he moved to stand in front of his friend, "you got to go easy on yourself. It wasn't your fault. And everybody around here knows it."

Ben frowned. "Yeah, well, that don't help much, does it?" Six months as sheriff, he thought, and in that time, there'd been the usual number of drunks and brawls, but no major trouble. Not until a few days ago.

Ben shoved the bandanna back into his pants pocket. He removed his hat and ran his callused hand through his sandy blond hair. A slight puff of wind teased his sweat-dampened skin, and he felt the relief of a temporary coolness. He stared solemnly into the too-bright sunlight and let his mind again rework the problem of the attack on Tenn Lane.

From the first time they'd met, Cable had envied Tenn Lane's easy way with people. Ben himself was oftentimes accused of being a cold, unfriendly man, which wasn't the case at all. He was simply uncomfortable in casual conversation. Never really sure just what to say. Especially around women. Not *all* women, he amended with an inward smile. Just the fragile, delicate, rosewatered females better known as True Ladies.

Deliberately Cable wrestled his mind back to the issue at hand. Tenn Lane. *Someone* had crept into the man's hotel room in the middle of the night, robbed him, then willfully shot him and left him for dead. That Tenn had managed to survive was a tribute to both the man's strong will to live and the excellent care he'd been given.

To make matters worse, when Cable's deputy had rushed in at the sound of gunfire, the thieves had shot him as well. Only in deputy Tom Stillwell's case, their aim had been truer. The young, eager lawman had left a widow and two children.

"Ben . . . Ben."

He shook his head and looked at Ike again.

"Tom knew what he was gettin' into the minute he strapped on a gun." Ike leaned closer and kept his voice down. These dang females around town had sharper ears than most hawks. "And Mary Stillwell ain't blamed you!"

Ben straightened slowly and settled his hat back firmly on his head, pulling the brim low over his sky-blue eyes. "It doesn't matter, Ike. Tom was young. He didn't have enough experience. It should have been me in that gunfight. Tom didn't stand a chance."

"He was young, all right," Ike agreed. "But as for experience . . . well, that comes with time. If you're lucky."

"It just doesn't make sense, Ike." Ben shook his head wearily. "Why would thieves pick out a tiny, spot-in-a-road town like Red Creek? And why were they so anxious to shoot their way out? There *has* to be a reason, Ike." He looked down at the shorter man. "And I *will* find it."

Ike met Ben's cold blue eyes and shuddered slightly, glad it wasn't *him* that Cable was after. "I believe you will, Ben. Just you be careful."

As Ike left for his store, Ben glanced at the late-afternoon sun. It was past time for Mick Owens to be back from the Lane ranch. He wished he hadn't had to send Owens . . . the man was unreliable at best . . . but there'd been no choice. Absently Cable tipped his hat to the group of ladies just passing him and thought disagreeably of the task still waiting for him. Dealing with Tenn Lane's sister. He didn't mind admitting, at least to himself, that he would rather be doing anything else. He hoped fervently to whichever gods listened to small-town sheriffs that she wasn't the fainting kind.

"Well, for heaven's sake. Would you look at that?"

The horrified voice of one of the women standing behind him brought Ben abruptly out of his reverie.

It was only then that his weary brain registered and identified the nerve-wracking series of yaps and growls as coming from Henry Jorgensen's ill-mannered hound. Someone down the street shouted at the dog, and he ceased his barking.

Ben looked up then and saw what had brought about both the matron's astonishment and the dog's ire. Slowly Ben tilted his hat back far on his head so it wouldn't impede his view, then he stared at the unexpected vision in the street.

A young woman . . . unlike any other woman he'd ever seen. She rode her horse astride and looked both proud and confident. He smiled and understood the reason for the older woman's reaction. The rider wore men's clothing, obviously cut down to fit. It clung to her every curve, and from what Ben could see, there appeared to be many of them. All in the right places. With her wide-brimmed hat, he couldn't quite make out her features, and she held her head steady, looking neither right nor left, preventing any further observation.

Ben's breath caught in his throat as he stood rooted to the spot, unable to tear his gaze away. She sat her horse like a queen . . . back ramrod straight, chin lifted. The woman seemed to be completely unaware of the stir she was causing, and, Ben acknowledged to himself, it was just as well. Judging from the whispered conversations buzzing around him, the good ladies of Red Creek were not at all pleased with the effect the young woman was having on their menfolk.

Surprisingly, neither was Cable. A flash of anger swept over him as he noticed the hungry male stares being directed at her. He fought down the sudden urge to do battle with every man on the street and tried to ignore the force of his own reaction to her.

His gaze followed her progress with fascination. Unable and unwilling to look away, Ben was drawn to the woman. Like a hungry bear to honey. He'd never experienced anything like this before. An immediate and overpowering urge ... no, *need* to make himself known. To talk ... to touch ... to taste the flavor of her mouth against his.

He shook himself, disgusted. He was no better than a schoolboy! Still, he watched her. She rode slowly past him, without so much as a glance in his direction. He couldn't stop himself. Cable stepped down from the boardwalk ... determined to follow and meet her.

And it was only then he noticed that she was leading Mick Owens's horse behind her own.

Two

Doc Burns, a middle-aged man from the East, practiced medicine out of his home. The small tidy house sat far back off the road, surrounded by carefully tended gardens of both flowers and vegetables. Several large pine trees gave their shade to the cottage, making a cool, inviting picture.

Dakota stepped down from her mount and tied both her horse and Owens's to the split-rail fence outlining the property. She breathed deeply in an effort to calm herself and was rewarded with the mingled bouquet of wild roses and pine needles.

First things first, she told herself. The single most important thing right now was her brother. Unbidden, tears welled in her eyes at the thought of Tenn lying wounded with only strangers to care for him. She blinked them back. He *was* all right. She knew it. He was much too stubborn to give up and die on her.

And once she'd seen him, she would gladly take on the sheriff. Ever since she'd left Owens behind, she'd been rehearsing the things she would say to the man who hadn't bothered to tell her about her own brother's condition! With every mile her anger had grown until now it was a fearsome beast crouching in her breast, waiting its chance to be released.

She'd already forged a mental picture of Sheriff Cable. In her mind's eye she saw him sitting in his chair behind a desk, feet propped up. Bald-headed and in desperate need of a shave and bath, his sweat-stained shirt straining over his considerable paunch, he would be rude, lazy, and dim-witted. Just like his no-account messenger. Dakota's lips twisted into a wry grin as she contemplated hearding the lion in his den.

Her horse snorted and snapped Dakota from her daydreaming. Quickly she walked up the path to the house. At the front door she brushed ineffectually at her dusty clothing and grimaced when she realized it was hopeless. Nothing less than a long bath would do to clean her up. Hesitating just a moment longer, Dakota lifted the brass knocker and let it fall.

The door flew open almost immediately. An elderly woman with soft brown eyes that inspected Dakota from head to toe stood in the opening. Apparently amused by what she saw, the woman smiled. "May I help you?"

"Yes. I'm Dakota Lane," she said, ignoring the old woman's expression. "I've come to see the doctor about my brother, Tennessee?"

Suddenly friendly brown eyes sparkled and a gnarled but strong hand grabbed Dakota's arm and pulled her inside.

"Come in, come in," the old woman urged. "I'm Edna, the doctor's housekeeper. We've been expecting you."

As she was pulled across the polished floor, Dakota yanked her hat off. She shook her head slightly as was her habit, to free her hair from the careless topknot. Long tresses tumbled loosely over her shoulders and down her back. The housekeeper almost gasped aloud at the transformation.

Why, the girl is lovely, Edna thought. The mass of shining brown hair framed an oval-shaped face, the skin lightly tanned to the color of a slightly darkened peach. Clear blue eyes were set under arching brows. Her nose was small and straight and her cheekbones high and pronounced, giving her a delicately exotic look. Her pink, well-formed lips were now shaped in a questioning smile, and Edna mentally shook herself.

"I'm so sorry the doctor isn't here. He's out at the Simpsons' delivering their latest baby."

"But, about my brother?"

"Now, don't you waste your time worryin' about that one! Oh, I'll admit, he gave us a scare right off." Edna's face darkened momentarily. "Nice young man like that. Gettin' shot in his sleep! What *is* this world comin' to?"

"But he's all right now?"

"Oh, land's sakes, yes!"

Dakota sighed, relief engulfing her.

"I tell you, that boy can eat like I don't know what! Anybody can put away as much food as him don't have to worry about dyin'."

Dakota smiled. "Can I see him?"

"Surest thing you know! He's been waitin' on you, like I said." Edna chuckled softly. "He told us that you'd hightail it into town. Said you never could take somebody else's word for anything. Always have to see for yourself."

"He *is* feeling better, then."

Edna turned and pointed at a door just opposite from them. "Your brother is right in there. Why don't you go on in, and I'll make you a nice cup of tea." The old woman smiled encouragingly and hurried off on her errand, leaving Dakota standing uncertainly in the hall.

She wished now she'd taken the time to stop at the hotel and wash up. The faint smell of beeswax and soap hung in the air, making Dakota feel even dirtier than she knew she was. A quick glance at the shining wooden floor illustrated her point.

From the front door to where she now stood, there was an easily seen path of dusty bootprints. She looked uneasily after Edna, then sighed heavily. Nothing to be done about it now. She walked quietly to the door, grasped the brass knob, turned it quickly, and flung the door wide open.

Immediately Dakota wished she'd knocked first. Her brother wasn't alone, and judging from the way he and the pretty woman leapt apart . . . they didn't want anyone to know they'd been kissing.

"Glad to see you're feeling better, Tenn."

He grinned at his sister unabashedly. The strips of white linen wrapped across his bare chest contrasted sharply against his skin, though his usual dark coloring did seem a little grayer than normal. But his brown eyes twinkled as always as he watched Dakota. The other woman in the room had jumped to her feet at the unexpected interruption and now stood at the window, her back to the room.

"Hello, Kota." His voice, so deep and familiar, sounded wonderful to his sister. "You got here almighty fast. Ben told me he sent out a messenger to the ranch only yesterday." He pushed himself a little higher against the pillows at his back and grimaced slightly at the movement. "Wasn't no rush. Didn't they tell you I'm gonna be fine?"

"Yes," Dakota answered as she darted a curious peek at the other woman's back, "they told me. But—"

"I know." Her brother laughed. "You had to see for yourself."

She smiled broadly at his obvious recuperative powers, stepped up to the bed, and kissed his forehead. "I'm glad I came. It's a relief to know you're really all right." Dakota touched the bandages gingerly. "You are, aren't you?"

"Oh, hell, yes!" He patted her hand. "Looks a lot worse than it is."

"If you'll excuse me, I'll leave you two alone." The woman spoke softly and stepped around the bed to leave. Tenn reached out and grabbed her hand.

"Now, wait a minute, Laura. I want you two to meet proper." He tightened his grip on the woman's hand, then raised his gaze to his sister. "Dakota, this is Laura Burns. The doc's daughter. She's been taking real good care of me."

A half smile crossed Dakota's face as she commented wryly, "Yes, I noticed."

Tenn's eyebrows drew together warningly. "You ease up on Laura. She's not used to that sharp tongue of yours." His expression said plainly that this was important to him.

Thoughtfully Dakota's eyes moved to the other woman, who was watching her hesitantly. A pretty woman, Laura Burns was everything that Dakota was not. Small, blond, pink-skinned . . . the delicate picture of femininity. Easy to see why Tenn was smitten.

It was bound to happen. They couldn't go on forever, just the two of them . . . brother and sister living out their lives on an isolated ranch.

In the lengthening silence Dakota sensed a growing apprehension in the other woman. Nervously Laura twisted her fingers, though she kept her gaze even, her chin high. And all at once, Dakota knew it would be all right. That this woman would truly be a match for Tennessee Lane. Even flustered, Laura Burns had sand.

"Thank you for your care of my brother, Laura. It can't have been easy."

The dainty blonde smiled in response and visibly relaxed.

"Here, now! That's no way to talk!" Tenn tried to look aggrieved, but in truth he was much too relieved.

Laura held out her hand to Dakota. "I'm so glad to meet you at last. You see, Tenn and I have been very good . . . friends for a long time. And he's told me so much about you." She smiled fondly at the wounded man and squeezed his hand.

"Well," Dakota said loudly, to get the attention of the other two, "now at least I understand all the extra trips to town Tenn's been making the last couple of months."

She tilted her head to one side and smiled. "*And* why he always found an excuse to go alone."

Tenn shifted uncomfortably, but Laura chuckled. "I came to join Father three months ago." She glanced at Tenn. "That's when we met."

"Where're you from?"

"Boston."

"Red Creek must've taken some getting used to, then."

"Oh, yes. It's all so different out here. But somehow . . ." Laura sighed. "Better. Cleaner, more open, more . . ."

"I think I know what you mean."

Tenn interrupted. "I don't know why I was worried about you two meetin'. You've both already forgot that I'm even here!"

"Well, now," Dakota said, "that's not likely. If not for you gettin' yourself shot, I wouldn't be in town to meet Laura!" They all sobered at the mention of the shooting. Finally Dakota asked, "Tenn, what the devil went wrong? What happened? Who shot you?"

He shook his head slowly, his shaggy brown hair falling over one eye. "You know, I'm still not sure myself. It took me near a week to arrange the sale, then when I found a buyer, a Mr. Gordon . . . he give me a bank draft for the cows." He looked up at Dakota and shook his head in disgust. "I had it in my hands, Kota. Top dollar he paid, too. Near ten thousand dollars." His head dropped onto the pillows. "He wanted his hands to start drivin' the herd so's he could leave that night for Reno to catch the train west. The boys handed the cattle over, then went off to celebrate. I came back here, had dinner with Laura and her pa, then went back to the hotel to sleep." He closed his eyes, as if he could block out the reality of that night. "Sometime during the night I heard a noise. When I sat up in bed, somebody shot me. That's all I know. Don't remember nothing after that."

"Why didn't you put the draft in the bank, Tenn?" Dakota kept her voice even, not wanting to upset him any further.

"Bank was closed when I made the deal. I had planned to deposit it first thing in the morning, then ride home and tell you." He opened his eyes and revealed the depth of his frustration. "I let you down, Kota. And the men. But I'll make it up to you all somehow. You'll see. Everything will work out."

Dakota smiled down at him. "Sure it will. And you've got nothing to make up for, Tenn. None of this was your fault. I am glad you're taking all this so well, though."

Tenn grinned and reached for Laura's hand again. "Hell, Kota . . . we've been broke before. So we don't buy the breeding stock right away." He looked up at his sister. "I'll find a way to meet the mortgage payment. Besides . . . the night I was shot, Tom Stillwell was killed."

Dakota gasped, her shock evident. Tom was such a nice man. Poor Mary. What would she do now?

"Yeah." Tenn nodded at his sister's reaction. "I was the lucky one. Ben Cable says he'll find the man who did all this, so I'm just gonna stay patient." He turned his gaze to Laura and smiled. "And real grateful to be alive."

"Sounds like good sense to me, Tenn." A new voice, deep, commanding, broke into their conversation.

Dakota turned around quickly to face the speaker and was met by eyes as blue as her own. The tall man stood just inside the door, hat in his big hands. Sandy-blond hair, clean and neatly trimmed, was brushed away from his tanned face. He had a strong jaw, his lips turned up slightly at the corners of his mouth, and pale blond eyebrows quirked questioningly as he stood silent under her inspection.

The breadth of his shoulders seemed to dwarf the room, and Dakota knew that *this* man was used to taking charge of any situation.

She felt the power of his even stare briefly before he turned, nodded approvingly at the other woman, and said, "Afternoon, Laura."

He then turned his eyes back to Dakota, and for the first time in a long while she found herself almost wishing she were wearing a dress. She raised her chin defiantly.

The left side of his mouth twitched slightly. "You, I take it, are Miss Dakota Lane?"

"That's right," she answered clearly. "Who are you?"

"Ben Cable." He inclined his head in a brief nod. "I'm the sheriff here."

She fought to control and hide her surprise. Hardly the man she'd imagined he would be! "Good. You've saved me a trip to your office."

Now *he* was caught off guard. Dakota saw it plainly in his eyes. She went on. "Would you explain to me why I wasn't told immediately about my brother?"

He crossed his arms over his chest and tilted his head. "Certainly. Just as soon as you explain to me why you were leading Mick Owens's horse when you rode into town."

"What?"

Dakota barely heard her brother. This was between her and the sheriff.

"Sure. Be glad to." Hands on hips, she took a step closer to her adversary. "I was leading that horse because Mr. Owens decided to *walk* to town."

Cable leaned casually against the doorjamb. "Now, why do I get the feeling you're leaving somethin' out?"

"I'm coming to that," Dakota assured him and took another step closer. "That *imbecile* you sent as a messenger boy *earned* his walk."

"How?"

Dakota met the man's steady gaze and paused. How to explain without embarrassing herself further? It had been bad enough dealing with Owens. She took a deep breath. There was only one way to handle this. Quickly and straightforwardly.

"He made . . . advances to me."

"He did what?" Tenn snarled and tried to move against Laura's restraining hands.

"I'm all right, Tenn," Dakota said clearly.

"What kind of advances?" Cable asked.

"Now, see here, Ben!" Tenn pushed fruitlessly at Laura's hands. "You got no call to talk to my sister like that. If she said Owens did something . . . he *did* it!"

"Simmer down, Tenn." Cable looked past Dakota to her brother. "And quit giving Laura a hard time of it. You'll get yourself to bleedin' again if you don't lay still."

"For heaven's sakes, Tennessee!" Dakota spoke sharply. She hadn't thought of his wound. "Lay down and hush up!"

"Hold on there, Kota. I think—"

"Hush, Tenn!" Dakota looked at her brother with a fierce light in her eyes. "Now, I mean it. If you don't lay back and be still . . . well, I'll finish this conversation with *him*"—she jerked her head toward Cable—"down at the sheriff's office."

Tenn did as he was ordered, a mutinous expression on his face. Laura sent Dakota a grateful look.

"As I said." Cable's voice demanded attention. "What kind of advances?"

"I had my eyes closed. I was . . . resting. I felt his hand on me. On my . . . shirt," she finished lamely.

"By thunder!" Tenn was shouting again.

"Oh, Lord," Laura groaned helplessly. She finally gave up trying to hold her patient.

"Ben! What are you gonna do about this?"

"What would you have me do, Tennessee? Hang him?"

"It's what he deserves, dammit!"

"Is it?" Ben turned once more to Dakota. His eyes gentler now. His strong features patient. "Did he . . . ah . . ."

"No." Dakota turned away from him. Somehow, he didn't fluster her nearly as much when he was angry. *This* Ben Cable was . . . disturbing. "He didn't."

"I *am* sorry about Owens." Cable's voice was soft, low. "If there'd been anyone else to send, I would have."

"It's all right."

"Well, dammit! It ain't all right with me!" Tenn was sitting straight up. "Something's got to be done about that man, Ben!"

Ben seemed reluctant to tear his eyes from Dakota, but he did. Facing Tenn, he said, "I'll have a word with him. But, generally, his kind don't learn till there's a gun pointed at him." Turning back to Dakota, he asked, "How far out did you leave him?"

"About ten miles."

Ben chuckled.

"What's so funny?" Tenn demanded.

"Nothin' special." Ben looked over at the man whose bandages were now turning a pale pink. "Just figured I'd go ahead and let him walk in. Who knows? Maybe it'll help."

Tenn returned the sheriff's smile and lay back down. "Prob'ly won't. But it makes me feel better just thinkin' about it."

As Laura flew into action, getting fresh bandages for Tenn, Ben looked down at Dakota. "How about you? Does it make you feel better, too?"

She met his eyes and smiled. "You know, I think I *am* feeling a little better at that."

In the cheerfully decorated, sunwashed parlor, Dakota perched uneasily on a dainty chair covered in a delicately flowered material.

"Our tea will be here in just a moment," Laura said as she stepped into the room and took a seat opposite the other woman. "Please. Relax," she said, smiling. "The chairs are here to be used, not looked at."

Grateful, Dakota sank back heavily against the chair. She hardly moved when Edna bustled in carrying an overburdened tray that held a tea service and a plateful of cookies. The freshly baked gingersnaps smelled wonderful, and Dakota managed to give the old woman a tired smile as she slipped quietly out of the room.

After calming Tenn down, they'd finally managed to convince him to get some rest. Ben Cable had excused himself quickly, leaving Laura and Dakota alone. And right now the woman who'd ridden all day just to get to town was more ready for a nap than conversation. But there were still too many unanswered questions.

Dakota accepted a steaming cup of tea and after eating three of the still-warm cookies she said, "I really feel awful. These dusty clothes of mine are going to ruin your pretty things. I should have stopped at the hotel before coming over here."

Laughing, Laura waved away Dakota's concerns. "You'd be surprised to know how often the furniture in this room has been cleaned or replaced. Believe me, my father has christened every stick in this house with muddy boots and/or clothing." She paused to sip at her tea, then shrugged her shoulders. "Naturally you came right here before stopping to clean up. You had to check on Tenn."

"It seems so strange," Dakota mused quietly. "To sell the cattle and have the money stolen the same night." She looked up and said, "Laura, do you know anything else about what happened to him?"

Shaking her head, the small blonde stood and walked to the open window, where a slight breeze ruffled the starched white curtains. "No. Nothing." She turned her head and looked at Dakota through suddenly serious eyes. "Ben brought him here right after the shooting, and to tell you the truth, I was simply too worried about him to concern myself with who shot him. And Ben hasn't offered any information. I don't think he knows much about it, either."

"What about Mary Stillwell?" Dakota stood and joined the other woman at the window. "Have you seen her?"

Laura shook her head slightly. "I don't really know her very well . . . and I didn't want to intrude on her now."

Dakota nodded. "I'll go see her this evening. But I'm also going to have another talk with Ben Cable. Somehow, I'll find out what he knows . . . if anything."

"He's a good man. I'm sure he'll find the thief."

"Maybe he will," Dakota said. "But will he be able to recover the money?" She looked down at the shorter woman. "Despite what Tenn says . . . we really do *need* that cash. I don't know how we'll keep the ranch without it."

As if she'd said more than she'd intended, Dakota turned, picked up her hat, and walked quickly to the door. Speaking over her shoulder, she said, "Thanks for the tea, Laura. I appreciate it. Think I'll go over to the hotel, though. I'm so tired, I might fall asleep in that chair if I don't get goin'."

Laura followed her out, and standing by the gate, she watched her new friend swing effortlessly into the saddle. Sighing, she said, "I *do* envy you the courage to wear britches for riding. Sidesaddles are such a bother."

"Make you a deal. For being such a good nurse to my stubborn brother, I'll take a pair of Tenn's pants and cut them down for you."

"Wonderful." Laura laughed. "Then all I'll need is the nerve to wear them."

Remembering the tiny woman's expert handling of Tenn, Dakota replied with a smile, "Don't worry, Laura. You've got the nerve."

Then she turned the big horse and started back for the center of town.

Three

DAKOTA'S knees poked up out of the water as she sat in the too-small bathtub. The desk clerk hadn't been very pleased with having to haul buckets of hot water up the stairs. But the luxury of soaking away the trail grime was worth earning that man's annoyance, she told herself. The hot water had soothed her tired body and restored her flagging spirits.

Sighing, she laid her head back against the tub's rim and stared at the ceiling. Red Creek's only hotel certainly wasn't fancy. Several cobwebs hung in long, filmy threads and danced slowly in the breeze from the open window. The glass chimneys on the lamps were covered in soot, and even the counterpane on the bed was stained with heaven knew what.

She shivered and reluctantly stepped from the tub of rapidly cooling water. Once dry, Dakota wrapped the scratchy towel around her body and walked up to the mirrored dresser against the wall. She picked up the hairbrush she'd packed and pulled it through her wet hair again and again until it was dry and crackling.

As her fingers lifted and combed through the heavy tresses, she looked into the mirror and noticed that on the far wall behind her there was the clear imprint of a boot about halfway up the wall. She turned, her head tilted to one side, and stared at it. Brow furrowed, she said aloud to no one, "Now I wonder how *that* happened!" She was glad she'd paid the hotel clerk extra to ensure clean sheets on the bed.

Dakota shook her head and smiled. Shabby hotel or not, this was the first time she'd ever been *really* on her own . . . and, now that she knew Tenn was all right, it seemed a shame not to enjoy it. At least a little. True, there were still a lot of questions to ask Sheriff Cable . . . and the worry over saving the ranch was never far from mind. But somehow, she couldn't quite ignore the bubble of excitement growing inside her.

Maria wasn't here to ride herd on her. Tenn was certainly in no shape to keep an eye on her, much less voice an opinion on her actions. She was on her own. For the first time.

She glanced over her shoulder at the door. Locked. Dropping the towel, Dakota reached for her chemise. She'd never admit it to Maria, of course . . . but she was certainly happy that the older woman had insisted on packing the few dresses she owned.

As she struggled to push the tiny buttons through the even tinier buttonholes, Dakota told herself that Ben Cable had nothing to do with her sudden desire to look nice. It was simply that while she was in town, a dress made more sense. After all, there was no reason to antagonize the ladies of Red Creek on purpose.

But still, she couldn't quite forget that thrill of excitement that had shot through her when Cable's eyes met hers. Dakota'd been around men all of her life. All kinds of men. Short, tall, thin, fat . . . yet *none* of them had affected her as *he* had in those few minutes.

She deftly twisted her hair into a topknot, allowing a few tendrils to fall and curl gently on her neck. Stepping back from the mirror, she gazed at her reflection critically. Though the green calico was definitely faded, its very softness seemed to lend itself to her . . . making Dakota appear, at least to herself, more gentle, refined . . . docile.

Hmmph! She laughed shortly. *Docile*? She picked up her black reticule and on impulse stuck her tongue out at the "docile" woman in the mirror and left the room.

A howl of pain brought Cable to his feet, and he hurried to the back of the jailhouse and looked in the open cell door.

Mick Owens lay on his stomach on the narrow cot, his head twisted around to glare accusingly at Doc Burns. "Goddammit, Doc! That hurts! Them feet are connected to the rest of me, y'know!"

The doctor shook his gray head. In disgust, he looked down at the brown wool blanket crumpled under Owens. He clucked his tongue at the liquid soaking in and spreading over the coarse material.

"Dammit, man," he growled. "See what you've made me do?"

Over the doctor's shoulder Mick caught sight of Cable and immediately pleaded, "Sheriff . . . call this butcher off me! He liked to burn my skin clean off!"

Cable's eyebrows rose slightly as he asked, "Doc?"

Doc Burns threw a quick glance over his shoulder, then returned his gaze to the reluctant patient. "Nonsense. No such thing," came his gruff reply. "Tried to pour some whiskey on these open blisters, and the damn fool jumped. Made me spill most of it on the blanket." His bushy gray brows drew together as he frowned down at Mick. "Terrible waste of good whiskey."

Ben swallowed a chuckle and instructed Mick sternly, "Lay still, Mick, and let the doc get on with it."

"Oh, Lordy, Lordy . . ." Mick dropped his face back into the flat pillow. Muffled words sounded in the small room, but whether he was praying or cussing, Cable couldn't tell.

Doc Burns once again turned his attention to the blisters on the soles of Mick's feet. Short but sure fingers explored the raw-looking surfaces with as much gentleness as possible. Examination complete, the doctor leaned back against the ladder-back chair. Ignoring Mick's heavy sigh of relief, the doc looked at Cable over the top of his wire-frame spectacles.

"He'll be all right, Ben."

"Yeah?"

Doc removed his glasses for a moment and rubbed the bridge of his nose before replacing them. "Yeah. Won't be doin' a helluva lot of walking for a few days, though. Those feet look like two slabs of raw meat!"

"Oh, Lord . . ." Mick whined piteously.

"Hell, man," Doc said impatiently, "it's your own damn fault! Those tall-heeled boots of yours weren't meant to be walkin' shoes! Especially if you ain't got the sense to wear *socks*!"

Ben Cable smothered a smile. An educated man from the East, Doc had slowly begun speaking like most of his patients ... and now he sounded as though he'd been born and raised under a cactus!

"You say a *woman* caused this?"

Cable saw the flash of humiliation cross Owens's face. Good for him, Ben thought. Perhaps this experience has been the best thing that could happen. At the very least he'd be a lot more careful around women for a while. Maybe this would even bring his pride and cockiness down a notch or two.

Maybe.

"A woman, Doc," Ben finally said. "Dakota Lane. Tenn's sister."

"Female from hell," Owens grumbled. Doc and Ben ignored him.

"Remarkable," Doc said with a low chuckle. "She must be quite a woman. Why, if that passing cowhand hadn't carried Mick in the last few miles, I bet he'd a been walkin' on two bloody stumps by the time he reached town!"

Another muffled groan sounded.

"Yessir ... I'm lookin' forward to meeting this young woman!" Doc gave Ben a knowing wink and added, "And a visit from his sister will give Tenn something to think about besides my daughter!"

Ben laughed gently. "She surely is something to think about. Dakota Lane wasn't anything like I'd expected her to be at all."

"That so?" Doc's head tilted to one side as he watched his friend. "What's she like, then?"

Ben crossed the cell to the barred window and stared out at the street. When he spoke, his voice was so low, the Doc had to strain to hear. "Strong ... oh, not physically, maybe. But strong where it counts, inside. She has a way of looking at a man that makes you sure she can see what you're thinkin'. Stood right up to Tenn and told him to hush." Ben chuckled. "Knows her own mind . . ."

Intrigued, the doctor asked quietly "What's she look like, this strong, sure woman? Face like a horse? Muscles instead of curves?"

Ben snapped a glance at the older man and saw his teasing smile. "She's beautiful. Soft brown hair that shines like wheat in sunshine . . . and a figure to take a man's breath away."

"Amen."

"That'll do, Mick," Ben advised. "That kind of thinkin' is what put you facedown on that cot!"

Owens's interruption broke the quiet spell, and the doctor decided to let the subject lie for a while. Instead he asked, "Ben . . . have you been to see Mary Stillwell?"

"No."

"She's been askin' for you."

Ben looked at the older man helplessly. "How can I go see her? What can I say? 'I'm sure sorry I got your husband killed for you, Mary'?"

"That's fool talk, and you know it!" Hands on his knees, Doc pushed himself to his feet. "Mary doesn't blame you. *No one* does."

"You're wrong, Doc." Ben sighed. "*I* do."

"Don't make no sense a'tall—"

"You shut up, Mick." Ben walked to the cell door. "Come on out to the office, Doc. Mick can stay right there till he's feelin' better."

Ben sat down in the chair behind his battered desk and looked up as Doc Burns stopped beside him.

"Lord knows, I hate to agree with Owens on any-thing . . . but he's right, Ben. You're not makin' any sense. The only one to blame is the man who shot Tom . . . and Tennessee Lane."

"I know." Ben leaned forward, elbows on his desk, hands running through his hair. "But . . . still. Mary's husband is dead. Those kids'll never remember their pa. They're too young. It'll be just like Tom was never here." He raised wounded eyes to the doctor. "And it's *my* fault. I knew Tom didn't have enough experi-ence. I should have been there with him!"

Doc shook his head. It was useless. No one would ever be able to convince this man that he was blame-less. Nonetheless, he gave it one more try.

"You couldn't be on duty all day *and* all night! A man's got to get some sleep sometime!"

Ben sighed.

"You go on over to see Mary, Ben. Might do you some good. Appears to me *she's* showin' a helluva lot more sense than you are right now." He patted the sheriff's shoulder awkwardly, taking the sting out of his words.

"All right. I'll go. Tonight."

"Fine, fine." The doctor picked up his bag and went to the door. "You'll see, Ben. I'm right. It wasn't your fault. Mary doesn't blame you."

The heavy door opened, then slowly swung shut again after the doctor. In the sudden silence Ben mut-tered, "What about Tom? Who does *he* blame?"

Mary O'Reilly Stillwell balanced her youngest child on her right hip and smiled at four-year-old Tom jun-ior, sitting on Dakota Lane's lap.

"Looks just like his da, doesn't he?"

Dakota smoothed little Tommy's hair back from his forehead. "Yes. Yes, he does, Mary."

"It's a blessing, that." The small redheaded woman chucked the baby under her chin. "Little Sarah here has got the map of Ireland all over her face. Can't see Tom at all in her . . . except for her temper, of course." Mary smiled and kissed the baby's forehead. "Ah, I shall miss Tom's temper most of all, I think."

"Why, for heaven's sake?"

"We had some grand shoutin' matches, Tommy and me. Me own temper's nothing to sneeze at, you know."

In spite of herself, Dakota had to laugh. She knew it all too well. The Stillwells' arguments had become legendary around Red Creek . . . as had their love for each other. The townspeople had often said that *nothing* could ever separate the couple.

But a bullet had done just that.

"Why, though," Dakota had to ask, "would you miss the shouting?"

Mary smiled softly, and her friend knew that she was walking in memories. "Where there's no arguin', there's no love."

"I don't understand."

"When you care for each other . . . no temper . . . no show of anger can harm you. Only someone who doesn't care what you do won't argue with you." She smiled through the tears welling in her emerald-green eyes. "My Tommy and me . . . we . . ."

"Oh, Mary . . ." Dakota set little Tom on his feet and stood to wrap her arms around the smaller woman. "I'm so sorry. I shouldn't have started you talking about Tom."

Mary patted her friend's shoulder and sniffed back the tears. "Nonsense! You couldn't stop me talkin' about him. I'll not pretend he wasn't here. I'll say his name often and talk of him to anyone who'll listen." She cupped her son's chin with her palm. "The little ones won't forget their da. Not while I'm around, they won't."

A knock came at the door, and Mary handed the baby to Dakota. After walking the short distance quickly, she threw open the door and gasped in delighted surprise.

"Ben! Ben Cable! It's high time you came!" She pulled him into the cozy parlor.

Dakota's eyes fixed on the doorway, waiting for him to appear. She held the baby tighter and fought down the surge of pleasure she felt at the sound of his name.

The sheriff looked extremely ill at ease. He clenched his hat in one hand, and when Tom junior threw himself at his knees, the man jerked as if he'd been shot. Mary released him, he threw his hat onto a chair, and effortlessly lifted the small boy to eye level. Solemnly he studied the boy's face as though waiting for a judgment to be handed down.

A silent spectator, Dakota held her breath as she watched man and boy communicate without words. Cable's jaw was clenched, and though his grip on the boy was gentle, she could see the rigid control he was exerting.

"Uncle Ben," the boy began and didn't notice how the man winced at his words, "my da's in heaven."

"I know, Tommy." The words were strangled, harsh.

"I want to go, too."

"Now, Tommy lad," Mary interrupted. "I've explained to you that it's not time yet for you to go."

He threw a mutinous glance at his mother. "You said I couldn't go live with Da. But I could visit. Just for a while." He turned his huge blue eyes back to Ben. "Couldn't I, Uncle Ben? I bet he misses me lots."

"I know he does, Tommy. Just like we miss him."

"See?" The little boy glared at his mother. "Uncle Ben knows. *He* says I can go! Didn't you?"

Dakota moved forward, somehow wanting to help the solemn man escape from Tommy's demands. But a brief shake of his head stopped her. She held her breath once more and waited.

"No, Tommy. I didn't say that." Ben held the boy easily and managed to keep from squeezing too hard.

"But I want—"

"I know. I know, Tommy. You just want to see your da again. So do I." How to explain, he thought. "But that will have to wait."

"How long?"

"Well, we don't know that." Not good enough, Cable, he told himself. "But until we do . . . there is something we can do for him."

"What?" The boy tilted his head suspiciously.

"We can try to be very good. To do all the things your da wanted us to do." Ben saw suspicion slowly give way to curiosity as Tommy listened intently. "Like you, for instance. I know your father wanted you to grow up big and strong . . . to help your mother and your little sister."

"I can do that." Tommy smiled slightly. "I already help Ma lots, don't I?"

"That you do, boyo," Mary whispered.

Dakota clapped her hand tight against her mouth.

"Well, sure you do." Ben set the boy down and squatted beside him. "And that's just what your father wanted. He's very proud of you, Tommy. And so am I."

The boy smiled suddenly. "I'll help now." He turned to his mother. "Can I take Sarah and give her a cookie?"

"She'd like that, I think."

Dakota held out the squirming toddler, who reached for her brother. Carefully Tommy clutched Sarah against him and walked determinedly to the kitchen. Just before he left the room, be turned back and said, "See, I'm big. I can carry her, just like Da did."

"So I see, Tommy. You're doin' fine, son." Ben fought to keep the quaver from his voice.

Alone again, the three adults stood in an awkward silence for a moment before Mary spoke.

"That was lovely, Ben. Thank you." She smiled and, though her lips quivered, her voice was steady. "I've had quite a time with that one. Even caught him packin' for a trip to heaven."

"Oh, God . . ."

Mary moved closer to the stricken man and laid her hand on his arm. "Here, now . . . that's enough of that." She looked up into his face and asked, "I saw you at the funeral, Ben. Why didn't you come to the house? Why didn't you speak to me?"

"I'm sorry, Mary. So sorry. I couldn't . . ."

Dakota moved sideways, slipping toward the front door.

"No, Dakota." Mary reached out for her. "Don't leave. Unless Ben would rather . . ."

He looked up, and Dakota felt a swell of sympathy for him wash over her. The pain in his eyes went deep and said more about the man than anything else could have.

"No. No, it's all right. Stay."

"Now, tell me why you've stayed away, Ben Cable. The children have missed you. So've I."

"How can you say that?" His gaze bored into hers. "Why would you miss me? It was because of me that Tom—"

"Hush!" Mary shook his arm. "Don't you even think that! For the love of Mike . . . Ben Cable, it was no more your fault than it was mine!"

"Yours?"

"Yes!" Her voice was firm, determined to reach him. "It was my idea to move West . . . if we'd stayed in Chicago, Tom might be alive now. And then again, he might've been run down by a streetcar."

Ben shook his head slowly.

"Don't you see, Ben?" Quieter now, but no less determined, Mary went on. "It was his time. I don't know why the good Lord chose to take him from me and his children. But it's not for me to second-guess Him. Nor for you." Her eyes filled with tears again. "I'll miss Tom for the rest of my days—God knows there'll never be another like him. And when it's my time . . . I'll go to him. And gladly." She forced a smile and waited until he returned it. "But for now . . . I'll go on livin'. It's what I've got to do. For the children . . . and for me. That goes as well for you, Ben Cable. You gave him the chance to be what he'd always wanted to be. He was a lawman . . ."

"Yeah. For a few months."

"You don't understand, Ben. It doesn't matter how long the dream lasts. It only matters that you have it."

"What'll you do now, Mary?"

She sighed. He obviously wasn't convinced yet. She took one of his hands, and with her other she reached for Dakota. "At first I thought I'd go back to Chicago. But now I think we'll stay."

"I'm glad," Dakota whispered.

Mary squeezed her friend's hand. "We've friends here." She looked at Ben meaningfully. "*Good* friends. Jacob has offered me a job in the restaurant . . . and we've the house. This is a good place. A grand place to raise the children. It was what Tom wanted for them . . . and I'll see they get it."

They sat in Jacob Gunderson's restaurant, their cups of coffee going cold, unnoticed. Dakota glanced up at Cable, then lowered her eyes again. He hadn't spoken more than a few words since they'd left Mary's house, and now she was reluctant to start a conversation.

Unwittingly she'd been a witness to something private. Something that he would, no doubt, like to pretend hadn't happened. Somehow, Dakota was sure that Cable was not a man comfortable with displays of sympathy. So she thought, perhaps the best thing to do is pretend with him.

"Sheriff."

He looked up, wary.

"Sheriff, I was wondering what you were planning to do about the thief who attacked my brother." She kept her facial expression bland and waited for his answer.

He stared at her blankly, as though he'd forgotten her presence for a moment She continued to surprise him. Before he met her, he'd been sure that she would

be one of those vapid, faint-hearted females that so
exasperated him as to leave him speechless. The wom-
en he'd grown up around in Georgia would never
have *considered* fighting off an assailant. Not that they
were incapable of it. The thought simply would not
have occurred to them. Females of his acquaintance
had long used the graceful swoon as their main artil-
lery. And to give credit where it's due . . . the ploy
usually worked.

But this woman was different. There was no denying the fact that she was every inch a lady . . . but she
was also a fascinating blend of qualities. A lady in
the truest sense of the word, there was also in her
the outspoken forthrightness of the members of her
sex considered a good deal less than ladies. And a
sense of justice combined with an ability to defend
herself more commonly seen in males.

Now, when most women would be fluttering over
him, offering concern and tender sympathy, Dakota
Lane did neither . . . for which he was grateful. Again,
a surprise.

Ben signaled to Jacob for more coffee. The old man's
ruddy face went two shades darker when he returned
Dakota's smile of thanks, and his tired eyes never
left hers as he filled Ben's cup. Soon the hot liquid
overflowed. Ben moved nimbly aside and shouted,
"Jacob!"

"Huh? . . . Oh, sorry."

Jacob hardly spared a glance for the sheriff as he
wiped the spill with the edge of his none-too-clean
apron, smiled again at Dakota, then returned to the
kitchen.

"Well, Sheriff? Your plans?" She was determined, if
nothing else.

Her husky voice sounded pleasant to him, and he smiled as he answered, "I plan to catch him."

"Yes, I understand that." Patience, Dakota, patience, she told herself. "But do you have any idea where to start?"

Ben leaned forward across the scrubbed-pine table. "I do have a couple of small clues that I intend to follow up on very soon. As I told your brother, you'll just have to be patient." Suddenly he reached for her hand.

His warm, callused fingers rubbed her knuckles gently while his thumb traced patterns on her palm. Dakota felt as though her hand were on fire. The heat seemed to build and grow from the tips of her fingers to the small curl of warmth she felt deep inside. She looked into Ben's eyes and watched them soften as if he knew what she was feeling. Her breath was coming in sharp, uneven gasps, and she shuddered slightly as Ben's fingers moved upward to encircle her wrist. This shouldn't be happening, she thought. How can the touch of a man's hand cause such a response? She closed her eyes helplessly as his hand gently stroked her forearm, and she felt the warmth spread quickly to the intimate parts of her body.

A soft tendril of fear overrode the sensations Ben was causing and prompted Dakota to pull her hand from his grasp. She tried to steady her breathing and regain control of the situation, but she could still feel his fingers on her skin. She rubbed her arm absently and thought there was no denying her attraction to Ben Cable. Even in a restaurant. A public place. Oh, Lord.

Never before had she experienced the emotions she felt when around Sheriff Cable. And *now* was certainly not the time to begin. She cleared her throat nervously and asked, "Would you mind telling me what these 'clues' are?"

He shook his sandy head regretfully. "I'm sorry, ma'am. But I think any information about the crime should remain with me alone. Don't you worry. I'll find the man. I want him as badly as you do." He stood slowly and put on his hat. "Now, if you'll excuse me . . ."

Moving toward the door, he knew without looking that her expression would be one of frustration. He couldn't really blame her . . . but at the same time he had no intention of sharing what little he knew about the crimes committed. With her capacity for doing the unexpected, there was no telling what she might get herself into.

She would bear watching.

Ben walked quietly along the boardwalk until he reached an alleyway between the restaurant and the town bank. Once there, he slipped unobserved into the shadows. Leaning against the rough wood siding, he rolled a cigarette, then cupped his hand around a flaring match to light it. The tobacco glowed brightly for a moment as he inhaled, then the alley was once again bathed in shadows.

The fingers of his right hand rubbed together as if in memory of the feel of her skin. Soft and smooth on the back of her hand and the palm slightly callused. A woman used to working. And taking care of herself. A woman to walk beside a man. Not behind him. Abruptly he jammed his hand into his pants pocket.

That's enough of *that* kind of thinkin', he told himself. He was in no position to be giving thought to a woman like that. What, after all, did he have to show for thirty-five years of hard living? A horse, a saddle, a few changes of clothes, and a star. He snorted derisively. Not exactly set up to go courtin'.

A door opened. Ben tossed the last of his cigarette into the dust as his gaze followed the slight figure in a dress crossing the street. In the deepening twilight she moved like a shadow . . . occasionally snatching glances over her shoulder as she went. Silently Ben backed farther into the alley.

He would admit to being intrigued by Dakota. In fact, he would give plenty to know exactly what was going through her mind right now. He'd be willing to bet she had no intention of giving up on her search for information.

A pale slit of lamplight shone briefly as she entered the hotel.

Ben stepped quietly out of the alley, his mind racing. He certainly didn't want her involving herself in his investigation. She could ruin any chance he might have of catching up with the killer. And dammit . . . he wanted that bastard more than anything in the world.

First, though, he had to find a way to keep Dakota out of it. For her own sake as well as his.

Four

OIL lamps in tarnished sconces hung on the hotel walls casting wildly dancing shadows on the stained, yellowing wallpaper. Stale cigar smoke hung heavy in the stuffy air, and from somewhere down the street came the muted sounds of a piano being played with more enthusiasm than talent.

A quick glance around the tiny lobby assured Dakota that she was alone in the room save for the young desk clerk, Andy. The tall, gangly redhead looked up when she entered the hotel and immediately flushed a bright scarlet. His freckles stood out in sharp contrast against the crimson of his skin, and as Dakota walked to the desk, she watched his huge Adam's apple bob up and down nervously.

"Hello, Andy," Dakota said, grateful she remembered overhearing the boy's name.

"Evenin', Miss Lane." His voice cracked slightly.

Dakota pretended not to notice. She sympathized with his obvious jitters, but, she told herself firmly, she needed information, and poor Andy would be a lot easier to get answers from than the surly clerk who'd been in charge earlier.

She placed her hand gently on the desk just inches from the boy's and said softly, "I was wondering if you could help me?"

"I'll surely try, ma'am."

"I'm just so upset over what happened to my brother," Dakota began. "I was hoping you might be able to tell me something about that night."

"Sure am sorry, Miss Lane," Andy said, his expression crestfallen. "But I don't know nothin' about it. Sheriff Cable already asked me himself."

She watched the knot in his throat jump up and down "Oh," Dakota countered as she lowered her lashes demurely, "surely someone as intelligent and important as *you* saw something? Anything? A stranger, maybe?"

His thin chest filled, and he stood straighter under her praise. "Well," Andy stammered slightly, battling his own shyness to answer, "I *did* see that Gordon gent who bought your brother's cattle talkin' to another fella the night of the, uh . . . shootin'."

The cattle buyer? But that wouldn't make sense, would it? "Do you know the other man's name?" she whispered.

His Adam's apple jumped again, and her heart sank as he replied, "No, ma'am, I don't. Never seen him before."

Andy pulled at his shirt collar, clearly uncomfortable with her close scrutiny.

"Could you describe him?" Dakota fought down her impatience. This could be the clue she'd been hoping for. After all . . . Mr. Gordon was a stranger in town, too.

"I think so." He tilted his head back and stared at the ceiling, concentrating. "A real big man, dark hair and eyes. Kinda dangerous lookin', if you know what I mean. Oh." Andy moved his gaze back to Dakota. "He had a small, half-moon-shaped scar on his forehead. I remember noticin' that, 'cause I tried to figure on what had done it to him."

"Did he stay here?" Dakota knew a moment's unreasonable hope, knowing even as she asked the question what the answer would be.

"No, ma'am, not here." He shrugged his bony shoulders and added, "Don't know where he stayed. Not real friendly, if you know what I mean. Didn't talk to nobody but Gordon."

"Anything else?"

"Only that they acted like they didn't know each other. Him and Gordon, I mean. I only saw them together once. Ran across them by accident out behind the livery stable. They was talkin' real quiet like. Couldn't hear what they was sayin'. And when they saw me, they split up right quick. Know what I mean?"

Had Gordon been behind the whole thing? Dakota asked quickly, "What about Mr. Gordon? What was he like?"

Andy smiled, glad to be on familiar ground and eager to help such a pretty woman. "That's easy. He was real different from folks around here. A dandy. Fine clothes and spoke real good. He give me a whole dollar tip just to bring him some clean sheets." The boy shook his head at the memory. "He was really somethin'. Can you beat that? A *dollar* for clean sheets?"

Having seen the condition of the hotel, that was

the *one* thing Dakota had no trouble at all under-
standing.

"What did he look like?" She tried to keep her
growing impatience out of her voice, but really Andy
was certainly taking his time about this.

"Big man, dark hair . . . handsome. Well set up."

For heaven's sake, Dakota's mind screamed! After
all of this . . . that's the best he can do? After I've
made a fool of myself battin' my eyelashes like
some simpering half-wit? That description could fit
half the Nevada Territory! She forced her eyes away
from that ridiculous jumping motion in his throat and
tried again.

"Is that all?"

"Well . . ." Hands on narrow hips, Andy tilted his
head to one side in thought. "There was somethin'
special he always had with him. . . ." He paused and
looked meaningfully at Dakota. "A walking stick."

"What's so special about that?"

He leaned toward her, shyness forgotten, and rested
his scrawny frame on the wide desk. "*This* stick was
special."

Dakota swallowed the impulse to shake the infuri-
atingly slow boy.

"Why?"

Andy smiled and glanced over his shoulder before
speaking.

"*This* stick had a solid silver tiger head for a knob."

"A tiger's head?"

"Yep." He nodded. "And he was always rubbin' it.
Surprised he hadn't wore it clean away, the way his
fingers was forever smoothin' it."

Certainly different enough, she thought. But where
do I start looking for this man?

As if he could read her mind, Andy said, "The night of the shooting, though, Gordon left town."

"I know," she said glumly. "West. But no one knows where."

He smiled. "San Francisco."

San Francisco? Dakota managed to hide the flash of despair that swept over her. If the thief really *did* run all the way to California . . .

"You're sure?"

"Sure as I can be. Heard Gordon tellin' the livery-man he needed a fast horse to get him to Reno in time for the train to 'Frisco."

"Did you tell the sheriff all of this?"

"Well, sure!" Andy straightened up.

"Then maybe," she said, more to herself than the boy, "that's why he seemed so confident of catching the killer. He has an idea of where to look."

"Oh, I don't think so." He shook his head slowly. "That's just Sheriff Cable's way. No. I don't figure him to be chasin' off to 'Frisco."

She nodded. "Suppose he won't. After all, he's got no legal power in San Francisco. He's only a sher-iff . . . not a territorial marshal."

"Hell—'scuse me, ma'am." Andy blushed furiously at his blunder. "That ain't why."

"What do you mean?"

He snorted in disgust. "You know how Yankees are! Notional. Just plain notional. Never seen a one that ain't."

"Yankees?" Dakota looked at the boy as if he were crazy. She could remember very clearly the unmistak-able slow drawl in the sheriff's speech. "He didn't sound like a Yankee to me."

"Well, he ain't a natural-born one. He was raised

up in Georgia." Andy's lips twisted distastefully as he continued. "But he's a Yankee sure enough. Wore blue in the war."

Something old and bitter coiled in Dakota's stomach. Though the war had been over for five years . . . some things didn't end. Memories of the Lane ranch in Texas swam before her eyes. The work, the plans, the sweat and blood they'd left behind when the Reconstruction people chased them off their land.

Reconstruction! Another word for thievery! The northeners who'd rushed to Texas at the end of the war had sounded just like Sheriff Cable. Helpful. Concerned.

At first.

But it hadn't taken long for their true colors to show. Under the guise of "Reconstruction"—rebuilding the country—they'd helped themselves to any land worth having. Most times, confiscating the property from families who'd been in Texas for generations!

Many good men had turned "outlaw" then. Hiding out in the thickets and the swamps, striking out at the interlopers whenever they had the chance. Called traitor for fighting in the Confederate Army and outlaw for fighting for their land.

Well, Dakota told herself with determination, we lost the Texas ranch. But we won't lose another. Not again.

"So, like I said," Andy spoke up again. "I don't figure the sheriff to walk off from his nice cozy job here to run down a killer in San Francisco."

"Perhaps not," Dakota agreed and mentally wiped out the lingering traces of her attraction for Ben Cable. She wouldn't be fooled by a fast-talkin' northerner this time.

"But I reckon what I said about Gordon don't do you any good, neither. With him in 'Frisco, you won't be talkin' to him any more than the sheriff."

Dakota smiled.

Upstairs in her room Dakota lay back against the carved, dusty headboard. Shifting position slightly on the lumpy mattress, she told herself that Andy's information wasn't much to go on . . . but it was all she had. And she'd never forgive herself if she didn't at least *try* to get their money back. Even though Tenn had bravely discounted its importance, she knew that without the cash money they'd been counting on, there was a better than even chance they'd lose the ranch. The final payment was due in a month or so.

Even if they *did* find a way to pay off the bank, there were so many other things they had to have. Sure, they could live without the new breeding stock they'd hoped to buy. But there were supplies to be bought, all the extras they'd need before winter, bills to settle up, wages to pay. A hundred and one things to do with money they no longer had.

And Dakota remembered those mooning looks Tenn had been sending Laura. It certainly seemed as though there would soon be another member added to the Lane family. A man should have some money in the bank when he takes a wife.

It just wasn't right that a thief and killer should get the money they'd worked so hard for!

Poor Tenn. It must be driving him crazy to be unable to go after the fella himself, she thought. To be stuck in a bed, helpless as a kitten, dependent on the abilities of a small-town sheriff to right the wrongs done to him.

Of course. She pulled her knees up to her chest and wrapped her arms around them. That's why Tenn's so willing to trust in Sheriff Cable. He knows he hasn't any choice. But she'd be willing to bet that he had no idea Cable had been in the Union Army. She couldn't imagine Tennessee trusting his future to a stinkin' Yankee!

No. He didn't know. And he wouldn't find out about it from her, either. It would do no good at all to tell him. Only serve to give him more to fret over. And Lord knows, she told herself, he's got plenty, now.

Tenn probably hadn't heard that the thief had gone on to San Francisco, either.

She stopped. Lifting her head, she stared across the room into the mirror. "Now, why," she asked herself out loud, "are you so all fired sure that the cattle buyer, Gordon, had something to do with all this?"

Mentally, she went over her reasons. He was seen sneaking around with the only other stranger in town. He was in a blamed hurry to get those cows moving. And he sure as hell left town quick enough!

"Besides," she told her reflection, "he's all I've got to go on."

Cable tilted his chair onto its two back legs and crossed his right ankle over his left knee. The thumb of his left hand thumped against the desktop rhythmically, steadily. He stared at the opposite wall, decorated with neatly aligned wanted posters, and pondered the question of Dakota Lane.

In the two days she'd been in town, she'd found time to talk to almost every living soul in Red Creek. Busiest damn female he'd ever run across. And everyone told the same story when he asked.

She was mining for information about the theft and killing.

In any other woman, he might suppose that it was simple curiosity regarding her brother's injury. But with *this* woman, he had an ominous feeling that it would prove to be much more. She hadn't bothered to question him again since her futile attempt at the restaurant, and that worried him.

He turned toward the windows when the sound of determinedly clicking heels penetrated his brain. Speak of the devil, he thought, and in she walks.

Dakota pushed the door wide and stepped inside the jailhouse. It took only a moment for her eyes to adjust to the relative dimness. Quickly she glanced at her surroundings.

A small, square room, sparsely furnished with a desk, two chairs, a tall, narrow cabinet near the windows, and a gun rack. An old stove that had been scrubbed and polished into a glossy shine sat in a corner and held a steaming pot of coffee. The bare wood floor was swept clean of dirt. Everything in the office spoke of order.

Her glance shifted to the sheriff, who was watching her expressionlessly. He sat, leaning back in his chair behind a huge rolltop desk, and showed no indication of moving. She stepped up closer to him and hid her surprise when he rose to his feet and inclined his head toward her.

"Afternoon, Miss Lane."

"Afternoon, Sheriff."

She moved to stand beside the desk and allowed her gaze to linger slightly on the papers stacked atop it.

Without a word Cable rolled the lid down, successfully hiding them from her view.

Eyebrows lifted questioningly, she asked, "Secrets, Sheriff?"

"Not at all. Merely official paperwork. Nothing to interest you, I'm afraid."

"I see."

Seating herself in the chair opposite his, Dakota took a moment to smooth the worn fabric of her plain cornflower-blue dress. Now that she was here . . . she wasn't quite sure where to start. She watched him covertly from the corner of her eye and was disgusted to find that his expression remained bland. Unreadable. He was rocking in that chair like he hadn't a care in the world.

The silence in the room stretched to an almost unbearable length, as if neither of them wanted to be the first to break it. She'd made up her mind to be polite. To be quiet. Gentle. If it killed her. She knew from experience she'd never get anything from him with anger. Finally Dakota could take the silence no longer.

She forced a smile. "Haven't seen you in a couple of days, Sheriff."

"Been busy."

"Tenn says you've been by to see him. I appreciate it."

"No need. I enjoy talking to him."

This was not going well. She swallowed her impatience and tried to start a friendly conversation.

"Have you seen Mary since the other night?"

His jaw tightened slightly. "No. Like I said. I've been busy."

Shouldn't have said that, she told herself. He probably doesn't want to be reminded that I witnessed such an emotional scene. Think of something else to say. Anything. Then it came to her. There *was* something she'd wanted to know.

"Yes. Well, I don't know if you remember"—she tried a smile—"the day we met? At Dr. Burns's house?"

He nodded.

"I'm curious. You see, you never did tell me why you waited so long to send for me after Tenn was shot."

"*That's* what you came to ask me?"

"Partly."

"I see." He leaned his head back and looked at her, his curiosity plain. "All right. I waited because it's been my experience that a woman is generally no use in an emergency."

She bit down hard on her bottom lip. She couldn't afford to make him angry yet. But really, how could *anyone* believe something so stupid!

"That explains why you didn't send for me the first day," she said through gritted teeth. "Now explain the other two days."

His chair slammed down onto all four legs. He leaned across his desk and met her angry stare with one of his own. "I shouldn't *have* to explain anything to you, Miss Lane. As sheriff, I do what I think is right. And frankly, I didn't want to be bothered with explainin' the situation to some woman who'd probably faint at the mention of the word *blood*!"

"I don't faint!"

"I had no way of knowing that, did I?"

Now is not the time for this, Dakota, she told herself. If you start arguing with him, he won't tell you a thing. Just find out what you came to learn, then leave. She took a deep breath and forced a smile.

"Tenn says you have a few ideas about the shooting?"

"A few."

The silence grew again.

Her fingers clenched in her lap. Cable's chair creaked noisily as he rocked it back and forth on its rear legs. Muffled sounds from the street emphasized the strained quiet in the jailhouse.

It wouldn't work. She simply hadn't the patience to deal with him politely. She doubted that anyone did.

"There are one or two questions I want to ask you," she said as she met his gaze. "*If* you don't mind."

"Not at all." His lips quirked in a lopsided smile. "Why, with the way you've been runnin' around town talkin' to anything that would stand still, I'd have been disappointed if you hadn't come to me, too."

"Fine." She straightened in her chair and ignored the fact that he'd been aware of her questioning the townspeople. He'd probably been expecting her to show up sooner or later. "Tell me, then, just what you're planning to do *exactly* to catch the man who shot my brother. *And* Tom."

"I already told you, Miss Lane, I don't think you should know those plans. That's business for the law."

"Fine. Then tell me this. Did you even *try* to find our cattle after the shooting?"

He brought the chair down onto all four legs again. "Now, why would you ask that? Your brother sold his cattle. Legally."

"I know. You didn't answer my question."

"So I didn't. Well, as a matter of fact, I *did* try to run down the outfit Gordon hired to move the herd."

"You tried?"

"Yep."

"Well?"

"Couldn't find 'em. Gone. Like they disappeared."

"A whole herd?"

"By the time I could go after them, the storm had washed every trace of them away."

"By the time you got around to checking, you mean."

He ignored that. "That herd could be anywhere by now." He stared at her, his eyes probing. "But like I said. Why would you ask? Those cows were sold."

"Yes. Sold. For almost ten thousand dollars. And that same night . . . the money was stolen, my brother shot, Tom killed, and the herd moved off." She returned his stare. "Doesn't that strike you as odd? A herd moving at night?"

He shrugged and leaned back. "Maybe. Maybe not. There's prob'ly a good reason for it."

"Sure. But we won't find out what it is, will we?" All attempts at patience gone, her voice rose dangerously as she faced the aggravating man. "Gordon's gone and the herd's disappeared."

"Look, Miss Lane—" His jaw tight, Cable stood, walked around the desk, and stopped beside her. Grabbing her elbow, he pulled her to her feet. He then guided her to the door, opened it, and held it for her. "Why don't you just let me do my job? Go home."

She jerked away. "I'll go home when I'm good and ready, *Sheriff*. And I wish you *would* do your job!"

He glared down at her.

She didn't flinch.

"Good day, Miss Lane."

"Good day, Sheriff Cable."

She swept past him without another glance. Somehow, he resisted the urge to slam the door. He crossed the room, picked up his coffee cup, then grabbed the pot off the stove.

"Dammit!" He dropped the red-hot container, spilling scalding coffee all over the floor and his best pair of pants. He shook his hand wildly as he paced the small office. A stream of curses flowed from him as he shouted his rage at the mule-headed female who'd just left.

Ben finally stopped at the front window and rubbed his aching palm as he watched her climb the steps to the hotel. Another burst of anger swept through him, and he kicked the tall cabinet beside him. That woman is gonna be nothin' but trouble, he told himself as he hopped over to his chair.

"Dakota, don't talk foolish!" Tenn's face was purple with anger. He stared at his sister as if she'd lost her mind and almost growled at the stubborn set of her jaw. "You can't go off to San Francisco alone. Dammit! Use the sense God gave you, woman!"

She didn't say a word. Ordinarily she wouldn't even have told him of her plans, expecting just this reaction. But in his present condition she knew he was in no shape to stop her. Paying no attention to the ranting curses filling the air, Dakota pulled at the bodice of her flower-sprigged, lemon-yellow cotton dress.

She'd been on the receiving end of Tenn's anger many times before and, no doubt, would be again. He would shout and rage, hurl dire predictions, and make empty threats before finally giving in. When all was said and done, her brother knew that she would do whatever she thought right.

And nothing would stop her.

"Dakota! Listen to me!"

"Tenn." She winced. Even wounded, Tennessee Lane managed to be louder than a herd of stampeding cattle. "By now I'm sure most of Red Creek is listening to you."

He rubbed a hand over his stubbled jaw and took a deep breath. Once calm, he tried a different tactic. "Where do you plan on getting the money for your fare?" His lips turned up smugly . . . sure he had her. "Or were you plannin' on ridin' your horse all the way to California?"

Dakota ignored the sarcasm. "Laura has been kind enough to loan me the money I need. Not a lot. Just enough to get me there. I'll get a job in the city."

Clearly thunderstruck, Tenn turned to face Laura. She'd been sitting quietly in the corner of the room, and he seemed bewildered that she was no more affected by his anger than Dakota.

"Laura, how could you do somethin' like that? Without saying anything to me?"

"Tenn, dear," Laura said as she stood and moved to his side, "it's my money, I can do what I like with it." She pulled and straightened the blanket covering him. "After all, we're not married yet. You really can't issue orders and expect me to jump." She patted his hand and gave him a quick kiss on the forehead. "Now. Calm yourself, say goodbye to Dakota, and wish her well." Laura smiled briefly at the other woman before leaving brother and sister alone.

His features tight, Tenn watched the door softly close. Dakota chuckled and he turned toward her. He scowled angrily. "It ain't funny, Dakota. She had no right."

"What do you mean, she had no right?"

"She shouldn't have butted in. This is between you and me. Family business."

Dakota shot him a disgusted glance. "I thought her being family was what you had in mind."

"Maybe I did." He inched higher in the bed. "But even so, she shouldn't have done something like this without talkin' to me first."

She knew the signs of his anger all too well. Guilt raced through her veins. If it hadn't been for her, Tenn and Laura would still be getting along just fine. Now it looked as if there was going to be rough riding ahead for them. She hoped Laura would give as good as she got.

"Don't you be a fool, big brother."

He looked up angrily.

"If you want some free advice, even when you're married, I wouldn't try issuing any orders if I was you."

"You're a fine one to be calling me a fool. Traipsin' off to California. And don't you be tellin' me how to handle Laura."

"Oh, I won't. I have a feeling she'll be doing that herself."

He pushed himself higher up against the headboard and clumsily shoved at the pillows behind his back. Dakota stepped forward, deftly rearranged the pillows, then eased her brother back against them. Before she could move away, Tenn captured her right hand in his. His face suddenly serious, he said, "Kota, I really wish you wouldn't do this. . . ."

He raised his left hand in the air as she started to interrupt him. "But I know that nothing I can say will stop you. If I thought you would be careful and use the sense God gave you, then maybe it wouldn't bother me so much." His eyes challenged her. "But you won't, will you?"

"Tennessee Lane. *You* of all people should know better than that." She glared at him, a little stung by his seeming lack of confidence. "It was you who taught me to shoot, to look out for myself. How to get along in a man's world. Are you tryin' to say you didn't do a good enough job?"

"No." His worried gaze swept over her. "No. You know what to do and, I hope, *when* to do it. But Dakota . . . sometimes you just don't think things through. And that troubles me some."

She leaned over and left a quick kiss on his forehead. "Don't worry. Why, I'll probably be back before you have a chance to miss me. And I'll bring the money back, too."

"Forget the money, dammit—"

Before he could get all worked up again, Dakota turned her back on him and left the room, quietly closing the door on Tenn's last-minute arguments.

In the hall Laura stopped her.

"No," she said softly, "I'm not going to lecture you or warn you. I know you'll take care. All I ask is that you write to us often . . . keep us up-to-date on where you are and what you're doing."

"I will. I promise." Impulsively Dakota reached out and hugged the other woman. "Thanks for the loan. I *do* appreciate it. But I think you're gonna have some trouble with Tenn about it."

"Don't worry about that. I can handle him. It's best that he find out before we're married that I have a mind of my own." She squeezed Dakota's hand. "I only wish I had more to give you."

"It's plenty. I'll find work."

"I know you will."

As she turned to leave, Laura's hand on her arm stopped her. "Watch yourself, now."

"Don't worry. And don't let Tenn worry, either. I've been watchin' out for myself for a long time."

"Yes, but a big city is different. Dakota, you don't know. You're used to life out here. Where a person's word means something. And most folks don't lie or cheat. You're used to knowing almost every soul in fifty miles."

Dakota moved impatiently. She appreciated the concern, but she wanted to get on with what she had to do.

Laura released her. "All I'm saying is that big cities are vastly different from what you're used to."

"I'll be all right."

"I know. Just be careful who you trust."

"I always have. But thanks."

Quickly then, Dakota turned and left the little house before Laura could start up again.

Peeking out the curtained front window, Laura watched the other woman walk purposefully down the street. Shoulders back, head held high, she walked with determination, the hem of her dress snapping about her legs with every step. Finally she rounded a corner and disappeared.

Dakota stopped when she was out of sight of the house. Leaning her head back against the comforting bulk of a weathered building, she took a deep breath and closed her eyes.

Laura's cautious words echoed in her head. She fought down a rising tide of fear. There was nothing to be done about it. She *had* to go to San Francisco. And fretting wasn't going to do any good. She would just have to face whatever problems she had when they came up.

San Francisco, she thought, more frightened than she wanted to admit. Alone in Red Creek was one thing. Alone in San Francisco was quite another. There would be no friendly faces. Nothing familiar. And she'd have to find work immediately. But what *kind* of work? And where? How would she live?

Her eyes opened and she stared at the wide azure sky above her. Quickly she sent a short but direct prayer to whoever might be listening. "If you're not too busy, I could surely use a little help."

Five

DAKOTA leaned back in her seat. The train ride would be a long one, and she wasn't looking forward to it. After the first couple of hours the exhilaration of traveling at such a fast pace had faded. Even the fact that the train was moving at almost twenty miles an hour couldn't ease her discomfort anymore. Yet she knew it would at least prove better than the stagecoach ride from Red Creek to Reno.

She brushed at the soot and dirt covering the bosom of her yellow calico dress and wished she'd been able to wear her shirt and pants instead. But that outfit was now rolled up and tucked away in her carpetbag.

For once Maria had been right, she thought wryly. If she hadn't packed Dakota's dresses, her trip would have been delayed for days while she went to collect them. Though faded and well worn, she would need them all in San Francisco. She only wished she'd been able to think of a way to bring her rifle along as well. But there was no way to pack it, and she couldn't very well walk down the streets of a big city with a rifle cradled in her arms. She *had* brought her pistol, though. Carefully wrapped in cloth, it lay on top of her clothes in the carpetbag. Knowing the weapon was close to hand gave her some comfort.

Even with her nervousness and the discomfort, Dakota couldn't quite overcome the knot of excitement that filled her. For almost three days she'd been traveling. Away from the family and home that had sheltered her, dependent on no one but herself.

That thought both thrilled and frightened her. She'd felt so confident. So sure of herself when telling Tenn of her plan. Of course, then she'd still been in Red Creek . . . safe in familiar surroundings.

She locked her fingers together in her lap and took a slow, calming breath. No sense scaring yourself, she thought firmly. Just put it out of your mind. Nothing to be done about it now, anyway. You're on the train. There's no turning back.

Deliberately she turned her thoughts to other things.

Before leaving Red Creek, she'd used the age-old rancher's method of delivering news . . . "put a kid on a horse." She'd paid a young boy to take a message to the Lane ranch, informing Jess and Maria of her plans. It brought a smile to her face, just thinking of Jess's reaction. And Dakota knew that she was infinitely safer on this train than anywhere near the foreman once he read her note.

Dakota stared out the grimy window as the landscape hurtled by. It was worth the risk of a hot cinder or two blowing in her half-opened window just to feel the air on her face. She was tired of the traveling and more than a little anxious about San Francisco.

Even as big a city as Reno, where she'd caught the train, would be dwarfed in comparison to the city built by gold. Her stomach tightened again. Really, she told herself, this is ridiculous. It would do no good to worry now. It was too late for that. Besides, after all her brave talk at home, she couldn't very well turn tail and run. Could she?

No. She wouldn't be able to face anyone. Especially her brother and Ben Cable. By now he must know where she'd gone. Tenn had no doubt told him. He's prob'ly expecting me to run home anyway, she thought. Well, she wouldn't give either of the men the satisfaction of knowing just how scared she really was.

She took a deep breath and glanced quickly around her. There were only a few other passengers in the car besides herself. Two ladies, obviously easterners, fanning themselves ineffectually with dainty lace handkerchiefs, a cowhand, hat over his face, sleeping so soundly as to be oblivious to his surroundings, and a heavyset, florid-faced man in a checkered vest.

Dakota sat apart from her fellow passengers. She was in no mood to talk. Especially with a stranger. There were far too many things for her to think about already.

The train rolled on through the day, making occasional stops in sleepy towns where the passengers disembarked to grab quick meals. Staring out at the countryside as the day passed, the sights seemed to blend together until one town looked much like the last. And the passing miles seemed designed to shake her confidence.

Dakota smiled and realized that she had yet to even see the face of the cowhand at the back of the car. He seemed to be sleeping most of the time, with his well-worn black hat constantly pulled low over his face.

As her gaze passed over the two ladies, now snoring softly, she glanced at the portly gentleman. When she did, his eyes caught hers, and he smiled lazily. She averted her eyes quickly but not quick enough. The heavy man seemed to take her glance as an invitation to join her. He rose, crossed the aisle, and took the seat next to her. Leaning over, he introduced himself.

"Maxwell Harrington at your service, miss."

Dakota turned her face aside to avoid the smell of whiskey his breath had directed at her. The lanterns hanging on the front of the car were the only lights in the otherwise dark car, and the shadows they cast leapt and shuddered along with the train's movement. The quiet was punctuated only by the sound of the steel wheels rolling on the tracks.

He made a useless attempt to pull his bright yellow-and-lavender-checked vest over his swollen stomach as he continued. "Yes, indeed. Maxwell Harrington." He seemed oblivious to the fact that she hadn't answered him. "And, miss, I represent the Coquette Corset Company."

A drummer. Dakota sighed at the thought of the tedious sales pitch she was going to be forced to listen to.

The huge man heard the sigh and remarked, "Ah, but with a figure like yours, you'll pardon me for sayin' so, what need have you to avail yourself of my wares?"

She gasped aloud, and her eyes widened at his audacity. Leaning closer to the window, Dakota put as much space between them as possible and tried to ignore the man.

It didn't stop him.

Harrington slicked back his oily hair, then grabbed

her hand before she could pull farther away and lifted it to his full lips. Gazing at her through liquor-hazy eyes, he murmured, "Surely I can't be the first to have complimented you on the lovely form you have been blessed with."

Revolted, Dakota managed to pull her hand from his grasp before his lips touched it. "You're drunk," she mumbled as she looked nervously around the darkened car for assistance.

He noted her gaze and glibly informed her, "Don't worry, my dear. We shan't be disturbed. Everyone else is fast asleep."

Realizing that she would have to protect herself, Dakota swallowed back a small flutter of unrest. Here, then, was her first test. She hadn't expected to be accosted by a man. After all, most times decent women were treated like sacred beings out West. And for a man to bother a lady . . . well, he was asking for trouble.

But whether she'd expected it or not, the situation was upon her, and she had to deal with it. Alone. Finally she found her voice and with more calm than she felt, said, "A scream would wake them quickly enough. And that's just what I'll do if you don't move on right now."

His small, glassy eyes narrowed perceptibly. "No one would take your word for anything. A 'lady' doesn't travel unaccompanied. No one will listen or believe you."

The smirk on his face was rapidly replaced by fear when a steely voice sounded directly behind him.

"I would."

The supposedly sleeping cowhand slowly rose from his seat and faced the now quieted salesman. Two blue eyes stared at the would-be Romeo, and the fat man visibly quaked at the danger he saw written in those eyes.

Ben Cable ignored Dakota's gasp of surprise. He moved swiftly, yanking the salesman from his seat. The calm expression on Ben's face couldn't hide the restrained anger pulsing through his body, and Maxwell Harrington felt only relief when he was hustled down to the end of the carriage and shoved onto a chair.

Cable's voice was low and furious. "The lady is traveling under *my* protection. Make sure you remember that."

Before the man could stammer a reply, Ben turned his back on him disdainfully. A few long strides and he dropped into the now empty seat beside Dakota.

He couldn't believe it! Ben had watched her since boarding the train in Reno, and he *still* couldn't believe she was here.

Dammit, he cursed silently. He never should have ridden his horse to Reno. If he'd stayed in town and taken the stage, he could've snatched her off the goddamn thing back in Red Creek! As it was, he couldn't understand what was wrong with her brother. How in the hell did he allow this stubborn . . . *female* to head off on a wild-goose chase?

He glared at her and was disgusted to see that she wasn't bothered in the least. No, she merely brushed at the front of her dress and smiled. Like she was at some damned *tea party* instead of fightin' off a drunken fool on a movin' train!

"Well," Dakota said softly, to avoid being overheard by the now wide-awake eastern ladies. "What do you have to say for yourself?"

"*Me*?"

"Yes, Sheriff. You. I don't remember asking for your help."

"Well, excuse *me*, Miss Lane. But it looked to me like you sure could use it!"

"You were wrong. I could've handled him myself."

He pulled his hat off and ran his hand angrily through his hair.

"Could you, now?"

"Yes."

"Well, I reckon we'll never know that for sure, will we?"

Silence, as wide and deep as a canyon, fell between them. Then they both spoke at once.

"Why are you— "

"What the hell— "

"You first," Ben muttered and slammed his hat back on.

"Fine. Why are you even *on* this train, Sheriff?"

"Me? That's just what I was fixin' to ask you!"

"I'm going to San Francisco."

"*What*?"

Dakota glanced over her shoulder at the obviously interested women, then looked back at Cable. "Lower your voice."

"All right. But what the hell do you *mean*, you're goin' to San Francisco?"

"How many things could I mean?"

"I don't believe this!" He stretched his long legs out to the seat opposite them and crossed his ankles. "I do not believe that your fool of a brother didn't have the sense to make you stay home where you belong!"

"My brother is no fool!" Dakota crossed her arms

in front of her. "And who are you to tell me where I belong? Nobody *makes* me stay anywhere!"

He shook his head and mumbled to himself. She only managed to catch a word here and there. "Fool . . . trouble . . . women . . . stage . . . and Red Creek."

"If you've got something to say, say it."

"You bet I will." He turned his icy blue eyes on her. "As soon as we reach Sacramento, you're goin' back to Red Creek."

"Not likely."

"Dammit, Dakota." He shifted position quickly, turning to face her, and grabbed both her elbows. "Can't you see what this trip is gonna be like? You think *all* men are gonna be as easy to get rid of as that drummer?"

She pulled free. "I can take care of myself."

"Well, you're gonna have to. 'Cause I'm gonna be too damn busy to look after you!"

"You just look after yourself, Sheriff." She tilted her head and looked up at him. "What do you mean, you're gonna be too busy? Just what are you doin' here, anyway?"

He sat back again and recrossed his ankles. "I'm after the men who shot Tom Stillwell and your brother." His face settled into grim lines of determination. "And I don't want to waste my time worryin' about you while I'm at it."

She ignored the second half of his statement. "You're a sheriff in Nevada. You can't arrest someone in California."

"I can do whatever has to be done." He glanced at her.

"How can you just pick up and leave like that? You were hired to watch over the town."

"I was hired," he said slowly, "on the condition that I could leave whenever I had a mind to."

"And that doesn't bother you? Walking out on people who depend on you?"

He turned away from her and stared down the dark corridor. "Folks shouldn't *depend* on anyone. Certainly not me. I never asked them to. Never wanted them to."

"Well, who's the sheriff of Red Creek while you're gone?" She demanded his attention again. "Or did you bother to find one?"

He rubbed his jaw and hesitated before answering. "Mick Owens."

"*What?*"

"Take it easy. Don't work yourself into a fit! It isn't permanent. Just till the town council can find someone better. Or until I get back."

"That shouldn't be difficult. Almost anyone could qualify."

He laughed then, a full throaty sound that sent flutters of pleasure through her.

"You really are somethin', you know that?" he asked.

She looked away from him, suddenly uncomfortable with the look in his eyes. Dakota was used to seeing admiration in men's eyes . . . and anger. But this was different. There was something else in Ben Cable's gaze. Something that made breathing difficult.

He seemed to sense her uneasiness and spoke softly as he leaned closer. "You do know that corset drummer was right."

She looked up to find his face only inches from hers. "What do you mean?"

"With a shape like yours . . . the last thing *you* need is a corset!"

Her breath caught in her throat. Mouth suddenly dry, Dakota ran her tongue over her bottom lip. No one had ever spoken to her like that before. A curl of something warm and exciting started in the pit of her stomach and quickly spread to places she didn't even dare think about.

His blue eyes were smoky now, and as he let his gaze sweep slowly over her, Dakota felt each glance as if it were a touch. Slowly he raised his right hand and cupped her cheek. It seemed natural to her to rub her head gently against the rough palm.

In his touch, the warmth of his voice, and the flickering lamplight, she forgot where they were. Forgot that those nosy women were probably watching them. She even forgot the disgusting drummer. Everything faded . . . everything but Ben Cable.

She watched through half-lidded eyes as his face came even nearer. Her breath stilled as their lips met. She shuddered slightly and felt his lips curve into a smile. Her eyes closed, she surrendered to the new feelings churning through her.

Her arms wrapped about Ben's neck, she met his kiss with every ounce of passion she possessed. His tongue forced her lips apart, and she gasped at the almost indecent warmth filling her body. Instinctively she pressed herself closer to him, searching for something she hadn't even known existed until a few moments ago.

His fingers, threaded through her hair, kneaded her scalp, and she softly sighed her pleasure. The kiss became gentle again, almost hesitant.

Then abruptly he pulled away. She could see that

his breathing was as harsh as her own, so she was surprised and disappointed when he stood and moved to the opposite seat.

He answered her unspoken question in a strangled voice. "I think it will be better if I sit over here."

The fire in her blood slowly cooled and with its absence came reason. She glanced frantically around the darkened car and noted with embarrassment that the two women were conspicuously looking the other way. Oh, Lord, she moaned inwardly. Whatever happened to me?

In the flush of a hungry kiss she'd forgotten everything. Her brother, the reason she was on this train in the first place . . . even the fact that Ben Cable was a man she didn't wholly trust.

She'd never experienced anything like that before! Even now, minutes after the kiss had ended, her breath was forced and uneven. She glanced at him and was suddenly glad he was sitting farther away. It was much safer.

He smiled softly, as if he could read her mind and the whirlwind of thoughts racing through it. "Another time, Dakota," he promised solemnly. "Another place. Where we can find the privacy we will need."

Her heart lurched, and she watched him warily until he pulled his hat down over his face. Only a few minutes later his even breathing told her he was asleep.

Dakota curled up uneasily on the uncomfortable bench seat. She would have to be more careful. It seemed that there were all kinds of dangers to be faced on this trip. Not the least of which was her attraction for Ben Cable. She told herself firmly that she must remember the reason she'd started this jour-

ney . . . and keep that reason foremost in her mind.
Not again would she allow the handsome sheriff to
so shatter her defenses.

With her silent vow she permitted herself to doze
off lightly, still prepared to keep a watchful eye on
Sheriff Ben Cable.

Sunlight shone hesitantly through the dirty windows of the train and lay across Dakota's closed eyes.
She woke slowly, reluctantly. Burrowing her head
closer against the firm pillow, she tried to stay asleep.

She shifted position slightly and sighed. Though
accustomed now to the movements of the train, she
was grateful to whoever had provided this pillow.
It was so comfortable. Perhaps a little too firm, she
thought as she moved her cheek against it once
more. But still, it even *smelled* wonderful. So tangy
and fresh . . . with just a hint of tobacco.

Tobacco.

Her eyes flew open. She managed to stifle a groan
as she realized that her "pillow" was actually Ben
Cable's shoulder.

Good Lord. And she'd done everything but slap and
plump it into shape!

When did he take the seat next to me? she wondered. And why hadn't she heard him move during
the night? She'd always been a light sleeper. Usually
the slightest sound would bring her awake and alert.
Years of taking her turn at standing guard or riding
night herd had set a pattern that had never been
broken.

Desperately she tried to think of a way to get out
of this situation without an embarrassing scene. Maybe, she told herself with a sudden, wild hope, he's

still asleep. His breathing was steady, and he hadn't moved a muscle. If she went carefully enough, perhaps he'd never know that she'd spent the night cuddled up against him.

"Now that you're awake, would you mind sittin' up? My right arm's about to fall off."

She pushed herself into an upright position and ignored his grunt of surprise when her elbow dug into his stomach.

Ben glanced at her, a sour expression on his face. She'd done that purposely, he knew. But looking at her, you'd never be able to tell. Butter wouldn't melt in her mouth. She was a portrait in innocence. Rumpled, sooty, a thick lock of her soft brown hair that had fallen free of the topknot now hung over one eye . . . and still, he found her beautiful.

And troublesome.

He'd known it all along. The minute he'd spotted her on the train, Ben had experienced a sinking feeling all the way to his toes. He'd managed, though, to hold on to a foolish hope that she was on some errand of her own . . . that she wouldn't have the nerve to be heading for San Francisco. He should've known better.

He'd decided to steer clear of her. Keep a safe distance. And he would have if it hadn't been for that damn corset drummer. Ben's teeth ground together in frustration. Everywhere she went, he knew it would be the same. With a face and body like hers, she'd have men trippin' over themselves trying to get close to her. Hell, he thought. She's already got me doing it!

Dammit! What in the blue blazes was he supposed to do with her now? He had a job to do . . . and it didn't include riding herd on a notional female! He moved his arm and flexed his fingers, trying to restore some life into them. It really hadn't been necessary for him to let her sleep on him all night. But somehow, he just hadn't been able to help himself. When she hit her head on the iron railing for the third time, he'd simply taken the adjoining seat and pulled her head onto his shoulder. It was nothing. It meant nothing.

He was lying.

He watched her as she tried to repair the night's damage to her hair and remembered the softness of her. Her gentle sighs, her warm breath on his cheek when she moved in her sleep, the curve of her breast against his chest. Ben felt a familiar tightening. It was bad enough that he'd gotten no sleep at all . . . he'd be damned if she'd make it impossible to *sit*, too!

"I, uh . . ."

"Yes?" he asked.

"I hope I wasn't a bother to you," she offered lamely.

A bother? He smothered a derisive snort. If she only knew what kind of *bother* she'd been! This is foolishness, he told himself. He couldn't afford to start acting like a thunderstruck cowhand at his first dance. There was too much at stake here. Somehow, he had to regain control of this whole thing.

Besides, the *last* thing he intended to do was get involved with Dakota Lane. She's not the kind of woman he could bed and walk away from. She's the marrying kind, he told himself grimly. And marriage was definitely *not* in his plans!

"Oh, no bother at all." He rubbed his right hand with strong fingers and kept his voice light, unconcerned. "Hardly knew you were there."

"Oh . . . good."

"Except for your snoring." He raised his eyes to her and watched them narrow dangerously. He was beginning to realize that she didn't take to teasing very well. Good. Better to keep her angry than all soft and tender.

"I *beg* your pardon?"

"Snoring. Loud. Like a hibernatin' bear."

Her mouth fell open And a slow flush spread over her cheeks. "I did not!"

"Yes, ma'am, you surely did." He was enjoying himself. "Kept me up all night." That was partly true.

Dakota gave Ben an icy blue stare that would reduce most men to giving stammered apologies.

Leaning forward, Ben smiled and said, "Those daggers you're shooting at me would most likely send our friend the corset salesman running for cover. But it won't work on me, Dakota."

"I don't know what you're talking about." She stood unsteadily on her feet and took a step. "Excuse me."

He rose and faced her, the teasing smile gone from his face. "Where are you going?"

"None of your business."

"Like I told that drummer, you're under my protection now, so where you go is definitely my business."

They stared at each other solemnly, neither one willing to give ground. Finally Dakota spoke.

"Sheriff Cable. When I got on this train, I didn't know you were on board. When you came chargin' to my 'rescue' last night, you weren't invited. I could have handled that man myself. You weren't asked to hold me . . . stand guard over me while I slept." Whispering hoarsely, she added, "So, would you tell me just how I came to be traveling under your protection?"

He leaned down toward her and in a voice that matched her whispered shout he countered, "When you didn't listen to me and stay home . . . when you took leave of your senses and boarded this train alone. When the first day on board, you have trouble with some fool man . . . *that's* when you came under my protection!" He tilted his hat to the back of his head and added, "At least until I can send you back to Red Creek."

Her smirk told him what she thought his chances of accomplishing that feat were.

He nodded abruptly as if in answer to a challenge. "Now. If you'll tell me where you're goin', maybe we can end this little sideshow." He inclined his head meaningfully toward the other passengers who were staring at them with keen interest.

"I need some air," she muttered and swept past him with what little dignity remained to her. His amused expression seemed to stay with her as she made her way to the end of the car. She opened the door and stepped out onto the tiny platform. Her fingers curled tightly around the handrail.

All I have to do, she told herself sternly, is try to stay out of his way until we reach San Francisco. She smiled slowly. In a city that size the chances of Ben Cable being able to keep track of her were about as good as a cowhand's chances of staying at the Palace Hotel!

But slowly she realized that the thought of losing Ben Cable in a crowd wasn't as appealing as it once was. Did she really *want* to get rid of him?

Six

Sacramento

EYES wide, Dakota stood in the park and turned in a slow circle. She wanted to see everything. But there were simply too many things to look at. The tall buildings; shiny carriages drawn by high-stepping horses; businessmen in fine, tailored suits walking with beautifully dressed women down broad sidewalks.

Never before had she realized how small and *quiet* the town of Red Creek was. As people pushed past her, the noise of the city surrounded her. Huge lumbering freight wagons driven by swearing men crashed down the street, narrowly missing encounters with sedate buggies. Pedestrians, who by necessity were nimble of foot, scooted in and out of the traffic with apparent ease. She shook her head, amazed at all the activity.

Dakota clutched her carpetbag a little tighter and smoothed the bodice of her rumpled gown. Such a big city, she thought with wonder. And so many people! And all of them rushing about as if there

wasn't enough time in a day to do all they wanted
to. She almost wished she didn't have to go on to
San Francisco. She would have enjoyed staying on
and wandering through this capital city.

But first things first.

She walked slowly down the street to the stage
depot, where she would board a stagecoach for the
final leg of her journey. Though she shuddered at the
thought of another jolting ride in a coach, at least it
meant the end of her trip was at hand. She looked
around and smiled. Cable was nowhere in sight.

As soon as the train had stopped, she'd grabbed her
carpetbag and hurried from the car, losing herself in
the crowd as quickly as possible. She knew that Ben,
too, would have to take the stage into San Francisco,
but these few moments alone, with no one watching
over her, had been worth it. The pleasure of being only
another anonymous face in a crowd was a marvelous
sensation. In Red Creek there were no secrets . . . or
strangers. Everyone knew everyone else's business
and generally made a habit of discussing said business at every opportunity.

Besides, she needed the time alone. Every moment
she spent with Cable was filled with apprehension.
With his teasing words and smoky blue eyes shadowed with unspoken promises, he sparked emotions
and feelings that were completely new to her. It was
unsettling.

She shook her head. No time for that now. As she
counted out the money for her fare, she saw with
dismay that the money Laura had lent her was almost
gone. She had only a few dollars left. A pang of worry
swamped her. What if she'd been wrong? What if she
couldn't find work in San Francisco? Then she'd be

stranded. Alone. With no way home.

No. It wouldn't happen. There was always a job for someone willing to work. She glanced down at the few paltry bills in her hand. She was more than willing. She would have to find work immediately. Her search for the thieves would have to wait.

Wearily she sank onto a bench just outside the stage office. The summer sun was climbing into the sky, growing warmer every minute. She could feel the perspiration rolling down her back, and the neck of her dress chafed against her skin with a combination of sweat and grime. She felt as though she'd never had a bath before. She knew she must look as awful as she felt, and though this fact would no doubt help keep unwanted male company away, Dakota would at this moment give everything she had for a tub of hot water.

With a clank of chains and grinding of wheels, the stagecoach careened around a corner and came to a stop directly in front of the station. Clouds of dust billowed up and settled gently on her, and with a resigned sigh Dakota stood and prepared to board the stage.

A grizzled, bearded old man with skin as dry and cracked as old leather climbed nimbly down from the driver's seat, opened the passenger door, and politely handed her inside. As she was the first passenger, she had her choice of seats and she chose to sit facing forward. Though she would undoubtedly receive more than her fair share of dust that way, riding backward always made her ill.

She kept her carpetbag with her, preferring to have her pistol handy, though the chances of having to use it were slim. Still, it made her feel better knowing she need not depend on anyone else for protection.

"We'll be just a minute, ma'am," the driver said with a friendly smile. "We're only waitin' on two more passengers—then we're off."

Dakota returned his smile, glad for the information. With only two more people in the coach, they would all be able to stretch out a little. That one of those two people would undoubtedly be Ben Cable was an unfortunate fact.

"Well, I'll be forever damned! Hello, Ranger! Didn't know you was out here!"

Grinning, the old man waited as Cable hurried up to him, hand outstretched.

"Hello, Jack. Good to see you again!"

The driver pushed his battered hat to the back of his head. Holding the younger man's hand in an iron grip and shaking it wildly, he exclaimed, "What're you doin' out here, Ranger? Huntin' somebody?"

Ben shook his head. "I'm not a Ranger anymore, Jack. You know that."

"Hell." Jack laughed. "Once a Ranger, always a Ranger."

"Today, I'm a stage passenger. I'll be riding to San Francisco with you."

"You huntin' for the law? I never knew you to be overly fond of big cities."

"You're right. I'm not. And soon as I can, I'll be back in the wide open. I've gotta do a little job first, though."

"Law?"

Ben hesitated before saying, "Personal."

Jack slapped Ben's shoulder. "If it's like that, I pity the poor fool you're after! But I'm right glad for your company. You can ride up top with me, son. We'll tell lies about the old days!"

"Sounds good."

Ben looked up and noticed Dakota for the first time. His eyebrows lifted, and he smirked at her obvious eavesdropping.

Disgusted to have been caught out, she turned her head away and leaned back in the seat. Wouldn't you know it, she thought. Just like him to come all the way to California and find old friends! Then something the old man had said struck her. *Ranger*? So, Sheriff Cable had once been a Texas Ranger. Interesting. Even more interesting would be finding out the reason he quit. Or did he quit?

"Mornin', ma'am."

Jack spoke and Dakota stirred and glanced over her shoulder. She was just in time to see both Ben and Jack effusively greeting a lovely young woman. As the driver took the woman's bag and tossed it to the rack on top of the stage, Ben took her hand gently and carefully assisted her into the coach.

The woman was beautiful. Not just pretty. Beautiful. Strawberry-colored hair was swept up off her neck and hidden under the most becoming bonnet Dakota had ever seen. It was a small straw, draped lightly with a short, ivory veil and tied under her chin with a lavender ribbon that exactly matched the color of the wonderful gown. Dakota's first stab of envy soared as she admired the pale, sunrise-colored dress.

Already feeling grimy, Dakota was completely dismayed now at the startling contrast between her and the other woman. They were as much alike as a porcelain doll and a corncob baby. When she caught the look of sympathy in the woman's eyes, Dakota could have screamed.

Though clothes had never meant much to her, she now realized that living on a ranch and living in the city were two vastly different realities. What did she know about city life? How did she ever imagine that she would be able to act as if she belonged in San Francisco? Slowly, thoughtfully, Dakota rubbed the worn material of her simple dress between her thumb and forefinger. She sneaked a furtive glance at the other woman's dress. Most likely silk, she thought glumly.

She shifted slightly and her foot kicked the corner of her carpetbag. Its heaviness reminded her that inside lay a pistol. A weapon she was at ease with. No. More than at ease with. She was a damn fine shot. Dakota straightened. No doubt the elegant creature opposite her wouldn't have the wildest idea how to use a gun or defend herself.

The stage creaked and leaned to the left as Jack climbed up to his perch and gathered the reins.

Removing his hat, Ben stuck his head inside the coach. He smiled warmly at the redhead, then glanced at Dakota. "Well, ladies, you'll be riding alone for this trip. I'll be up top with Jack. Settle back and try to get comfortable. It's a long ride to the stage station where we'll spend the night." He touched his forehead to them and added, "If you need anything, just yell out." Then he climbed to the top of the stage.

As the coach took off with a lurch, the two women eyed each other warily. After a long moment of silent inspection, Dakota said, "My name's Dakota. Dakota Lane."

The other woman's gaze took in her traveling companion's trail-worn appearance, then nodded shortly. "Janice Van Dyke." She sniffed daintily, then turned and stared out the window.

Well, Dakota thought, she hadn't really wanted to talk to the woman anyway. And she was far too tired to worry about the deliberate snub. She didn't even care that Ben Cable obviously admired the woman. Turning sideways and stretching her legs out on the seat, she settled back against the side of the jouncing coach, closed her eyes, and hoped for sleep.

Much later she woke with a start just in time to keep from rolling off the seat as the coach lumbered through a hole in the road. Mumbling and moaning softly, Dakota sat up, feet firmly on the floor, and took count of the new bruises setting in on her body. Every muscle ached, and she felt as though she'd been run over by a herd of cattle. Why, her behind hadn't been that sore since Tenn had taken a switch to her when she was ten!

And if she weren't feeling bad enough, one glance at Janice Van Dyke would have taken care of it. The woman was in the same position she'd been in hours ago. That pretty dress wasn't made of silk. Had to be iron. Nothing else could have held her in place so long. Even her hair was perfect. The only sign that she was alive were the tiny beads of perspiration on her forehead and upper lip . . . and those were being delicately blotted with a lace handkerchief.

Reluctantly Dakota had to admit to a bit of admiration. If nothing else, the woman had staying power. Ruefully she pushed at her own messy, damp hair and brushed ineffectually at her even dirtier dress.

All at once Dakota fell forward and caught at the

half door to keep from tumbling to the floor. The stage was stopping. What in heaven was going on? Didn't they know better than to stop so suddenly? She lifted the shade slightly and looked out.

Something was wrong. *Very* wrong. They were in the middle of nowhere.

Janice started to speak, but Dakota held up her hand for silence. Going down on her knees, she peered carefully out the window, keeping herself well hidden. She stifled a gasp of surprise. There were two men at the side of the road. They had their rifles aimed at Jack and Ben.

A holdup!

For a frantic moment Dakota's heart stopped. With one shot Ben Cable could be dead. Gone. Mouth dry, she forced herself to think. To do *something*! They weren't paying any attention to the passengers yet. Now might be the only chance she got. Then one of them spoke.

"Throw down the box, old man. We ain't got all day."

She ventured another glance. The speaker stepped down from his mount while his partner kept a rifle aimed at Jack and Ben.

"You won't get much, mister," Jack cautioned. "Just some mail. That ain't hardly worth your time, is it?"

"I'll decide that." The bandanna over his mouth muffled his speech slightly. He walked closer to the stage, his spurs jingling.

"Throw down your guns." The other bandit's voice, hollow and dead-sounding.

Dakota's eyes flashed to him. A big man in a filthy shirt and pants, holding a well-kept rifle in steady hands. Her heart sank as she heard the soft thud of the weapons being tossed to the ground. Then, something heavy hit the dirt.

"All right. You got the box." Jack sounded angry. "Now you back off and let us get on."

"What's your hurry?" The first thief spoke again. He was much closer to the stage now. Dakota pulled back into the shadows of the coach. She'd seen enough. From his swaggering steps to his cold, black eyes.

"What's happening?"

Dakota glared at Janice and held her fingers to her lips for silence. Then slowly, hardly daring to breathe, she reached under the seat for her carpetbag. She had no idea what Jack and Ben were planning, but she knew she'd feel better with her own gun in her hand. That man out there had the look of a dangerous man.

There was just no telling what they might do next. And there was a gun still aimed at Ben. She knew it. She could *feel* it.

A single gunshot echoed through the uneasy stillness as the bandit shot the lock from the iron box. Janice gasped and Dakota fought down a sudden, panic-filled urge to run.

"What'd we get?"

"Shit." The first bandit's voice held a note of disgust. "Ain't nothing in the damn box but some letters."

"I already told you that, mister."

"Shut up, old man!" the big man with the rifle shouted. "Now what, Harry? You said this goddamn stage would be carryin' cash!"

"Well, we ain't." Ben's voice sounded wonderful to Dakota. "Now what say we just move along? You didn't take anything. Nobody's been hurt."

"Shut the hell up. We'll go when *I* say so." Harry turned to his partner. "You watch 'em while I check the passengers."

"Now, hold on here. You get to botherin' my passengers, and the stage company's gonna come down on you like a rock wall. They won't take kindly to that at all, boys."

Dakota's gun was loaded and ready. She bit her lip and took a deep breath.

The hammer of a gun was drawn back. Its distinctive *click* was unmistakable.

"Mister, I told you to shut up."

"Old man, don't you go worryin' Decker." The first bandit spoke softly. "He don't like bein' told what to do."

His spurs jingled again. He walked slowly, like a man used to walking carefully. Absently Dakota noted that Janice was crying.

She held her breath and waited.

The handle turned and the door was pulled open with a jerk. At once the would-be robber stuck his head inside where Dakota's pistol greeted him.

He raised his gaze slowly from the barrel of the gun and met hers. His black eyes narrowed as she cocked the pistol.

In only a moment Dakota had inspected him thoroughly. He held his rifle casually in the crook of his arm, as if it were an extension of his body. Every bit as dirty as his partner, menace flowed from him as surely as the stench of his unwashed body. Dakota stared into eyes as flat and black as a rattlesnake's and swallowed back the wave of revulsion that threatened to overwhelm her. She had to appear confident. At the slightest show of weakness she knew this man would kill her.

He would kill them all.

"Harry?" the other bandit called. "What's goin' on over there?"

"Answer him."

The man looked closely at her, shrugged, and yelled, "Shut up, Decker."

"Now. Tell him to throw his rifle down. You can drop your own as well."

An eternity passed before he complied.

"Why in hell should I throw down my gun?" Decker called.

"Ma'am, why don't you answer him? Appears you're in charge of this setup now."

She wasn't fooled by his quiet words. This was a man who would kill without batting an eyelash. The knowledge was written in his black, expressionless eyes.

"Step back slowly, drop your rifle, and we'll show him."

He started to move but stopped when she added, "And mister, don't make me shoot you."

"Dakota?" Ben's voice. "What in the hell is goin' on down there?"

"Dakota." The man cocked his head. "That you?"

She moved the pistol fractionally. "Step back. One step at a time. Carefully."

"Oh, yes, ma'am."

The bandanna still hid his face, but Dakota didn't need to see the mocking smile. It was plain in his tone. He did as he was told, though. And as his rifle hit the ground, another soft thud came to her, and she knew the other bandit had been disarmed. Slowly Dakota followed the man out of the stage.

"*Have mercy!*" Jack muttered as she stepped into view.

"Son of a bitch," Decker mumbled.

From the corner of her eye she saw Ben jump nimbly down from his seat. Quickly he scooped up his and Jack's weapons. At the same time a flash of movement from the mounted bandit brought a shouted warning from Dakota.

She had just enough time to see Ben throw himself to the side and hear a gunshot before she herself was locked in a struggle for her pistol. Her captive had taken advantage of her momentary distraction, and now his huge hand was wrapped around the barrel of the gun as he tried to twist it out of her grasp.

Dakota was no match for his strength. With a final wrenching motion, he took possession of the weapon and shoved her from him. Everything seemed to slow down. Every action took forever. Every movement a lifetime. Sprawled in the dirt Dakota held her breath and watched helplessly. The bandit brought her pistol to bear on Ben. The hammer was drawn back. She saw the chamber move into position. She heard the shot.

The bandit rocked slightly on the balls of his feet. With his free hand he reached up and pulled the scarf away from his face. Dakota's gaze followed his shocked one to the center of his chest where a dark stain blossomed and grew, soaking into the dirty blue material.

He looked up then, his eyes wide. Surprised. Dakota's pistol dropped from his nerveless fingers moments before he slumped facedown into the dirt.

She couldn't seem to stop looking at him. She kept

waiting for him to get up again. To aim the gun again. To focus his ugly eyes on her again.

Someone grabbed her and pulled her to her feet, and still she watched the motionless form.

"Dakota. Dakota." Ben's voice sounded far away. "Dakota. Are you all right? Were you hit? Goddammit! Say something!" His hands cupped her cheeks, forcing her to look away from the body. He held her face until he saw recognition and awareness sparkle in her eyes. Sighing, he kissed her forehead. "You're all right."

"Yes," she said finally. "Are you? I heard a shot. Saw you fall."

He shook his head. "No. I'm all right. I didn't fall. I jumped. The other one"— he jerked his head in the direction of the other body a few feet away— "had a knife." Ben turned around slightly, never releasing his hold on her. "His aim was bad."

Dakota stared at the huge blade imbedded in the side of the coach. A sudden, ghastly image pushed through her mind. Ben laying on his back, the knife sunk deep in his chest, his blue eyes wide and blank. She shuddered and leaned against him.

His arms folded around her, pressing her body to him with steady strength. She heard the rapid beat of his heart and knew he was as shaken as she.

"Missy."

She pulled away from Ben and glanced up at Jack. Floating wisps of gray hair surrounded his smiling face.

"You can ride my stage anytime. You done just fine." As an afterthought, he asked, "How's Miss Van Dyke doin'?"

Dakota hadn't given the elegant Janice a thought during the last few minutes. Now, though, she looked through the open door of the stage and was surprised to see the woman in a very unladylike position on the floor.

"She must have fainted," Dakota said as she climbed into the coach.

"You need some help?"

She looked up at Ben, who stood just outside the door. "No. I'll take care of her."

"Hmmph!" Jack snorted. "Eastern women. Never did have no use for 'em myself! Ben, let's get those two loaded up top and their horses tied on to the back of the stage. We'll leave the bodies at the station."

"Right." Ben watched Dakota in thoughtful silence for a moment before going to help the old man.

The coach rocked and swayed as the two dead men were hauled to the baggage rack. Dakota patted Janice's limp wrist gently and remembered the feel of Ben's arms around her. The warm, gentle strength of him. A deep breath steadied her still-pounding heart but did nothing to calm the other feelings racing through her body.

The stage station was a welcome sight. Made of adobe and surrounded by scrub pines, it was hardly a fancy hotel. But after the hours spent bouncing around inside the stage coach, both women looked at the small building as if it were a palace.

The proprietor, Angus Patterson, was a huge man. She guessed him to be at least six feet six inches tall, with hamlike hands and arms almost as big around as her waist. The bright blond shock of hair belied the deep wrinkles in his tanned, impassive face. He walked slowly, with his mighty shoulders hunched as if apologizing for his great size.

She watched as Angus led the tired horses to the corral, followed closely by Jack, gesturing wildly. Dakota correctly guessed the old man was regaling Angus with the story of the would-be holdup, and she smiled at the effort Jack was making to get a reaction from the bigger man.

Stepping into the station, the relative coolness of the interior soothed Dakota like a gentle touch. Angus's wife, Ada, a short, quick, round woman with a ready smile, had already set the trestle table with what seemed a banquet.

After supper, while Janice excused herself to go lie down, Dakota stepped out into the yard to enjoy the night air.

She strolled across the dusty yard until she reached the well, shaded by one lone pine. Leaning against the cool stones, she stared up at the darkening sky, watching as the stars slowly made their appearance, one by one. A full moon lit the yard with a soft glow, and somewhere nearby a chorus of crickets serenaded her.

Dakota breathed deeply, inhaling the scent of pine mingled with the damp, slightly musty aroma of the well. The cool night air touched her warm skin, and she relished it. It was so good to be alive. Her mind reached back to the holdup attempt, and she shivered involuntarily. It might have ended so differently.

They might have been killed. *Ben* might have been killed. Like Tom Stillwell, his life would have ended in an instant.

She stared off into the darkness and admitted to herself that she'd been scared. Not only for herself. For Ben. And that in itself was frightening. When had she begun to care so much about him?

"Dakota?"

She turned quickly. Ben stepped out of the shadows and asked, "Are you all right?"

She shook her head.

He took a step closer.

Dakota's breath caught, and she ran to him, throwing her arms around his neck. After a moment's hesitation Ben's arms encircled her gently.

She cried in the safety of his embrace. For the first time in her life Dakota felt no need to hide her tears.

Seven

Red Creek

LAURA opened the bedroom door while balancing Tenn's dinner tray with her other hand. She saw him glance her way before turning his back again. She crossed to the bed, suddenly determined to end this ridiculous game he'd been playing. Ever since Dakota left for San Francisco, Tennessee had been behaving like a spoiled child.

He'd barely been civil to her. And all because she'd done something without asking his permission first. Well, Laura had taken all she was going to take. It was time he learned a few things.

She set the tray down with a clatter on the small end table beside the bed. Hands on hips, she challenged, "All right, Tennessee, this has gone on long enough. Why don't you just say what you have to say and get it over with?"

His lips narrowed into a thin line, but he didn't say a word.

"I mean it, Tenn. If you're angry with me, come out with it."

He glared at her out of the corner of his eye. "There's nothin' to say. You know good and well what I'm mad about."

"Yes, I do," she said, sitting down on the edge of the mattress, "but I think you should say it."

"All right, fine." He turned to look at her directly. "You had no right givin' Dakota that money. It wasn't your place."

"Really?" Her eyes narrowed and her brows shot up. "And just what is my place?"

"Now, don't you climb up on your high horse! You know what I mean."

"I don't believe I do. Perhaps you'd better tell me, so I won't make the same mistake again."

"Fine. Dakota's *my* sister. *My* responsibility. And *I'll* make the decisions where she's concerned."

She shook her head. "Dakota's old enough to make her own decisions, Tenn. And so am I."

"Not when you don't know what you're doin'!"

"Who says we don't know what we're doing?"

"Me! I say so."

"Well, you're wrong, Tennessee." She leaned toward him, meeting his hurt glare with a steady eye. "We both know. We knew you'd be angry, too. But we also knew what had to be done."

"But— "

"No *buts*." She smiled at him. "You raised Dakota yourself, Tenn. You of all people should have more faith in her."

His shaggy head shook slowly, his brow wrinkled with worry.

"And as for me"— she leaned closer and brushed his lips with her own— "I'm going to be your *wife*, Tenn. *Not* your child. I'll always do what I think best."

He frowned. Laura could almost see him thinking. She paused for a moment, letting her words sink in. Finally she went on. "Sometimes, you won't agree with me."

"Hmmph!"

She took his hand and squeezed it. "But I will promise you one thing."

He looked up, wary. "What?"

"I won't do anything that might worry you without at least telling you first. Fair?"

"Oh, you'll tell me. Not ask me. Then you'll do it anyway?"

She smiled, and reluctantly he returned it.

"Well," Tenn said on a resigned sigh, "at least I'll get some advance warning next time." He reached for her and she went into his arms willingly. "I've missed you sorely, woman," he whispered, then kissed her hungrily.

After a few moments Laura sat up fanning herself with one hand. She took a deep breath, straightened her hair, and picked up the dinner tray. Gently she set it on Tenn's lap and spread out his napkin.

He glanced down at the steaming bowl of broth and grimaced. "Laura, when am I gonna see some real meat?" He pointed at the open window. "I swear, if a horse wanders too near that durn window, I just might eat it. Hide, hooves, and all."

She laughed delightedly, relieved he was back to his old self. Though she knew she wouldn't be giving in to him all the time, Laura didn't want to fight with him, either. She loved the hardhead. "There's plenty of beef flavor in this soup, dear."

"By the time you get around to fixin' some real food, I'm likely to forget how to chew." He picked up the spoon and grudgingly began on the steaming broth. "You figure Kota will be all right?"

"I'm sure of it." Laura tugged at her apron, straightening the folds. "She's very capable, you know."

"Yeah, but what about all those city men? How's she gonna look after herself in a place that big?" He waved the silver spoon at her. "Y'know, most fellas can think of a hundred different ways to get around a girl."

"Is that right?"

He grinned, then suddenly frowned again. "She ain't been around a whole lot of people before, Laura. What happens if some handsome gent starts sparkin' up to her? Then what?"

She ignored a sharp stab of apprehension and answered with more confidence than she felt. "She can handle herself, Tenn. You'll see."

"I surely hope so." He sipped at the broth again. "I'd hate to have to go all the way to California just to kill the fool who trifles with her."

"Tenn!" Laura reached over and patted his strong, sinewy arm. "It won't come to that. We're being silly. We've both forgotten that Ben's gone to San Francisco, too. Why, they're probably on the same train. You trust Ben, don't you?"

"Yeah . . ."

"Well, then. You can relax now. Ben will protect her."

Tenn hesitated, obviously mulling that thought over. Finally he glanced up at Laura and smiled. "You know, you're right. As long as Cable's around, Dakota will be safe enough. I can't imagine *any* fella fool enough to go after Dakota with him around." He set the spoon in the empty bowl and leaned back against the pillows. "You don't know how much better I feel. Dakota's in good hands with Ben."

His hands moved up and down her back in slow, rhythmic circles. Soothing, comforting, Ben held her and felt the tremors in her body as if they were his own.

They stood together, locked in the silence of the night, each drawing strength and comfort from the other. Minutes passed and neither of them noticed. Dakota's tears soaked through his shirt and touched his skin. He held her tighter. Her fingers clutched at his shoulders. He bent lower, so she might reach him easier. She drew her head back and looked at him. Her warm breath fanned his lips. He kissed her.

Tenderly his mouth touched hers. He tasted the salt of her tears and tightened his arms around her. Straightening, he smiled down at her. His fingers moved to wipe the damp from her cheeks.

"Better now?" he whispered.

She nodded. "I'm sorry. I didn't mean to— "

"Shh . . ." He wrapped his arms around her again.

Her tears finished, she leaned into him, her cheek against his chest. His heart beat steadily, and for a moment, Dakota couldn't help but think that had the holdup gone differently, it would be silent now. She snuggled closer and felt the strength of his arms as he cradled her body against his own.

"About today."

She pulled away slightly and looked up at him.

"I didn't get a chance to thank you."

Her jaw dropped and he laughed softly. "I see you weren't expecting a compliment."

"No." She smiled and rested her head against his chest again. "I kind of thought you'd complain about my 'interfering.' "

"Well, you *did* interfere. . . ." He tightened his arms about her suddenly ramrod straight form. "But this time I was glad for the help. If it hadn't been for you surprising them like that— "

"I don't want to think about it."

"I know. We got lucky. You gave us the chance we needed."

She shuddered and stepped out of his embrace. He was right. They *had* been lucky. Dakota was suddenly swamped with a flood of emotions. It was all too much. The trip, the holdup, the threat of what might have been, and his gentleness. What was happening between them? What would happen now? She couldn't understand what had made her go to him like that. So naturally, as if it were where she belonged. And the way he'd opened his arms to her, almost as though he'd been waiting for her.

She shook her head and tried to ignore the rush of questions and unfamiliar feelings that swept through her. Turning toward the well, Dakota dropped the bucket into the darkness. The resulting splash echoed loudly in the stillness.

"I'll get that for you."

She moved aside, leaned on the well's cool stone ledge, and stared down at the inky water below. The sudden quiet between them was almost as disturbing as the embrace they'd shared only moments before.

"How's Miss Van Dyke doin'?"

"Oh, she's better now," Dakota said, grateful for the change in subject. "She *did* have quite a bit to say about the 'uncivilized West.' "

"I can imagine."

"She was raised in the East, you know. Probably never even seen a gun up close." She looked up at Ben. "I can understand why she fainted." She knew *she'd* wanted to.

He pulled on the well rope and easily lifted the heavy, water-filled bucket from the depths. Gently he set it down on the ledge.

"Hmmph! I suppose you're right. But I never could stand swooning women. Make me nervous." He dipped his neckerchief into the cool water, wrung it out into the dust, and retied it around his neck.

Dakota stared at the tiny droplets of water as they slid down his neck and over his chest. She had a sudden urge to touch him again. To feel the texture of the golden curls just visible in the vee of skin at his open collar. To lay her hands on his broad chest once more and sense his heartbeat through her palms.

Ben moved then and began untying the bucket of water from the well rope. Glancing over his shoulder, he said, "I'll carry this to your room for you. I imagine you'd enjoy a good wash. Even with cold water."

They regarded each other silently for a moment. The pale, unearthly light of the moon drew them together, encircling them in a hazy, shimmering world of complete privacy.

He cleared his throat uneasily, then took her arm. Quietly they walked across the dusty yard to the house. Only one lamp burned inside. Everyone else, it seemed, had already retired in preparation for an early start in the morning.

As there were so few passengers this trip, the women had each been given their own rooms. At the end of the hall Ben stopped and opened Dakota's door. Moonlight streaming through the solitary window was the only light as Ben walked silently to the small table against the far wall. There was a momentary brightness when he struck a match, then cupping the flickering flame in his hand, he touched it to the lamp wick.

A hesitant light grew, dimly illuminating the plain, serviceable room. Dakota watched as Ben poured some water from the bucket into the washbowl on the table. When he finished, he walked toward her, the half-full bucket in his hand.

"My room is just across the hall," he whispered huskily. "After I've washed up, I'll come back and empty your washbowl."

"You don't have to."

"Back in a few minutes."

The door closed behind him leaving Dakota in a thoughtful silence. Slowly she walked across the floor toward the washbowl, struggling with the buttons of her dress. As she removed her clothing piece by piece, the cool night air from the open window caressed her naked flesh.

She took her plain cotton nightdress from her carpetbag and laid it on the foot of the bed. Then, using a corner of the towel provided by her hosts, she dipped it in the fresh water and rubbed at the grime on her skin. Staring at her reflection in the small mirror nailed to the wall, Dakota pulled the pins from her hair and let the heavy tresses fall free. Her eyes dreamy, she looked into the reflection as if watching the memory of Ben's embrace. The warmth of his arms, the strength of him.

A slight sound, barely heard, and she muttered, "Yes?"

In the mirror Dakota watched the door open behind her.

Her skin glowed like fine ivory. Ben's eyes followed the lines of her waist to her gently rounded bottom. Her long legs, lean and trim from years of riding horses, were shapely and graceful. In the mirror he could see her face and her beautiful blue eyes watching him with candid interest.

Suddenly she spun about and grabbed her nightgown. Her tawny brown hair swirled enticingly around her and then settled back to frame her face. The face that so enchanted him.

Without a doubt he knew he should turn and leave the room . . . but he couldn't. Not willingly. He saw the same knowledge written on Dakota's face as he walked slowly toward her.

Fear and desire came together in her eyes and fought for the upper hand.

Nothing in her life had prepared Dakota for the sensations coursing through her body. As he steadily closed the gap that separated them, a voice in her head screamed at her to stop this before it was too late. But the events of the day came together again in a rush, sending her common sense into exile.

She clutched at her nightdress, holding it up under her chin. Her breath came in slow, shallow gulps, and she felt the gooseflesh rise on her skin when he stopped just inches from her.

He didn't speak. Ben knew that if he tried, he wouldn't be able to find the right words anyway. His gaze moved over her features longingly. And though he knew this was wrong, knew that he had no business even contemplating what he was about to do . . . he couldn't stop himself.

A fragmented memory of her holding a gun on the deadly thieves flashed into his tortured brain. He remembered the heart-stopping fear that had claimed him. And also, the flash of pride as she successfully held the men off until Ben could act. He didn't want these feelings for her. But they seemed to have blossomed despite his efforts.

Lifting her chin with his fingers, he stared into her eyes, willing her to understand what he couldn't explain to himself.

Dakota didn't require words. His need for her was in his eyes. Instinctively she leaned toward him, ignoring her mind's silent scream for sanity. This need, this wanting, went against everything she'd ever known. Everything she'd ever been taught or believed in. But at this moment she didn't care.

In memory she could still see rifles pointed at Ben's chest. Only that afternoon he could have been killed. Gone forever. Was it really so wrong to want to be close to him now?

When Ben lowered his mouth to hers, she knew that it was already far too late to stop. Even if she had wanted to. His kiss slowly built in intensity as he ground his mouth against hers. Forcing her lips apart, his tongue dipped sweetly into the recesses of her mouth, caressing and teasing. Ben's lips seared Dakota's with all the passion she had ever dreamed of.

She reached up and entwined her arms about his neck, her nightdress falling unnoticed to the floor. His strong hands roamed freely over her body, then with a groan he pressed the length of her against him.

The coarse fabric of his clothing rubbed against her sensitive skin, and Dakota's breasts ached, her nipples hardening against his chest.

His hand curved around her bottom, pulling her tighter, closer to him. The cold metal of his belt buckle bit into her abdomen, and through the confining material of his pants, she felt the rigid proof of his need rub against the throbbing center of her. She moaned softly and dug her nails into his back as she tried unsuccessfully to mold herself into his body.

Ben tore his mouth from hers and struggled for breath. His eyes were glazed as he stared at her. Slowly he moved his hands to cup her face, then tenderly he touched his lips to hers. Her tongue reached out to lick her lips when the kiss ended, as if to recapture the taste of him.

"Dakota," he said in a strangled whisper, "are you sure?"

She knew what this effort had cost him. And somehow, his question made her more sure than before. To be separate from him now, even for a moment, was painful. Her eyes spoke volumes, though all she managed to say out loud was, "Yes, Ben. Please."

He released a pent-up breath and lifted her in his arms. She settled against him with a contented sigh. With a quick motion he threw the crocheted coverlet back and gently deposited her in the middle of the bed. He took a step back and smiled when she held her arms out to him.

Dakota watched in hungry fascination as he quickly removed his clothing. His broad chest shone golden brown in the lamplight, and her gaze followed the trail of pale hair over his flat belly. His fingers tugged impatiently at his belt buckle, and she looked away.

Embarrassment battled with a newly awakened raw desire as she lay naked and vulnerable under his hot, liquid gaze. A soft breeze drifted in the open window and brought chills to her already sensitive skin.

Moments later he lay down on the bed, half covering her with his body and embarrassment faded away at the touch of his warm flesh against hers.

"So beautiful," he muttered and moved his mouth down the curve of her throat, placing small damp kisses along its length. His hand slowly circled the mound of her breast, and his long fingers teased the dark bud erect.

She moaned softly at the tingling, pulling feeling that spread down to her toes. When his tongue touched the tip of her already tender nipple, fire shot through her veins and she thought she would come off the bed as his mouth closed over it. He sucked at her breast, his teeth nipping her flesh gently.

She watched him with clouded eyes and sensed the fire build at the sight of his lips pressed against her. He chuckled softly when she wove her fingers in his hair and pulled his mouth more firmly to her breast. His tongue drew lazy circles around the tiny peak, and she arched her back in response. Raising his head slightly, he smiled at her, then moved to kiss her dry lips. The soft, moist heat of his tongue drove Dakota to the brink of insanity.

His right hand held her head firmly in place as his left drifted over her eager flesh. First one breast, then the other felt the magic of his touch, and she moved against him helplessly. Softly he moved his hand lower, caressing the rise of her hips and the smooth length of her thighs.

Ben dipped his head to her breast once more as his

left hand moved to the inside of her thighs, stroking her body tenderly.

Dakota's mouth was dry, and she twisted about on the bed, trying at once to bring him closer . . . and to move away. The strength of the feelings he created were so overpowering, she didn't know what to do. She gasped aloud as his hand found the center of her pleasure, and suddenly all thought of escape fled.

Gently his fingers touched and probed the secrets of her body, and she moved her hand down to cover his.

"Easy, Kota," he whispered, his fingers still wondrously touching her soul.

She felt the slick moisture build between her legs, but was helpless to do anything about it. Under his incredible hands, she lay transfixed, swept away to a place where only the unbelievable need she felt mattered.

Slowly Ben raised himself over her, spreading her legs apart with his knee. Dakota opened her eyes and looked up at him. Passion and tenderness filled his eyes, and she smiled softly, trustingly. She arched against him again and twisted her hips while his thumb stroked the tender flesh between her thighs. She knew he watched her and didn't care. Nothing mattered anymore. This building fire must be quenched.

He touched the core of her once again, then slipped his fingers deep inside. Her eyes flew open at the invasion.

"It's all right, darlin'," he coaxed. "Relax now, let me love you. . . ."

She nodded and closed her eyes again, lost in the wonder of him touching her so deeply. When he pulled his fingers away, she almost cried out in despair. But before she could, he pushed his body gently into hers.

Moaning softly, a spasm of delight washed over her. He filled her so completely. They were one. Their bodies no longer separate, but each a part of the whole. A short, slight pain began and ended quickly, then a flood of sensation washed over her once more and she knew nothing beyond the driving need to somehow release herself from the torment he'd created.

He lifted her hips and thrust deeper inside her. Dakota wrapped her legs around him and squeezed tightly. Her nails raked at his shoulders as she struggled toward the distant peak of satisfaction.

Instinctively her hips moved with him and with each thrust the tension built even higher. He leaned over and captured her mouth, successfully swallowing her moans of pleasure. His tongue darted in and out of her mouth even as his flesh entered and left her body.

When she thought she couldn't stand any more of the loving torment, a blaze of light engulfed her. Her body shuddered with the force of it, and she knew she was going to die. As if from far away, she heard Ben's harsh cry, then slowly they returned to earth, still wrapped around each other . . . locked together.

He rolled to the side, but kept his right arm around her, holding her close. When the wonderful throbbing finally stopped and Dakota thought she could speak again, she whispered, "Ben, I've never done that before."

She heard his soft laughter before he answered, "I know that, Dakota."

With the cooling of passion, reason returned. And with reason came the first wave of shame and guilt.

She'd behaved no better than a common trollop. Dear God, she moaned silently. Every lesson she'd ever learned about decency and morals had been thrown to the winds in a moment! How would she ever be able to look Tenn, Maria, and Jess in the face again?

"I shouldn't have done it now," she whispered plaintively.

Ben put his free arm behind his head and stared at the ceiling. "It was my fault. I'm sorry."

She raised up on one elbow and stared down at him. "It was no one's *fault*. It just happened. But," she added slowly, "it can't happen again."

Her mind was working frantically. How *could* she have allowed herself to be so overcome? Great God in Heaven! She'd just made love to a man she'd only known a week!

Lord. If Tenn ever found out, he'd kill Ben in a heartbeat. And now she had to spend the rest of this already disconcerting trip with the added burden of her awakened desire for Ben Cable. It was too much.

There was only one thing to do. No matter how difficult . . . she must keep her distance from Ben.

"Good." His voice broke into her train of thought.

"Good? What's good?"

"You finally agree." He moved his gaze from the ceiling to her confused face.

"Agree to what?"

"To go back home, of course." It was the only solution, Ben thought. He had to get her away. He wouldn't allow himself to stumble into emotions better left alone.

He looked at her speculatively. Her passion and wild abandon only served to point out the fact that she was ready for a man. A steady man. Her untried feelings would soon convince her that she was in love with him. And he couldn't accept the responsibility of *that*.

Grabbing the coverlet, Dakota threw it around her shoulders, sat up, and faced the man still lying naked on her bed. "Who said I was going home?"

Ben snatched his pants from the floor and pulled them on. It was amazing, he thought, that a woman could change so rapidly. One moment more passionate than anyone he'd ever known, the next, stubborn as hell. Well, by heaven, he wasn't going to stand for it.

"I said it. I knew it wouldn't work out. You coming to San Francisco." He swept his arms wide, encompassing the bed and added, "And this just proves it."

"This proves nothing!" She slipped off the bed, still holding her makeshift robe tightly around her. "I didn't count on it happening. . . ." She looked confused briefly, as though she were trying to understand exactly how the loss of her virginity *had* occurred. The whole thing was a blur.

"But it *did* happen, Kota." His voice was soft, consoling.

She nodded and her eyes filled with tears that were blinked back before they could fall.

"Kota, I . . ."

"No. I will accept the responsibility for what happened." Her eyes dared him to defy her as she promised, "But, Ben, it will *never* happen again. It can't." She pulled herself up to her full height and faced him.

He stared at her silently. Fully prepared to let her down as easily as possible—he was at a loss with the shoe on the other foot. Dakota was dismissing him.

And as much as he willed it otherwise, it hurt.

"So," she said, breaking into his thoughts, "you'd better go back to your own room. The stage will be leaving bright and early in the morning." She raised her chin. "And I'm not gonna miss it."

Ben took several sharp, stabbing breaths and ran a hand over his face. His expression murderous, it took all of Dakota's nerve not to back down. Finally he bent and retrieved his shirt, hat, and boots, then bowed with a sarcastic flair and stomped out of the room.

Eight

BEN'S fury grew during the night. In the predawn light he shouted at the horses and urged them backward, lining them up in front of the stage. It was actually Angus's job to hitch up the animals, but Ben needed to be busy.

He hadn't slept. His own traitorous mind had seen to that. Every time he closed his eyes, he saw Dakota's body innocently opening to him.

A virgin! By all that's holy, he'd taken a virgin! And not just *any* virgin! No, *he* had to seduce the sister of one of his very few friends! He swallowed the lump of anger in his throat. He was asking for trouble. Good God! Ben had been able to avoid any entanglements for years! And now, not only was he involved with the residents of Red Creek and *their* problems . . . there was Dakota!

This wasn't supposed to happen. Being a small-town sheriff should have been just another aimless job to keep him fed while he drifted. Dammit! He didn't *want* a home! He didn't *want* to care!

One of the horses nipped at him and Ben just managed to keep from slugging the animal. But it wasn't the horse's fault. Like everything else that had happened since last night, the fault lay entirely at Ben Cable's door.

Mumbling angrily, he went through the motions of strapping the harnesses onto the horses. He'd done the job so many times before, his mind was, unfortunately, free to wander again. Naturally it dredged up the haunting specter of Dakota.

He'd known it was a mistake. Right from the first. He never should have gone back to her room. But there wasn't a man alive who would have been able to keep him from it. And he doubted that any man would have been able to leave that room without touching her, having her. Maybe a saint. He snorted derisively. Lord knew, Ben Cable was no saint.

Finished with his chore, Ben stomped over to the corral, propped one foot on the lower bar, and leaned his forearms on the top. He'd steered clear of virgins over the years. Their very innocence scared him off. He'd always believed there was more pleasure to be had with a woman who knew what she was doing . . . and who had no personal interest in who she did it with.

He was wrong. There was something to be said for being the teacher. For being the first to taste the honey.

Dammit! He shifted position uneasily. At this rate he might never have a good night's sleep again. Even the thought of her brought his body to eager attention. He gritted his teeth and stared off at the first rays of sun poking over the far-off hills.

He could still hear her voice telling him that it shouldn't have happened. Well, hell. *He* knew that better than she did! And then she announced that it would never happen again. Hmmph. That's the trouble with virgins. They had no idea what they were getting into when they left their chaste life behind. She thought it would be so easy. But she didn't know that doing without something you've never had is far easier than trying to live with the knowledge of what you were missing.

He rolled a cigarette thoughtfully, then struck a match and held it to the twisted end of paper. He inhaled deeply, feeling the bite of the tobacco go deep into his lungs. If he were completely honest with himself, he would have to admit that it wouldn't be easy on him, either. And it wasn't only her delectable body driving him to distraction. There was so much more to her than that. Her pride. Her strength. Dammit, even her fierce loyalty to Tenn. Something he'd been sure he wanted no part of anymore.

Even before he'd bedded her, Ben had found things in Dakota to almost make him wish he were a different kind of man. The kind she needed. The staying kind.

But he wasn't. He'd learned the hard way, a long time ago. It just didn't pay to have people depend on you. Count on you. Love you.

The hurt goes too deep when it's taken away.

He pinched out the smoking end of his cigarette and tossed the remains into the dust. Straightening, he pulled his hat brim lower over his eyes and glanced toward the station house. Soon she'd be stepping outside, ready to board the stage. She shouldn't have had to wake up alone this morning. She deserved better. Dakota deserved soft words and strong arms.

Ben looked down, disgusted with himself. He wasn't looking forward to seeing her. He already knew that she would have an expectant look in her eyes when she saw him for the first time.

And he knew that he would have to ignore it.

Dakota's body slammed hard against the backrest as the stage hit a hole in the road. Grimacing, she straightened up again and smiled halfheartedly at Janice, across the way.

Before boarding the stage, she'd been so worried that somehow, someone would know . . . would be able to tell by her face what had happened to her during the night. She'd worried for nothing. No one seemed aware of anything different about her. Not even Ben. Why, he'd hardly glanced at her.

That fact brought with it a wave of regret. She didn't know what she'd expected from him. But surely, a kind word or two wouldn't have been too much to ask. Just remembering what she'd done with him . . . how brazenly she'd behaved, was enough to bring a rush of color to her cheeks. He'd probably lost all respect for her after the way she'd tumbled into his arms so greedily. He *must* have. Or he wouldn't treat her with such disregard.

She blinked back tears for what couldn't be changed and stared out at the land. Hours crawled by. The drought that had held California in its grip for so long had wreaked havoc on the countryside.

All around her the earth was dying. It was a world of brown. Even the evergreen trees were a bedraggled beige with the layers of dirt that covered them. The summer heat seemed more intense when the eyes could find no spot of cool to rest on.

When the stage stopped for a change of horses, Dakota climbed gratefully down from the confines of the coach. Ben was off helping the hostler ready the next team as she walked to the well for a drink of water.

"Scorcher, ain't it?"

Dakota turned and smiled at Jack. "Sure is."

The old man took off his hat and wiped the sweat band with his bandanna. "I don't mind telling you I sure am glad to have the Ranger along on this trip. He's doing a lot of my work for me." Chuckling, he sat heavily down on the low front porch. "Must be gettin' old." He squinted up at Dakota. "But don't you tell nobody, y'hear?"

" 'Course not." She winked at him and added, "Besides, no one would believe me anyway."

He shook his shaggy head and laughed softly. Motioning for her to sit beside him, he said, "You're all right, missy. You surely are. I never had much truck with females, but you'll do."

She smiled.

Shrugging toward the barn, Jack said, "Why, even the Ranger was commentin' on how handy you come in sometimes."

"Oh, was he?" Before or since last night? she wondered.

"Yes, ma'am. And that there is mighty high praise from a Ranger. Specially *that* Ranger."

Curious, Dakota asked, "How long have you known him, Jack?"

"Oh, 'bout five years, I 'spect."

She glanced across the yard and studied Ben's back for a few moments. Here was her chance to find out more about Ben Cable without having to ask him.

Lowering her gaze, she told herself perhaps she'd even be able to understand why he was treating her so coldly now after a night of such heat.

"How did you two meet?"

Jack reached into his shirt pocket for his block of chewing tobacco. He pulled off a chew with his teeth and began his story.

"Well, missy . . ." He spoke slowly, jawing his tobacco. "It was back over to Texas, not long after the war. I was driving the stage line. Now, I usually had someone riding shotgun for me, but on this particular run I was alone. Well, everything was going along as it should till I come to the base of these mountains."

Dakota leaned back against the porch rail and gave him her full attention. Jack clearly enjoyed being the teller of the tale.

"Now, these mountains end in what is pert near a perfect point at their bottom. With all the brush and such sproutin' up all over, why, a dozen men could hide in there and go unnoticed." He spit some juice into the dust and looked Dakota square in the eye. "Howsomever. There wasn't no dozen. Just three of them. And pure-dee mean, too. They called down the cashbox and then, keeping me covered, ordered me down, too."

"What about the passengers?" Dakota was outraged.

"Now, missy," he chided, "who's tellin' this story?"

Her face fell and Jack patted her arm clumsily. "That's all right. Wasn't no passengers that time. Only the mail and some little bits of cash. Nothin' to stir any self-respectin' outlaw's juices!"

She smiled.

"Anyhow, most times a man is robbed, the thieves'll more'n likely just take his cash and skedaddle. Not this bunch. Without so much as a whisper, one of 'em put a bullet in me while the other two laughed."

Dakota leaned forward, completely caught up in the story.

"Well, sir, they stampeded that coach and the horses, and after riding their animals up and all around me, took off and left me layin' there. Now, missy, I ain't too proud to admit that that bullet was almighty uncomfortable. Hurt like hell. No water. No horse. I was as good as dead . . . and they knew it. I must have laid there for a couple of hours when up rides this handsome young fella on a tall black horse. By this time I didn't much care if it was them robbers come back to finish me off. I was *that* tore up. But this young fella, he picks me up like I was a baby and carries me off the main road behind some of those bushes. Before I knew it, he had him a fire going and coffee brewing."

"Ben?" Dakota whispered.

"Nobody but." Jack grinned. "Well, gentle as a woman, he dug that bullet out of me and fed me some coffee and jerky. Right quick I started feelin' better. I wanted to go after those boys who hit my stage, but Ben, he wouldn't hear none of it. He set me up with firewood and plenty of water, then after I fell asleep, he took off."

She gasped and threw a surprised glance at the far-off figure of Ben Cable.

"Now, missy, let me finish."

She looked back at the old man.

"Anyway, about dawn I woke up and I was alone. Figured that Ben had done what he could and then lit out. Just like you was figurin'. But pretty soon,

who should come into camp but Ben, ridin' that big
black and leadin' three horses. Each one of them with
a layin'-down passenger. You can imagine my surprise
when Ben plops down that strongbox. Calm as you
please then, he pours himself a cup of coffee and sets
down. 'So what happened?' I said. He just looks up
and says, 'They had a change of heart, old timer.' Well,
I finally dug it out of him exactly what happened.
He tracked those buzzards down just like an Injun.
Then rides right into their camp, guns blazin'. And
him outnumbered three to one." He smiled in fond
memory. "Lordy, that's one fight I wish I'd seen."

"I had no idea," Dakota said, clearly showing her
surprise.

"Missy, he's quiet, and it's always the quiet ones you
got to watch out for. 'Cause ol' Ben over there . . . why
he's just likely to beard the devil in his own den!"

Dakota looked over at Ben, where he was hitching
up the horses. Not moving her gaze, she asked, "What
happened then, Jack? Finish your story."

Wearily he pushed himself to his feet, then offered
her his hand and helped her up. "That *is* the end, missy.
Ol' Ben, he took care of me till I was fit to ride, then we
went on in to the nearest town."

"Was anything said about the dead men?"

"Hell, I mean shoot, no. They was thieves and most
prob'ly killers. And Ben was a Texas Ranger. Nobody
needed to know more than that." He glanced over at
the stage. "You best get aboard, ma'am. We'll be fixin'
to leave any time, now."

She barely noticed the jarring ride that day. Instead,
her busy mind went over and over Jack's story. She
knew every word was true. The old man was a plain
speaker and wouldn't have bothered to lie about Cable.

Besides, his admiration for the ex-Ranger was obvious. The story explained it.

Dakota had to rethink her opinions of Ben Cable. At least, on the subject of his capabilities as a sheriff. She shook her head, remembering how she'd thought Cable would never be able to track down the men who'd attacked Tenn. But then, hadn't her older brother always warned her about jumping to conclusions?

And hadn't she gone ahead and jumped to more than one conclusion about Cable? Just last night she'd assumed that he cared for her. Not love. Just *some* kind of feeling besides lust. His gentleness, his patience, his tender kisses had all convinced her that perhaps the growing interest she felt for him was returned. But judging by his behavior in the morning light, she'd again been wrong about Ben.

And as for her own interest, she was ashamed to admit that far from easing the desire she'd felt for him, their coupling seemed to have only strengthened it. All day visions of him swam before her eyes. She saw his tanned hand cupping the white flesh of her breast. She saw his soft smile when her body jumped as his fingers entered her. Over and over again her weary brain played out these images until she thought her body would burst from the renewed and now unsatisfied need.

Dakota opened her eyes wide and stared out the half door. She must somehow banish these memories. It was perfectly obvious that Ben wanted nothing more to do with her. And she couldn't blame him. The only thing left for her to do was to continue with her original plan.

She would need all her wits about her in the city. First, she would find a job. Then, somehow, she would recover her brother's stolen money and go home. She glanced at the roof of the stagecoach. If Ben is as good as Jack says, she told herself . . . let *him* find and arrest the men. She wasn't interested in justice anymore. She only wanted to save Tenn's future. His dreams.

She wouldn't stand by and watch him lose his home again.

Dakota'd never seen so many people. All kinds of people. Some dressed in the height of fashion, others as though they had just come off a long trail. But all of them moved as one. Hurrying up and down the wide streets. Pushing and shoving, determined to reach their destinations in as short a time as possible.

She had a sudden, overwhelming urge to be back in quiet, slow little Red Creek.

Just getting off the stage and to the sidewalk seemed a formidable task. Standing on the wide boardwalk, Dakota planted her feet firmly and withstood countless bumps and jostles. Dismay filled her. How would she ever even begin to find two thieves in the sea of people? Where should she start? Where should she go?

For the first time she felt real doubt about her trip. She didn't know anyone. Why, she'd probably get lost just trying to cross the broad street! Maybe, she thought, she should do what Ben wanted and go back home.

No. She squashed that thought firmly. She'd never been a quitter. All her life there had been some kind of problem to deal with. Some hurdle to overcome. And she had always faced it head on. Never had backed down from a fight. She stood taller. Someone in the city was living very well on hers and Tenn's hard-earned money. And they'd shot Tenn and killed Tom Stillwell to get it.

By the lord Harry, Dakota vowed silently, they won't have it long.

"Now do you understand, Dakota?"

She turned and looked up to the driver's seat of the coach. Ben looked down at her, shook his head, and continued. "Now do you see why I didn't want you to come out here?" He swung his long legs over the side of the coach, jumped to the ground, and landed inches from Dakota.

"Look at this place!" His arm swept around. "Hell, you'd probably get lost in no time. And I just don't have the time to guide you by the hand."

"I didn't ask you to guide me." She gripped her carpetbag tighter. Honestly, sometimes it was as if he could read her mind. "I can find my way over wide-open rangeland—I suppose I can do it here." She hoped her voice sounded convincing.

He shook his head, clearly exasperated. "Look. I've got to go to the stage depot. Tell 'em about those two we buried back at the station. It'll only take a few minutes, then I'll find you a hotel." He turned and walked away, but after only a few steps, he looked back and warned, "Stay here."

She watched in silence until the crowd of people swallowed him, then turned away. She had just a few minutes to make her decision and be gone before he returned. She'd *known* he'd be impossible as soon as they reached the city. But somehow this was worse than she'd imagined. He hadn't spoken to her all day. Hardly even noticed her. And then, when he *did* speak, it was an order.

Well, he's got a surprise headed his way. She wouldn't be stopped. Not by him and not by the overwhelming city. Grimly determined, she started off down the street at a fast walk. In the opposite direction from Ben Cable.

"Hold up there, missy."

Jack hurried to catch up with her, tossing a glance over his shoulder at the same time. He snatched his hat from his head and asked, "You got yourself a place to go?"

"No," Dakota admitted softly.

"Well, I don't know why the Ranger's in such an uproar, and I reckon it's none of my business." He scratched his whiskered chin. "But, missy, I reckon I owe you somethin' for your help out on the road. Now, I know of a place."

"Where?"

Jack cautioned, "It ain't nothin' special . . . but it *is* respectable. It's a restaurant. Run by an old friend of mine. Her name is Molly Malone." He chuckled and said, "Fierce old woman, but a heart as big as the outdoors. Reckon she'd give you a job and could prob'ly even find you a place to stay. You just tell her Jack sent you."

"Thank you." Dakota kissed Jack's leathery cheek and smiled as the old man blushed.

"I'll tell you how to get there," he said. "But you got to be right careful. It's down on the waterfront, and there's some mighty shady folks down there. Most times a good woman will be safe. But it don't pay to take no chances."

The Irish Lady restaurant was not exactly the Union Plaza, but it looked clean. And right now, Dakota thought, she was so tired, she wouldn't have cared if it had been a drafty tent. Besides, she told herself as she stepped out of yet another stumbling drunk's way, anything would be better than simply standing on the corner much longer.

She took a deep breath, straightened her shoulders, and started for the swinging door. Just at that moment a cowhand came running out of the restaurant, his arms wrapped around his head.

A huge woman was right behind him, swinging a broom and shouting, "I told you, I don't like gunplay in my place of business."

The cowhand stood shamefaced in the middle of the street as an appreciative crowd gathered.

The woman went on, barely pausing for breath. "Now, Travis . . . when you can behave yourself, you can come back. I'll hold on to your guns for you till then."

Clearly intimidated, the cowhand pleaded over the laughter of the crowd. "Shoot, Molly, I might need them guns."

Molly Malone, gray-streaked russet hair blowing about her face, stared him down and shook her broom at him. "Any fool knows that the only man who needs a gun is the man who carries one!" She pushed her hair aside, toward the sloppy knot at the back of her head. "If you ain't got that pistol, you'll be a sight more careful of what comes out of your mouth." She shook the broom at him menacingly. "Now, you git, Travis. And think about what I told you."

The man was beaten and he knew it. He kicked at the ground ineffectually for a while, then walked off down the street. A roar of laughter from the men who'd been witness to Molly's latest lesson in good manners followed him.

As she turned to go back into the restaurant, Molly noticed Dakota. Slowly the older woman's gaze traveled up and down her tired, trail-worn appearance. She shook her head as if trying to figure out how a girl like her came to be on the "Coast."

"Molly Malone?"

"That's me," the old woman said, her head cocked, her eyes suspicious.

"Jack sent me." Dakota paused a moment, waiting for some sign of recognition. "He's the stage—"

"I know him." After studying the young woman's face carefully for a moment, Molly's eyes mirrored the sudden smile that stretched across her features.

"Well, dearie, you look like you've been riding a rough trail. Why don't you come and sit down. I'll get you some coffee." She took Dakota's arm and ushered her inside. "And you can tell me why in the hell Jack sent a girl like you down here."

Entering the restaurant, Dakota almost sighed with pleasure. Warm and friendly, the small place was filled with large tables covered by different-colored lengths of calico. Bright curtains hung at the sparkling clean windows and when the wind blew in, Dakota was sure she heard them rattle from all the starch that had been ironed into them. The walls were painted a fresh white, and almost every square inch of them was covered by either a painting, a drawing, or a daguerreotype. Except on the far wall. There, on wooden pegs, hung at least thirty guns in their holsters.

From a table near the window Dakota watched as Molly climbed up on a chair and hung still another holster and gun on an empty peg.

She studied the older woman unobserved. Though they were about the same height, where Dakota was slim, Molly was stout. The woman gave no impression of being fat, however, and Dakota guessed that every pound on Molly was pure muscle. Her skin was burned brown from the sun, and long lengths of her hair straggled free of the confining pins. She wore a plain black skirt so long that it swept the floor and above it, a serviceable white shirt stretched tautly across her ample bosom.

Dakota smiled as Molly climbed down from the chair, showing that beneath her skirt, the big woman wore a pair of well-worn cowboy boots.

She disappeared into the other room and came quickly back carrying a pot of coffee and a plate of sandwiches. She sat down opposite Dakota and said, "Now, you get some of this inside you before we talk."

As she ate, she listened to Molly banter good-naturedly with the customers, and she relaxed for the first time since leaving Red Creek.

When most of the coffee had been drunk and half the sandwiches eaten, Molly finally asked, "All right. Tell me your story, girl. How come you to be on the waterfront? Why would Jack send you here?"

So, without leaving out a thing, Dakota launched into the story about what had brought her to San Francisco and why Jack sent her to the Irish Lady.

"Well, then," Molly commented when the story was finished. "Seems you come in pretty handy in tight places."

Dakota smiled.

"Oh, that Jack," Molly said, a faraway look in her eyes. "There's a wild one for you."

"Jack?"

She laughed. "You young folks are all alike. You see the gray hair and a few wrinkles and figure we're all the same. Old and quiet." She leaned back and smiled at the ceiling. "No such thing." She shifted her gaze to Dakota. "You remind me sometime to tell you about Jack and me and himself . . . Mr. Malone, God rest his soul. Oh, those were excitin' days."

Abruptly Molly pulled out of her reverie. "Dearie, I owe Jack a lot. Even my business here. Jack was a good friend to Mr. Malone, God rest his soul, and after he went . . . to me." The big woman leaned over the table and patted Dakota's hand. "But this time Jack's made it easy for me to repay good turns. You're a good girl, Dakota. I like you. Would you be willin' to help out around the restaurant? Cookin' and servin'?"

"Yes!"

"Well, that's settled. And as for rentin' a room, I've got a couple extras right upstairs. You can stay there . . . no charge."

"I'd have to pay you something."

Molly laughed and stood up. "Don't you worry about that. With all the cowhands and sailors that come streaming in here to eat and drink . . . you'll more than earn your keep. Besides"—she winked— "I'll enjoy the company. Me and himself . . . well, we was never blessed with children." Her face saddened for a moment before she went on. "Now, I'll take you upstairs and give you a chance to get washed up. You look all worn out, dear. So don't you worry about coming down to help tonight. Tomorrow will be soon enough."

Dakota followed the seemingly tireless older woman, forcing her legs to climb the flight of stairs. Molly stopped at the first door she came to and opened it. Pointing farther down the hall, she said, "That door down there is mine. So if you need anything, you just step over."

Alone in the small but immaculate room, Dakota walked across the polished floor and threw open the window. A soft ocean breeze touched her. She ignored the distinct odor of rotting fish and turned to take a good look at her new home.

Sparsely furnished, the room held a dresser, a small writing table under a small hanging mirror, and a nightstand with two lanterns atop it alongside the bed. The water pitcher on the dresser was empty, and suddenly Dakota was sure she didn't have the strength to fill it, let alone wash up.

Maybe a nap, she thought as she stretched out on the bed. She lay on her back, staring up at the whitewashed ceiling, and smiled as she thought of Ben Cable's reaction when he found her gone. Dakota knew he would find her. Probably by tomorrow, she thought. But by then she could tell him that she'd found a job and a place to stay. She was almost looking forward to it.

A gust of air whispered through the open window, and she turned her face toward it. With her eyes closed, she savored the cool evening breeze and the soft bed beneath her. Still, her tired mind resolutely began forming a plan, but before she'd made any progress, the soft featherbed had lulled her into a deep sleep.

Ben marched down the sidewalk toward the waterfront and Molly Malone's restaurant. His anger mounted with each step, and he knew that waiting until morning to confront Dakota had done nothing to improve his temper.

After finding her gone from the stage station, Ben had spent most of the night trying to locate Jack. He'd been sure the crafty old coot had had a hand in Dakota's disappearance. He'd finally caught up with the old man in a saloon on the Barbary Coast, and after Jack told him what he'd done, it had taken all of Ben's self-control to keep from strangling his old friend.

He snarled at a drunk who had the misfortune to stumble into him. The damn place looked even worse in daylight. How did he get involved in all this? he asked himself. Taking a job as sheriff in a small town? Or was it the steady gaze of sky-blue eyes that had pulled him into this mess?

All he knew was that Dakota had better not give him any arguments this morning. He wasn't in the mood.

Nine

DAKOTA heard him before she saw him.

As she stood in the kitchen, making yet another pot of coffee, Ben's voice, calling her name, rang out loudly over the muffled sounds of men eating.

How had he found her so quickly? She'd thought she'd have at least a couple of days to settle in before doing battle with Cable.

Ben stepped into the kitchen and glared at her for a moment before a sudden lunge brought him to her side. He grabbed her shoulders and squeezed. Pulling her tight against him, he gave her a fierce hug, then let her go again. "Why did you leave the depot? I *told* you to wait for me. Dammit, don't you *ever* do what you're told?"

Dakota pulled free and turned away from him. "Who are you to tell me what to do?"

"I'm . . ."

"Yes, Ben? Who?" She turned back and looked up at him. "You didn't even *speak* to me yesterday. After, after . . ." She shook her head. "So don't pretend you

139

care about me. What I do and where I go is no business
of yours."

He gripped her elbow tightly and pulled her to the
far corner of the steamy room. Bending down, he said,
"I've been all over town lookin' for you. Dammit to hell
and back, you're gonna make me an old man before my
time!"

He didn't look like he'd had much sleep. She pried
his fingers from her arm. "Well, now you've found
me. So you can quit worryin'." She stepped away. "I
have to get back to work."

Ben watched her walk to the stove and wondered
where she'd gotten the outfit she was wearing. He
never would have believed that a simple black skirt
and white shirtwaist could look so damn fetching.
With her hair piled on top of her head, the long,
elegant curve of her neck beckoned him.

Then a rowdy shout from one of her customers
snapped him back to reality. Ben walked over to the
stove and pushed his hat to the back of his head. "You
have any idea what it's like on this waterfront? Women
down here are not 'nice' girls from good families. Down
here, they're fair game. That means you are, too." She
turned away from him and he followed her. "The men
around here aren't gonna ask, 'Please, ma'am, can I
have a kiss?' They're just gonna grab hold and take
what they want!"

She resisted the urge to push the lock of sandy-blond
hair off his forehead. "Then I'll have to teach 'em
different. If you remember, Mick Owens learned his
lesson pretty well."

"Not the same at all, Dakota." He pounded his fist
against the wall. "Mick's just a fool. *These* men, the
ones who live on the waterfront . . . they travel in

packs. Like wild dogs. No woman is safe on the Coast. Especially at night."

She wasn't convinced.

Ben took her in his arms, forcing her to hold still and listen. "The other night. What happened between us. That was good, Kota." Amazing, he corrected mentally. Just holding her, even in this blazing-hot kitchen, was enough to fan the flames of his desire for her. He'd never been so affected by a woman. Looking down into her deep blue eyes, he felt himself falling into their depths and lowered his head slightly to taste her lips again.

Suddenly, though, he stopped. Forcing himself back to the subject at hand, Ben straightened and continued. "Dammit, Dakota . . . what could happen to you down here . . . unprotected . . ."

She swallowed and tried to push away from his embrace. "Are you trying to say that now that I have known the 'wonders' of a man's bed, I'll be an easy target for any man anywhere?"

"No!"

She gave him a shove and managed to put a little distance between them. "That *you* of all people would talk about protecting me from men!"

That little barb stung. He was feeling bad enough about bedding her. But he wasn't about to let her get away with making it look as though he'd raped her.

"At the time you didn't seem to think you were being forced." He leaned toward her and gave her a wicked smile before adding, "And I have the scars on my back to prove it."

Dakota slapped him. Hard. She straightened her spine and lifted her chin haughtily. "A *gentleman* wouldn't speak like that to a lady."

"And a *lady* wouldn't have damn near set my bed on fire, Dakota. But you sure did."

He watched her face crumple and could have cut out his own tongue. Dammit. He hadn't meant to say that. Not even to imply it. He knew, better than anyone, that Dakota was a lady. Every glorious inch of her.

But, hellfire, a man could take only so much. He knew she'd enjoyed their lovemaking. She knew it, too. But she was too damn stubborn to admit it. It was easier to place the blame on him.

The slight color in her cheeks was the only sign of her embarrassment. In a quiet, steady voice she told him, "It won't happen again, Ben Cable. And as for any other man with the same idea, well . . . I brought my gun with me."

They stood several feet apart, glaring at each other. Neither one willing to back down.

"You all right, Dakota?" Molly's calm voice cut into the silence. The big woman stood in the doorway, holding a double-barreled shotgun pointed at Ben.

Dakota nodded, smiled, then faced the man opposite her. "As you can see, Sheriff, I have all the protection I need." Her eyes never left Ben's face as she said, "Molly Malone, meet Ben Cable."

"The Ranger, Ben Cable?"

Dakota's jaw dropped, and a tiny smile touched Cable's lips.

"You know each other?"

Molly set her shotgun down and walked toward Ben with her right hand out. "Never met him. But Jack's told me the story about how they met so many times, I tell it better than him." She shook Ben's hand firmly and returned his smile. "Any friend of Jack's and Dakota's is all right with me, boy."

"Oh, for heaven's sake," Dakota said disgustedly. Then she picked up the pot of coffee and walked out to her waiting customers.

The restaurant closed and locked up, Dakota sat at a table with a pot of steaming tea. She still hadn't seen Ben or Molly. They'd been in the kitchen for what seemed an eternity. The restaurant had slowly emptied of customers and still the two hadn't appeared.

Finally Molly came in and sat down opposite her. Dakota knew she should open the conversation with the older woman, but she didn't know what to say. Lord only knew what Ben had already told her. After all, she didn't know Molly very well. Maybe she'd take Ben and Jack's side against her.

"Ben left the back way," Molly stated. "But he sure had a lot to say before he went."

"I'll bet."

"Y'know, I figured him for a quiet one. But tarnation, when he gets goin', there's just no stoppin' him."

Dakota grimaced. She could imagine.

"Yessir. That man surely does have some opinions." Molly's eyebrows rose considerably. "And most of them are about you."

"That's not surprising."

"Didn't figure it would be." The older woman leaned back gratefully in her chair. "Any woman worth her salt can tell when a man's interested."

"Interested?" Dakota shook her head. "I don't think so." Not hardly. Why, the things he'd said to her in the kitchen were hateful. Besides, if he was so "interested," why did he ignore her very presence the morning after he'd . . .

Molly poured herself a cup of tea and, holding it between her hands, allowed the warmth to seep into her fingers before continuing. "Well, that's really neither here nor there."

"What do you mean?"

"Ben says he told you not to make this trip. That you'd be in the way and that he'd take care of everything."

"That's all true"—Dakota met Molly's gaze steadily—"but it was *my* brother who was almost killed. Someone shot him and stole the money we've worked hard for. I had to do something."

"Reckon I can understand that."

"Hmmph! I wish Ben did." She leaned back against her chair. "Those men are somewhere in San Francisco. I know it. And I can find them."

"Then what?"

"What?"

"I said—then what?" Molly eyed her seriously. "These men, whoever they are, are not gonna be stopped by some snip of a girl."

Dakota gasped.

"Now, don't get your back up, honey. Just listen for a minute. Say you *do* find these men. What are you gonna do? Arrest 'em? Ask 'em please, sir, can I have my money back?"

Stunned into silence, Dakota's mind whirled. That had never occurred to her. She'd never thought about what she would do when she found the thieves. She had no proof. No evidence to give to a sheriff. Would she be forced to steal the money back? And if she could manage to do that . . . would *she* then be the criminal? No, she told herself. Handle that problem when you get to it.

"I'm not interested in arresting them. Ben can have them. I just want to get our money back."

"Got any ideas how you're gonna do that?"

"No. Not yet. But I will."

"Maybe you will." Molly shook her head slowly. "But it ain't gonna be easy. A female just don't march down the street—especially on the Coast—demandin' that stolen money be handed over to her."

"Then what am I supposed to do? Go home and wait for Sheriff Cable to solve everything, like a good little girl?"

Molly laughed, as much at the statement as at the look of disgust on Dakota's face. "All I'm sayin' is that you should go a little easy. Have some kind of plan. First off, you don't have any idea who these men are. Cable will find out eventually. His kind always do. That man is tough as nails. The trick is for you to find out first."

Dakota smiled. "Thanks, Molly. I'm glad you're on my side."

For more reasons than she cared to go into, Molly was indeed on Dakota's side. The older woman's mind flashed instantly back over the years. To the many times, both here and in Ireland, that she had gone for help to the men in power. And gone away empty-handed.

In the Old Country it was the British who would just as soon spit on an Irishwoman as help her. She'd lost her land, her parents, her very way of life because men in power didn't care.

And here. In San Francisco, when Mr. Malone was shot down in the street by some thug . . . the men in power had called it self-defense. Self-defense, she thought with a snort. And Mr. Malone not even owning a gun.

Oh, yes. She'd help Dakota. Any way she could. *And* she'd do it without the sheriffs of the world. Not that she didn't trust Ben Cable. But this went deeper than that.

She sipped at her tea, then warned, "You got to go careful. This is not the kind of place folks take kindly to questions. You got a gun?"

"In my room. My six-gun."

"Won't do." Molly shook her head as Dakota started to argue. "You can't wear a holster over your skirts. First thing tomorrow you go down to the gunsmith and get a little derringer. It's only a two-shot weapon, but if you're careful, that'll be enough. I'll loan you the money. And I want you to keep that gun with you all the time down here. As much as I hate the blasted things, you'll need the protection."

"I don't know what to say."

"For starters, say good night. It's late and this old woman has got some thinking to do." Her smile took the bite out of her gruff words. "You go on up."

At the top of the stairs Dakota turned and looked back. A new confidence surged through her. With Molly on her side, Dakota was more sure than ever that what she was doing was right. Smiling, she watched her friend pour another cup of tea, then turned and went to her room.

When the gunsmith showed Dakota the Remington over-and-under double-barreled derringer, she knew it was the right choice. Small, the barrels were only three inches long, one on top of the other. It weighed almost nothing and fired a .41 cartridge. The smith told her its range was fifteen to twenty feet, but it worked even better closer.

"My most popular lady's weapon," he added with a proud smile.

She balanced the gun in her hand, amazed at the light weight. It would fit easily into a reticule, or she could fix up some kind of strap and wear it on her leg.

"It'll do fine. How much?"

"Well, that plain model you're holdin' with just a polished wood grip'll run you eight dollars. For ten dollars more, I can get you somethin' real nice with ivory or pearl stocks. Even engrave your name on it."

She smiled and shook her head. "As long as it shoots. That's all I'm interested in. How much for cartridges?"

"I'll throw a box in. No charge."

"Thanks. I appreciate it."

"No need. Any friend of Molly's . . ."

The man moved off to get the ammunition, and Dakota smiled, thinking just how often she'd heard that particular sentence. Molly, at fifty, had lived in San Francisco half her life. She'd lived through the Gold Rush, survived the fires that had plagued the city in its early years, and watched a sleepy village grow into a magnificent city. As most of the longtime residents could tell you, she was more a part of the city than the bay.

At the restaurant, at any given time, you could find cowhands seated alongside seamen and city officials. From the very rich to the poor looking for a handout, they all eventually found their way to Molly's place. The food was good, the prices reasonable, which in San Francisco was a thing to be relished, but the main attraction was Molly herself.

After paying the smith, Dakota slipped the pistol and ammunition into her reticule and stepped out onto the busy street. She walked directly to the telegraph office, sent a wire to Tenn and Laura, then decided to treat herself to a little sightseeing.

San Francisco had grown a lot in its short history. From its early days as a Mexican military post, through the hundreds of tents blossoming during the Gold Rush, into a city of staggering riches and terrible poverty. Even with the Rush long over, there were still many prospectors hoping to find some untouched vein of gold and become instant millionaires. Fabulous wealth was displayed in the luxurious hotels, and even the business buildings were ornately designed.

But in the midst of abundance was an undercurrent of fear and poverty. Thousands of people were arriving in San Francisco, and there were simply no jobs for them. They ended up living on the streets, turning to crime, or being shanghaied out of one of the Barbary Coast saloons.

Dakota shuddered at the thought. She'd heard more and more about the money being made in the shanghai business. Some poor unsuspecting fool would go into a saloon, order a drink, and wake up on board a ship. Where he would stay for two years or more. If he survived.

A heavyset man in a black broadcloth suit bumped against her in his haste. She stepped back against the window of Lily's Millinery Shop and sighed in relief. It was a pleasure to be out of the direct path of so many people. If only for a moment. Holding her reticule up against her waist, Dakota turned and stared in the window at the pretty bonnets on display. One in particular caught her interest. A delicate straw with yellow ribbons, it also had a tiny bunch of yellow daisies on the side of the brim.

A step sounded behind her. Dakota's breath caught. Even before she saw his reflection behind hers in the glass, she knew it was Ben. She felt his presence as surely as she could the sun's. In the shine of the windowpane she studied him. He seemed hesitant, unsure of himself.

"Hello, Kota."

She nodded at his reflection.

He breathed deeply and expelled it in a rush. As if groping for something to say, he asked, "Buyin' a hat, are you?"

"No."

"Oh." He pulled his hat off and twisted it in his hands. Mumbling "Excuse me," he stepped up beside her, moving farther out of the way of the passing crowds. He pointed at the little yellow bonnet and smiled. "That one would look real pretty on you."

Somehow, she wasn't surprised that he'd picked the hat she'd been eyeing. What *did* surprise her was the trouble she was having trying to talk to him. She settled for a half smile.

"Look, Kota," he said softly, "I want to say something."

"Yes?" She looked up at him.

He couldn't look her in the eye. Instead, he stared down at his hat brim as if it held the answers to his problems. "I, uh . . . oh, hell." Ben forced his gaze up and noticed the rapid rise and fall of her chest before meeting her eyes. "I just wanted to say I'm sorry for the things I said yesterday. At the restaurant."

She cocked her head.

"You know, what I said about settin' fire to—"

"I remember," she interrupted hastily.

"Oh, well. Yeah, I guess you would, at that."

"Yes."

"I don't know why I went on like that, Kota. Never should have said something like that to a lady."

She smiled.

"You were right, y'know. A gentleman wouldn't have." He didn't need to add that he'd been kept up all night remembering the stricken look on her face. He'd never insulted a lady in his life. Or felt so wretched.

"Thank you."

"Oh, no need to thank me." He smiled his relief.

"After all, what we did together didn't need talkin' about, we both know. And I don't think either one of us is likely to forget it. At least, I know *I'm* not gonna—"

"*Ben.*"

"Sorry. Doin' it again, aren't I?"

Despite his dredging up the memories of that night again, Dakota chuckled softly. She had the distinct feeling that Ben Cable didn't apologize very often. He certainly seemed as though he hadn't had much practice at it.

"It's just that," Ben whispered, "every time I see you, I remember. Just standing here with you, I want to touch you, kiss your—"

"Ben, please." Dakota straightened nervously and glanced quickly around. The blood was rushing to her cheeks. No one was paying the least attention to them. If they'd been in Red Creek right now, half the town would be talking about them before sundown. She had to make him stop.

"But, Dakota," he went on, "you have to understand what it's like for me. What goes through my mind every time I'm near you."

"I do understand." Better than you know, she thought. In spite of her best efforts, deep inside herself Dakota knew exactly what he felt. Because that feeling echoed in her. And now, knowing that he *did* care about her, even if it was only this overpowering need, the wanting would be harder to ignore than before.

But if Dakota let Ben know that she felt the same, she wouldn't get the chance to ignore her desires. There was only one thing to do. Lie. She just had to make him mad enough to leave her alone. Because she wasn't sure she'd be able to say no again.

"I do understand, Ben," she said softly. "It's just not like that for me."

His jaw dropped.

"I'm sorry."

Ben tilted his head back and snorted derisively. "Well. That should teach me to keep my mouth shut."

"Ben."

He straightened and shook his head. "Please. Don't apologize again. Once was enough."

Dakota winced at the sneer in his voice.

He took her elbow in a firm grip. "I'll walk you back to the restaurant."

"You don't have to. I can take care—"

"Of yourself. I know." He yanked her elbow. "I'll walk you anyway."

She didn't see the crowds, couldn't hear any noise, she only sensed the widening gulf that separated her from the man who walked by her side.

*   *   *

"Molly, where are the doughnuts?"

"Gone."

Dakota turned and stared at her friend. She knew that any kind of sweet sold quickly, but *all* of them gone? Already? "But we only made them this morning! The customers must've been hungrier than usual."

"Didn't say they'd been bought. They're just gone."

"What do you mean?"

Molly straightened up from the dishpan. Putting her palms against the small of her back, she arched and groaned in pleasure at the stretch. "Well, I left half of the batch on the windowsill to cool. When I come back a few minutes later, they were gone."

Dakota glanced at the empty sill. She crossed the room and stared out the window at the alleyway. Dark and empty, it told her nothing.

"You mean somebody stole 'em?"

"Guess so."

She turned and looked at Molly again. "Does this happen a lot?"

"Sometimes. There's a sight of hungry folks around here."

"But you give out free meals all the time. To whoever needs one. Why would they steal from you?"

"Maybe they got too much pride to take charity."

"But not too much to be a thief?"

Molly shook her head and turned back to her dishes. "Don't get yourself all worked up, girl. It's just a few doughnuts."

"But you can't let it go on."

"Don't seem to be much I can do about it."

Dakota'd had enough of stealing. Just because

she was having trouble finding one set of thieves, though, didn't mean she couldn't find another. Her lips pursed together, she set her mind to working on the problem.

"There must be something," she mumbled to herself as she stared out the window into the dark, quiet alley.

"What'd you say?"

"Nothing." Dakota turned from the window, a thoughtful look on her face.

Ten

"WHAT'LL you do with 'em when you catch 'em?"

"I don't know yet," Dakota mumbled as she carefully balanced the stick on the edge of the plate. Finally satisfied, she stepped back with a proud smile on her face. "That should do it."

"Dakota . . ."

"No, Molly. It'll work. You'll see." She pointed at the windowsill. "See. The stick that holds up the window is balanced on the edge of the plate of doughnuts. When the thief moves the plate, the stick falls away and the window crashes down." She grinned.

Molly shook her head. "You don't even know he'll show up again."

"For doughnuts? He'll come."

"Can't understand why you're so het up over this nonsense. It's just a little flour and sugar." Molly picked up the coffeepot and headed out to the dining room.

Dakota couldn't explain it, but catching the food thief had become very important to her. She'd been in San Francisco two weeks now and was still no closer to recovering the stolen money than the day she'd arrived.

She saw almost nothing of Ben anymore. Oh, he came by the restaurant every evening for supper, but he didn't speak to her. Not since the day she'd lied to him.

But he looked at her. His gaze was enough to start a brushfire. She felt the heat of it from across the room. And still, they didn't speak, because there was nothing to say. He'd made it plain that he wasn't interested in love. Every time he reminded her of their night together, it was desire he spoke of. Not love. Dakota's nerves were strung as tight as a banjo. If something didn't happen soon, she knew she'd go out of her mind.

A rustling in the alley shook her from her thoughts. Stepping back away from the window, she lifted her chin and tried to see more clearly. A small, dirty hand reached out slowly toward the plate of doughnuts, and Dakota held her breath. Quickly the thief began to take the sweets from the plate, obviously passing them on to a confederate. Dakota inched her way forward, staying out of sight.

When there were just two doughnuts left on the plate, she made a grab for the dirty hand. Too late, Dakota remembered her trap. As the thief's fingers were pulled from her reach, the stick was knocked aside and the heavy window came crashing down on Dakota's wrist.

She yelped and heard a giggle from the darkness. Molly came at a run.

"What is it? What happened?"

Dakota pulled her hand free, turned toward the door and wrenched it open. Disgusted, she sighed at the sight of the empty alley. She heard only the sound of people running away. Stomping her foot and rubbing the red spot on her wrist, Dakota answered, "Blast it anyway! They got the dang doughnuts and durn near broke my hand doin' it!"

Dakota heard a muffled snort from behind her and spun around. Molly held her hand to her mouth, trying unsuccessfully to hide her smile. "Ready to give up?"

"Not by a damn sight!" She turned back and peered into the darkness. "You just wait and see. I'll get 'em." Looking down at the ever-reddening skin on the back of her hand, she added, "And when I do, they'll be sorry they ever thought of thievin'!"

Red Creek

Tenn left the banker's office in disgust. He twisted around and glared through the window at the bald man hunched over his desk. It looked as though the little man had already wiped all thoughts of the Lane ranch from his mind. And why not? Tenn asked himself. No skin off the banker's nose to foreclose.

He shouldn't have been surprised. It's not like he really expected Bathgate to extend the damn mortgage. But what would it have cost him to give the Lanes a little more time? There wasn't exactly all kinds of folks linin' up outside that damn bank waitin' for a chance to buy a ranch!

Tenn stepped into the stirrup and swung aboard his horse. Hands gripped together on the pommel, he sat quietly for a moment, staring off down the street toward Laura's house. Reluctantly he pulled at the reins and urged his horse forward. He'd have to tell her. No way around it. He knew she was already getting things ready for their wedding. A wedding that probably wouldn't happen now for quite a while.

The horse plodded slowly as if too tired to move, but Tenn didn't mind. He wasn't in any kind of hurry to tell Laura about all this. They only had one chance left. Dakota. He never would have believed it, but he sure was glad that his sister went to San Francisco. He only hoped she'd be able to get the money back in time. There was only a month left.

Tenn looked up at Doc Burns's place. Inside, he knew Laura was happily preparing for the wedding. His lips twisted in frustration as he nudged his horse in the ribs. The big animal took off like a shot. We still have a month, he thought. No sense in tellin' her anything yet. Not while there's still a chance.

Laura pulled the white curtain aside and watched curiously as Tennessee Lane rode past her house like the hounds of hell were chasing him. It wasn't like him not to stop. She frowned. And he shouldn't be riding that hard so soon after healing. What could have happened?

Suddenly she knew. Just the week before, Tenn had said something about having to see Mr. Bathgate at the bank on his next trip. She squinted into the sunlight, trying to keep his receding figure in sight. He must have had bad news from the banker. That was the only explanation. Glancing down at the fine lace she'd been stitching onto a camisole for her trousseau, she had a moment's panic. It would be just like Tenn to call off the wedding if things didn't go just right for him.

She tossed the material onto a chair, hurried to the hall coat tree, and took down her bonnet. Quickly she tied the ribbons under her chin, took a fast look in the mirror to check her appearance, then went outside. With a determined step Laura headed for the bank.

Dakota's head pounded in time with the tinny music from an old upright piano someone had dragged out onto the street. She glanced out the front window of the restaurant and grimaced. Two more "musicians" had joined the drunk banging on the piano. Now the screech of a badly played concertina and a banjo were contributing to the discord.

She rubbed her temples in a futile attempt to soothe her aching head, then turned when a customer shouted out that he wanted more coffee. Moving purposefully toward the kitchen, Dakota thought that if nothing else, this trip had proved to her that she didn't belong in a city. She could hardly wait to finish her task and go home. Back to the wide-open spaces where the only sounds were nature's own and you saw only the people you wanted to see.

Coffeepot in hand, she wove her way through the clamoring crowd as though she'd been doing it for years instead of two weeks. Two frustrating weeks. She poured the hot black liquid into an upraised cup and fought down a wave of defeat.

She tossed a glance at the far corner where Ben sat, as he did every night, eating supper. He wouldn't speak to her, she knew. But, though he was silent, he was always around. And his eyes seemed to follow her everywhere. Like now. She tried to shrug off the heat of his gaze, but it was impossible. She could just as easily stop breathing.

Ben cursed silently and lowered his eyes. This wasn't doing either of them any good. She'd already let him know very plainly that his attentions weren't wanted, and for the life of him, he couldn't understand why. *Or* why her rejection had upset him so. It should have pleased him!

Hell, he'd been worried that she might take that night they'd been lovers and build it into some kind of romantic fairy tale. But she didn't. And it was driving him crazy. He took a swallow of the scalding coffee. For God's sake, he lectured himself silently, don't you know when you're well off? Haven't you had enough of people close to you turning their backs? Do you *have* to have more pain? Wasn't your father enough?

He lifted a spoonful of stew to his mouth and frowned. Tasted like sawdust. Disgusted, he dropped the spoon back into the bowl. Damnation, he couldn't even eat anymore! Nothing had any flavor. Nothing held his interest, except for a pair of shuttered blue eyes.

Leaning back in his chair, he forced himself not to watch Dakota as she worked. The sight of her bending and stretching over other men was simply too much to bear. How in the name of heaven had he, Ben Cable, come to this? Instead of doing the job he'd come all this way to do, he spent his time riding herd on a troublesome female who wanted nothing to do with him! He shifted uneasily as he admitted he hadn't even been very successful at that!

An inexperienced woman had somehow managed to outdo him at every turn. She'd found a job and a decent place to stay, which, he thought with a shudder, was more than he had done. He was still sharing a room on the waterfront with three other men and several large, noisy rats. Of course, he really hadn't had much choice about that. He could have withdrawn some money from an account he kept at a bank in town, but all of the decent hotels were far from the Barbary Coast. He couldn't bring himself to be too far away from her, in case she needed him. Which was beginning to look less likely every day. She already had the best protection on the Coast. No one in town was more formidable than Molly Malone.

Disgusted with himself, Dakota and the whole miserable situation, Ben picked up the spoon again and forced himself to eat.

"How many for tonight?" The dapper man studied his partner across the room.

"Three." The man with the tiny horseshoe scar over his eye grinned. "A farmer, a soldier boy from the fort, and some no-count China boy."

The other man nodded. "Six thousand. Not too bad." He looked up from his ledgers. "But about the soldier . . ."

The grinning man belched, then rubbed his stomach gratefully. "Shit, man. No time to start worryin' now. Them soldiers is always desertin' anyways." He laughed shortly. "This one's just takin' a lot longer trip than he figgered on. I'm gonna give him to Cap'n Jonas."

Quickly the other man scanned the ledgers and shipping routes. He smiled. "Good. China should be far enough to keep him quiet. By the time he gets back—if he gets back—no one will even remember him."

"Wouldn't count on comin' back if I was him. Jonas is awful hard on his crew. Why, he's bought more 'sailors' from us than any three of the other captains."

"Yes, well." The ledger book was slammed shut and tucked away on a bookshelf behind the huge desk. "It's the strict disciplinarians, like Jonas, that keep our pockets so well lined." He looked over at the disreputable man who'd become such an integral part of this operation. "Have you had any further trouble with Mother Bronson?"

"Nah." He scratched his chest, then shook his head. "Glad, too. That is the biggest damn woman I ever saw." He looked up. "You know she does her own crimpin'? She don't use laudanum or opium in the whiskey like the rest of us. She just pops a man over the head, then hefts him and carries him all by herself to her pickup point. I tell you, a couple more like her, and we'd have to get out of the shanghai business altogether."

"Never mind all that. Did you convince her to stay away from our saloon?"

"Oh, hell, yes. She don't care. Only did it that one time for somethin' different. She gets all the fools she needs right in her own boardin' house over on Steuart Street."

"Good. I don't want any trouble. Soon, if things continue going along well, we won't have to bother with small change like procuring sailors."

"Or buyin' cattle, then stealin' the money back?"

The man swung his head around and glared at the unkempt man in the big chair. He was becoming unreliable. The day would come, in the not too distant future, when something would have to be done about him. But not yet.

"That's right. I don't want to risk what could be the biggest profit-making venture ever, over these little deals." A sudden thought struck him. "You're sure you killed both of those men in . . ."

"Red Creek." He pushed himself to his feet and grinned again. "I'm sure. I never miss what I aim at." He hadn't missed the speculative gleam in his partner's eye. "You best keep that in mind, *partner*."

Tension filled the air, and for a few long moments the only sound in the room was the muted noise from the saloon below. The two men stared at each other, and the distrust and hatred swirled in the silence. Finally the dapper man shrugged.

"No need for warnings, my friend." He bent at the waist slightly and lifted his walking stick from the desk. Running his manicured fingers over the tiger's head knob with slow, almost sensuous strokes, he added, "I'm well aware that we need each other. See that *you* remember that."

"Yeah," the man answered, tearing his gaze from the other man's hypnotic action with the stick. "I'll do that, *friend*."

Stick tapping on the floor, the man moved to the back door. Before he touched the knob, he said quietly, "Blow out the light. I don't want to be seen leaving this place. Too many questions."

The other man moved to the kerosene lamp and hesitated. In the dark a gun could be pulled and fired without being seen. Dare he trust the fancy man who so obviously despised him? He put his hand on his own pistol, then blew out the flame.

A chuckle in the darkness. The door opened, then swung slowly shut again.

Quickly the man struck a match, removed the globe, and lit the oil-soaked wick. A sputtering, flickering light dimmed, then grew steadily. Uneasily he replaced the globe and sank down onto his chair. He had a feeling he'd just been tested. And he'd lost.

*   *   *

"You gonna talk to that man?"

"Hmm?" Dakota turned away from the pot of stew holding the two full bowls she'd come into the kitchen for. "What'd you say, Molly?"

"I *said* are you gonna talk to him?"

"Who?" She knew very well who.

"Ben Cable." Molly set a stack of plates down on the countertop. "He's been comin' in here every night for two weeks and starin' at you like a moonstruck calf."

Dakota looked away.

"And you're no better!" Molly shook her finger at the younger woman. "Lord's sake. The way you two carry on. You're both actin' like a couple of bullheaded younguns."

Dakota looked for a way out of the conversation. "I've got to take this food out there before it gets stone cold." She pushed against the swinging kitchen door with her hip, looked out at the crowd, and stopped. Smiling, she whispered, "Molly! Look who's here!"

She took a quick look, patted Dakota's arm, and said, "You deliver those, then come back for another bowl. I'll have it ready."

"Howdy, Ranger!"

Ben looked up. "Jack!"

The old man pulled out a chair opposite Cable and sat down. He eyed the younger man, noting the tired lines around his eyes and mouth. Didn't look like things were going too well for him. "Reckoned I might find you here."

"Good to see you. Been awhile."

"Surely has, son." Jack pulled his hat off and set it on the edge of the table. "The durn stage comp'ny don't care if a man's old. Run your legs off as soon as look at you!"

"You wouldn't have it any other way, you old liar!"

He snorted. "Prob'ly not. Likely, I'll throw in my chips while sittin' atop some stagecoach."

"Jack!" Dakota's welcome broke into their conversation. She slid a bowl of stew in front of the old man and smiled. "Saw you come in. Molly figured you might be hungry."

Jack grinned and picked up the spoon. "Like I said before, missy. You'll do. Been thinkin' about Molly's stew all day long." He took a bite and sighed. "Ah, good as ever." Sneaking a sidelong glance at Dakota, he hinted, "Only thing missin' is some fresh bread to soak up that *de*licious gravy!"

She laughed. "Be right back!"

One look at the cooling shelf was all it took to get Dakota's temper rising again. There *had* been three loaves of bread on that shelf. Now there were two. Dakota stomped across the kitchen floor and threw open the back door. Stepping onto the narrow porch, she glared at the empty alley. Hands on hips, she ignored the stench of the rotting fruits that littered the darkness and tried to imagine the face of her opponent. Old? Young? Man? Woman? It didn't matter. Not anymore. By heaven, she told herself, she was going to catch that thief if it was the last thing she did.

Mumbling angrily, Dakota turned back inside. She didn't see the two small figures rise up from behind an abandoned packing crate and move off into the deeper shadows.

*   *   *

When the last customer was finally shooed from the restaurant, Molly and Dakota joined the two men still sitting at the corner table waiting for them. Setting the big coffeepot down next to a fresh apple pie, Molly groaned tiredly as she sank onto a chair.

"Lordy, I must be gettin' old," she mumbled. "Don't know what I'd do without Dakota around to help."

Jack pinched her cheek. "You ain't old, Molly. Just seasoned."

She laughed and took the coffee Dakota held out to her. "Maybe so, but hell, I don't even remember how I run this place before she come to town." Glancing at Jack, she asked, "So, how come you're in here on a Wednesday, Jack? Somethin' in the wind?"

"Maybe." The old man looked at Cable. "How's your hunt comin', Ranger?"

Ben shook his head wearily. "It's not."

"Ain't surprised."

"What?" Ben's gaze narrowed, and he saw Dakota lean forward eagerly. "What do you know about it?"

"A man hears things . . ."

"What'd you hear, Jack?"

Ben glared at Dakota.

The old man looked at the two young people curiously. There's more here than meets the eye, he told himself. He hesitated and Molly spoke up.

"That's enough, Ranger. Reckon we all want to know what Jack here's found out."

Dakota smiled softly. Ben shifted his glare to Molly.

"Won't do no good to fish-eye me, Ranger. You ain't gonna run me off. Nor Dakota, neither." She looked at her old friend. "Go on, Jack. What'd you hear?"

"You know Old Tom? That prospector I been haulin' free for some twenty years?"

Molly nodded. "He's been eatin' free here for that long at least."

"Well . . ." Jack picked up his coffee and took a sip. "I seen him yesterday. Said some girl workin' for Molly was askin' a whole mess o' questions that was liable to get her hurt real bad." He raised his gaze to Dakota. "That right?"

"Yeah, she has," Ben said, frowning at her.

"Well, Tom says everybody knows this man she's been askin' about, but nobody wants to say so."

"Who is he?" Molly's voice came soft, wary.

"Name's Ellis. Hank Ellis."

"Oh, Lord."

Dakota glanced at Molly. "You know him?"

"Know *of* him."

Ben's patience was gone. "Well, is somebody gonna tell *me*?"

Jack toyed with his cup, spinning it in wet circles on the table. "This ain't a man you want to be messin' with."

"Why?" Dakota demanded.

"Reason why folks won't talk about Ellis is, they're scared. Ellis don't have any enemies." Jack met Dakota's gaze worriedly. "They're all dead."

A cold chill spread through her veins. If Ellis, one man, could spread that much fear through the waterfront, maybe Ben was right about all this. She looked at Molly. The older woman's face was etched in worry. What kind of man *is* Ellis, she thought, to create such a dread in people? She inhaled deeply and forced herself to ask, "Then why would Tom talk? Isn't he scared, too?"

Molly chuckled halfheartedly. "Hell. Tom's too old and too tough to be scared. 'Sides, he spends most of his time up in the mountains . . . still lookin' for the Mother Lode. If he had to, he could hide from Ellis and others like him forever."

Jack nodded. "That's about what the old coot said."

"What about the other man I'm lookin' for?" Dakota asked. "Gordon."

"Says he don't know him."

"But they were together in Red Creek!"

Jack shrugged.

Molly poured more coffee into her cup and stared into the flame of the oil lamp. Almost to herself she muttered, "Well. We got a name, anyway. It's a place to start."

"To start *what*?" Ben asked angrily.

"To start gettin' Dakota's money back." The old woman stared at Ben as if daring him to contradict her.

"Goddammit!" Ben's fist smacked down on the table as he glared at Dakota. "See what you're doin'! With your foolishness, you're draggin' Molly into something that could get her hurt . . . or worse!"

"Now, see here, Ranger," Molly warned before Dakota could manage a word. "I been on this waterfront for more'n twenty years. And in all that time ain't nobody—not even himself, Mr. Malone, God rest his soul—told me what to do! Nor what I can't do. And it ain't about to start now."

Dakota interrupted before Ben could answer. "Molly, maybe you should stay out of this."

"What?"

"I mean it. It isn't your fight, Molly. I don't want you to get hurt."

"First time you've made sense in weeks," Ben mumbled.

Molly ignored him. "That's mighty nice of you, honey. But I've been taking care of myself for a long time now. And if I need 'em, there's plenty of men around here I can call on for help. Don't you worry."

"But why? Why are you risking your life for me?"

"Not just for you, dearie." Molly's eyes took on a faraway look. "When Mr. Malone was shot down in the street, nobody said a thing. Nobody *saw* a thing."

Jack nodded and Molly continued.

"The fella who killed him was a lot like this Ellis." The old woman turned her gaze to Dakota, and the younger woman was surprised to see the venom in those usually placid eyes. "Everyone down here was too scared to talk. And when I tried to do something about it, I was shushed." Her eyes filled with tears. "So my man died, and that trash got clean away with it. Mr. Malone, God rest his soul, didn't deserve that."

"Amen," Jack muttered.

Molly sniffed loudly, rubbed her eyes, and gave Dakota a weak smile. "This time . . . this time, Dakota, I mean to get rid of the trash."

Dakota jumped up, went around the table, and hugged the other woman. For a moment Molly's strong arms squeezed back tightly, then she released her. "But for now, why don't you go get us some more coffee? We can make some war plans while we eat this apple pie."

Taking the pot, Dakota walked to the kitchen. While she filled it, she heard the door swing open, and without turning around, she knew it was Ben. She worked silently, determined to make him be the first to speak. Finally he did.

"At least you tried to get Molly out of this."

She turned and frowned at him. "Of course I did. I don't want her to get hurt because of me."

He pushed away from the wall he'd been leaning against and walked to her side. Building up the fire, he took the coffeepot from her and set it on the stove. "And what about you?"

"What?"

"It's all right for *you* to get hurt—or killed?"

"Won't happen."

"How do you know that?" He gripped her shoulders tightly. "Why is the money so goddamn important to you?"

She pulled away. "You wouldn't understand."

"*Make* me understand!"

"Fine!" Eyes blazing, she faced him. "We've got to get that money back. Without it, we'll lose everything! The land, our home, everything!"

"Good God!" He took a step closer even as she backed away. "You can always find another ranch. Another place. Is it worth *dyin'* for?"

"Listen to you!" She crossed her arms and stalked around the kitchen. "Do you know how many people like you said that to us in Texas?"

"People like me?" Ben ran his hand through his hair. "What the hell does that mean?"

"You. Northerners!"

He threw his arms up. "*Northerners*! I'm from Georgia!"

She smirked at him. "Yes. But you fought for the North."

He turned away slightly, his lips turned in a mockery of a smile. "Yeah. Yeah, I did."

"Well, you don't know what it's like to lose, then, do you? After the war, the Reconstruction people swarmed into Texas like locusts and took over everything! About broke Tenn's heart to lose our place."

"But—"

"No!" She shouted it at him. "I won't let that happen to him again!"

"Even if you get yourself killed tryin'?"

"Yes!" Tears were too close to the surface right now. She turned away.

"You think it'll go easy on Tenn if he only loses his sister?"

"He won't!"

"How the hell do you know that?" He crossed to her and spun her around to face him.

"You don't know what it's like losin' everything." She kept her eyes downcast as she spoke.

Ben laughed derisively. When she looked up at him he said, "Yes I do."

Dakota turned her head away, but he gripped her chin and forced her to look at him.

"You know I fought for the North. Well, my daddy was just about as disgusted with me as you are." His gaze bored into hers. "He disowned me. Said he had no son. I was as good as dead to him." She gasped and he let her go. Stepping back, he went on. "I said I was from Georgia. Well, I am. Atlanta."

She gasped and he nodded. "General Sherman burned my house down along with everyone else's."

"Your father?"

"Oh," he said, his face tight, eyes haunted, "he wasn't there. He'd already died. One of my old 'friends' said he left this world cursing me."

"Oh, God, Ben—"

"So don't tell me I don't know what it's like to lose something! I lost everything! My home, my father, my friends." He smiled softly, sadly. "And you know somethin', Dakota? It taught me somethin' you ought to have figured out by now. Havin' a family and a home doesn't mean you're safe. It only means you have more to lose."

His fingers on her chin tightened as the memories overtook him. Dakota, appalled at his story, tried to tell him so with her eyes. She'd been so wrong. Too caught up in her own problems and worries to see his pain. But how could she have known? "Ben, I'm—"

He released her and slammed his hat on his head. "Don't say you're sorry, Dakota. That's the past. It doesn't matter anymore. But you do." Ben sighed heavily. "God knows I wish you didn't."

Her brow furrowed. She didn't understand. Suddenly Ben knew he had to *make* her understand what he meant. Grabbing her and pulling her body tightly against his, he lowered his head and claimed her lips with a fierce intensity. Their breaths mingled and became one as his tongue forced its way into the warm cavern of her mouth. He pressed the length of her against him and knew she felt the hardened evidence of his desire.

Breathing was difficult when he finally let her go. Stepping back, he said softly, "Just think about what you're doin' here. And if it's worth it."

Walking to the back door, he paused before stepping outside. "Tell Molly I couldn't stay. I'll see Jack later." His eyes touched her for a moment. "Good night, Dakota."

The door closed and she was alone.

Eleven

Red Creek

"NOW, Tennessee," Dr. Burns said soothingly, "don't get all het up until you hear the whole thing."

Tenn shifted uncomfortably in the tiny chair. He frowned at Laura, who smiled back at him.

"The upshot of it all is, I'd like to invest in your ranch."

"Why's that, Doc?"

"Oh, I think we all know why." Doc tamped the tobacco in his pipe bowl. "You and Laura are all set to get married, and I'd like to help."

"Yeah." Tenn looked at his future father-in-law and tried to be angry at the interference. "What if I said I don't need help?"

The older man held a match to the tobacco and sucked in his cheeks as he drew on the stem. Finally satisfied, he answered with a smile. "You wouldn't be telling me the truth, son."

"Look, Doc"—Tenn stood up and twisted his hat in his hands—"I thank you for the offer, but—"

"Tennessee . . ." Laura spoke softly.

"Now, now, Laura honey," her father said, "let us men finish this. Why don't you go make some coffee?"

She sat back in her chair. "No. This is *my* future, too."

Doc shook his head as he watched her, then glancing at Tenn, asked, "Are you sure you *want* to marry a woman who argues with everything you say?"

Tenn glared at her. "No, I *ain't* sure."

"Well, I am," she said.

"All right, all right, enough of this foolishness." Doc stood up and faced the younger man. "Now, Tenn, you would have been willing to take an extra loan from that skinflint Bathgate down at the bank."

"Yeah, but—"

"No *buts*. My money's every bit as good as his"— he winked—"and I'm not about to foreclose and have my daughter come back and live with *me* again!"

"Father!"

"Hush." Doc barely glanced at her. "Tenn, you're one of the hardest-workin' men I've ever seen. I know you'll make a success of that ranch, and I'm willin' to back my belief with cash."

"I don't know. . . ."

"Let me do this, Tenn." The old man held his hand out. "I have the money. I don't need it. And you can buy me out whenever you want to."

Tenn looked from the doc to Laura. Her eyes were pleading with him to accept her father's offer. Well, he reminded himself, she *had* warned him that she would do whatever she thought was right whether he agreed or not. But she shouldn't have told her father about the mortgage on the ranch.

He stiffened. The thought of taking charity went against everything he believed in. But if Doc was a partner, then it wouldn't really be charity. Would it? He looked back at Doc's outstretched hand and, after hesitating only a moment longer, grasped it.

"All right, Doc." The old man smiled, and Tenn heard Laura sigh with relief. "From now on you're a full partner."

Doc grinned. "Make that a silent partner, hmmm? You don't tell me how to doctor . . . and I won't tell you how to handle cattle."

"Deal." Tenn turned as Laura ran to him. He wrapped his arms around her and swung in a circle. "Get yourself ready, woman! I'm sendin' a wire to San Francisco, and as soon as Dakota comes home, we're gettin' married!"

Dakota stifled a moan. Her leg was so cramped she doubted she'd be able to move at all when she had to. She'd been crouched down behind a smelly crate in the alley for what seemed hours. A quick glance told her the batch of doughnuts was still sitting on the cooling shelf. Well, of course they are, she thought disgustedly. No one but she had been in the filthy alley.

Where is that thief? she wondered as she tried to stretch out her left leg. Maybe he's tired of doughnuts. She should have made a pie. Nothing worse than a persnickety thief. Hell, she thought. Maybe Molly's right. Maybe I *should* forget about catching this fella. Concentrate on finding what I came here for.

That stray thought brought Ben Cable to mind again. Truth to tell, though, he was never far from Dakota's mind. She hadn't seen him since the night before, when she'd said all the wrong things. When she'd brought the memories of pain into his eyes. When he'd branded her with his kiss.

But she hadn't known. She leaned her head back against the edge of the crate. Still, she hated reminding him of his loss. She hadn't considered that other people might have been wronged during that damned war. That she wasn't the only one with old wounds and scars. But Ben's seemed somehow sharper ... deeper.

At least, she told herself grimly, she was beginning to understand why Ben never spoke of love. He was too afraid of it. He didn't trust it. And she couldn't blame him. To have his own father disown him must have been dreadful.

She sat up and shook her head to clear it. What was done was done. Maybe if he came back, they could talk without their pasts coming between them. He *had* to come back.

Dakota moved slightly and her knee cracked. If the thief didn't show up soon, she'd have to give up. She couldn't very well leave Molly all alone to serve the supper crowd.

A moment later there was a rustle from down the alley. Dakota went perfectly still. Hardly daring to breathe, she peeked around the edge of the crate. From the darkness two shadowy figures moved slowly toward Molly's. They held hands, with the taller of the two leading the smaller one along.

As they came closer to the light, Dakota just managed to stifle a gasp of surprise. They were children! The tall one looked to be in his teens, while the other couldn't have been more than nine or ten.

She waited until the taller one released the young

one's hand and reached for the plate of doughnuts. Then she leapt out of her hiding place and made a grab for the little one. Her arms closed around the slight body, and the child screamed. The older one jumped, knocking the doughnuts off the sill and sending them rolling all over the alley.

Dakota shouted as the squirming child she held gave her a good kick in the shins. She and the bigger one stared at each other for a moment, then Dakota was locked into a tug-of-war for the small thief. She kept a firm grip, though, and after only a few minutes' struggle, her opponent dropped the child's hand and ran down the alley into the darkness.

The wildly fighting child ceased his struggles immediately and screamed "Joe!" at the retreating figure.

"You shouldn't trust a thief, boy," Dakota said, tightening her grip.

He kicked at her again, but this time she was ready and outstepped him. "What do you know, lady? Let go o' me!"

"Nope! Not till I find out who you are and where I can find your folks."

"Don't got none!" he bellowed and twisted viciously in her arms.

"Ow!" Dakota yelled as the boy bit her hand. "That does it!" She threw him over her shoulder. When he kicked again, she swatted his backside. "No more. Understand?"

Silence.

Well, she told herself, it was better than his howling! He weighed almost nothing. Practically skin and bone, she thought sadly. No wonder they were after the doughnuts. Dakota took a last glance down the

alley, though she didn't really expect to see the other
thief, then went into the kitchen.

Ben walked into the Irish Lady restaurant and
stopped in his tracks. The silence in the crowded
room was deafening. He'd never known a room full
of men to be so quiet. His every sense went on alert,
sure there was trouble. Then he heard it.

A bloodcurdling scream from upstairs. He took
three quick steps before he stopped again and looked
around. No one else had moved. Now, that was
unusual. Not that these men would run to offer help
to someone in trouble. But they would, ordinarily at
least, rush to watch the fight. Cable glanced around at
the upturned faces, each of them watching the stairs as
though they could see whatever was going on. Most of
them wore smiles.

He took another slow step toward the staircase and
stopped again at the loud crash that echoed down
through the restaurant. What the *hell* is goin' on up
there? he wondered. A belligerent stream of colorful
cursing in a high-pitched voice followed the crash,
and Ben couldn't stand it any longer. He took the
stairs two at a time.

Uncertainly he stared at the doors lining the hallway for a moment until he heard Dakota yell, "Ow!"

He threw open the nearest door, his hand instinctively reaching for his pistol. He never touched it.
Instead, he relaxed against the wall and smiled at the
sight that greeted him.

Dakota had the half-dressed boy by one arm, dragging him toward the iron bathtub situated near the
fireplace. The boy had dug in his heels, and the
throw rug under his feet was bunching up before

him as he fought against the woman.

Ben chuckled and winced as the boy cut loose another scream. The kid had quite a voice.

"Will you stop that screaming!" Dakota shouted.

"No, I ain't!" The boy twisted and turned, pulling his scrawny body with all of his might.

"It's just a *bath*!" She grabbed his other arm, too, and doubled her efforts. "I'm not gonna cook you for supper!"

"You ain't stickin' me in no tub of water, neither!"

"Oh, yes, I am!" She blew at the stray lock of hair that hung over her eyes and backed up another step closer to the tub. "You stink like that foul alley. And by heaven, you're gonna have a bath!"

"No!" He reached out and kicked at a small table in their way, sending the pitcher and bowl crashing to the floor.

Ben looked around quickly. It looked as though this fight had been going on for some time. The room was in a shambles. Counterpane torn from the bed, the blankets were bunched in the middle of the mattress. A kerosene lamp lay on the floor, its chimney smashed. Pictures on the walls were left hanging at absurd angles. He shook his head in admiration. So much destruction from one small boy.

Dakota yelled again. "Don't you dare bite me! Not one more time!"

Cable laughed out loud, and she turned her head. She didn't smile or frown, simply shouted, "Don't just stand there laughin'! Help me!"

"Do what?"

"I am *trying*"—she grunted as the boy's foot met her stomach—"to get this, evil-smelling child into that tub!"

"Is *that* all?"

The boy jerked one of his arms from her grasp, and Dakota teetered, slightly off balance.

"Help me!"

Cable glanced at the boy and frowned. Looking at the boy with his shirt off, he could actually count the boy's ribs, he was that skinny. And ripe. Ben could smell him from the doorway. She was right. The kid needed that bath something awful.

"You stay out o' this, mister!" The scrawny child glared at Ben. "This here's between her and me! And ain't no woman gonna set me down *naked* in water like I was some infant!"

"I don't blame you."

"*What?*" Dakota spared a moment to look in astonishment at him. She could just barely make him out through the strands of hair hanging down in front of her face.

"I said I don't blame him." Ben stood away from the wall and took a cautious step closer to the two combatants. "No woman would've been able to give me a bath at his age, either."

"Ben!"

"However, at my *advanced* age . . ." He couldn't resist winking.

"There! You see?" The boy tried again to pull free. "Now, leave go o' me, lady. You got no right!"

Cable made no move to come closer, but he did ask, "How did you happen to get into this mess, Dakota?"

She blew at her hair again uselessly. "I caught him. Him and his brother have been stealing food from Molly."

Ben frowned at the boy. "A thief?"

"Me and Joe ain't thieves!" He reached for Dakota's wrist with his teeth, but she was too fast for him. "We was just hungry!"

"Ben Cable, are you just gonna stand there, or are you gonna help me?"

She was a mess. Hair stringing down, her dress askew, her cheeks flushed, she was also clearly tuckered out. If he hadn't come in when he did, Ben thought, the little scamp would've won the fight just by wearing her down.

He took a few quick steps and picked the boy up. Holding him under one arm and ignoring the amazing collection of curses the child knew, Ben said, "I'll do it. You go on."

"But you'll need help. . . ."

"Dakota, the day I can't manage one rawboned, gutter-mouthed child is the day I take to a rocking chair and stay there."

"Who you callin' rawboned?"

"But—"

"No *buts*, Dakota. Go on and have some coffee. I'll be down in a while."

She looked from Cable's confident face to the wildly twisting body of the determined boy and gave a sigh of relief. Whatever happened . . . at least she wouldn't be there to see it. She nodded gratefully. "Thanks, Ben. He about tired me out." Dakota glanced across the room into the mirror and groaned. She looked as if she'd been living in a cave for years. "I can't go downstairs lookin' like this."

He smiled and used his free hand to cup her chin. "I think you're beautiful," he whispered.

She stared up into his eyes, suddenly glad for the boy's presence. She couldn't think of a thing to say.

"Oh, Lord," the boy groaned. "Ain't it enough you're gonta' stick me in water and make me catch my death? Do you have to make me throw up, too?"

Ben tapped a finger to the boy's head. "Quiet, you!"

Dakota cleared her throat nervously. "I'll, uh . . . go now. Just give a yell when you're finished."

"I think we can count on our friend here to do the yellin'!" Ben grinned at her, then gave her a gentle shove toward the door. "But I will surely need my supper when this is over."

"It'll be ready."

She left them, closing the door on the boy's latest stream of curses. Smiling, Dakota thought, Give it up, boy. You don't stand a chance against him.

Ben came down the stairs to the kitchen an hour later. His shirt was soaked through, his hair a mess, but there was a victorious smile on his face.

"Where's the boy?" Molly asked.

"Asleep." Ben shook his head and plopped down at the nearest table. "Guess between the warm water and all that fighting, he just wore down."

"I'll just go check him," the old woman said as she left the room.

Dakota brought Ben's supper to the table, and he sighed hungrily. Steak, fried potatoes, and coffee. She took the seat opposite him, and he was suddenly overwhelmingly happy.

She was more glad to see him than she would have thought possible. Truth to tell, she'd been worried that he wouldn't be back, after all the things he'd said the night before. He was such a private kind of person, she'd been afraid that he'd be too self-conscious to face her after revealing so much of himself.

"He's sleepin' sound." Molly interrupted Dakota's thoughts. The older woman joined them at their table. She'd chased off the rest of the customers and closed the restaurant. With all the noise coming from upstairs, the men hadn't been eating anyway. "But what about the older one you saw, Dakota? Think he'll be back?"

"I do." She set her cup down and looked up at Ben. "Would you mind stayin' around for a while? I don't think I can handle the big one on my own."

His eyebrows shot straight up. "Why, Dakota, I believe that's the first time you've ever admitted you couldn't do something all by yourself."

Dakota's lips twisted in a wry grin as Molly laughed. "He's right about that, dearie!"

"Well," Dakota said, her eyes on Cable, "maybe I'm learning a few things about myself and . . . people."

His gaze met hers as he nodded and said, "Maybe we've all been learning a few things."

Molly looked from one to the other of them and smiled. "Then you sure won't need me." She stood up and started for the stairs. "Think I'll go get me some sleep. You have any trouble, just yell."

They didn't hear her.

They sat side by side in the darkness, their backs against the wall. The open bedroom window just to their left and the sleeping boy on their right.

Listening to the sound of his deep, gentle breathing, Dakota whispered, "Poor little thing. He must've been dog-tired."

Ben chuckled softly. "If not before the bath, he sure was after. What a fighter!"

She smiled. "Oh, yes. It was a good thing for me

you turned up. He about had me beat."

Ben shivered.

"Didn't you change shirts yet?"

"Nah."

Dakota felt around in the dark and found the dry shirt that had belonged to Mr. Malone. "Don't be foolish, Ben. Take yours off and put this dry one on. It'll fit. He must've been a big man."

"He would've had to be to hold his own with Molly."

"Come on, now," Dakota insisted. "Take off that wet shirt before you catch pneumonia!"

He sighed. "Yes, ma'am."

She could just make him out in the dark, and when he slipped the sodden shirt off his shoulders, Dakota reached up to help. Her fingertips brushed over his clammy skin, and she held her breath, remembering the feel of his back under her touch.

He stopped moving and turned his head slightly, trying to read her expression. It was too dark. Instead, he had to content himself with the wonder of her fingers against his flesh. Holding perfectly still, he waited, praying silently that she wouldn't take her hands away.

She didn't.

Of their own accord, her hands moved over his shoulders, pushing the wet fabric down his back. Her fingertips traced the line of his spine, then she moved her palms to his shoulder blades. His skin warmed beneath her hands, and she heard his labored breathing match her own.

Slowly, careful not to break the spell that held them, Ben turned toward her. Her hands skimmed across his flesh with the movement, and when he faced her,

Dakota's palms slid over his chest. Coarse, golden hair curled beneath her fingers, and she felt his breath catch when her nail scraped over his nipple.

She moved closer to him and raised her eyes to his. In the shadowy light Dakota saw the tense set of his jaw and moved to kiss him lightly on his lips.

He didn't move for a long moment, then suddenly she was held in a viselike grip against the warmth of him. His mouth covered hers in an assault that broke down all barriers. Ben's fingers moved to the row of dainty buttons on her shirtwaist and in seconds had them undone. His hand cupped the fullness of her breast as his fingers stroked the bud through the sheer material of her camisole.

Dakota moved against him, and when he tore his mouth from hers and moved to her neck, she tried to get closer still.

"Ben . . ."

"Shh." He whispered against her skin. "God, Dakota, I've missed you so. I need you so." His tongue traced warm patterns down the length of her neck. "I tried not to . . . God knows I tried."

His mouth descended on hers again, and she didn't mind the fierceness of it. She matched it with every ounce of need that had been building in her for weeks.

At a scrape against the side of the building, Ben lifted his head, putting his fingers against her mouth for silence. Another scrape and a dull thud. A glance at the bed told Ben the boy was still sleeping. He set Dakota aside and assumed a crouching position alongside the window.

Hastily she buttoned her blouse. There would be time again for her and Ben to continue what they'd started. She wouldn't pretend any longer that she didn't need him. She did. As much as she needed air or water. She needed Ben Cable. And he needed her. It was enough for now.

Dakota looked up at the window. Past the breadth of Ben's back, she could just make out a long leg stepping into the room. She held her breath.

As soon as the intruder was fully inside, Ben sprang. In seconds the struggle was over. The tall thief was no match for Cable's strength. Now the stranger lay on the floor, Ben sitting on his middle.

The curses ringing in the air woke the boy. His voice joined the melee as he jumped from the bed. Dakota grabbed him as the bedroom door swung open. Molly stood in the doorway, holding a lamp high. The light spilled into the room, illuminating Ben and his opponent.

The boy screamed "Joe!"

And at the same time Ben and Dakota said together, "A girl!"

"I almost hit her!" Ben shook his head and took another sip of coffee. "I've never hit a female in my life!"

"Oh, for heaven's sake, Ben. You didn't know she was a girl. And you didn't hit her!"

Dakota poured herself another cup and glanced at the stairs. What a night!

"You think Molly's all right with her?"

"Yes. Molly can handle just about anything. Besides, she didn't want any help, beyond filling that blasted tub again." Dakota looked across the table at Ben. "Where have those kids been living? I've never seen anyone so dirty!"

"On the streets, most likely." He sighed. "There's

lots of kids on their own down here. Too many."
His gaze narrowed as he remembered something.
He'd meant to ask her earlier but had gotten dis-
tracted. "Did you see those strap marks on the boy's
back?"

"Couldn't help but see them. They looked mighty
fresh. As though someone was beating on him just a
few days ago."

Ben stood up and walked to a window. Staring out at
the darkness, he muttered, "Never could understand
whippin' a child." He turned to her and grinned sheepishly. "Oh, a spanking now and then, that's almost
expected. But to flay a child with a strap? No."

She crossed the room to him and wrapped her arms
around his middle. His left arm encircled her shoulders, and she smiled. "I know. I'd like to find out who
it was did that to him and give him a taste of his own
medicine."

"I can tell you who did it."

They turned as one to face Molly. In her billowing
floor-length white nightgown, the older woman looked
three times her normal size. She wore a disgusted
frown as she dropped into the nearest chair.

"There's the same kind of marks on the girl. Older,
though, and more of 'em."

"Someone beat a girl?" Ben said in a hushed, outraged voice.

"Often." Molly threw some coffee down her throat
before continuing. "I asked her who and she told me.
Their ma's boyfriend did it."

"And she let this happen!"

Molly smiled sadly at Dakota. "Honey, there's lots
of fool women out there. Women that'll do *anything*
to keep their man."

"I'll find this woman," Dakota started, "and when I do—"

"She's dead."

"What?"

"The girl, 'Josephine' "—Molly smiled—"says their ma died. Says since then, the boyfriend's gotten worse. Keeps findin' them wherever they are. Makes 'em steal for him, beats 'em . . . though she says she's been able to protect the boy some."

"If he always finds them, how did they manage to be on their own now?"

Molly poured more coffee for the three of them. "They got more reason than just a beatin' to hide better now." Her lips curled in a sneer. "He's been trying to sell her to Flat Nose Kate."

"Jesus!"

"Who?"

Ben looked at Dakota. "Kate runs one of the shadiest bordellos on the Coast. She's an evil, twisted woman who pays top dollar for girl children. The younger the better."

"Good Lord."

"Exactly," Molly breathed. "Well, the old bitch ain't gonna get this one. Not if I can help it."

"Not if *we* can help it," Dakota corrected solemnly and laid her hand over Molly's.

Ben's hand covered both of theirs as he vowed, "She won't get this one."

Twelve

"Is that right?"

Molly looked over at the lopsided cake and smiled fondly. "It's just right, Josie."

Dakota shook her head gently. The change in the children was amazing. Only three days in the safety and warmth of Molly's place, and they'd both blossomed. Eager to help, Timmy was constantly running from room to room, cleaning, carrying food and coffee . . . doing everything he could to prove himself indispensable.

Dakota's gaze shifted to the boy's sister. Tall and pretty, with the grime of her disguise removed, Josie was a new person. She wore one of Dakota's threadbare dresses and preened in front of the mirror as if the yellow calico were the finest silk. The girl's shining brown hair was tied back with a ribbon, and her eyes glowed with happiness under Molly's indulgent gaze.

Though the threat of their mother's "friend," a man named Dietz, still hung over them, the children were able to let go of their past and their worries to embrace the new world that had opened up to them.

Dakota looked away, suddenly ashamed of herself. Compared with them, she'd lost little. Yet she was only now releasing the bitterness of the past.

"Dakota."

She looked up.

Molly glanced over her shoulder, making sure that Josie was out of earshot. "We ain't had much time lately to talk about Ellis."

"Oh," Dakota said quickly, "Molly, it's all right. The kids are more important right now."

The older woman smiled gently. "Ain't they somethin', though? Hardest-workin' younguns I ever saw."

"They want to please you."

She wiped her hands on a dish towel. "Hell," she said gruffly, "they do that just by bein' here. Y'know, me and Himself, we always wanted children. . . ." She shook her head. "That's not what I wanted to talk to you about, though. It's about Ellis."

"What?" Surprised, Dakota realized that she wasn't as interested as she would have been just a couple of weeks before.

"There's somebody comin' over tonight. After we close. She may be able to help us."

"Who?"

"Molly." Timmy called from the other room, "where you want I should put this damned coffeepot?"

The woman rolled her eyes. "Can't seem to make that child stop cussin'." She looked back at Dakota. "We'll talk more later."

Dakota watched Molly go, then turned back to the mountain of bread dough she'd been kneading. Somehow, she wasn't looking forward to their visitor.

* * *

With the restaurant closed for the evening and the children upstairs, Molly and Dakota were alone when their visitor slipped in the back door. She stood uncertainly in the lamplight and waited silently under Dakota's openmouthed stare.

Her dress of bright blue satin was cut unbelievably low, revealing generous breasts. Her legs were encased in netlike tights, and she had the whitest hair Dakota'd ever seen. What was once a pretty face was covered under layers of makeup, and her amazing hair was tied to the side of her head, with a blue feather stuck into the mass of curls.

Though about the same age as Dakota, the woman's eyes were old. Ancient. As though she'd seen far too much pain to remain unscathed. Finally those green eyes narrowed slightly as she asked, "Seen enough, honey?"

"I'm sorry . . . I—"

"Forget it," she said, walking to the table, "I been stared at before." She dropped into a chair and smiled when Molly handed her a cup of coffee. After taking a quick gulp, she set the cup down and said, "Let's get on with it. I gotta get back."

"Fine," Molly said and looked at Dakota. "This is Shelley. She's a friend of mine." The older woman paused, then added, "She also works for Ellis."

Dakota's gaze shot to the other woman.

"Shelley says she can get you into Ellis's office." Molly watched Dakota carefully. "You could snoop around some, see if you could find anything interestin'."

She nodded.

"It ain't all that easy, y'know," Shelley cautioned.

"If he should come in while you was there . . . you'd be on your own."

Dakota nodded. But suddenly curious, she asked, "Why would you do this for me? I don't even know you."

Shelley drew back and gave the other woman a long, assessing stare. What she saw in Dakota's face seemed to reassure her because finally she shrugged. "Let's just say I got no reason to like Ellis. And I owe Molly plenty."

"But—" Dakota started.

"Look." Shelley stood abruptly. "If you ain't interested, just say so."

"I'm interested."

"Sit down, Shelley," Molly urged.

"Tell me what to do," Dakota said.

The old prospector walked up to the door of the Irish Lady at the same time as the messenger boy. The kid peeked inside and groaned at the sight of the crowd. It would take forever to get the woman's attention in a bunch that size. If he didn't deliver the dang wire, though, and *quick*, his ma would have his head. He'd already been home late for supper three nights running.

"Well, c'mon, boy" the old man grumbled. "Go in or get out o' the way. Some of us want to eat tonight."

The boy looked down at the name on the telegram, then glanced up at the prospector. "You know who Dakota Lane is?"

"Sure do." He nodded. "Works for Molly."

The boy shifted his feet nervously. It was getting later all the time. "Look, mister, I got to get on home . . .

and you're goin' inside anyways . . ."

"Spit it out, boy!"

"Will you see she gets this wire?"

The old man sighed. "Sure, if it'll get you movin' faster."

"Thanks." The boy tipped his hat and took off down the street at a run.

"Hmmph! Reckon he *can* hurry when he's got a mind to," he mumbled, hand on the door.

"Pete!"

The old man stopped and turned.

"I got your order set," a man called out from the store across the street. "Come over and get it."

The prospector looked longingly at the food-laden tables in the restaurant, then let the door swing shut. First things first. Got to get his supplies if he was going to be leavin' town at first light. "I'm comin'!" he shouted, absentmindedly crumpling the piece of paper in his hand and tossing it into the mud.

Dakota stood in darkness at the foot of the staircase. Though she was heartily sick of hiding in smelly alleys, she had to wait where Shelley'd told her to. Nervously she patted her right calf, checking for the tenth time in as many minutes that her derringer was indeed in place.

She wasn't at all sure that this was a good idea. After all, anything could happen. Even Shelley admitted that Ellis didn't always take an hour for supper. What if he came back early? What if he found her in his office?

Stop it! She paced anxiously and threw another glance at the back door at the head of the stairs.

She already knew what she would do. She reached into her pocket and pulled out the tiny brown vial Shelley had given her.

A sleeping powder. And according to Shelley, there was enough in the vial to put a man to sleep almost immediately. It seemed that all the "girls" carried the stuff because, as her new friend had said, "Sometimes the customers get a little *too* rough." All Dakota had to do was get him to drink it in a glass of whiskey. From what Shelley'd said about the man's drinking, that shouldn't be difficult.

The door opened, sending a small shaft of light into the alley below.

"Dakota!" Shelley's whispered shout reached her.

"Here," she answered, climbing the stairs quickly.

"Well, c'mon, then."

Dakota stepped across the threshold and into the dimly lit office. As the door clicked quietly shut behind her, she fought back a wave of panic.

"Hurry up. Ellis has already left," Shelley said as she moved toward the other door. "I couldn't get away any quicker." She glanced around her, then looked at Dakota meaningfully. "You hurry up and get what you need—then you get the hell outa here. Understand?"

Dakota nodded. "Thanks, Shelley."

"Like I said. Don't thank me. I owe Molly . . . but more than that, I hate Ellis. You take care o' him, that's thanks enough for me."

The other woman left the office then, and Dakota was alone. In the light of a solitary lamp she looked at the room for the first time. Her lip curled in disgust. It was filthy. The floors hadn't seen a broom in years, and the gaudy red wallpaper was peeling. A massive oak desk stood near an empty fireplace on the far wall, and there were heavy damask draperies pulled shut over the windows.

She shuddered and swallowed her urge to run. It was suddenly hard to breathe in the small, dark room. She wished fervently that she'd never come. Forcing a deep gulp of air into her lungs, Dakota determinedly walked across the room to the desk. The sooner she finished, the sooner she could leave. The only problem was, she had no idea what she was looking for.

Papers were strewn across the desk, with others sticking out haphazardly from the cubbyholes under the open rolltop. Sighing, she began her search. Rifling through the papers as quickly as she could, her eyes strained to read the crablike handwriting.

Glancing repeatedly at the closed door, Dakota swallowed nervously. Her mouth dry and her stomach tied in knots, she rummaged through the disorganized mess. There wasn't enough time, she told herself. She'd never be able to look through everything in an hour. Her fingers flipped through page after page of indecipherable writing while her mind conjured up images of Ben and what he would do if he ever found out about this.

Suddenly she stopped and cocked her head to listen. Dakota dropped the papers back onto the desk and quickly moved around and took the chair on the visitor's side. The door flew open a moment later. Heart pounding, she glanced over her shoulder and gasped at the sight of the big man filling the doorway.

"Who the hell are you?" he shouted as he stepped into the room and slammed the door behind him.

A huge man, he appeared to be just as much fat as muscle. His clothes were covered with layers of grime, and even at a distance, the stink of him reached

her: She swallowed back her revulsion, clutched her
shawl tighter about her, and gave the answer she'd
rehearsed just in case.

"I'm . . . uh, lookin' for a job."

His tiny brown eyes narrowed even further. He
stared at her for what seemed an eternity, then crossed
the short distance to her chair and pulled her to her
feet. Dakota turned her head away, but he pulled her
chin back firmly.

"Gotta get a good look at ya, honey," he said,
grinning. His right hand shot up and pulled her shawl
away from her crossed arms. "Don't hire just *anybody*,
y'know. My girls has got to have what the men want."
He ran the flat of his hand over the mound of her breast
and laughed when she shuddered. "You seem mighty
promisin', honey. . . ."

She stepped back. He followed.

"You're awful skittish, though."

"I, uh . . . I've never done this before."

"That's easy enough to see." He rubbed a big meaty
hand over his unshaven cheeks. "Undo some of them
buttons."

Her eyes flew to his.

"I ain't gonna hire what I ain't at least seen."

Dakota glanced around the room uneasily. He was
between her and the back door. Going out the main
door would do her no good. She'd simply end up in
his saloon, where he could have any number of people
stop her.

"C'mon, now. I ain't got all night." He stepped closer and reached for her. "Or do you want ol' Hank to
do it for you?"

"No. No, I'll do it." Her hands moved to the buttons
at her throat. Think, she told herself. Think. Then all

at once, she remembered the powder Shelley'd given her. Of course. "Uh, could we have a drink first?"

He cocked his head and looked at her. "A drink, huh? You ain't a drunk, are ya?"

"No, I'm just . . . nervous."

He nodded and pointed to a table in the far corner. "All right. Pour us some whiskey, then." As she moved off, he continued, "I mean, it don't matter to me if you're a drunk, but I like to know that kinda thing right off. Gives me an idea how much good you'll be at the job."

While he talked, Dakota poured amber liquid into two dirty glasses. With her back to him, she slowly reached into her pocket for the vial. Dumping the powder into his drink, she was pleased to see that it dissolved immediately. She took a deep breath and walked back to the heavy man.

He lay sprawled out on an old, horsehair sofa. His booted foot was propped on the arm over an especially large hole where the stuffing was spilling out. Ellis accepted the drink and tossed its contents down his throat. Then he pulled his filthy shirt out of his pants and ripped it apart, sending buttons skittering over the wood floor. His massive chest was completely covered in a mat of black and gray hair that he scratched as if it was infested with bugs.

Dakota swallowed.

"Well, c'mon, honey. Let's see it." He loosened his belt and began to tug at the buttons of his pants.

"What?" she breathed, averting her eyes.

"Goddammit. Either you take that damn dress off, or I do. Now."

She turned and saw him move. Hastily she backed off, took a drink of the raw whiskey, and welcomed the fire trailing down her dry throat. "No. I'll do it."

"Then get at it." He lay back against the sofa again and in the lamplight Dakota saw him return to unbuttoning his pants. Her fingers went again to the top button. She had no choice. But maybe, if she moved slowly enough, the powder would work on him before she finished. Why hadn't she asked Shelley how quickly the drug worked? Why had she gone on this fool's errand in the first place? Why hadn't she listened to Ben?

Oh, God, Ben. Where was he? Had he found out where she was? What she was doing? The second button slipped free and she heard Ellis sigh. Sneaking a sidelong glance at the man, she watched with revulsion as his hand slipped into his pants and rubbed at his crotch with concentration.

Third button open, and her stomach tightened. Dakota couldn't breathe in the little room. The whiskey she'd drunk had gone straight to her head. She felt dizzy.

"Hurry it up!"

She jumped. Fourth button and the material of her dress hung wide over the top of her chemise. Ellis yawned and she chanced another look at him. He shook his shaggy head as if to clear it, then tried to focus on her. Fifth button. Soon she'd be down to her underthings. His head flopped back against the sofa, and he seemed to be having a hard time lifting it again.

"Go on . . . I'm watchin'."

She didn't think so. Dakota redid the fifth and fourth buttons and waited. Nothing. His eyes were closed now. Quickly she buttoned up the rest of her gown and walked closer to him. The disgusting man's breathing was deep and even. His jaw hung open and an echoing snore filled the room. He lay just as before, with one foot propped up and his hand in his pants. It was all she could do not to gag.

Thank you, Shelley, Dakota sighed. Quickly she turned to his desk. Having already checked the desktop, she moved on to the drawers. Hurrying, she pulled open one after another, looking over then discarding countless worthless papers. With only one drawer left, Dakota had about decided the entire plan had been a waste of time. But inside the deepest drawer was a leather case tied shut with a rawhide thong. She looked over her shoulder uneasily. Ellis was still snoring.

She sat down gingerly on the edge of the chair and tugged at the string. She found several papers, each with a list of dates, times, and money amounts. Scanning them hurriedly, a horrible realization began to take shape. Carefully Dakota went back to the beginning of the lists. She studied the small, crabbed handwriting closely. There was no mistake.

A loud snore erupted from the sofa. She sent the revolting man a venomous glare, then shifted her gaze back to the list.

Not list. *Lists.* Shanghai lists. Filled with page after page of descriptions of men. There were no names. The poor souls had lost not only their freedom, but their identity as well. Alongside their descriptions was the price paid for their delivery. At the bottom of each page was the name of the sea captain who had bargained for the men. And one other name was there. A name that seemed to leap out at Dakota.

Gordon Tyson.

Gordon!

It had to be, she thought. It had to be the same man. She read through the papers again. Slowly, carefully, she tried to memorize as much as she could. She couldn't risk trying to make a copy of the lists. Anyone could walk into the office at any time. Already, she'd stayed too long. She slipped the papers back into the folder, then returned them to the drawer and closed it firmly.

She'd found what she needed. She was sure of it. Pulling her shawl tight around her shoulders, Dakota moved to the back door and opened it a fraction. After a moment she ducked outside quickly and shut the door behind her. As she moved down the stairs and onto the crowded street, Dakota breathed easier. She knew she'd been lucky. She even knew it had been a foolish thing to do. But it was worth it. At least she had a name now. And when she told Ben, she was sure he'd understand.

Once she'd passed the line of saloons, the crowds thinned to just a few people wandering in and out of the shadows. She wondered briefly if she ought to stop and get her derringer out, but then decided to keep going. She wouldn't feel really safe until she was back at the restaurant.

Fog drifted in off the bay and swirled damp fingers over the dark streets. Dakota shivered and stepped up her pace. Her footsteps seemed to echo on the wooden sidewalk, and she fought down an eerie sensation of being watched.

Almost there, she told herself. In the distance she could see the vague outline of the Irish Lady. Faint glimmers of lamplight shone like stars in the mist. She smiled, then felt a strong hand close around her arm. Before she could scream, another hand covered her mouth roughly as she was dragged into the darkness.

Dakota clawed and kicked. Her nails dug into the hand keeping her quiet. She brought the heel of her shoe down on the man's foot and heard him grunt in pain. But his hold didn't loosen. She twisted and turned like a cat in a sack, but it did no good. His grip only tightened.

All the warnings from Molly and Shelley and Ben came rushing back to haunt her. She couldn't even reach her gun. His iron band of an arm held her own arms too tightly. Fighting even harder, she finally managed to clamp her teeth down hard on the man's hand.

"Goddammit!" Ben hissed. He released her and shook his hand up and down vigorously. Glaring at her, he inspected his flesh closely while she staggered to regain her balance. "I think I'm bleedin'!"

"Good." Her relief at hearing his voice was gone. "Why did you grab me like that? You nearly scared me to death!"

"Yeah?" Ben stepped closer. "I damn well meant to. Now you know how *I* felt, standing in this damn alley waiting for you to come out of that place alive."

"Waiting? How long have you been here?"

"Too damn long," he snarled. "And so have you!" He grabbed her shoulders and jerked her close to him. Ben never wanted to relive anything like what he'd experienced standing in the dark waiting for her. If she hadn't come out when she did, he'd have gone charging in, and the hell with his investigation! Now that she was here, though, all he could think was, thank God she was safe. His arms closed around her, and after a minute's hesitation, Dakota lay against him willingly. "I've never been so scared in my life!"

She leaned back, and he felt her shiver. "Me, nei-ther."

Some of the anger drained away at the sound of her hollow voice. He pushed her head back down to his shoulder. "Well, at least you had the sense to be scared."

"How did you know where to find me?" Dakota's fingers toyed with the lapel of his coat.

"Shelley told me."

She stiffened. Shelley? How did he know Shelley? Was he one of her customers?

He chuckled as if he could read her mind. "Molly told me about Shelley . . . and when I went to see her tonight, she told me where you were." Ben leaned back to watch her face. "I couldn't believe you went to see a man like Ellis alone. Are you all right? He didn't hurt you? Or . . ."

She burrowed closer to his warmth and gratefully inhaled the clean scent of him. "No. He didn't hurt me. And he didn't 'or either.' "

Ben released a long, pent-up breath and held her tighter.

She leaned back. "Now will you tell me why you grabbed me like that?"

"Because I wanted to scare some sense into you! This isn't Red Creek. These fellas are dangerous. More dangerous than you would believe. You've got to start trustin' me, Dakota. When I tell you something, I'm not makin' it up." His gaze bored into hers. "You've got to believe that maybe I know more about these things than you do."

"I do believe you," she said softly. "Now, more than ever." She wasn't even angry at having to listen to yet another lecture. The fear she'd just experienced in Ellis's office was still too real. "But are you sure that was your only reason for scaring me? Aren't you a little mad, too?"

" 'Course I was mad."

"No." She shook her head. "Not 'cause I was in there, but because maybe I found some information about Ellis before you did?"

His arms dropped and he took a step back. Ben stared at her through wide, disbelieving eyes. *She thinks this is some kind of game! It's like there's a damn race between us!*

"Dammit, Dakota! I'm not *stupid*! Believe it or not, I was a lawman long before I met you . . . and I even managed to catch a few outlaws now and then." He took a deep breath and finished, "I found out about Ellis a while ago."

She felt the sharp, swift stab of betrayal. "Then why didn't you say anything?"

He sighed and looked up at the hazy, fog-enshrouded lamplight. "Because I didn't want you running off half-cocked and getting yourself killed, and because I didn't have proof. Just suspicions. Since then I've talked to the marshal here, sent out a few telegrams, and I think I've got enough to hold Ellis now." He lowered his gaze to hers and smiled crookedly. "He's a very popular man. At least three states want him."

"Well," she said softly, "you could've told me."

"Yeah, I could've. But like I said, I was afraid you'd rush out and do something—"

"Foolish?"

"And you didn't disappoint me."

She smiled. "All right. But why don't you go and

arrest him, for heaven's sake?"

Ben pulled her back against him and said patiently, "First, because I'm not a federal marshal. Just a small-town sheriff from Nevada. That's not all, though. The marshal here would be glad to lock him up. But"— he sighed—"I still don't know anything about this Gordon fella. And Ellis is the only clue to him I've got."

She leaned back and smiled up at him. She *did* know something he didn't. Images of those lists in Ellis's office swam before her eyes. She could hardly wait to see Ben's face when she told him.

Thirteen

"GORDON Tyson?" Molly's voice betrayed her surprise. "Are you sure the name was Gordon Tyson?"

Dakota nodded. "I read the papers carefully. Twice. It was Gordon Tyson."

Molly stood up, rapped her knuckles on the tabletop, then walked to the front window. Staring out into the darkness, she said, "Well, fancy that."

Ben looked at Dakota, and she shrugged. She'd expected surprise from him when she'd told the two of them her news. But Molly's reaction she hadn't counted on. A hint of a smile had crept onto the older woman's face at the mention of Tyson's name. It was still there.

"You gonna tell us, Molly?" Ben asked quietly.

She turned to face them squarely and smiled more broadly. "You two been spendin' so much time down on the waterfront . . . you forgot there's an *uptown* in this city, too." She paused and studied their faces. "And this Gordon Tyson is a mighty important man there."

Molly walked back to the table. Bending down, she

set her hands on the cloth-covered top and leaned forward. "He's got more money than God. Hobnobs with all the fancy gents. Nobody knows how he got his money. And nobody asks, either." She eased herself down into a chair and continued. "But Tyson . . . guess he's got a sight more ambition than the rest of them people uptown. Lately, there's been talk of runnin' him for mayor." She threw her head back and let her booming laughter surround them for a moment before quieting and throwing a guilty look at the stairs. She didn't want to wake the kids. Slapping the tabletop with the flat of her hand, she crowed, "Shanghai King runnin' for mayor!"

Ben and Dakota stared at each other, openmouthed.

Finally Dakota said forcefully, "We have to tell people. Tell 'em what we found out!"

Ben shook his head wearily and rubbed his jaw. "No. We don't have any proof. It'd be your word against his." He stared hard at her. "Besides, I want you out of this now. You've already done enough."

"Oh, no," Dakota countered. "You can't stop me now. You wouldn't even know his name if not for me. And if you need proof, why don't we just go back to Ellis's office and steal the lists?"

"What's the matter with you, anyway?" Ben couldn't believe it. "You just barely got out of there tonight. And what makes you so sure those lists are always so handy? Even Ellis isn't stupid enough to leave 'em just lyin' around all the time. Tonight you were lucky. You can't count on bein' lucky all the time."

"We could try—"

"No, *we* can't." He grabbed her arm, more to get her attention than anything else. "You don't know that this is the Gordon who was in Red Creek. There's lots of people named Gordon in the world. You never saw the man back home, and you've never seen *this* Gordon, either."

A sudden hope struck her. "Did you see our Mr. Gordon in Red Creek?"

He shook his head. "No. I was gone most of the time Tenn was in town. By the time I got back, there was so much to do at the office, paperwork and such . . . no."

"Well, I *can* see this Gordon. And I know something about the other one, too. At least enough to go on." She pulled her arm free. "I'm *going* to find Tyson."

She'd almost quit trying to find the man before tonight. She'd reached the point where she'd almost forgotten the fear of losing the ranch . . . the anger over Tenn's injury and Tom's death. What had happened? Was it simply being so far from home? That so much time had passed since the shooting? Dakota glanced over at Ben. Or was it her growing fascination with Cable that was dimming her resolve?

"Not without me."

"What?"

"I *said* you're not going anywhere, lookin' for anyone, without me." He wouldn't go through what he'd experienced tonight again. Not if he could help it. "I can't be following you around all the time. And if this *is* the same man, he's got a lot to protect. He'll do anything to keep his secrets."

She met his determined gaze and knew he was right. But she wouldn't run and hide, either. She had to make Ben see that she *needed* to be a part of his plan. Whatever it was. "All right. We'll find the proof we need together."

Ben glanced at Molly and frowned. She was grinning from ear to ear. Rubbing his tired eyes, he wondered why he could never seem to win an argument with Dakota. Maybe he should be happy with this. At least she was willing to compromise. He looked at her and tried to ignore the warning twinge deep in his gut. It would be dangerous. If anything happened to her . . . but if she was with him, he'd have a better than even chance of protecting her. He swallowed heavily. "Deal," he said.

Red Creek

Tenn slapped the heavy beam with pride. The new room was really starting to take shape. He smiled at Diego, the young carpenter, then stepped into the open framework.

In his mind's eye he saw it so clearly. He would come in from the range and find Laura here, in her new parlor, sitting by a fire. The flickering light would be dancing on her hair, and she would smile softly at him. There would be time for quiet talks, for loving, and he wouldn't have to leave her to go home to a cold bed. It was getting harder to wait.

The way Diego was working, it was beginning to look as if the new room would be finished before Dakota got home. Tenn pulled off his hat and pushed his hair back out of his face. Strange he hadn't heard from his sister. He would've bet she'd take the first train home after receiving that wire.

No. He tamped down the vague worry that nibbled at the edges of his mind. If there *was* a problem, Ben would have let him know.

Replacing his hat, Tenn crossed the room to the far side. Staring out the window frame at the valley beyond the ranch house, he reassured himself. With Doc's help, they now had a chance to build the Lane ranch into something he'd always dreamed it could be. And he wasn't about to start courting trouble that wasn't there.

"Tenn!"

He stuck his head out the window opening. "Yeah, Jess, what is it?"

The old man chuckled. "If you're all through playin' house in there, the boys have got the new corral posts ready."

Tenn frowned. It was a good thing him and Laura were getting married soon, he thought. Much longer and folks were gonna start thinkin' his bread wasn't quite done. He turned and stalked to the doorway. Ignoring Diego's muffled laughter, Tenn took another look at the place. Hurry up, Dakota. I can't wait forever.

"Dakota," Josie gasped and backed away, "you're beautiful. Just like a princess."

"She's right, dearie." Molly pulled at the delicate material gently, straightening the hang of the skirt. "If you don't knock Cable's socks clean off . . . he ain't wearin' any."

Dakota smiled at the compliments. She *felt* pretty, too. She only wished there was a big mirror somewhere around so she could be sure. Her hands ran over the bodice of her new gown, then she looked up at Molly and smiled. "I feel sort of guilty, spendin' so much of the wages you paid me on one dress." She bit her bottom lip. "Are you sure you can afford to pay me? I mean, we never talked about a wage. Just room and board."

Molly shook her head. "Don't you worry about that. All the work you done around here, you're worth plenty more than what I gave you." The old woman laid her arm around Josie's shoulders. "Did you ever in your life see a dress like that one, child?"

"No, ma'am."

Dakota knew exactly what they meant. The minute she'd seen the gown in a small dress shop on Montgomery Street, she'd known she had to have it. It fit her as though it had been made for her.

Yards of beautiful burgundy silk floated around her body, falling gracefully from the tight-fitting waist. The bodice was cut daringly low, and stretched across the open vee of her bosom was a black net so fine, it might have been spun by spiders. Her arms were encased in long, tight-fitting sleeves, and she wore black fingerless gloves on her hands. Her hair was swept to the top of her head and held in place with ebony combs, while tiny burgundy ribbons shot through the mass of curls and hung daintily down her back.

"Hey, Dakota!" Pounding feet ran up the stairs, and Timmy threw open the door. The boy stood in the threshold, his eyes wide, staring openmouthed at Dakota. He didn't move for a full minute, then finally he pursed his lips and gave a low whistle. "Well, goddamn, if you ain't a sight."

"What'd I tell you about cussin'?"

He flicked a glance at Molly. "Sorry, Molly. But she surprised me some." He looked back at Dakota. "You're mighty pretty for a girl."

She laughed.

"Timmy, why'd you come up here anyway?"

He didn't bother to look at his sister. His eyes still on Dakota, he said, "Ben's here. He wants to know what the hell's keepin' you."

"*Timmy!*"

"Sorry, Molly."

Dakota took a deep breath and picked up her matching silk reticule from the bed. Slipping the drawstrings over her wrist, she lifted the hem of her gown and left her room.

She stopped at the head of the stairs and looked down. Ben's gaze crashed into hers, and she was delighted to see the same stunned expression on his face that Timmy had worn only moments ago. Her heart pounded heavily in her breast as she noted how handsome Ben Cable was. His tailored black suit clung to his body, and his gleaming white shirt was starched to perfection. He wore a black ribbon around the collar of his shirt, tied in a bow. His sandy-blond hair was combed back from his tanned face, and without his hat brim to shade them, Dakota could read the desire in his eyes.

Slowly she descended the stairs, her gaze never leaving his. As she moved closer to him, Dakota realized that she didn't need a mirror after all. In the reflection of his blue eyes, she saw that she was indeed beautiful tonight.

Twenty minutes later her fingers tightened on his arm, and Ben smiled. Gently he laid his left hand over hers. He felt the admiring glances cast their way, and he swelled with pride. Every man in the room would be looking at him with envy. And he didn't blame them. But it wasn't just Dakota's beauty that so captivated him. She had an inner fire that warmed him. That touched him deep inside. Where no other woman had ever been.

Passion for her flooded his body, and it took every ounce of strength he possessed to fight it down. He wanted her more than he'd thought possible. And no other woman would do. In the past he would have sought out any willing female with a generous heart and no expectations beyond mutual pleasure. But since that one night with Dakota . . . his desire for any woman but her had gone.

He hesitated to call this new feeling love. Mainly because he'd spent so many years hiding from that word. Over the years he'd deliberately avoided getting close to anyone, until Dakota. Now, since meeting her, the fates had seen fit to taunt him at every turn. He hadn't had a peaceful moment in weeks. When she wasn't with him, he was thinking about her. He'd surely had a lot fewer worries before Dakota Lane came storming into his life.

Although, truth to tell, being alone suddenly seemed too miserable to think about. She shifted position slightly, and he looked down at her.

She held herself like a queen. Sure, confident, as though she wore elegant gowns every day of her life. If not for the grip she had on his arm, he would never guess that she was nervous.

The maître d' hurried over to them and bowed with a courtly air to Dakota. She dazzled the poor man with a smile, then followed him, Ben's hand on her back, to a table in the center of the room.

After seating her at the linen-covered table, Ben watched her as she stared with open fascination at their surroundings.

The marble floors and pillars shone with a warmth all their own. Highly polished silver fixtures caught and held the fire of hundreds of candles in crystal chandeliers. Waiters moved with quiet grace through the maze of tables while muted conversations and the soft clink of elegant goblets drifted through the air. A young woman sat in a shadowed corner, plucking daintily at the strings of a golden harp, sending ripples of quiet music over the well-dressed crowd.

A waiter appeared and set a silver bucket on their table. Inside, resting on a bed of cracked ice, sat a bottle of champagne.

Dakota looked at Ben questioningly.

"This *is* an occasion"—he smiled—"isn't it?"

"Yes." She lowered her gaze as the waiter poured sparkling wine into delicate glasses. When he left them alone once more, she looked up to find Ben holding his glass and staring at her.

"Pick up your glass, Dakota," he urged quietly. She did and met his gaze evenly. "Let's drink to tonight. For just a while, let's . . . pretend."

"Pretend what?" Her breath was coming quickly, and the curl of excitement in her stomach spread.

He leaned forward and gently clinked his glass against hers. "Pretend that we're here for the same reason every one else is. To enjoy each other's company."

Dakota smiled. It was as if he could read her mind. She even found herself hoping that Tyson wouldn't show up at the restaurant they knew to be one of his favorites. She didn't want anything to spoil this evening. Lifting the glass to her lips, Dakota took a sip of the bubbly wine and smiled. "I'd like that."

Violin music drifted into the room, and Ben glanced

to the alcove where the harpist sat. She'd been joined by three men in high collars and black suits. They stood in the shadows playing their instruments.

Abruptly Ben rose from his chair and came to her side. "It's been a while since I've been on a dance floor. But if you don't mind taking a chance, I'd love to twirl you around the floor."

"Mr. Cable," she said as she put her hand in his and stood, "I'd love to."

They joined three or four other couples as the music began. Ben led her lightly around the dance floor, and Dakota gave silent thanks for the hours of instruction Maria had enforced on her. Despite what he'd said, Ben was a wonderful dancer. His hand pressed against the small of her back sent spirals of heat through her body. She stared into his eyes and heard her own heart beat furiously in response to the desire she saw there. Reluctantly she lowered her gaze and tried to think of something to say.

"Red Creek must pay their sheriffs well. This is a *very* nice suit."

He led her through a quick turn, then smiled down at her. "No. The pay's not that good, I'm afraid. A few years back I was in San Francisco and grubstaked a man down on his luck. Guess I'm a good judge of character. He did well and so did I." He laughed. "So I'm a sheriff, just not a poor one."

"That's wonderful," Dakota said. "Does that mean you've moved out of that awful boardinghouse on Pacific Street?"

One of Ben's eyebrows rose. "And how did you know about that place? Been asking questions about me?"

"No!" She certainly wasn't about to admit to that. "People talk . . ."

"Sure." He laughed again and spun her exuberantly around the floor.

The evening passed quickly. Ben and Dakota were oblivious to their surroundings. There'd been no sign of Tyson. But she didn't mind. Tonight, she was happy to pretend. For a few hours she wanted to believe they were just like any other couple.

Finally, though, it was time to leave. As Ben slipped her shawl around her shoulders, a commotion by the entrance caught their attention. A group of people were clustered there, loudly welcoming someone. Amid much laughter and hearty conversation, the group slowly parted and a lone man made his way into the room.

Elegantly dressed in a fine gray suit, he entered the main dining room, stopping every few feet to greet friends. In his forties, he looked a perfect gentleman. From his silk cravat down to his shiny leather shoes. But what caught Dakota's eye was the walking stick he carried. Its knob was a silver tiger's head.

Gordon Tyson . . . Mr. Gordon.

She would have moved forward, but Ben's strong grip on her arm restrained her. She glanced at him and saw that he, too, had noticed the stick.

Ben glared at her and whispered, "Not now, Dakota. Let's leave. Quietly."

"But that's him."

"I know," Ben replied curtly as he pulled her to her feet. "That's what we came for, Dakota. Now we know for sure. There can't be too many of those tiger sticks around town. He *has* to be Gordon."

He cut off any further discussion by guiding her

firmly toward the exit. They passed close to Tyson, and when they were near enough, Dakota stopped suddenly, jerking Ben to a halt.

"Excuse me," she said clearly. "Mr. Tyson, isn't it?"

Ben groaned as the dapper man turned toward her.

Gordon Tyson faced the lovely young woman with open interest. His thin mustache curved upward as it rode a smile that never warmed his eyes.

"Yes?"

Dakota stared at the man she had come so far to find. His quiet elegance did nothing to hide the cold, unfeeling glint in the brown eyes that met hers in question. She had spoken on impulse, unwilling to leave the restaurant without making some sort of contact.

Seeing him here, surrounded by what appeared to be wealthy, influential friends, wasn't as easy as she'd thought it would be. Somehow, she hadn't really believed Molly's stories of the man's popularity. Was she wrong about the man? Was it really him? Yes. She looked into those flat brown eyes again and knew she was right.

She had to say *something*. Everyone was staring at her. She could feel Ben's anger. Before he had a chance to make an excuse to Tyson, she plunged in.

"Oh, I was sure it was you!" She smiled coquettishly at him. Turning slightly and playfully tapping Ben's chest, she continued, "See, dear . . . it *is* Mr. Tyson."

Ben nodded, forcing a grim smile.

Dakota addressed the barrel-chested older man nearest Tyson. She ignored the look of consternation on his face as she said, "Forgive me for interrupting, Mr. . . ."

"Allen," the man said. "Foster Allen." He nodded at the quiet redheaded woman wearing an expensive but drab beige gown next to him. "My daughter, Margaret."

The poor shy woman flushed to the roots of her hair, so Dakota quickly turned her attention back to Mr. Allen. "You see, Mr. Tyson is a friend of my brother's."

"I'm sorry . . ." Tyson began, obviously confused.

Leaning forward slightly, Dakota chuckled. "Surely you remember Tennessee Lane? Red Creek, Nevada?"

His gaze hardened and he glanced quickly at Allen's expression.

"You see," Dakota went on, "Mr. Tyson bought some cattle from my brother just a couple of months ago." She had Allen's and everyone else's attention now, so she continued, ignoring Ben's low growl of warning. "He paid a fair price for 'em, too. But I'm sure that doesn't surprise any of you."

Her refined listeners smiled pleasantly, though they were clearly puzzled.

Tyson, though, knew exactly what Dakota was doing, and he made an attempt to forestall her. "It's very kind of you to—"

"Nonsense." Dakota cut him off and returned her attention to his friends. "Mr. Tyson created quite a stir in Red Creek. It's a small town, and men like him seldom visit us." She smiled. "He surely did make an impression on the townspeople."

Her audience nodded benignly, sure of their own impact on a small town.

Suddenly Dakota snatched the walking stick from Tyson's hand. She stared at the silver tiger. Oblivious to the others, she looked at the emerald eyes of the carved predator. How many others, she wondered. How many men like Tenn and Tom Stillwell did it take to own such a thing?

"This lovely tiger's head," she said softly, "was talked about a good deal."

Tyson stood speechless as Dakota returned his stick. Their eyes met in a silent duel.

Then Foster Allen spoke up. "Not surprised to hear that, m'dear. That tiger's head is one of a kind. I remember when Gordon commissioned it."

Tyson shot the old man a venomous look that went unnoticed by all but Ben and Dakota.

Her mouth suddenly dry, she prodded the older man. "Really?"

"Oh, yes." He closed his eyes, thinking. "Almost two years ago now, wasn't it, Gordon?"

Tyson agreed abruptly, having no other choice. Then he turned and formally addressed Dakota. "I *am* sorry, young lady. But I'm afraid that I don't remember your brother." Bowing, he turned away.

Ben grabbed Dakota's arm. Furious, he wanted to get her away. Someplace quiet. Where he could strangle her!

But Dakota wasn't finished.

"That's all right, Mr. *Tyson*. We remember you." She threw her head back proudly before continuing. "By the way, perhaps you didn't know. My brother was shot and robbed the night you left town."

A collective gasp came from the people listening, and Tyson swung quickly around to face her. His eyes were cold. His thin lips set in a rigid line.

"It seems," Dakota said, "the thief knew that Tenn would still have the bank draft with him. Whoever it was broke into Tenn's room at the hotel and shot him. Then stole the money." Murmured sounds of sympathy washed over her, but she didn't stop. "But that wasn't enough for this thief. When our deputy, Tom Stillwell, heard the gunshots and came runnin', they shot him, too. Killed him. He left a wife and two babies."

"Oh, my dear, how dreadful," an old woman said softly. Dakota glanced at her audience. Foster Allen was watching Tyson suspiciously.

Shifting her gaze back to Tyson, Dakota wasn't surprised to see the man's hate-filled eyes boring into hers.

"My brother survived, though," she said directly to Tyson. Then, to worry him a little more, she added, "And he can identify the thief. That money was important to us, Mr. Tyson. It meant the start of a dream we had been living on for a long time. But more important than that . . . someone shot my brother and left him for dead. That same someone killed my friend, Tom." Meeting Gordon Tyson's gaze evenly, she promised solemnly, "We'll find him. If it takes forever."

Fourteen

DAKOTA rubbed her temples and stifled a yawn. Her head ached, and she was tired enough to crawl onto the tabletop and fall asleep immediately. But Ben wouldn't let her.

"Dammit, Molly, you should've heard her!" His voice was low and shook with anger. "In front of a room full of people, she stopped just short of calling him a thief!"

"I did not!" Lord, they'd been arguing over the same territory ever since they'd left the restaurant. "All I did was let him know that *I* know who he is."

"That's *all*?" Ben's fist crashed down on the table. "With a man like Tyson, that's plenty!"

She opened her mouth to contradict him again, but Molly stopped her. "He's right, Dakota." She sat at the table and stared hard at the younger woman. "This fella's got a lot ridin' on what folks think of him. He's got to keep his secrets secret."

"And now, 'cause of your own mule-headed foolishness," Ben interrupted, "he knows about you. He'll figure out that we've been lookin' for him. Won't be hard to discover you've been askin' a lot of questions." Dakota simply stared at him, unconcerned. His frustration boiled into anger. "Can't I make you understand that you're in danger? He can't let you shoot off your mouth all over town."

"For heaven's sake, what can he do?" Dakota snapped at both of them. "Have me killed? We all know that western people wouldn't tolerate a woman killer."

Ben moved to the chair beside her, pulled it out and straddled it. He leaned forward, his face only inches from hers and his voice deadly calm, and said, "You're right. But an *accident* can happen to anyone. And livin' down here on the Coast, folks would take you for just another dead whore."

Dakota gasped, outraged, and glanced to Molly. She nodded in agreement.

"You're not safe here, Kota," Ben continued softly. "A single woman can't fight men like Tyson. Not alone." He held her gaze with his own. "Go home. Leave this to me."

His soft voice and the images he'd created had almost lulled her into consenting. Almost. She had to force herself to look away from him. "No."

Ben's head dropped onto his chest.

"Absolutely not!" Dakota jumped to her feet and faced him. It always came back to this, she thought. When was he going to realize that she wasn't about to turn tail and run home? "I'm not gonna leave till this is finished."

Ben grabbed his hat from the table and shoved it down on his head. His gaze swept over Dakota with an infuriating slowness. "I thought we'd found something tonight. That we'd finally reached a point where you trusted me enough to have faith in my judgment." He shook his head. "Guess I was wrong." Then he stepped closer and whispered for her ears alone, "I hope you know what you're doin'."

Outside the Irish Lady restaurant the shadowed figure stood in the darkness. Hidden by the black night and the creeping fog, he stared at the quiet building across the street. He'd followed the couple from the Palace, then slipped into the alleyway to wait.

He smiled to himself. She was even lovelier than he remembered. He'd watched her as she danced with the tall man and had worried some when she'd looked so taken with him. But on their carriage ride home they'd fought like two cats in a sack. He smiled. The man must mean nothing to her.

The restaurant door opened, and the watcher stepped back farther into the alley. The tall man was leaving, and he didn't look happy. The watcher smiled and waited. He stared as inside the building the lamps were blown out one by one. In the vague half-light he caught a fleeting glimpse of her moving around the room. He waited. Minutes crawled by. A lamp was lit in a second-story room. He watched the flickering light for another long moment and cursed himself for a fool.

He'd been hanging around the restaurant for the last two weeks, had eaten more food than ever before and still was no closer to talking to the woman than the first day he'd seen her. But he was through with waiting. No more of this little-boy-lookin'-in-a-candy-store-window nonsense.

He smiled and pulled his collar up around his neck. The damp night closed around him. Tomorrow, he told himself, he would be back again. And this time, it would be different.

He walked quietly away and in seconds was enveloped by the shrouding mists.

Ben glanced uneasily over his shoulder as he left Molly's place. The hairs on the back of his neck stood straight up. He was being watched. He could feel it. He knew it was probably some waterfront rat hoping to rob him. Well, he told himself, let 'em try it. The mood he was in, he could use a good fight.

Hands jammed in his pockets, Ben left the quiet darkness of Montgomery Street and turned onto Pacific. The burly toughs he passed took one look at the thunderous expression on his face and steered a wide path around him.

He kicked at a rock in the street and watched it skitter off into an alley. He couldn't stop thinking about that scene with Tyson. Ellis, he wasn't worried about. Ben could have the marshal pick him up anytime. It was only professional courtesy to Cable that the marshal had waited anyway.

But Tyson, he knew, was a different story. A respected businessman with influential friends, Gordon Tyson would not be easy to deal with.

And Dakota! She'd really stirred up the fire. Of course, she'd been doing that right along. He'd never known a woman to cause so much trouble. A man shouldn't have to put up with this much interference.

All the women he'd been raised around were nothing like her. They'd been good, quiet wives, content to stay home and take care of their men. They never had opinions on anything! Or at least, if they did, they had the good sense not to hit their husbands over the head with 'em!

He stopped suddenly. *Wives? Husbands?* What was he thinking? Ben jumped backward as a man came flying out the batwing doors of the nearest saloon. A quick glance told him the man was all right, just drunk. He sighed heavily and walked on.

God, he hated cities. He wanted nothing more than to finish this business and go home. To get Dakota out of this miserable place called the Barbary Coast. She didn't belong there. She was too straightforward. Too honest. Too reckless. Too lovely.

He reached into his pocket for the makings and rolled a cigarette as he walked. Taking a deep pull at the tobacco as the match flared, Ben remembered how good the evening with her had been before Tyson showed up. She was everything any man could ever want. But did he want a wife?

Trying to think logically, Ben admitted to himself that as a married woman she would have the protection of his name. He wasn't completely without power. Whether he wanted to remember or not, his father had been an important man. And Ben had added some weight to the Cable name over the years. Even Tyson would have to think twice about arranging "accidents" for Mrs. Ben Cable. He smiled. There was also the fact that as her husband, Ben would have more control over her actions. Legally, at least.

He sucked the smoke deep into his lungs as he recalled again the passionate night they'd spent together. His mouth suddenly dry, he acknowledged that having the right to take her to his bed was an added incentive. He rubbed his jaw absently. Might as well be honest with yourself, he thought. It was more than just wanting to protect her. More even than bedding her.

For the first time in years, Ben knew he wanted to belong somewhere. With someone.

He was surprised to find himself in this fix, too. But he was in this muddle up to his neck, and he realized the thought of marrying Dakota Lane didn't make him want to run. Instead, he wanted to hold on to her, lose himself in her. Had he finally put his past to rest?

He stopped in front of the shabby boardinghouse that had been his home for far too long. The strong smell of boiling cabbage twisted his lips into a grimace. Another good reason to talk her into marrying him. He could move out of this hellhole.

"You said you took care of the Lane man." Gordon Tyson faced his cohort angrily. All pretense of the elegant gentleman gone, his cold eyes glinted with malice as he stared at the disreputable man across from him.

"Hell," Ellis whined, "who'd a thought the kid would pull through?"

Tyson paced the darkened office of the Last Chance Saloon like a caged animal. "Not only pull through, you idiot, but be able to identify you! How could you have made such a blunder?"

Hank Ellis stirred uncomfortably. He wasn't afraid of his fancy partner, but he didn't like having his ability questioned. "I'll just go back to that hick town and finish him off."

Tyson stared at him, amazed at the man's stupidity. The time to end their partnership was long overdue. The old days of making a quick profit by swindling small-town cattlemen were over. He'd *known* they shouldn't have bothered with Lane. But it had seemed so easy. One last time. For old times' sake. He'd been stuck in that godforsaken backwater town anyway. It should have been simple. God knows, they'd pulled the same swindle hundreds of times before. Now look what it had gotten him.

Well, Tyson told himself, things change. There were bigger goals now. He counted some very important people as friends. There was no telling how far he could go in politics. Maybe even governor.

Ellis belched and Tyson sneered at him. There was no room for Ellis in Gordon Tyson's plans. After Dakota Lane was taken care of . . . well, everyone knows that Ellis drinks too much, Tyson thought. Maybe one night the poor drunk will stumble into the bay. Poor man.

For now, though, he needed him

"Stay away from that town," Tyson ordered. "And the Lane kid." He went on almost to himself. "I can't understand how a plan that has worked so smoothly in so many towns could go so wrong." He smoothed the sides of his hair back. "Damn that Dakota Lane. In front of everyone!"

"Dakota?" Ellis mumbled thoughtfully.

"Yeah. Pretty girl. Brown hair, blue eyes. Razor-sharp tongue."

Oh, Hank told himself, he would *enjoy* this. A *pretty* one!

"She'll have to be discouraged," Tyson said.

"I understand."

"No, you don't. I won't have her killed. That would look too suspicious now." Uneasily he remembered some of the rather pointed questions Foster Allen had asked after the Lane girl left. "Just see that she leaves town," Tyson said. "I don't care where she goes or how you do it." He glared at his partner. "Just do it soon."

The big man laughed when Tyson left the office. Imagine, he thought. Gordon Tyson being pushed to the wall by a slip of a girl.

He leaned back in his chair and propped his booted feet on the desk. Licking his too-full lips in anticipation, he reached for the whiskey bottle standing nearby.

She stood outside the building and wondered again if she was doing the right thing. Dakota rubbed her tired eyes. She'd tossed and turned all night while her mind conjured up taunting images of Gordon Tyson.

In spite of Ben's lengthy lecture, she knew she had to do something now that they'd finally found the man they'd searched so long for. But until that morning she hadn't known what. Then, while serving breakfast, she'd overheard two of her regular customers laughing about an article in the newspaper. *The Weekly Observer*, they said, was famous for printing what they considered to be the truth. No matter who the story was about. While the other papers in town treaded softly around the wealthy and the powerful, *The Observer* delighted in harpooning the city's heroes.

She'd also been told that though the paper was looked down on as being no more than a gossip sheet, other newspapers often took up the banner that *The Observer* had raised.

Dakota lifted her gaze and looked over the varied signs on the buildings. She would tell her story to the paper. If the rumors were true, and he did have his eye set on becoming mayor, well, the best way to stop him was to expose him. She had to reach the people whose opinion mattered to Tyson.

Then she saw it. A small place tucked in between two three-story offices. Hurriedly she dodged the busy traffic that clogged the street.

When she opened the door, a wave of heat engulfed her. The stuffy atmosphere carried the odors of ink, machinery, and stale sweat. She stepped up to the narrow counter and waited until the young man seated at a table looked up from his paperwork.

His frustrated features melted into a smile when he saw her. "Can I help you?"

Leaning her elbows on the counter, she said, "I hope so."

He stood up and straightened his ink-stained vest.

She introduced herself, then said, "I have some information about someone that I think people should hear."

"Why us?" he asked. "There are several papers in town. Most of them much bigger than mine."

"Because I heard you're not afraid to print the truth."

He nodded, pleased.

"What I'm gonna tell you could cause a lot of trouble. For you and for me."

He leaned toward her. "I'm intrigued. And I've been in trouble before." Reaching for a pad and pencil, he said, "Let's hear it."

"Really?"

Smiling, the young man's eyebrows rose and fell quickly. "I'm the curious sort, miss. And you have me so interested, it would surely drive me out of my mind *not* to hear your story now."

As she talked, the young editor's only comments were a few low whistles and an occasional chuckle. He scribbled furiously on his pad, shaking his head in wonder. When she finally finished, Dakota asked, "Well? Will you print it?"

He set his pencil down on the counter and flipped back through his notes. "Miss," he said, smiling, "I will look into this myself."

Dakota smiled.

"There've been rumors before about the 'illustrious' Mr. Tyson." He nodded his head at her in approval. "But nothing so substantial as this. You say you actually *saw* the papers? The shanghai lists?"

"Yes," she said, suppressing a shudder at the reminder of the night in Hank Ellis's office.

"You didn't by chance, uh . . ." He groped for the right word. "Appropriate any of them?"

"No. I didn't dare to."

"Ah, well." He sighed. "No matter. I have other sources. There are a few seamen I may be able to convince to talk to me." He grinned sheepishly. "Anonymously, of course."

"Then you will print it?"

"Probably in a couple of days." He reached for his coat and snatched it off the back of a chair. "First, I will personally check out your story." He threw the coat on hurriedly, not bothering to straighten its collar. "I do thank you for bringing me this story, Miss Lane." He grinned again. "For a long time I've wanted to do something about our Mr. Tyson."

She couldn't hide her surprise.

"Not all San Franciscans are fools." He wagged a finger at her. "To be as clean as this man has pretended to be . . . one would have to be a saint."

Dakota smiled. She'd done the right thing, coming here.

"And now," he said, stepping out from behind the counter, "you go home. Leave the rest to me." He held the door open with a flourish. "And watch the papers!"

On the long walk back to Molly's, Dakota thought how strange it was. When the editor told her to go home, she did it. When Ben said the same thing, she was furious. Strange.

Josie tugged at the ten-pound sack of coffee. "Was it beautiful, Dakota?"

"Hmmm?" She searched through the storeroom shelves for the last of the potatoes. "Was what beautiful?"

"The Palace." The young girl sighed dreamily as she clutched the coffee beans to her breast. "Did you dance? Was there lots of pretty dresses? As pretty as yours?"

Dakota straightened and looked at the girl. Her eyes were closed, and there was a soft smile on her face. After the kind of life she'd had, Josie was still able to hold on to her dreams. And Dakota suspected that the girl was a little sweet on Ben. She couldn't blame her.

"Yes, Josie. It was beautiful." She walked over to the daydreamer. "Just like I told you this morning."

Josie's eyes flew open, and she smiled guiltily. "I don't mean to bother you none . . . it's just that Ben was so handsome." She looked up at Dakota quickly. "And you looked so pretty. Just like a princess."

"You'd better get that coffee inside before Molly has to come out lookin' for it."

"Yes'm."

Dakota watched the girl until she was safely inside, then turned back to the storeroom. A princess. She shook her head and walked to the far corner of the building. Pulling at the burlap bag, she chuckled. The princess and the potatoes.

He stood outside the restaurant watching the customers filing in and out. He'd been there over an hour. The place was practically empty now. Most of the supper crowd had been served and sent on their way.

Reaching up, he ran his finger around the tight collar of his stiff new shirt. Damn uncomfortable things, he told himself. Felt too much like a noose for his tastes. He rubbed the toes of his boots on the backs of his pant legs. After smoothing his hair back, he ran one hand across his bearded jaw. Probably should have shaved the beard. Hell, he told himself, chances are she won't even speak to him. No reason why she should. She's most likely sick and tired of seein' him at the restaurant starin' at her with big ol' cow eyes.

He shifted uneasily and asked himself for the hundredth time what he was doing there. Standing out in the street in a fancy suit, like he was some wooden store dummy. He jammed his hands into his pants pockets. This was a stupid idea.

If his friends ever found out about this . . . *him* goin' to call on a lady? They'd never stop talkin' about it. He pulled at his collar again. This could ruin a fella's reputation.

Suddenly he turned his back on the restaurant. He'd just leave. No one would ever have to know.

"Dakota!"

He turned involuntarily at the sound of her name.

Snorting derisively, he thought, for godsake, it's just a female. He'd never had any trouble dealin' with women. What kind of man are you anyway? Too scared to walk into a restaurant and see a woman? So go on, fool, he told himself firmly. Stop standin' around out here and get it over with.

Determined, he crossed the street and, before he could talk himself out of it, pushed the doors to the restaurant open. He glanced around quickly. Just like he thought. Place was almost empty. He took a seat in the back of the room, away from the few remaining customers. Then he waited.

Dakota came through the kitchen's swinging door, carrying the coffeepot. She refilled several cups before noticing the customer in the corner. She sighed. She'd thought she was finished. She was tired and hot from a long day's work, and her visit to the newspaper office still weighed heavy on her mind. All she wanted was a quiet place to sit down, cool off, and relax. And she knew the sooner she served the man, the sooner she could do just that.

She walked quickly to his table, filled his coffee cup, and asked, "What can I get you?"

He raised his gaze to hers. "Well, ma'am . . . I was hopin' . . ."

Oh, no, she thought tiredly. Not tonight. She just couldn't deal with another love-struck cowboy. He'd always been so quiet. So polite. Almost shy. He'd hardly spoken at all in the last two weeks. Why now?

"Look," she said kindly but firmly, "I'm not on the menu. So, what would you like to eat?"

"Now, that's a shame. You'd probably make a mighty sweet dish," he said, and grinned.

Dakota looked at him more closely, surprised at his forwardness. She had to admit, there was something about the man. That grin of his. And his voice. Deep and warm, tinged with humor. He even had a nice face. What she could see of it. He had a full beard and mustache, neatly trimmed. His dark brown hair curled down over his collar and his warm, coffee-colored eyes held a glimmer of amusement.

She couldn't help smiling back. "I'm sorry, but it's late and . . ."

"You're tuckered," he said, his grin still in place.

He pulled out the chair next to him and motioned for her to sit down. Grabbing an extra cup from the table, he took the coffeepot from her and poured them both some of the steaming black brew.

"Thank you."

He nodded, pleased. "Look, I know you're tired out, but I was kinda hopin' we might go and get a bite to eat somewhere."

"I don't even know you."

"I can take care of that real quick." He took her hand in his and gave it a formal shake. "Name's Cheyenne Boder. From Texas."

"I'm . . ."

"Dakota Lane. I know." At her questioning glance he shrugged and laughed. "You don't think I come in here all the time just for the food, do you? Hell, I never ate so much in my life."

Dakota chuckled softly.

"Now you know my name." He leaned toward her and grinned again. "And you sure as hell have seen enough of me in the last two weeks to know I don't cause trouble much . . ."

"That's true, but still . . ."

"Don't say no right off. I give you my word that I'll be a real gent. Even watch my language. At least, I'll try to."

"That's not it, it's only that . . ."

"You're tired. I know. But you got to eat sometime, don't you? Wouldn't it be nice to just sit down and let somebody else serve you for a change?"

"Yes, but . . ."

"Now I ain't talkin' about the Palace, you understand. Won't be nothin' like you got there the other night."

She drew back and stared at him through narrowed eyes. "How did you know I went to the Palace?"

Cheyenne flushed slightly and cleared his throat. "I was passin' by and I seen you leave the place with that big blond man. Now, I figure he ain't your fella, not the way you two was fightin', so what did I have to lose by tryin'?"

She frowned, remembering their fight all too well. "You're right." She sighed. "Ben's not my fella."

So, he thought ruefully. That's the way the wind blows. Ah, well, the good ones are always spoke for. But, he reasoned cheerfully, if she don't realize how she feels for the big blond, *he* sure wasn't gonna be the one to tell her.

"Good." Standing, he pulled her to her feet. "Then let's you and me go get something to eat."

Molly and Josie came through the door just then, and the older woman urged, "Go ahead on, Dakota. Nothin' much goin' on here. Me and Josie can handle it."

"Go ahead, Dakota," Josie added her voice and smiled hesitantly at Cheyenne.

"There you go!" Cheyenne waved his hand at the

two women. "When two pretty ladies tell me what to do, I durn well do it."

Molly laughed, Josie preened, and Dakota gave up. Maybe he was right. Maybe this was just what she needed. A chance to laugh and enjoy herself with a *very* handsome man. She grabbed her shawl from the peg beside the door, took his arm, and stopped outside. She took a deep breath and sighed.

Cheyenne smiled down at her. "That ocean sure does smell good, don't it?"

She looked up at him, smiling, and started to answer when Ben's voice shattered her thoughts.

"Don't you want to introduce me to your *friend*, Dakota?"

Fifteen

DAKOTA spun around. Ben Cable stood just inches from her. His blue eyes were like chips of ice as he took in both her and her escort.

"Isn't this nice? A lady and her 'gentleman' caller stepping out for the evenin'."

Cheyenne stepped boldly forward and pulled Dakota to his side. "Mister," he said quietly "you just move along. You had your chance last night. *This* night's mine."

Dakota frowned at him and pushed away slightly.

"What's that supposed to mean?" Ben moved closer, shifting his gaze between Dakota and Cheyenne. "What are you talkin' about?"

"Just what I said." Cheyenne shifted position slightly, putting himself between the other two.

"And what do you know about last night?" Ben's eyes narrowed at the protective move the other man made.

"He watched us." Dakota said it softly and both men turned on her.

"Watched—"

"You don't have to explain nothin'—"

"For heaven's sake, stop it. Both of you!" She looked around anxiously. No one was paying any attention. Yet. In a low voice Dakota said, "Ben, you've probably seen my 'friend' Mr. Boder, before. He's one of my customers."

Ben looked at the other man sharply. Carefully he studied him, ignoring the stupid grin. She was right. He *had* seen the man around a lot lately. "Boder?"

"Cheyenne Boder. The one and only," he answered. Then he turned to Dakota. "Let's get goin', huh?"

"All right," she said with a hesitant glance at Ben.

"Just wait a damn minute." Ben grabbed Cheyenne's arm and pulled him around. "You're not takin' her anywhere."

"Don't do that, mister."

"Dakota," Ben went on, "you can't be serious. You're letting a no-account *stranger* take you out walkin'?"

"Careful what you say about me, all right, *friend*?" He pulled his arm free. His grin was gone, his brown eyes hard.

"You stay out a this," Ben snarled. "This is between me and Dakota."

Dakota looked from one man to the other helplessly.

"Not anymore, it ain't."

"Will you two stop?" Dakota noticed a few people standing on the outskirts of their three-sided argument. "People are watching."

"Hang those people!" Ben shouted.

"I don't much care for that word, friend." Cheyenne grinned at Dakota.

"And you're not my friend!" Ben rubbed his hand viciously across his face. He'd only come to the restaurant to apologize to Dakota for shouting at her the night before. And *now* look at him!

"Well. We agree on somethin' anyway," Cheyenne said with another smile. "We both like Dakota." His smile faded as he added, "And we ain't friends."

"That's enough!" Dakota had to shout to make them listen to her. The whole thing was ridiculous. She didn't even have to be there. The two fools were going at each other like she didn't exist!

"Stay out a this!" both men shouted back at her.

"You can't talk to her like that," Ben ordered.

"You did."

"That's *my* business."

"And *this* evening is my business!"

"Like hell." Ben finished his short statement with a sharp jab at Cheyenne's chin.

Cheyenne staggered a little with the force of the blow, then charged at Ben like an angry bull. Suddenly the street was crowded with cheering men and women. They came from everywhere and formed a circle around the two battling men, shouting encouragement.

Dakota stared disgustedly at Cheyenne and Ben rolling around in the dusty street, punching and gouging at each other. A big man beside her shoved her in his haste to get closer to the action. She elbowed her way back to the front of the circle, glaring at a man she heard taking bets on the outcome of the fight.

She watched as Ben took a powerful blow to the stomach. Gasping for air right along with him, Dakota tensed as Cheyenne moved in close to deliver a blow to the back of Ben's neck. But Ben was too fast. He sidestepped Cheyenne easily, then threw a round-house punch to Cheyenne's jaw. Scrambling over each other, they grunted, punched, and swore.

She flinched at the sound of fist meeting bone and told herself there *must* be a way to stop them. But she wasn't willing to go down and try to come between the battling fools. She'd probably get her teeth knocked out before they knew she was there. A glance at the cheering crowd told her she wouldn't find help there. Nothing these people liked better than a good fight.

Desperately she tried to think. Inspiration struck her when she spied an empty bucket standing by the door of the restaurant.

At the edge of the crowd Dakota ran into Molly and the kids, who'd come to see what was going on. She barely spared them a glance as she went for the bucket. Stooping to fill it in the watering trough, she vaguely heard Molly's whoop of encouragement. The older woman had guessed Dakota's intention and was cheering her on.

"Atta girl, Dakota! Show them two who's in charge!"

Dakota blew at the hair falling in front of her eyes and pushed her way through the crowd once more. Cold water sloshed over the side of the old bucket, soaking her dress, but she didn't notice. Getting as close as she dared to the two combatants, she tossed a wave of water over both of them.

The men stopped their fight and came up sputtering. Covered in water and mud, they sat up and looked at her in surprise. They looked so much alike, it would have been comical if she hadn't been so angry.

The disappointed murmurings of the crowd meant nothing to her as she said much too calmly, "I told you to stop it. You"—she looked at Cheyenne—"can leave. I'm not goin' anywhere with you."

Ben grinned and slapped Cheyenne on the back in sympathy. Then she turned on him. "And you! I never want to lay eyes on you again!" She threw the empty bucket at them, then turned and ran around the corner of the restaurant, headed for the storeroom . . . and privacy.

The two men sat where she'd left them, in the middle of the street. The unhappy crowd slowly filtered away, until there was only Molly and the kids left on the boardwalk. She shook her head at the men. "You two take a good look, now," she said to Josie and Timmy. "See what fools men make of themselves over womenfolk?"

"They done all that over a *girl*?" Timmy was astonished.

Josie lifted the hem of her skirt as if she could be muddied just standing there.

"All right," Molly said as she ushered them back inside. "Let's leave 'em be. They got some thinkin' to do."

Ben and Cheyenne looked at each other, smiling reluctantly.

"Wasn't exactly how I planned to spend the evenin'," Cheyenne commented.

"Me, neither."

Cheyenne followed Ben's gaze to the corner where Dakota had disappeared. Then, turning back to his opponent, he said, "You're a lucky man, friend."

"I know, friend." Ben smiled and pulled his hand free of the muck to shake Cheyenne's. "I know."

Dakota sat down on a new fifty-pound sack of potatoes. She shook her head and gripped her hands together tightly in her lap. Imagine those two half-wits grappling in the middle of the street! As if she were a bone tossed to a couple of hungry dogs.

And that crowd was no better! Cheering and laughing.

Her lips twisted suddenly. All right, she could understand the laughter. She covered her mouth with her hand, determined not to laugh. But then she remembered her last sight of them. Sitting straight up, covered in mud, and *so* surprised! Their eyes had opened so wide, it was a wonder they hadn't popped clean out of their heads.

She leaned back against the potato sack and let the laughter loose. Her body shook with it as she rolled from side to side. Tears pooled in her eyes and she was gasping for breath. A showdown in the street, ended by a bucket of water!

Ben walked slowly down the boardwalk, the only sounds that of his heels on the wood and an occasional plop of mud dropping off his clothing. With the fight over and Cheyenne gone on his way, Ben knew he had to find Dakota. He had to try to make her understand why he'd acted so rattle-brained.

Dammit, he'd simply lost control when he'd seen her with another man! He'd always laughed at other men when they made jealous asses of themselves. Finally, now, he understood. He could even understand how people could kill while under that white-hot flash of rage. Because when that fight with Cheyenne started, he'd wanted nothing more than to rip the man's head off.

His mouth set in a grim line, he looked down at himself. Dripping wet and covered in mud, he'd been saved from making a complete jackass of himself by a woman. Never mind that it was the same woman who'd driven him loco in the first place.

Ben stopped in front of the storeroom. The little building stood alone in the alley, surrounded by darkness. At least no one else had to see him like this, he thought lamely. He brushed his grimy hands against his even dirtier pants and lifted his hand to knock. Then he stopped. Cocking his ear to the door, he listened carefully.

Laughter?

She was laughing at him?

Somehow, that was harder to take than her anger. He quietly opened the door, stepped inside, and closed it again. Deliberately he shot the locking bolt closed.

At the sound Dakota's laughter died. She sat on the mound of potatoes, her skirt hiked up, elbows on her knees. They stared at each other in silence for a long minute.

Then, without warning, she started laughing again.

"What's so damn funny?"

She fell back, lifting the damp hem of her skirt to her mouth. Pointing at him, she choked out, "You. You're filthy!" Her laughter turned into breathless giggling.

His head tilted, he stared at her, disgusted, until he couldn't stand it any longer. Covering the small room in a few easy strides, Ben pulled her to her feet.

"So you think mud's funny, do you?" With a quick tug he jerked her close against him. Running his still wet hands up and down her back, he held her tightly, pressing himself against the length of her.

"Ben!" she cried, pushing futilely at his chest. "Stop. Let me go!"

"Oh, no," Ben said, a smile on his splotchy face. "This is funny, Kota. Remember?"

"It *was*." She grimaced at the feel of the mud seeping into her clothes. Dakota looked up at him. She saw the humor in his eyes, and something more. Her right hand reached up and pulled a particularly large clod of mud from his hair. She dropped it to the floor.

Their eyes met and they stood silently, each gripped by the knowledge of their desires.

Suddenly conscious of every nerve in her body, Dakota rubbed her breasts across Ben's chest. Her nipples tingled and ached for more. Her mouth craved the taste of him. Her hands moved over the solid strength of his shoulders, and she felt him shudder at her touch.

Soft moonlight filtered through the tiny windows at the top of the storeroom's walls. The little place was filled with the odors of the foods stored there. Onions, garlic, even a few oranges from the surrounding farms.

Ben lowered his head slowly. Tantalizingly. Tenderly. Finally he stopped. Mere inches from her face, he stopped. She felt his breath on her cheeks. The scent of him filled her, obliterating any other. She ignored the mud and grime covering him, put her hands on his face, and drew his lips to hers.

He groaned when she parted her lips and slipped her tongue inside his mouth. Wickedly her tongue darted in and out, teasing, toying, exploring. Her hands weaved through his hair and held his head firmly on hers. She pulled at him. She nipped his tongue with her teeth, then moved her own tongue over his lips.

His breath came fast and heavy as he forced her back a few steps. With her back against the fully stocked shelves, she stared at him through glazed eyes. Her chest heaved with the effort of breathing.

Ben's hand ran down the length of her neck as he stood between her spread legs. His fingers stopped at the vee of her blouse. She nodded slightly, and Ben pulled the fine material open. Smoothing the straps of her chemise down, he ran his thumb over an already erect nipple. Dakota bit her lip and silently willed his mouth to her breast.

Encircling her waist, Ben lifted her gently, propping her against the shelves. His kiss began at the hollow between her breasts, and she shuddered when his tongue moved against her warm skin. Mercilessly he moved over her flesh, branding her with his touch. When his lips closed over her tender nipple, she moaned and arched against him. She opened her eyes and watched his tongue flick against the hardened bud. Dakota's hand went to the back of his head and pressed him tightly against her, wanting, *needing* more.

He pulled away and, ignoring her groan of disappointment, set her down on her feet. Lifting her skirt inch by inch, he then pulled off the pantalets she wore. The cool night air on her skin felt wicked, and Dakota shivered.

Ben lifted her leg until the back of her knee rested on his hip. She leaned back and raised her leg even higher when she felt the warmth of his hand caressing her inner thigh. His hands moved lovingly over her body. His mouth clung to hers, and his fingers explored her depths.

Bracing herself against the shelf, Dakota raised her other leg and wrapped both of them about his waist. Only his strong arms supported her. She fumbled anxiously at his belt then finally her clumsy fingers managed to undo the buttons of his pants.

Ben gasped aloud as her hand closed over him, rubbing, stroking, enticing. She pushed her hand even farther down and gently cupped him. He arched suddenly and slammed her against the shelves. She felt no pain. She felt only his hands. Everywhere.

One hand cupped her bottom, allowing one finger to thrust into her from behind. A sensation of shock mixed with pleasure brought a groan from deep in her throat. With his other hand Ben kneaded her soft, damp warmth. His thumb teased the center of her as his fingers plunged deep inside. Then he began to suckle and pull at her nipple, and it was as if she would lose her mind. He surrounded her. He was everywhere at once. Ben. Only Ben.

Finally his hands left her, and he lowered her onto his body. Their cries of pleasure mixed and joined, and their lips came together in a hungry frenzy.

Up and down he moved her, and she cried out with the overpowering sensations coursing through her. Again and again they rocked against the shelves. They noticed nothing. Not even the flour bag falling from the shelf and bursting open.

Dakota gave herself over to the feel of him. Her fingers in his hair, she gripped and pulled as her body throbbed in release. Awash in a wave of contentment, she held Ben close as his body joined hers in satisfaction.

Locked together, their breathing labored, neither of them was willing to leave the closeness of being one. Then, with a final, tender kiss, Ben moved to free them from their position. Slowly he lifted her, and they both groaned softly at the parting.

Ben smoothed her skirt down and reluctantly pulled the edges of her blouse together. He smiled as he reached out to touch her hair.

Her honey-brown tresses were covered with a fine white dust. He looked down at himself. They were *both* covered with it.

Dakota brushed at his hair uselessly. Then Ben eased his forehead down against hers, and they chuckled together softly.

They hadn't noticed the flour bag spilling open. They hadn't noticed being coated with the fine white stuff. They hadn't noticed the mess they were making of Molly's storeroom.

And they didn't care, now.

"I'll walk you back to the restaurant," he offered.

"All right."

He opened the door and looked quickly around. With the condition they were in, it wouldn't do to see anyone. In the empty alley Ben walked her the short distance to the back door. Before she went inside, though, he claimed her for one more kiss. Their lips met in a gentle caress, and for a moment Ben wanted to refuse to let her go.

But Dakota stepped back, breaking the spell. She reached up and stroked his cheek, murmured "Good night," and slipped inside.

Ben stood alone in the darkness, unwilling to leave. His body ached from the fight with Cheyenne, he was covered in mud and flour, and he'd just had the most incredible experience of his life.

He should be exhausted. But he wasn't. He wanted her again. Now. Just the sight of that old storeroom stirred the smoldering fire in his blood into a raging wildfire, and he felt himself harden in response.

Ben glanced at the upstairs window. A light came on. Dakota. She would be washing. Nude. His mouth was dry, and he drew a deep breath to steady himself.

He couldn't walk down the streets looking like he did. Only one thing to do. Turning, he moved off toward the beach. He'd just walk into the ocean and rinse off. Besides, he thought dismally, the cold water might be just what he needed.

As his shadow passed the restaurant, Molly dropped the curtain back into place. She rolled her eyes up as she realized what a mess her storeroom must be. *Both* of them covered in flour! She smiled wistfully.

"Ah, Mr. Malone," she whispered aloud, "it's times like these I miss you the most."

Two days later all of San Francisco was laughing at Gordon Tyson. True to his word, the editor of *The Observer* had printed the article Dakota'd given him. And it hadn't taken long for the other papers in town to pick up the story. Though they were hesitant about being the *first* to denounce a powerful citizen, it seemed they had no compunctions over jumping onto an already moving bandwagon.

The heat in the kitchen coupled with the teeming crowd of men drove Dakota into the night for a breath of cool air. Her customers had been gathering together and laughing over the newspaper article all afternoon. She'd never seen the restaurant that crowded. Silently she thanked the editor for leaving her name out of the whole thing. If Molly's patrons knew that the story was Dakota's doing, they wouldn't give her a moment's peace.

She lifted the edge of her apron and ran it over her face. Even the night air carried a damp heat that exhausted her. Leaning back against the side of the restaurant, Dakota wondered again about Tyson's reaction to the article. She'd give just about anything to know what the "great" man was doing at that moment.

The editor of *The Observer* should be safe enough from any fancy lawyers Tyson might have. Though the paper was plain in its accusations, it also openly stated that there was no real proof. But judging from everyone's response to the story, the allegations were surely strong enough to start folks wondering about Gordon Tyson.

Dakota sighed and tilted her head back to look at the black, star-studded sky. She would probably never recover the money that was stolen from Tenn. Ben had been right all along about that. Forcing a small smile, she consoled herself with the knowledge that at least she'd been able to stop Tyson's political plans. Small consolation, though, when she tried to imagine breaking the news to her brother.

But maybe Ben had been right about that, too. Maybe Tenn *would* be able to withstand losing another ranch. Maybe it was enough that they still had each other. And more than that, Tenn had Laura. The tiny blonde certainly didn't seem the type of female to turn her back on a man because of some bad luck.

Dakota chewed her bottom lip thoughtfully. Tenn had Laura. Whom did *she* have? She smiled softly, remembering the night in the storeroom. A flush crept up her cheeks, and she fanned herself with her hand. Surely a man who made love with such eager abandon felt more than a casual fondness. Could it be that despite his words to the contrary, he actually loved her?

She closed her eyes. In the last two days he'd come to the restaurant for his meals, as always. He'd acted no differently toward her than before the incredible encounter in the storeroom. But she *had* caught him looking at her when he thought she wasn't paying attention. Was it possible?

Her eyes opened again slowly. When had *love* crept into this? There'd been no lightning bolt. No bells ringing. She hadn't known that love could arrive quietly. Without fanfare. Now she knew. Dakota smiled. She loved Ben Cable.

A shout from inside shattered her train of thought. Reluctantly she turned to go back inside. A deep voice stopped her.

"You stay real quiet, girlie. Come on over here to me."

There was no mistaking that voice. Ellis.

She peered into the light-dappled darkness of the alley. She hesitated, wondering if she could make it to the back door before he could reach her. He must have read the thought on her face.

"Don't. Don't you try it, little girl." He shook his shaggy head, a half-smile on his face. "I'll stop you. One shot. That's all it would take. I don't want to kill you. But if I have to . . . so be it."

She opened her mouth, and he cautioned quickly, "Don't you scream for help, neither. First one out that door dies. Then you."

Dakota swallowed heavily. She believed him. Her mind worked frantically. He would remember her, she knew, as soon as he got a good look at her. Then what? With no other choice she walked toward the sound of his voice. After only a few steps she moved through a slash of light thrown from an upstairs window.

"Stop!"

She did.

He laughed deep in his chest. "It's you! Huh! Guess you wasn't really lookin' for no job, were ya? Well, now, I'm gonna enjoy this more'n I thought. I owe you, girlie. That headache you left me with like to tore me in two."

Dakota didn't say anything. There was nothing she *could* say. Now that he'd recognized her, she knew there would be no escaping him.

"C'mon," he ordered. "Keep walkin'." He backed away as she came closer, and he kept moving until she was in the farthest corner of the alley behind the restaurant.

Mouth dry, her stomach tightened, and she fought down the wave of nausea threatening to overtake her. Risking a glance toward the street, she hoped desperately to catch someone's eye. But there was no one. She was alone.

She would have to get herself out of this situation. Gratefully she remembered the two-shot derringer strapped as always on her right calf. Somehow, she had to reach it. It was the only chance she had to stop Ellis.

"See, darlin'," the big man said softly, "I'm s'posed to get rid of you." He took a step closer. "And it don't matter how." Another step. "So, 'fore I take you over to Fat Annie's, I reckon I'll have me a little fun." Closer.

She knew he was taking his time purposely. Taunting her.

Dakota shuddered and took a small step back, hoping he wouldn't notice. Fat Annie! Next to Flat Nose Kate, Annie ran the most disgusting house on the Coast. If Ellis *did* manage to get her there, no one would ever see her again. She looked around the darkness again, frantically.

"Here I am, girlie."

She knew where he was. She could smell him.

Suddenly he reached out and shoved her. She stumbled to the ground and heard him laugh again.

"We can get acquainted right here. Kinda get you used to bein' in the dirt. Then you can tell me why you was at my place that night."

Dakota rubbed her leg as though she were injured.

"Aw . . . did you get hurt? Now, that's too damn bad." He moved toward her, and Dakota seized her chance. Slipping her hand under her skirt, she pulled the little gun free, cocked it, and fired.

The sharp report of the gun echoed in the alley. Ellis howled in pain and rage as he crumpled to the ground clutching his left knee, trying to staunch the blood.

Loud voices and running feet sounded sweeter than any music to Dakota. She crossed her arms over her upraised knees and laid her head down atop them. In seconds the first man entered the alley.

Ben took in the scene immediately. His body tensed, and white-hot anger coursed through him. He hardly spared a glance for Dakota as he rushed toward her fallen assailant. He jerked the huge man to his feet as though he weighed nothing.

With deliberate fury he crashed his fist into the man's face again and again until Ellis was unrecognizable. Ben felt the other man's nose break, but he couldn't stop. It was as though he had no control. He knew only the driving need to destroy.

A spectator from the gathering crowd finally pulled Ben off and held his arms back until he sagged,
his rage spent. Cable stood bent over, gasping for air.
His heart crashed against his rib cage in a pounding
fury, and he tossed a hurried look at Dakota. She
was staring at him as though she'd never seen him
before.

Hank Ellis lay unmoving, sprawled in the dirt with
the rest of the alley trash.

"Somebody get a rope."

"I'll do it."

"Hang the son of a bitch!"

The cries of the crowd grew louder and more
demanding. Dakota looked from the screaming men
back to Ben. He watched her for a moment, then
noticed Molly heading for her.

"Nobody's gonna hang that man!" Ben had to shout
to be heard over the angry men. "I'm takin' him to the
marshal." Now that his head was clear, that decision
came easily.

Disgruntled murmurings swept through the crowd.

Ben pulled his gun from its holster. With his other
hand he yanked Ellis to his feet. The big man swayed
drunkenly. "Now, clear out. Excitement's over."

Molly gently helped Dakota up and guided her
through the onlooking throng, who parted soundlessly before them.

When the women were gone, an angry voice shouted
out, "Who the hell are you to be tellin' us what we're
gonna do?"

Ben turned toward the voice and answered in a
calm, steely tone. "I'm the man who'll shoot whoever
gets in my way."

Ellis moaned and Ben shook him. Just being that close to the man threatened to set off the fury that had claimed him before.

"Yeah," someone called out, "that's pretty big talk, mister. But you cain't shoot *all* of us!" A few of the man's friends chuckled.

"No. I can't." Ben waved his pistol barrel over the crowd, stopping every now and then at a particular man. "But I sure as hell can get some of you." He cocked the pistol. "Who wants to be first?"

One or two of the men looked as though they'd like to challenge Ben's authority, but when they met his hard gaze, they quickly changed their minds. Slowly, uneasily, the crowd moved away, disgusted to have been cheated out of a hanging.

Ben waited another full minute or two, then, gritting his teeth, gave Ellis a shove. The man staggered and lurched down the alley, moaning through puffy lips.

The pig had no idea how close Ben had come to letting the crowd have him.

Sixteen

"DRINK it down now, all of it." Molly handed her a small glass of whiskey. "We've got to get some warmth back in you. You've had a nasty shock."

Dakota's fingers trembled. She hoped Molly was right about the liquor, because she'd never felt so cold. She tilted her head back and drained the amber liquid. The coughing fit started immediately, but after a few moments it was over, and Dakota *did* feel a welcome warmth spread through her body.

She set the glass down and locked her fingers together in her lap. She couldn't stop thinking about it. Ellis. The shot. And Ben.

Suddenly his rage-contorted face flashed through her mind. Her breath came faster. Her fingers tightened spasmodically. As the memory came tumbling back, she saw Ellis's fall. Ben's appearance. Then the brutal, methodical beating.

Ben would have killed him. If someone hadn't pulled him off, Dakota was sure Ellis would be dead now. She still couldn't believe it. In those first, frantic minutes in the alley, Ben Cable had been a stranger.

She shook her head. No. Not a stranger. She'd simply never seen that side of him. He was always so calm, so competent, so controlled. Deliberately Dakota collected herself.

She knew he'd be back, and when he returned, she had to be ready for him.

A knock on the door a few minutes later announced his arrival. Ben nodded at Molly as she held the door open for him, then his gaze went directly to Dakota. Her chin came up in a defiant gesture that didn't fool him. The eyes that met his still held traces of fear.

"Did you have any more trouble?"

He looked over his shoulder at Molly. "No. Around here, most men think death is better than jail. So I guess they figured Ellis'd suffer more if they gave him to me." Ben turned back to Dakota. "Anyway, right now he's in the city jail with a doctor digging a bullet out of his knee."

Dakota shuddered and her gaze dropped fractionally.

"It was a good shot," Ben said. "Not fatal. Just enough to stop him."

She looked away. "I've never shot a man before."

He had to strain to hear her voice. "You shouldn't have had to this time," Ben countered.

Her gaze snapped up to his, challenging. In a loud but quavering voice she demanded, "What choice did I have?"

"None!" He shouted at her and crossed the room in quick, angry strides. "You already made your choice when you decided not to trust me." Hands on the table, he leaned toward her, his eyes blazing. "You didn't *have* to be in danger. You chose to. *You*, Dakota. You won't listen to anybody but yourself." He grasped her chin and forced her to look up at him. "You had to shoot Ellis. Fine. He deserved it, and I'm glad you're all right. You're safe. But I'm tryin' to tell you that none of this would have happened if you'd listened to me!"

God Almighty, since he'd seen that damn article in the paper, he'd been running all over creation looking for Ellis. Ben had known Tyson wouldn't do anything himself. He couldn't risk it. He was the kind who hired out his dirty work. All day Ben had searched the Coast for Hank Ellis. But the man had more holes to hide in than a snake.

Then at dinner, when he'd heard the shot . . . his heart pounded erratically just remembering it. He'd *felt* Dakota's danger. He still couldn't recall just how he'd gotten into the alley. And even the beating he'd given Ellis was fuzzy. But the rage. The desire to kill was something he'd never forget.

"All right," Dakota admitted, "I was wrong." She bit her lip in an effort to stem the tears threatening to fall and added, "Does it make you happy to hear that? Now, will you just let it go?"

He released her and sat down opposite her at the table. "If I thought you would go home and leave the rest to me, maybe I could. But I know you, Dakota. And leaving is the last thing on your mind right now." He reached up and pulled his hat off. After staring blankly at the brim for a moment, he said softly, "But I *do* have an idea. One that should keep you safe . . . even from Tyson." Ben looked at her. "Are you willing to listen?"

She nodded.

"Good." He turned to Molly. "I know this is your place, Molly, but would you mind leaving me and

Dakota alone for a few minutes?"

The older woman watched him carefully, and Ben knew she was trying to decide if he was calm enough to be left alone with Dakota. He smiled sardonically. "I'm through yelling, Molly."

She nodded. "All right, then, I'll just go up and tell the kids that the excitement's over. At least for tonight."

"Molly," Dakota said, "you don't have to leave."

"Oh," she answered with another quick look at Ben's face, "I think I do. You two got some talkin' to do."

Ben waited silently as Molly climbed the stairs. Once she was out of sight, he set his hat on the table beside him and ran his hands through his hair. "Now, you'll listen to everything I have to say before you butt in. Right?"

"Yes."

"Good. Well, even you admit that you're not safe on your own anymore." He stood and began pacing around the table. "Ellis is in jail, but Tyson will only hire somebody else. Someone we won't know about. Won't recognize."

"Yes, but—"

"Quiet." He rubbed his jaw as he spoke. "And if you're here, that leaves Molly and the kids in danger, too."

"You want me to leave Molly?"

He glared at her. "You *said* you'd listen."

Dakota crossed her arms in front of her and nodded.

"What I'm gettin' at is, if you were married, even Tyson would think twice about going after you again." She started to speak, and Ben hurried on. "A woman alone could meet with an accident and maybe no one would ask any questions. But a respectable married woman would be missed."

"Married?"

He ran his finger around his collar. "That's the only way I can think of to keep you safe, Kota."

She stared at him. Her mouth dropped open and her heart skipped a few beats. *Married*? He expected her to marry someone as protection against Tyson? Good heavens! Dakota tried to remember his fight with Ellis. Maybe he'd been hit on the head.

"Well? Aren't you gonna say anything?" Ben rubbed his jaw again.

"Married?" She shook her head slowly. He'd really caught her by surprise. For the life of her, she couldn't seem to make her mind work. Finally she stammered, "Who?"

"*Who?*" His eyes widened. Hands on his narrow hips, he shouted, "Who the hell do you think? Me, that's who!"

"You?"

Ben pushed his hand through his already tousled hair. "Goddammit, yes!" He marched around the table again, shaking his head and talking out loud to himself. "She asks me *who*? Hellfire and damnation, we nearly tear Molly's storeroom apart just two nights ago . . . she was a *virgin* when I took her, I'm the only man she's ever been with, and yet she asks me *who?*"

"Can't you be a little quieter?" Dakota looked over her shoulder at the staircase.

He sucked air into his lungs in an obvious attempt at self-control. "I'll try." Then, his good intentions apparently shot to hell, he shouted again, "What in the name of all that's holy is wrong with you, Dakota?

Of course I'm talkin' about me! What the hell did you think I meant? That I was gonna raffle you off at the saloon like a box lunch?"

"Well, I don't know. Maybe." She stood up and faced him. All of her earlier illusions about him being in love with her had shattered. If he was in love, he was doing a good job of hiding it. "Why do you want to marry me?"

"Dammit! Aren't you listening? To keep you from getting yourself killed, that's why!"

"That's not a good enough reason to marry *anybody*."

He turned away and stalked to the window. Silently he stared out at the night for what seemed an eternity, then just as quietly, he returned to her side. After a quick glance at the empty stairs, he said in a hushed voice, "Besides, after the other night . . . Hell, Kota, you might be pregnant now."

He was right, she knew. She'd spent an uncomfortable couple of weeks after their first time together, waiting to see if she was carrying his child. But she hadn't been pregnant then. So there was a good chance she wasn't now, either. "I wasn't the last time. I won't be now."

"You don't know that."

"I will in a few weeks."

He gripped her arms. "You don't *have* a few weeks. Jesus, Dakota. Look what almost happened tonight."

Her gaze fell and the blood rushed from her face. She didn't want to think about Ellis. About those terrifying moments alone with him. But Ben didn't stop.

"Do you think Tyson is just gonna lay down and forget all about what you've cost him?"

"Tyson . . ." she echoed thoughtfully,

"What?" Ben's voice was soft, suspicious. "What are you thinking?"

She looked up at him. "In the alley. Ellis recognized me from that night in his office."

He sighed heavily.

"What if he gets a chance to talk to Tyson? Then *he'll* know that I was snooping around."

Ben threw his arms high in the air, completely exasperated. "Hell, he knows that now! Oh, maybe he doesn't know about you sneaking around Ellis's office, but he's sure as hell figured out by now that it was *you* who talked to the paper!"

"But about Ellis?"

He shook his head. "Ellis won't be talking to anybody for a long time. And it's for damn sure Tyson isn't gonna go anywhere *near* Ellis."

"Good." Dakota stepped away from Ben and began to walk around the room. She chewed her bottom lip as she tried to make sense of the wild thoughts racing through her mind. Any other time she would have been delighted with Ben's proposal. But now . . . well, she didn't want to marry a man who was doing it for all the wrong reasons. She stole a covert glance at him. Whether he knew it or not, Dakota was sure that he cared for her. He'd just been alone too long. He was too used to drifting in and out of people's lives.

He was staring at her. His gaze was worried, hesitant. She was glad that he couldn't read her mind. Or her heart. She took a deep breath and straightened her dirty white shirtwaist.

His plan made sense, she knew. She would marry him.

And after this whole mess was settled, it would be easy to convince the bullheaded man that he loved her. After all, once they were married, time would be on her side.

"All right, Ben. I'll marry you."

He almost sagged with relief.

"On one condition," she added suddenly.

He straightened and glared at her. "What?"

"That you let me help you catch Tyson."

"Dakota . . ."

She shook her head. "I mean it. I've already told you that I wouldn't leave until this is finished. And you just said yourself that if we're married, I'll be safe."

"Safer."

"Safer. Well?"

"Dammit." He jammed his hands in his back pockets. Silently he stared at her. Dakota knew he was trying to think of a way to say no. Finally though, he gave up. "I guess so. But only if we're married. At least then I wouldn't have to spend all my time watchin' over you."

She nodded, then suddenly decided to see if he'd thought at all about what would happen when the chase was over. "What about later?"

He looked up.

"After Tyson's caught. What then? We'll still be married."

He didn't say anything for a long moment, then his head dropped back and he stared at the ceiling. On a sigh he said, "When this is over, we'll get a divorce as fast as we can." He looked away as he told that lie. It was hard to even say the word *divorce*. Once they were married, he knew he'd never let her go. But he couldn't risk her saying no. And she was just stubborn enough to do exactly that if she felt she was trapped. Why weren't things simple? Why was he having to trick a woman into marrying him by promising her a divorce? He hoped he wouldn't choke on the lies he would have to tell. "Don't worry. I don't like the idea of marriage any more than you do."

Stung, Dakota inhaled sharply. She shouldn't have asked. It would have been easier not knowing how he really felt. But how could she have been so wrong about him? Thank God he didn't know she loved him. At least she'd been spared *that* humiliation.

If that was the way he wanted it, then that's how it would be. She wouldn't confess loving him. She wouldn't try to hold him. Obviously the closeness they'd shared meant far less to him than it had to her. Dakota forced air into her lungs. He would never know from her just how much his indifference hurt. Her pride had taken enough of a beating.

Feigning a smile, she said softly, "Fine. When does this 'temporary' marriage take place?"

He slammed his hat back on his head. "Couple of days. I'll take care of everything. Just get your gear together. Once we're married, we'll move into the Fremont Hotel."

"Wait," she said, and he stopped on his way to the door. "I'll stay here. With Molly. This isn't a *real* marriage. It's just . . . business."

"Wrong, lady." He crossed the room to her and grabbed her arms. "This marriage will at least *look* like a real one. Or it'll do no good at all."

"If you think I'm going to—"

"You made a deal, Kota." He bent closer and claimed her lips with his own. All his frustration, fear, and anger seemed embodied in that kiss, and Dakota responded to him hungrily, instinctively. Then as quickly as it began, the kiss ended. He pulled away, sucking air into his lungs like a drowning man. "You just be ready. Day after tomorrow, you're gettin' married."

He released her, turned on his heel, and marched to the door. Pausing to look back at her, he said through gritted teeth, "Good night." Then he threw the door wide and disappeared into the gathering fog.

Red Creek

"They're what?"

Tenn handed Laura the wire he'd received only that morning. "See for yourself. Ben says him and Dakota are gettin' married. Tomorrow."

She read it quickly, then raised her gaze to the big man beside her. "What on earth do you suppose happened?"

He gripped his hat tighter and shook his head. "I don't know. Can't figure it out. But I got a feelin' there's a whopper of a story behind it."

Laura handed him the wire. He folded it and jammed it into his shirt pocket. "What are you going to do?" she asked.

"What *can* I do? Too damn far away to go ridin' off and check up on things." He laid his arm around her shoulders and absentmindedly stroked the smooth fabric of her rose silk gown with his thumb. "Tell you one thing, though," he said suddenly. "If they're gettin' married, there's no reason for us to wait for Dakota to get back."

Laura leaned back, a soft smile on her face. "What are you saying?"

He grinned. "I'm sayin' let's get married this Sunday. After services the reverend can do us up real quick."

"*This* Sunday?"

"Why not? Diego's about finished with your new parlor. Won't take but a few more days . . ."

"Oh, that's not it. It's only that I don't know if we can get everything ready by Sunday."

"What're you talkin' about? All we really need is us."

"Yes . . ."

"Then it's settled?"

"But my father . . ."

"Will like the idea," he finished for her. "Probably be relieved to get me out of his house. Hell. I spend more time here than I do at the ranch!"

She laughed and laid her forehead against his broad chest. His arms closed around her, and she sighed with pleasure. Laura knew he was right. Besides, she longed for the opportunity to be alone with Tennessee. In their own home. Together. Did it really matter if she didn't have the big, fancy, "proper" wedding she'd planned on? His heart pounded beneath her cheek, and she realized the answer was no. The only thing that mattered was being with him.

"All right. Sunday."

Tenn leaned down and kissed her parted lips gently. Tenderly. He held his desire for her on a tight rein. Only a few more days. She slipped her tongue into his mouth, and his breath caught. Reluctantly he pulled away from her and stepped back. The disappointment on her face tugged at his heart, and he reached out to touch her cheek. "You keep kissin' me like that, darlin' . . . and we won't wait for Sunday."

She smiled.

Miserable, Dakota shifted position and sighed. She'd been standing still now for twenty minutes, and Josie showed no signs of completing her task.

"Are you about finished?"

"Almost." The girl tucked another tiny white daisy into the shining brown curls hanging down Dakota's back. Reaching up, she adjusted one of the pale blue ribbons that held the mass of hair in place and smiled. "You're gonna look so pretty, Dakota."

She smiled wistfully. "Thanks, but I don't think it'll matter."

Josie laughed. "Course it matters. Lord's sake. It's your weddin' day."

Dakota shook her head and ignored Josie's "tsk-tsk." The spur-of-the-moment wedding had really captured the fifteen-year-old girl's romantic fancies. She'd talked of little else for the past two days. And though Josie's enthusiasm was wearing, Dakota didn't have the heart to tell her the *real* reason for the marriage. No point in destroying Josie's dreams just because her own had taken a beating.

"This dress sure is a pretty color. Makes your eyes look all soft."

Dakota smiled halfheartedly at the girl tugging and straightening the fall of her dress. It was true. The gown was the pale blue of a summer sky just as dawn touches it for the first time. With full-length sleeves, pearl buttons, and a bit of lace at the throat and cuffs, it was a simple dress that somehow seemed just right to the cheerless bride.

"Finished!" Josie stood back and smiled at her friend. "Ben's gonna just love you. I'll go tell Molly we're set."

Dakota nodded and walked over to her bedroom window. If only that were true. But it wasn't. Ben didn't love her. The whole marriage meant nothing. Through the sparkling windowpanes she saw that for the first time in weeks banks of threatening gray clouds moved across the morning sky. She opened the window a few inches hoping for a breeze. Instead of lowering the city's temperature, the stormy skies only served to blanket San Francisco in a damp, smothering heat.

Resting her forehead against the cool glass, Dakota closed her aching eyes. The past two sleepless nights were making themselves felt. Tears welled up and she straightened, blinking furiously. Over the years, whenever she'd had the time to imagine her wedding day, she'd never once thought that it would be a ceremony without meaning or celebration.

She'd always harbored a secret dream of a flower-decked church, surrounded by friends and family. And the faceless groom she'd envisioned would hold out his hand to her, loving her, wanting her.

Now, though, she was about to marry the man she loved, knowing full well that he didn't love her. That it was only a temporary solution to an immediate problem. That he could hardly wait to be rid of her.

"Hey, Dakota!" Timmy yelled at the top of his lungs. "Come on down. Ben's here and we're fixin' to go."

She lifted her chin and took one last look in the small mirror hanging on the wall. It was too late now to stop the marriage. And too late to keep from loving him. Quickly she turned away from the solemn woman in the mirror and headed for the door.

A bride should be able to smile.

Then she did, unexpectedly. At the foot of the stairs Timmy waited impatiently for her. As he tugged at his new suit of clothes, Dakota could hear him grumbling.

"All this sissy stuff just to go watch some fool get hitched." He yanked at the collar of his new shirt and stretched his scrawny neck, hoping for some relief. His short pants ended just below the knee and his socks were already dirty and falling down. His clean brown hair, once neatly combed, stood straight up on his head. "I swear, these womenfolks got me lookin' like a dang girl."

"I think you look very handsome, Timmy," Dakota said.

He glared up at her. "Don't you go playin' none with me, Dakota. I ain't in no mood. I look like a dang fool, and you know it same as me."

She bit the inside of her cheek to keep from smiling again. "Then why are you dressed up?"

His lips twisted and he shrugged. "Aw, Molly bought this here outfit, and she puts some store in it."

"Well, I think it's real nice of you to go along with it for her sake."

"Hell . . . I mean, heck, it won't last long." He looked up hopefully. "Will it?"

"The wedding?" She sobered quickly. "No. I don't think so." Probably won't take more than a minute in some dingy little room, she told herself.

He grabbed her hand and pulled. "Well, then, let's get a move on, huh? Ben and them's out front waitin'."

Dakota let herself be dragged toward the door, but as she stepped outside, she came to a sudden stop.

On the street sat a shiny black carriage drawn by a pair of matched gray horses. Molly and Josie had already taken their seats, and now Timmy ran to join them as Dakota followed more slowly. Garlands of flowers outlined the splendid coach and their mixed bouquets sweetened the sultry air. Her pace slowed even further as she noted the driver, high on his perch, wearing a spotless black coat and tall hat.

Ben walked to meet her, brushing needlessly at his finely tailored black suit. His blond hair was combed neatly back from his freshly shaven face, and he held his hat in one hand as he stretched out the other to his bride.

Her heart stumbled, then beat again more quickly than before. Ben helped her into the carriage and took the seat beside her, opposite Josie, Molly, and Timmy. He set Dakota's carpetbag on the floor between his feet and turned his attention to her.

"Isn't this about the prettiest thing you ever saw?" Josie sighed.

"Yes, it is," Ben agreed, his eyes never leaving Dakota.

She looked away before he could read the confusion in her eyes. Why did he look at her like that? Why did he have to pretend so well?

The resplendent carriage wound its way through the crowds of San Francisco, and as they left the business district of the city behind them, Dakota's bewilderment mounted. Ben wouldn't answer any questions, though. Instead, he laughed with Molly and Timmy, flirted shamelessly with Josie, and only spared an occasional, secretive smile for Dakota.

They turned down one of the many residential streets just outside the business district, and she occupied herself by staring out at the houses under construction. Once the area had been filled with temporary, readymade houses of corrugated iron or wood. But now they were steadily being replaced by the more expensive and more permanent brick ones.

The carriage rolled on, down a wide avenue shaded on both sides by huge, stately trees. Dakota breathed deeply, hoping the quiet, peaceful neighborhood would calm the flustered, fidgety feeling that gripped her.

Their coach made a sharp turn suddenly and followed a meticulously kept drive to a beautiful house, surrounded by towering pines. With pale, almost rose-tinted walls and a red tiled roof, the one-story home sprawled across its lot. Dakota stared openmouthed as the still silent driver brought the horses to a stop opposite the ornately carved front doors.

"It's *pink*!"

"Hush, Timmy," his sister warned.

"That's all right, Josie." Ben laughed. "It's made of adobe, Timmy." The boy looked at him. "Adobe is a kind of clay mixed with straw. Sometimes it has a little color to it."

"Pink's an awful silly color for a house. Why didn't they just use bricks or somethin'?"

" 'Cause, adobe walls are about two feet thick. They keep the house nice and cool all summer long. And warm in winter." Timmy didn't look convinced. Ben smiled again. "I think you'll like the place. There's lots of big rooms, and right in the center there's a patio with a water fountain."

"Still seems dang silly to me."

"Hush!" Josie grabbed her younger brother and dragged him down from the coach. Ben stepped out and helped Molly down. Then he turned back to his bride.

Dakota stared up at the imposing house for a moment, then shifted her gaze back to Ben.

"Kota," he said softly, seeing the curiosity on her face. "Just this once"—he reached for her hand—"trust me. Please?"

Seventeen

HE waited silently for her answer.

Dakota studied him for a moment. She knew he had earned the right to expect her trust. In the space of a single heartbeat, images of him raced through her mind. He'd always been close whenever she'd needed him. He'd saved her from Ellis. He'd agreed to accept her help in capturing Tyson. He was even *marrying* her for her own protection. Yes, if she couldn't give him her love . . . she could at least trust him. She flashed a brilliant smile.

And he smiled in answer. A wide, charming smile that warmed her soul and made her wish again that their wedding was real.

As Ben helped her down from the carriage, the front door opened. A tall, muscular man who looked to be in his sixties stepped out. Dressed formally in a dark blue suit, he was a formidable-looking character. He sported a handlebar mustache that was as snowy white as the full mane of hair that fell carelessly about his head. His bright green eyes sparkled with delight as his wide mouth broke into a grin. Nodding at the small group on his porch, he moved toward the carriage with a speed and agility that belied his years.

Grabbing Ben's hand, he pumped it vigorously. "Ben, m'boy! You look well!" Then he turned his attention to Dakota. He placed his huge hands gently on her shoulders and laughed aloud. "Oh, she's a pretty one, you lucky devil. You've done all right for yourself!" He planted a hearty kiss on each of her cheeks and said again, "Yessir. Mighty pretty!"

Dakota blushed.

Ben shook his head at the older man, then addressed Dakota. "Kota, I'd like you to meet Judge Henry Stone. Judge, Miss Dakota Lane—my bride."

She looked at him sharply as she heard a note of genuine pride in his voice.

The stately man bowed low over Dakota's hand and placed a gentle kiss on her wrist. "A pleasure, my dear."

After the introductions were completed, the judge asked, "Shall we go inside?"

"Why don't you take Molly and the kids on in, Henry," Ben said. "We'll be along directly."

The older man nodded briefly, offered Molly and Josie his arms, and escorted them inside. Timmy followed, dragging his feet, hands jammed in his pockets.

Dakota stepped away from Ben and walked to the yellow rosebush guarding the front door. Her fingers gently tracing the outline of a fragile bud, she asked, "What's going on, Ben? Who is the judge? How do you know him?"

He walked up behind her, plucked the rosebud

from its home, and handed it to her. "The judge is an old friend of my father's." He sighed before continuing. "He left the South some time ago. Long before the war he opened a law office here. He's a good man, Kota. About the only friend from back home I've got left."

She looked up at him, and he traced his finger down the line of her cheek. "When I went to him about marrying us, he offered us the use of his home. I thought you'd like it more than a tiny courtroom somewhere. Was I wrong?"

"No." Dakota smiled, touched by his thoughtfulness. "Of course not." She swept her arms out. "This place is beautiful. But Ben, does he know the reason for our marriage?" Does he know, she added mentally that I love you and you don't love me?

"No. He doesn't." Ben's features tightened slightly. "As a matter of fact, he thinks this is a very romantic, very sudden elopement." He took her hand in his. "Why don't you and I think of it like that, too?"

"That would be too hard, Ben," she said regretfully and pulled her hand free. "*I* know the truth."

"And what truth is that?" He took her hand again.

"The fact that you're only marrying me to protect me." Suddenly she tore her gaze away. "To protect me from Tyson. And because I *might* be carrying your child."

He squeezed her hand. "Kota, if all I wanted to do was protect you, I could have kept you in the city jail, under armed guard." With the touch of his finger under her chin, he brought her gaze back to his. Ben hated to see her this unhappy. Especially today of *all* days. "There are easier ways to safeguard a person than by marrying them."

"And what about the chance of me being pregnant?"

He grinned. "Like you said, we would've known that in a couple of weeks."

"Then why?" Her eyes clouded. "Why all this?"

"Let's just say I'm a romantic." Ben smiled and looped her arm through his proprietarily.

Her big blue eyes stared up at him. "That's not much of a reason."

Leaning down, he touched his lips to hers. When he pulled away, his gaze moved over her face as though burning this image of her into his brain forever. "All right," he said softly, "a hurried ceremony in a crowded courtroom wouldn't look real. But a private ceremony held in Judge Stone's home does. It also tells Tyson that we have some powerful friends."

"Oh."

He saw her disappointment and tried to stem it. "But, Dakota, this is also our wedding day. For however long it lasts, our marriage begins here. Now. I wanted it to be . . . special." Ben cupped her cheek in his hand. "I'd like you to try to enjoy today. For Henry Stone's sake, if not our own. All right?"

She looked up into his eyes, and Ben almost told her the whole truth. That he loved her. That he needed her. That he couldn't live without her. But he didn't. The time wasn't right yet. Once this whole Tyson mess was over, *then* he would somehow prove to her how good they would be together.

Dakota nodded her agreement, and they walked to the door side by side.

Judge Stone's house was lovely. Heavy, dark furniture was distributed sparsely on the gleaming oak floors, giving the huge uncluttered rooms a cool, open feeling. They walked under a wide, curved archway to the patio, where Judge Stone, Molly, the kids, and a few other people waited.

A lone musician, dressed in black and silver, softly strummed his guitar to the accompaniment of subdued conversation and water splashing in the center fountain. The rich bouquet of wild roses floated on the still air of the shade-dappled patio.

Huge porcelain vases holding masses of flowers were set all over the brick patio, bringing a wild array of color into the sheltered terrace. There were even liveried servants standing serenely behind a table laden with champagne and a carefully prepared dinner.

Dakota shook her head.

"Do you like it?"

She looked up at him. "Of course. It's beautiful. But Ben, why did you—"

"I told you." He shrugged and smiled over her head at the judge. "Henry's an old family friend. *Most* of this was his idea."

"Oh."

If he heard the disappointment in her tone, he gave no sign as he led her over to stand before the judge. They stood solemnly during the short ceremony. Ben knew that she wasn't really hearing any of it. He'd even had to nudge her when it came time for her to say "I will."

He'd done the best he could. His mind told him that of course, she was feeling let down. After all, she'd had nothing to say about her own wedding. But still, his heart wished that she could simply accept it. That she could *see* why he'd done all this. That she could *feel* his love for her.

She went through all the proper motions. Ben stood

at the edge of the patio and tossed back a glass of champagne. It was his own fault. If he'd only told her the truth, maybe the day would have been different. He shook his head. And maybe the wedding wouldn't have happened. There was no telling with Dakota. She was so stubborn. So prideful. She might very well have refused to marry him. And he knew he couldn't have borne that.

Ben watched silently from the edge of the patio as Henry Stone led her through a dance. He suddenly wished he could hear what they were saying.

Henry smiled. "Well, *Mrs. Cable*, I hope Ben's arrangements for today pleased you."

"What?" Dakota looked up, startled at the use of her new name.

"I asked if you approve of Ben's preparations." He swept her into a turn and continued with a smile. "You should have seen the boy. I'll wager he hired every youngster in the area to go out and buy all the flowers they could carry from the flower shops in town." He shrugged. "I thought my roses would do nicely by themselves . . . but you know Ben. Mind of his own. Said it had to be just right. By thunder, looking at the place now, I'd have to agree with him."

Her steps lighter, her smile brighter, Dakota waited for him to continue.

"Ah, well," the judge said softly. "Here comes your new husband to claim you, so I will reluctantly return you to him. Think I'll give that champagne Ben brought a try. If you'll excuse me—" He slipped away as the groom stepped up.

Ben smiled as he took Dakota in his arms and began to dance her across the patio. Nodding his head toward a shadowed corner, he said, "Looks like Josie's found herself an admirer."

"Who is he?"

"It's all right, Dakota." Ben chuckled. "That's Bill Butler, the judge's nephew."

It appeared that the two young people were trying to teach each other to dance. She smiled, then rested her head on Ben's shoulder and asked, "Wasn't it nice of the judge to go to so much trouble for us?"

"Uh-huh." He rested his chin on the top of her head. "I told you he was a good man."

Dakota kept her smile hidden as she asked softly, "Could we sit down for a minute?"

"Sure. Are you all right?"

"Fine. Just tired."

Ben held her hand tightly and led her to a quiet, shady corner away from the other guests. He sat down beside her on the bright green bench. A long minute passed before Dakota said, "Judge Stone called me Mrs. Cable a while ago. I was so startled, I couldn't think of a thing to say."

He chuckled. "It'll take some getting used to, I guess. But that *is* your name now." Ben's eyes darkened before he turned away. Looking around the patio, he added hopefully, "It was a nice ceremony, though . . . wasn't it?"

"Yes, it was."

"Glad you liked it. The judge had to put it together so fast, he was worried."

"Ben"—she laid her hand over his—"why do you want me to think Henry did all this?"

"Hmmm?" He turned away, his face deliberately expressionless.

"Ben Cable . . ." She tilted her head and willed him

to look at her. "*You* did this. All of it. The flowers, champagne, everything. Why?"

His forearms on his thighs, Ben squinted off into the distance and said softly, "It's not so hard to understand."

She touched his arm, and he grabbed her hand. "I just wanted to make it as pleasant for you as I could. I know I forced you into this. But there was no reason for anyone else to know that." He squeezed her hand gently and looked into her eyes. "A woman like you, Kota"—he smiled helplessly—"you should be able to look back at your wedding day and smile. I only wanted to try to make it something special."

"But you said we'd get a divorce as soon as possible. Why go to all this trouble for a temporary arrangement?"

Dropping her hand, he stood abruptly and thrust his hands into his pockets. "I know what I said." His voice was raw, controlled. "But we *are* married, Dakota. And you gotta admit, when we're together, there's a lot of . . ."

She flushed and looked away.

Ben knew she was remembering the night in the storeroom. The memory carried with it a dull throbbing ache, and he wondered if she was as easily aroused by that recollection. He cleared his throat, suddenly uncomfortable.

"Anyway, we *do* have something together, Kota." Looking out at the judge dancing with Molly, he forced himself to say, "You can still get a divorce as soon as you want to, once this is over. But is there any reason for making even a *temporary* wedding a dismal one? One to be shuddered at even in memory?"

She stood and faced him. "Thank you, Ben."

"What?" His eyebrows drew together, and his eyes questioned her.

"I said thank you. It was a lovely day."

"The day was nice," he corrected, his hand on her cheek. "*You* were lovely."

She raised her hand to his and covered it. The touch of her flesh against his sent a thousand curls of heat through him. Her lips parted and her breathing was harsh.

Staring down at the smoky depths of her eyes, Ben traced her jawline tenderly with his finger. His thumb moved slowly over her mouth, and her tongue darted out to lick suddenly dry lips. He took a long, strangled breath.

She leaned forward and, with both hands cupping his face, guided him down to her. Her mouth teased his, her teeth nibbling at his bottom lip. Ben stood quiet under her gentle assault, letting her be the aggressor. When her tongue forced itself between his lips and caressed the inside of his mouth with warm, sure strokes, though, his control snapped.

Ben's arms closed around her, cradling her body along his. One hand at the back of her neck, the other against her bottom, he pressed her form into his own. His mouth returned the caresses she'd given him and Dakota moaned softly at the onslaught of undeniable desire.

He broke away suddenly, and they stood enfolded in each other's arms, gasping for air.

"Can we . . ." she asked in a breathy whisper, "leave now?"

He squeezed her once more for good measure and answered, "We'd better. Or I'm going to fill you right here on the bricks in front of God and everybody."

She trembled slightly. "Then let's go now, or I'm going to let you."

He raised his head to look at her and saw the raw desire in her eyes. More than a match for his own. Not trusting himself to speak, he only nodded, took her hand, and led her to where the judge and Molly were standing.

Hastily they said their goodbyes, enduring the older couple's knowing looks. As they moved quickly to the doorway, Josie intercepted them.

"Are you leaving already?"

"Yes, Josie." Dakota groped for something to say. "I'm, uh . . . awfully tired."

"Oh. Well," the girl said quickly, "I only wanted to thank you both for invitin' me today."

"Josie, you don't have to thank us for that," Ben said quietly.

"Yes, I do." She smoothed the starched fabric of her new peach-colored gown. When she looked up at them again, her old-young eyes were filled with tears. "I never had nothin' this nice before. And I never been to a place as pretty as this one."

Dakota stepped up to her and hugged her tightly. Ben's hand lay awkwardly on the young girl's shoulder. After a moment Josie looked up and blinked back her tears. Smiling, she nodded toward the corner of the patio where Bill Butler stood watching her. "Bill's teachin' me to dance." Lowering her gaze, she added, "He says he wants to come by the restaurant . . . maybe take me on a picnic." She looked up again, a shining hope on her face. "You think it'd be all right?"

"I'm sure it would. Why don't you ask Molly?"

"Oh, I will. I just wanted to tell you, too." Impulsively the girl hugged first Dakota, then Ben. "I'm so happy!" Then she turned and walked back to her young man.

"Isn't she somethin'?"

"She surely is," Ben agreed. His hand moved down Dakota's back, tracing the length of her spine. She shivered.

"What hotel did you say we were stayin' at?"

He, too, struggled to speak as he answered, "The Fremont. Let's go."

Their laughter echoed down the halls of the prim and proper Fremont. Ben opened the door, and they fell into the room dripping water all over the highly polished floor.

The storm clouds that had hovered so threateningly over the city had split open, releasing a torrent of much needed rain. The deluge that had soaked them in their open carriage had done nothing to cool their desires, though.

Ben hurried to light a fire, both to ward off the chill and to dispel the growing darkness. He didn't want to light a lamp. He preferred the flickering glow of flaming shadows.

Dakota's hair hung in a sodden mass down over her eyes as she bent over, trying to undo the long row of buttons down her back. But between her chilled fingers and the delicate size of the pearl studs, she couldn't manage. Ben had already peeled off his shirt and shoes, so he quickly stepped up behind her to help.

As he pushed the first dainty button through its hole, he left a kiss on the back of her neck. Then slowly, lingeringly, he went down the row of fasteners in the same manner.

Gently he eased the drenched material down over
her shoulders and drew it down her arms. As the
dress dropped to the floor, she stepped out of it and
bent to pick it up.

Ben's hands spanned her waist and held her tightly
to him. She straightened slowly, forgetting about the
soaking wet dress lying puddled at her feet. Carefully
he turned her around to face him, never releasing his
hold on her waist.

Leisurely his fingers plucked at the ribbon on her
wet chemise. As the ribbon fluttered free, inch by
tantalizing inch, Dakota's breathing sounded harsher
in the silent room.

Ben was aware of everything around him. Her breath
on his cheek, the crackle and hiss of the growing fire,
and the spreading flames in his own body. If he
couldn't proclaim his love until she was free of the
danger that threatened her, he could at least proclaim
his need. And at the same time convince her how much
she needed him.

Slowly she raised her hand to touch his bare chest.
Tiny rivulets of water ran down his flesh, hung on
the short, golden curls, and shone like diamonds in
the firelight. His big body trembled slightly as her
fingers moved over his skin. Laying her palm against
him, she moved over his flat nipples and heard him
suck in his breath.

He continued down the length of tiny bows, his
fingers pulling at them with less and less patience.
The soaked-through material hid none of her body
from his eyes, yet she knew they both wanted and
needed more. Finally the last of the ribbons floated
free. Tenderly he slipped the straps of her chemise
from her shoulders. Gazing at the full swell of her

breasts, he inhaled sharply. "God, Dakota, you're so beautiful," he whispered.

She smiled, an ancient, knowing smile, and stepped back from him. Watching the flame of desire in his eyes, she slowly untied the strap of her petticoat. She held the edges of the garment with her fingertips, then suddenly let it fall.

He groaned softly. Soaked to the skin, her sheer pantalets clung to her belly and legs.

Ben took a step nearer, but Dakota stepped playfully out of reach. Her gaze locked with his. Her hands slipped inside the waistband of the gauzy cloth. Slowly, deliberately, she moved her hands down the length of her legs, revealing herself to Ben by inches as she pushed the pantalets down.

He didn't move. Dakota heard his harsh breathing and realized anew how powerful their need for each other was. She stepped free of the clothing piled on the floor. She walked slowly toward Ben and felt the fire in his eyes warm every inch of her.

Every other time she'd been with him, she'd enjoyed it, but there had still been the secret fear of discovery to cloud her passion. Tonight there was no cloud. They were legally married, and for however long that lasted, she would give herself to him with no reservations. She remembered all he had done to ensure that she would have lovely memories of her wedding. And now she would do all she could to create a wedding night that would live forever in their hearts.

His arms reached out for her, but smiling softly, she brushed them aside. She stepped up close to him and grasped his wrists, holding his arms down to his sides. With a feather-light touch, her lips kissed his chest. Moving over his warm skin, her mouth tasted and teased him. When her teeth nipped gently at his flat nipple, he groaned and tried again to reach for her.

Dakota looked up at him from the corner of her eye. She smiled and said softly, "Let me do this, Ben. Let me love you."

He groaned, threw his head back, and nodded.

She released his wrists and moved her hands sinuously over his broad chest. Her fingertips twirled the golden hairs curling over it, and she felt the heavy pounding of his heart.

Running her hands down over his flat belly, she stopped at the waistband of his pants. She smoothed her finger just under the material, and his stomach quivered at the contact.

Dakota looked up at him and saw that he stared straight ahead, his lips compressed tightly. She smiled knowingly, then slowly undid the buttons of his trousers, lingering over each one. She reached the last button and paused, then freed it quickly. Her hand slipped inside. She rubbed the smoothness of him and felt his throbbing need.

"Enough!"

Ben reached for her, pulled her head back, and lowering his own, claimed her mouth with a fierce, driving passion. In one smooth motion, his lips still clamped over hers, he swept her up in his arms and lay her on the bed. Its feather softness surrounded her, and she moved sensuously against it. Ben stood and tore off his pants. His breath ragged, his patience at an end, he stretched out beside her.

Dakota's damp hair lay like gold satin on the white sheets. She stared up at her husband bracing himself over her and felt her desire grow beyond anything she'd ever known. She reached up and pulled his mouth down to hers.

Ben's hands roamed over her back, pulling her ever closer, as though he sought to mold them into one body. She pressed her lips to his neck, then moved her tongue over his throat, loving the taste of him. When he pulled back from her, she groaned, and he smiled as he pushed her back down on the bed.

"Oh, no, my love," he said softly, "you've had your fun." Smiling wickedly, he continued, "Teasing me, driving me mad. Now it's *my* turn."

He lowered his head to her breast and took one of her upright nipples into his mouth. His teeth nipped lightly at her tender flesh, then his tongue drew lazy circles around the darkened bud. Tenderly he worked her breasts, each in turn. Dakota wove her fingers through his hair and pulled his head closer, increasing the pressure on her nipple, unable to believe the sensations he was creating.

He raised up and she grabbed for him, afraid he would stop. His lips touched hers in a gentle promise. "Patience, my love, patience." She felt his warm, sweet breath on her face and smiled. Her eyes closed, she relaxed and surrendered her body to him.

Ben's strong hands glided knowingly over her skin, his lips and tongue following their path. His fingers moved lower and lower, stroking her heated body. When his hand found her center and touched the tiny, sensitive core of her, Dakota arched her body up. She spread her legs wider for him, and he smiled before taking her nipple into his mouth and sucking at it with a slow, steady pull.

Dakota didn't know which way to turn. One hand held his head to her breast while the other cupped his fingers as they stroked her body into madness.

He raised his head and smiled. She licked her lips feverishly and twisted beneath his hands. Sliding his free arm under her, Ben moved his hand down her back until he cupped her bottom. His right hand still kneaded the damp center of her, and now he entwined her fingers with his as he dipped inside her body.

Dakota's eyes flew open, the feel of her own damp warmth startling her. She pulled her hand free and reached to bring his mouth closer to hers. He smiled and shook his head. His hands were everywhere, but somehow his fingers never seemed to leave her core. She groaned aloud when his hands suddenly worked together, holding her legs wide. His thumb moved across the too-sensitive nub, and her body jerked in response. She opened her eyes and looked at him. He lifted her hips, his gaze never leaving hers. Then his mouth came down on her, and Dakota gasped in shock. She twisted and tried to pull away.

He held her still and soothed her. "It's all right, Kota. Let me love you."

She couldn't speak. She only nodded and lay back.

Ben's tongue caressed the tender spot his fingers had teased only minutes before. Licking and stroking, he introduced her to feelings she'd never imagined. Dakota's head tossed from side to side, her only thought now a fervent prayer that he never stop. She shuddered as his mouth moved over her. Initial embarrassment long gone, she gloried in the feel of his tongue running over her flesh. The warm, wet sweetness of it. Arching against him, she reached out and pulled his mouth down harder.

Deliberately she opened her eyes and watched him. Her fingers threaded through his blond hair, his hot breath stirring her fires even brighter, she moaned deep in her throat. His lips clamped down, and she felt the throbbing, shuddering release draw near. Soon she would burst, and she needed him inside of her when it happened. She needed his hard strength plunging into her.

"Ben," she gasped, "please . . ."

He looked up and met her eyes. "Yes, sweetheart. Now." Ben moved his body over hers, covering her with the length of him. His lips nuzzled her neck, and she thought she heard him murmur, "Now and always."

He entered her swiftly, and they gasped in unison at the joining. Dakota's hands moved erratically over his back, pulling and scratching at him. Urging him on. Urging him deeper. So deep inside her that he would never be able to leave.

Ben set their pace, thrusting slowly in and out, building their passion into a frenzied peak, until finally, exhausted, they tumbled over the precipice together. They remained locked together, their breathing slowed, their heartbeats evened.

Finally he rolled to his side, keeping his arms wrapped tightly around her. Dakota moved languorously against him, cuddled in close, and together they slept.

When the fire had been reduced to a few smoldering bits of wood, Ben awoke. He opened his eyes to see Dakota's radiant face just inches above his own. When he smiled a tired greeting, she touched his lips with her own tenderly.

Slowly then, she moved her leg over his inert form and straddled his body.

"What's this, madam?" Ben groaned.

"This"—she smiled—"is a wife's right. And *duty*." She grinned knowingly. "To see that her husband awakens to a smile."

She leaned forward, her brown hair falling like a curtain on either side of her face. Bending lower, she rubbed her breasts against his chest lightly, bringing a low moan of pleasure from Ben's throat.

"Haven't you had enough for a while?" Ben asked, smiling.

"Never," Dakota challenged on a throaty sigh.

"You should be tired," he said, amazed. "I know *I* am."

She moved against him once more, rubbing her center across his belly. Her fingers toyed with his nipples, and behind her, she felt the hard shaft of him. Chuckling, she said, "Not *too* tired, though, I see."

"Witch!" He reached for her.

"No, Ben, you're tired."

She rose to her knees and writhed sensuously over him. His hands reached out and grasped her breasts, softly kneading the tender flesh. She sighed as his fingers began to pull gently at her hardened nipples, and she leaned closer, giving him easier access.

Parting her lips, Dakota kissed him, moving her tongue over the inside of his mouth with slow, deliberate strokes. Her hips continued to move across his body, and when he tried to roll her underneath him, she held his shoulders down.

"No." She leaned back and raised herself high above him. Then, agonizingly slowly, she lowered herself again. When the tip of his hardened manhood touched her, Dakota moaned.

Ben lay still beneath her, his gaze following her

every movement. His hands slid up her thighs until he held her hips. He guided her as she came down on him until he was tenderly sheathed inside her warmth.

She sighed as she sat impaled by his body. Rocking gently to and fro, she threw her head back in pleasure. He filled her. She could feel him in every part of her body. In her soul.

This was why she had awakened to such an over-powering desire for him. This glorious sensation of being complete. His body joined with hers. She arched higher as his fingers touched her sex.

Looking down, she saw her own passion mirrored in his eyes. She smiled softly and began to move with him.

Eighteen

DAKOTA smiled and stretched contentedly as the morning sun spilled in through the open curtains. Never in her life had she gone with so little sleep and still felt so marvelous. Smiling slightly, she turned to wake Ben.

He was gone.

She sat up quickly and looked around the empty room. Their clothes were gone, too. Someone had taken them from the floor. Carefully, Dakota swung her legs off the bed and groaned at her aching muscles. Grinning, she rubbed the sore spot on her inner thigh as she remembered the source of that particular ache. A very active man, that Ben Cable, she told herself. And so inventive.

She reached for the top sheet when she heard the door handle turning. Holding the white cloth high in front of her, she watched with relief as Ben entered the room carrying a tray loaded down with food.

He smiled and asked, "Is the sheet really necessary, Mrs. Cable?" Eyes sparkling, he added, "I believe I've already seen the charms you're trying to hide."

Dakota dropped the sheet and walked to him. Quickly he slammed the door shut.

"What a wonderful idea," she said as she took the tray from him. "For some reason, I'm *starving* this morning." She turned away and, swaying her hips deliberately, carried the tray to a table on the far side of the room.

He watched her for a moment, admiring her naked bottom as it moved invitingly from side to side. Then, in a few quick steps, he caught up to her and swatted her backside.

"Ow!"

Ben turned her around and pulled her up against him. He ran his hands over her body, feeling each familiar curve and swell. "If you don't behave," he warned with a smile, "I'm gonna plop you right back on that bed, and you'll never get to eat!"

Dakota rubbed her bare breasts against his shirt and sighed. "We have to eat. Got to keep our strength up." Her lips curled in a satisfied smile as her fingers undid his top two shirt buttons. She kissed his exposed skin, running her tongue over his flesh.

Ben's hands moved to her bottom, and she felt his grip tighten. She pushed another button free and moved her lips over him again while her hand slipped to the waistband of his pants.

There was a knock at the door. Ben sighed regretfully.

"Don't answer it," Dakota urged, her breath brushing his chest. She would never know what he might have done, because a voice from the hall called out, "Are you Cable? Got a message for you from Molly!"

"Molly?" It was as if she'd been dunked in ice water. Dakota instinctively moved toward the door. Ben caught her, threw the sheet around her nudity, and motioned for her to get out of sight.

"What is it?" Ben asked, slipping his gun from the holster. Just because the stranger *said* he was from Molly didn't make it so. There was still Tyson to be considered.

"You Cable?"

Ben eased the door open an inch or two. In the hall was a man he'd seen many times at the Irish Lady. "Yeah. I'm Cable. What do you want?"

"I don't want a damn thing!" The old man straightened. "It's Molly. She says you and the girl should come to the restaurant. It's important."

"Did she say what it was about?"

"Shit. Molly ain't about to tell me her secrets. Me nor anybody else. She just said to come on the double."

"All right, thanks." Ben dug in his pocket and came up with a dollar. He flipped it toward the man, who snatched it out of the air with lightning speed.

"Sure thing, mister."

Ben shut the door and looked at Dakota. The playful shine was gone from her eyes. Replacing it now was a cold, dark fear. "What do you think—"

"I don't know, Kota." He reached for her, gave her a quick squeeze, then released her. "But Molly wouldn't have sent for us today if it wasn't important. Hurry and get dressed."

Dakota watched him walk to the window overlooking the street. A cold sense of dread washed over her as she saw him flip open his gun's cylinder and check the loads. She hurried to her carpetbag.

The Closed sign on the Irish Lady shook them both. Molly wouldn't have closed the restaurant unless something terrible had happened.

After pounding on the door for what seemed an eternity, waiting for a response, Timmy's tearstained face peeked out from between the curtains. Seconds later the boy had the front door open and his arms wrapped around Cable's knees.

Dakota's eyes widened as she stared at the sobbing child.

Ben reached down and picked him up, cradling the thin body tenderly. His hand patted the boy's back, trying to soothe the gulping sobs that shook him. "Shh, Timmy. Shh." He walked into the restaurant and Dakota followed him, then closed and locked the door behind her.

"What *is* it, Timmy?" Dakota asked in a hushed tone. "Where's Molly?"

He raised his head from Ben's shoulder, and she bit her lip as she brushed away his tears.

"Molly's upstairs. In"—he hiccuped—"Josie's room."

"Josie?" Dakota caught Ben's eye and saw her own fear echoed there. "Ben . . ."

"Come on." He continued patting the almost hysterical boy as he took the stairs two at a time. Dakota was right behind him.

Molly stood at the broken bedroom window, staring down at the shards of glass littering the floor. She lifted her ever-present apron to her eyes, then looked up when Dakota spoke.

"Molly? Molly!" She ran across the room to the older woman. As her fingers probed the cut on Molly's forehead, Dakota demanded, "Who did this to you?"

"Doesn't matter."

"Like hell." Ben set Timmy down on the bed and joined the women. "That's a nasty cut, Molly," he said as his strong fingers turned her face toward the early-morning sunlight. "What happened?"

Molly pulled away. "I told you, it don't matter about me. That ain't why I sent for you. It's Josie."

"She's gone."

Dakota glanced at Timmy. "What do you mean, gone?"

"Just what he said." Molly stepped over the broken glass and joined Timmy on the bed. She pulled the little boy to her and stroked his hair as she told them the story. "We got home kinda late last night. The judge was real nice, and Josie"—her breath caught— "Josie was havin' so much fun with that young Bill that, well, time got clean away from us.

"Anyway, we got home nigh on to midnight and went right on to bed. We were all pretty tuckered out. Even Josie, though her little face was just shinin'. I guess I was more tired than I thought. Slept real sound. Didn't hear this glass breakin'. Didn't hear nothin' till Josie screamed." Timmy flinched and burrowed closer to Molly. "I come runnin' in here and seen a real big fella draggin' Josie outa her bed. So I went after him."

Ben stepped up beside the old woman, and Dakota slipped her hand into his. He squeezed it, hard. "What happened then, Molly?" he asked.

"Hell, I must be gettin' old. He knocked me down like you'd swat a fly. Musta hit my head, 'cause I don't remember nothin' after that till about a hour ago."

"Timmy," Dakota said softly. "Did you see what happened?"

He nodded into Molly's shoulder.

"You have to tell us, Timmy. We have to find Josie,

and we need your help." Ben's voice was calm, even.

The boy raised up and looked at them. His eyes red and streaming, his mouth twisted with hate, the boy said venomously, "It was him. Dietz."

"Oh, my Lord . . ." Dakota gasped and Ben's fingers tightened even further around her hand. How could they have forgotten about that man? she asked herself. They should have remembered. They should have been watchful. They should have protected her.

As if he could read her mind, Ben said softly, "It's over and done, now. All we can do is find her. Quick." Turning back to the boy, he said, "Finish your story, Timmy."

He sniffed. "Like Molly said, Dietz knocked her down and was draggin' Josie off. I *tried* to stop him. Honest! But he just laughed at me. Said he didn't need me no more. That Josie would be plenty. Josie bit him and he hit her. Hard. And she just slumped over." His voice broke. "Dietz threw her over his shoulder and went back out the window. I stayed with Molly to take care of her."

"You did right, Timmy." Dakota smoothed his hair back.

"He done fine," Molly agreed. "As soon as I woke up and Timmy told me who the fella was, I figured I best send for you." She looked down. "Couldn't think of nobody else."

Ben laid his hand on her shoulder and patted it. "You better *not* call anybody else when you need help, Molly. I'd be right hurt."

She gave him a watery smile.

"Now," Ben said with a confidence he didn't feel, "let's get your cut taken care of and figure out how to get Josie back."

*   *   *

"She ain't much to look at," the blowsy woman with copper-colored hair sneered. She snapped the peephole on the door closed and looked at Dietz. "I'll give you a hundred."

"You said *two*!"

Her harsh laughter barked at him. "So? Changed my mind. She's older than I usually take 'em."

"She's only twelve!" The fat man wiped sweat from his forehead. All he wanted was his money.

"Twelve, my grandma's ass!" She shoved the roll of bills back into her cleavage. "That kid's at *least* sixteen!"

"Fifteen!" The word came out before he could stop it. It was too hot in the damn saloon. Especially here, on the top floor. If he didn't get out soon, get a drink . . .

"I thought so." Flat Nose Kate opened the peephole for another look. The tearstained face of a too-thin girl looked back at her. "How do I know she's even a virgin?"

"I told you she was, didn't I?"

Kate looked away from the girl, who was wearing only her nightgown, cowering in a corner. "And I'm supposed to *trust* you?" Dietz rubbed a bandanna over his face. "Why would I lie to you, Kate? I know your boys'd track me down."

"You best remember that, too." She turned her thoughtful gaze back to the girl. "Well, a little makeup, some pigtails, oh, I guess she'll do."

"Two hundred?"

"One fifty." She lowered the hole cover again and dipped her fingers into the bodice of her dress. Pulling out a thick wad of bills, she slowly counted off the right amount and handed them to the man. "Remember. I already let you have one of my best girls for more'n two hours . . . no charge. I ain't runnin' no charity here."

The bills were still warm. His small eyes greedily watched her tuck the remaining money between her generous breasts. For a moment he considered trying to steal it. If he could get his hands on that much cash, he could finally leave this crummy town. Maybe buy himself a good saloon somewhere. Never have to buy his own booze again.

"Don't try it," Kate warned in a steely voice. "I'd cut your heart out."

He blinked.

"But if you could lay your hands on another one . . . a little younger . . ."

He rubbed his hand over his jaw. Suddenly he knew he'd do anything to get ahold of that money. "What about boys? I know where I can get a *real* young boy."

Kate tapped one long, red fingernail against her chipped front tooth. "Hmmm. A boy. Well, why not?" She threaded her arm through his and led him toward the stairs. "I'm sure a few of my . . . clients would like something different."

"I'm telling you the best time to do this is the middle of the day." Ben looked at Dakota in frustration. "At night this place will be crawlin' with people. During the day the girls in there"—he nodded at Kate's place across the street—"sleep while they can."

"All right," Dakota said, "but in the dark it'd be easier to hide."

"Won't have to hide. Once we get Josie out of there

and onto the street, we should be safe enough."

"Why?"

"None of these folks down here want anyone to know that some of them like little girls."

Dakota shuddered.

"What they can do and get away with in the dark in a room at Kate's is one thing. Chasin' down a young girl on a crowded street is another."

"Oh, God," Dakota mumbled. "Do you think she's still all right?"

Ben didn't know. But there was no sense in telling her that. "Probably. Kate probably waits a couple of days to put 'em to work. Get most of the fight out of them." He squeezed her shoulder. "Are you ready?"

"Yes."

He smiled down at her outfit. "It's a good thing it's so early in the day. Otherwise, you'd create quite a stir in your britches. 'Specially with that holster and pistol."

A reluctant smile crossed her face. She never would have thought that she'd need her pants for sneaking into a whorehouse, but thank heaven she'd brought them along. They'd be a lot easier to move in in a hurry.

"I wish I could have left you at Molly's." Ben breathed heavily as he pulled her into his arms.

"I had to come," she answered, returning his embrace. "Josie may need a woman to be with her. We don't know what they've . . . done to her."

His arms squeezed her tightly. "I know. But be careful. And do everything I tell you, all right?"

She nodded.

"All right, then, let's go." He took her hand and ran quickly across the street. Slipping along the side of the building, Ben was looking and hoping for a back entrance. Finally, on the far wall of the old three-story building, he found what he was looking for.

They stared at the flight of steps leading to a second-story doorway.

"All set?" Ben looked down at her and pulled his gun out.

Dakota nodded and tightened her grip on her own pistol. She desperately hoped she wouldn't have to shoot . . . but if she had to in order to get Josie out safely, she would.

Crouching, Ben went up the wooden steps quietly, Dakota in his wake. He turned the doorknob slowly and smiled triumphantly at her when the old door opened. They crept into the second-story hallway and stood quietly for a moment, letting their eyes adjust to the darkness.

A dirty red runner covered the length of the dusty hallway. Stale sweat, cigar smoke, and cheap perfume hung in the stuffy air, and Dakota longed to go back outside. Instead, she moved down the hall behind Ben.

At the first closed door, he stopped. Carefully, quietly, he turned the tarnished knob and looked into the room.

A loud snore reached Dakota before he closed the door again. He shook his head. They went on. One by one, they checked the rooms lining the hallway. The only occupants were Kate's girls, catching up on their sleep. Dakota gave silent thanks they'd seen no children yet. She didn't know if she'd be able to keep quiet then.

As they reached the last door, Ben held up his hand. She stopped short. Straining, she was able to make out the sound of voices. A man and a woman. The woman was angry about something.

Ben pulled the hammer back on his gun and nodded at her to do the same. Then he eased the door open an inch. They listened as the woman said,

"The stupid son of a bitch tried to rob me. I told him what'd happen."

"Now what do ya want me to do with him?"

"I don't care. Drop him in the bay. He already brought me the girl."

Ben looked at Dakota. They both knew what the woman was talking about. There was a dead man in that room. It had to be Dietz. And that meant that Josie was definitely here. Somewhere.

Ben nodded at her, then threw the door wide. The room's occupants turned, startled at the interruption. At once Ben knew he'd made a mistake. He shouldn't have gone crashing in. They should have crept in quietly, sneaking up on the occupants instead of alerting them so abruptly.

A tall, cadaverously thin man and a copper-haired woman stood over the inert body of a huge man lying on the floor, wearing a bloodstained shirt.

The tall man turned when they entered, his hand already drawing his pistol. Ben shoved Dakota aside as the gunman's bullet struck his shoulder. He staggered slightly and pulled the trigger. He fired again and watched the falling man's eyes widen in shock before glazing over.

Dakota's heart stopped when she saw her husband slowly slide down to the floor. Quickly she stepped between Ben and the frantic, desperate woman across the room. Dakota raised her gun and took aim even as Kate dropped to the floor, scrabbling for her dead gunman's pistol. Dakota pulled the hammer back, hoping the sharp click would stop the other woman. It didn't.

As Kate reached across Dietz's prone body for the fallen weapon, the body beneath her suddenly shifted and her jaw dropped. Eyes wide, Kate stared sightlessly at Dakota before slumping facedown onto the floor.

Carefully, swallowing down her revulsion, Dakota inched her way toward the woman. A knife handle protruded from her back. Dakota looked away in time to see a satisfied smile cross Dietz's face as he died.

The gunshots had wakened the whole place. Stumbling, half-dressed women were crowding the hall as Dakota helped Ben to his feet. He brushed aside her anxious concern as they walked into the throng of chattering women.

Ben grimaced against the fiery pain in his shoulder and shouted for silence until the women quieted down.

"That's better," he said when he had their attention. "All we want to know is where Kate kept the kids hidden."

A few of the women shot hard glances at the wounded man and the woman at his side.

"Why the hell should we tell you anything? You just killed Kate."

Ben's gaze found the woman who'd spoken, and he answered tightly, "I didn't kill her. Dietz did. Just before he died."

"And why should we believe you?"

"Not askin' you to. I just want the girl Dietz brought here this morning."

"Go to hell."

Dakota took a step toward the blonde with shadowed eyes, but stopped when another voice spoke up.

"Aw, shut up, Lily." A woman in a see-through wrapper walked away from the crowd and glared at the outspoken whore in the rear of the crowd. Then she looked at Ben. "Why do you want the kid?"

"We want to take her home," Dakota answered.

The woman clutched the flimsy material tighter across her flaccid breasts and studied Dakota's face for a long minute. Then her tired eyes swept over the britches Dakota wore, and just for a moment a half smile touched her face. Then she said, "Good. She don't belong here. None of 'em do."

"Dora, you hush."

"I told you to keep quiet, Lily." Dora pointed at a stairway. "The kid's up there."

Ben turned for the stairs, but Dora's hand stopped him. "Just one thing, mister."

"What?"

"There's two other girls up there. You gotta take them, too. Kate hadn't started 'em yet. Get 'em out a here before this is the only place they belong."

"We'll take them, too."

She nodded and turned toward the other women. "All right, go back to bed. Show's over."

"Who put you in charge?"

"Me, Lily. *I* did." Dora's balled fists rode her wide hips. "And if you don't like it, leave."

A few of the others snickered.

"I didn't mean nothin'," Lily whined before moving off down the hall.

Dora looked back at Dakota. Ben was already on his way up the stairs. "Don't you worry about them in there," she nodded in the direction of Kate's room.

"I'll take care of that mess." She glanced over her shoulder at Kate's room. "I'll send one of the boys for the marshal. There won't be no trouble. Kate killed Dietz. Dietz killed Kate. The gunman just got in the way." Dora snorted derisively. "Hell, the marshal will most likely be pleased as punch. Kate was no prize, y'know."

"Appreciate it, Dora."

Dora waved her thanks aside. "Always wanted my own place. And Kate never was any good at it. You go on now. Get those kids and get out. Go back where you belong."

Dakota watched the other woman signal to a man downstairs. She glanced around the darkened hallway, now empty again, and shuddered. Thank God they'd been in time. Quickly she turned and followed Ben up the steep, narrow staircase.

He'd already opened the first door. A girl about ten stood in the hall rubbing her eyes. Dakota took her hand and called out loudly, "Josie?"

A moment passed, then she sighed with relief as the girl started pounding on the far door in answer, yelling, "Dakota! Dakota! In here!"

Ben rushed down the length of the hall, threw back the bolt, and staggered under the force of Josie's hug. Wincing slightly, he pulled her arm away from his shoulder.

"You're hurt!" she cried and brushed at her tears.

"Not bad." Ben kissed her forehead, then turned her around and pointed her off down the hall. "Go wait with Dakota. I'll be along."

The girl sped down the hall on her bare feet and threw her arms around Dakota as she sobbed out her thanks. "I was so scared. I didn't know what to do.

He hit Molly. Is Timmy all right?"

Dakota patted the girl's back and tried to answer all of her questions. "Everything's all right. Molly's fine. So is Timmy." She pulled back and held Josie's face between her hands. Running her thumb gently over the growing bruise on the girl's jaw, Dakota added, "And so are you."

Josie's eyes filled again, but she smiled and nodded determinedly.

Ben joined them after freeing the other two girls, both younger than Josie. He held two little hands in his and smiled down at his wife. "Let's get out of here. I'm hungry."

Dakota smiled and kissed him.

There was no other way, Ben told himself. He stood outside the stage station on the muddy sidewalk and stared down at the ticket he held in his hand. Abruptly he jammed it into his pocket, pulled his hat brim low over his eyes, and squinted at the busy street.

The storm had raged almost continuously for three days and nights. Now that the sun was finally shining again, the same people who'd cursed the drought were shouting obscenities at the rivers of mud flowing through the city.

Shaking his head, Ben realized that the shouting in the street would be nothing compared to what Dakota would say when she saw the ticket he'd just bought for her. And heaven help him, he knew he would deserve it. But he had no choice.

He turned and slowly started for the Fremont, where Dakota waited for him. His mind jumbled with images of the last three days, he scarcely noticed the bustling crowd around him.

Since rescuing Josie and the others, he and Dakota had become even closer than before. It was as if working together had forged their already existing bond into something indestructible. At least, he *hoped* so.

He sighed. Timmy and Josie had found a permanent home with Molly. The two other girls were being cared for by the marshal and his wife until their relatives could be found. Ellis was about to be transferred to Arizona, where he'd be tried, and probably hanged, for murder. The only remaining problem was Tyson.

Ben shoved his hands into his pockets and winced at the ever-present ache in his shoulder. Bitterly his fingers made contact with the stage ticket. To solve the final problem, he had to risk everything he'd built with Dakota.

But there was no other way. It was only chance that had saved him at Kate's. If the gunman's aim hadn't been off because of his turn, Ben would most likely be dead right now. *Then* what would become of Dakota? With no one to protect her, she would be an all-too-easy target for Tyson.

He hadn't considered the possibility of his own death before. But the gunfight had convinced him. Dakota *must* be safe. He couldn't take chances with her life. He wouldn't. If anything should happen to her . . .

Ben inhaled deeply and hurried his strides. Best to get this over with.

Nineteen

DAKOTA twisted her hair to the top of her head and secured it with a thin violet ribbon. Brown curls fell and danced lightly on the neck of her new lavender dress. Standing, she did a slow turn before the full-length mirror, holding her skirt out at her sides. She moved her head to catch her reflection from all angles. It was wonderful. She could hardly wait for Ben to see it.

A soft smile on her face, she crossed to the window and looked out at the street below. Everything was working out so well.

Just yesterday she'd seen proof of that. Dakota grinned at the memory. Despite the crowded restaurant, and men bellowing for their meals, Josie had floated through the room, her happiness unshakable.

She had changed overnight from a haunted, fearful girl into a blossoming, confident young woman. All because of a dozen roses. The scene flashed before Dakota's eyes again.

"Aren't they beautiful," Josie had said with a sigh. The girl had rearranged the blossoms three times in the space of fifteen minutes.

"Yes," Molly agreed, "but you best quit fiddlin' with 'em like that, or they're gonna wear out."

"Why don't you put 'em in your room?" Dakota suggested.

"All right."

Josie moved up the stairs, her nose buried in the soft fragrance, and Molly had laughed gently.

"That young Butler won't ever know what he did for that child—sendin' her flowers."

"She's amazing." Dakota shook her head. "Nobody would guess what she's been through just by lookin' at her."

"I know. But it's over now. And I think knowin' that she don't ever have to worry about Dietz again is the best medicine in the world. Anyhow." Molly had smiled and pushed her hair back from her face. "I finally got me some children. And all three of us is gonna do fine."

"Molly!" Timmy poked his head into the kitchen. "There's a cowhand out here wants his damn guns back."

She glared at him.

"*Dang* guns back," he corrected with a smile.

Molly shook her head at him, but her disapproval was lost in the grin she couldn't contain.

Dakota sighed as the pleasant memory faded. She was glad that Molly and the kids would have each other. It would be easier to leave for home when the time came, knowing her friends were happy.

Home. How she missed it. She looked around the hotel room and realized that the fancy hotel and the big city held no attraction for her. All she wanted to do was get back to Red Creek. Back to the ranch.

Ben's coat hung over the back of a chair. Dakota ran

her hand over the fabric and thought of her husband.

Her marriage had been everything she'd ever dreamed of and more. Whatever his reasons for marrying her, Ben had been the best of husbands. Loving, gentle, *very* attentive. She caught herself hoping that he *did* love her. That he didn't want a divorce as he'd said he did. Maybe, after his father's betrayal, he couldn't bring himself to be the first to declare his love. Maybe he needed *her* to say the words. To be the one to risk all.

She wrapped her arms tightly around herself. If she did tell him that she loved him, only to have him push her away, what then? Well, she told herself, she would be no worse off than she was now. He could get his divorce, and she would go home. Alone.

But it wouldn't happen like that. She knew it. She could feel it. He *did* love her.

His key sounded in the locked door, and she turned to face him. She would tell him today.

"Ben! What do you think?" she asked and turned slowly for his inspection. She was suddenly very glad she'd worn the new dress.

"Very pretty." He stepped farther into the room.

"Pretty enough to get you to take me out to supper?" She smiled and walked closer to him. "We've hardly left this room for the last three days."

"Not tonight, Kota." He pulled his hat off and tossed it onto the dresser.

"What is it?" Her hand on his arm, she looked up into his eyes. Something was wrong. Very wrong. Foreboding spiraled through her. She waited anxiously for his answer.

He squeezed her hand, then moved away. Holding

the edge of the curtain back, he stared out the window for a moment. "Have you wondered *why* we haven't left this room much?"

"No." Dakota moved to the bed and sat down. "I just thought that you . . ."

"That I'd rather be makin' love to you than anything else?" Ben turned to stare at her, his gaze bleak.

"Well . . ." What had happened? The warm glow inside her drained away, giving rein to a feeling of dread so overpowering she could scarcely breathe. Whatever he was about to say, she knew she didn't want to hear it.

"You were right. I would. If I could, I'd keep us both in that bed right there for the next forty years or so." He looked away. "But I can't."

"Ben, what is it? What's happened?"

"Nothin' yet. And that's how I want it to stay." He took a deep breath, dropped the curtain, and turned to look at her. "Dakota, it's time to finish this business with Tyson."

She smiled and shook her head. "You had me scared." Rising, she walked over to him. "I thought something was wrong."

He only looked at her.

Dakota spoke quickly, saying anything. Anything at all to fill the empty silence that separated them. "I'm glad to hear you say so. I was just thinking that it was high time for us to be gettin' home. What are we gonna do first?"

He looked away and drew a deep breath.

"*We're* not doin' anything."

"What do you mean?" She took a step back.

"I just bought you a stagecoach ticket home."

She stood stock still. Even her heart seemed to stop.

"The stage'll take you to Sacramento," he said quickly. "Then the train to Nevada. I'll finish up here, then join you at Tenn's ranch."

A cold like nothing she'd ever known settled over her. Dakota heard the slow pounding of her heart. She watched his chest rise and fall with his rapid breathing. The clock on the mantel sounded unnaturally loud in the deafening silence.

"You're sending me home?" Her voice cracked. "Just like that?" All of her childish fancies came flooding back to taunt her.

"It's not 'just like that.' I've thought it all out. This is the only way."

"When did you decide this?"

He shook his head.

"When, Ben?" Her throat was closing. She swallowed past the lump and fought down tears. She refused to cry. "Today? Yesterday? Or did you have this in mind all along?"

"Dakota . . ." He took a step toward her.

"No!" She raised her arms as if to ward off a blow. "Don't." Eyes filled with unwanted tears, she asked again, "When, Ben? Was this the plan from the start? Was it the reason for our 'marriage'?"

"Dakota, no." Ben jammed his hands into his pockets. "I swear to you, no."

"I don't believe you, *Sheriff*. You never intended to let me help you catch Tyson. You just went along with whatever I said. You would have said anything to get me to agree."

He didn't answer, but his gaze never left hers.

"You *used* me!" The tears spilled over and ran down her cheeks unchecked. She couldn't stop them any more than she could stop the words that tumbled from her lips. "You planned to pack me off like a child right from the first. You just thought of a way to get me into your bed at the same time. Why now? Why do I have to leave today? Have you finally had enough of me? What's the matter, are you tired of my body now that you've had your fill?"

"Stop it!" He moved quickly and grabbed her shoulders. "Stop it. That's not true, Dakota, and you know it."

She pulled away. "I don't know a thing about you. *Nothing!*" Turning her back on him, she added on a mirthless chuckle, "You did a good job, Sheriff. You kept me busy. Made sure I was happy. Drove my body to distraction to keep my mind occupied."

"Dakota . . ." He moved closer. His voice came softer. "It wasn't like that. I only wanted to protect you. To—"

"To what?" She whirled around and glared at him. "To *love* me?"

He stopped. His jaw tight, his eyes grim.

"I thought not." She stepped up close to him. Her breath came faster, and despite her anger and hurt, Dakota felt her body respond to his nearness. To the scent of him. "All right, Sheriff. I'll leave. I guess I don't have a choice. You are my *husband.*"

He winced.

She looked up at him through teary eyes and knew this blurred image of him would be her last. But she wanted him to know what he'd done. What he'd lost. "Before I go, though, there's something I want you to know. I'd made up my mind to tell you today, no matter what."

Ben watched her, his face unreadable.

"I wanted to tell you"—she inhaled sharply—"that

I loved you." She saw the impact her words had on him. She was sure he'd swayed slightly. "See, I was convinced"—Dakota laughed—"that you loved me. That the only reason you hadn't said so was because you were afraid of being betrayed again. Being hurt again."

"Dakota . . ." He breathed her name like a dying man.

"Don't say anything else. Please." She turned away. "I'll be packed and ready in a few minutes."

A long moment passed in silence and carried away her last hope.

"I'll wait for you downstairs."

She nodded.

Red Creek

"You sure you're not disappointed?"

Laura snuggled up against her husband and stared into the fire. A satisfied smile curved her lips as she ran the flat of her hand across his bare chest. "Why in heaven would you think I could be disappointed about anything?"

Tenn stroked her arm and kissed the top of her head. "Well, I know you kinda had your heart set on a fancy to-do for your weddin' day and . . ."

She tilted her head back to look at him and laid one finger across his lips. "It was perfect. Better than perfect." Boldly she placed a gentle kiss on his nipple. "We're together, Tenn. That's all I care about."

"All?" He grinned at her.

"Well," Laura added as she moved away from him to stretch out on the blanket spread in front of the fireplace, "maybe not all." She held her arms out for him. "I *am* awful new at this . . . Is it too soon for you to give me another lesson?"

Tenn's gaze swept over his wife greedily. The reality was far better than the dream. She was here. In her parlor. And as the firelight danced on her naked body, he knew he'd never be able to enter this room without seeing her like she was now, in his mind and heart forever.

She gave of herself so freely, so lovingly, he didn't understand how he'd managed to live so long without her. Tenn pulled her into his arms and kissed her with gentle adoration while his hands slid over her fine ivory skin. "Oh, darlin'," he finally managed to say, "you don't need no lessons."

Ben helped her inside the coach, then handed her the carpetbag. He'd never felt so helpless in his life. Or like such a low-down, shoddy excuse for a man. If anyone else had hurt her like he had, Ben would have killed them.

If only she'd say something, he told himself. Anything. Even one of her white-hot bursts of temper would be easier to bear than this cold, controlled despair. Maybe he was doing the wrong thing. Maybe she *should* stay. As soon as the thought blossomed, he squashed it. No. He was doing the only thing he could do. He had to make her see that.

"Dakota," he tried again.

Her empty blue eyes flickered over him, then away again.

"I know I've hurt you, but—"

"You don't know."

His heart stopped for a moment. At least she was speaking to him again. That was a start.

"If you had any idea what you've already done to me," she said slowly, "you wouldn't still be standin' here talkin'."

Ben swallowed and hung his head for a moment. "All right. I'll go." He reached into the stage and grasped her chin with his fingers. Turning her face to his, he met her gaze and said, "But I'll be coming back to Red Creek. To the ranch. To you."

She pulled away and stared out the opposite window. She didn't see him walk away.

The stage hit a rut in the road and Dakota's head slammed back against the wall of the coach. She was almost glad for the pain. The throbbing in her skull gave her something to focus on.

She hadn't even been able to say goodbye to Molly and the kids. It hardly seemed possible that she'd been in San Francisco barely two months. So many things had changed. Her entire life had been altered.

The simple gold band on her finger caught her eye, and she fought down a sudden urge to pull it off and toss it out the window. She couldn't do it. After the last few days with Ben, she might well be pregnant. And Dakota refused to bear an illegitimate child. She couldn't subject any child, not even Cable's, to being called a bastard all its life. Oh, Lord, she groaned silently, please, no baby. She didn't know if she could bear being bound for life to a man who would lie to her and use her like Ben Cable had done.

It wasn't right. He shouldn't have been able to get rid of her so easily. Oh, she could have fought him in town. But causing a scene wouldn't have done her any good at all. She knew very well that Ben would have tied her hand and foot and stowed her on the luggage rack if she hadn't agreed. But there were so many things she wanted to say to him. To call him. Now that the hurt and shock were beginning to fade, she was beginning to think clearly again. It was almost a relief to feel the anger building inside. Anything was preferable to the pain she'd already lived through.

How *dare* he pack her off like a ten-year-old? Just because he was her husband, she was supposed to go along with everything he said like a docile fool? And didn't she remember him saying something about coming out to the ranch to see her? Wasn't *that* just like him? He would come to her. Whenever he was ready. To do what, explain? There was no explanation for what he'd done to her. But she was supposed to just sit quietly at the ranch and wait for him to decide what to do.

"Hmmph!" She would *not*! Why, as the miles crawled past, Dakota was having a hard time figuring out just what had happened. How in thunder had she allowed him to get away with this? For heaven's sakes, *no one* had *ever* treated her like she didn't have a mind!

Dakota straightened in her seat. Her fingers tightened around the gold ring on her left hand. He's in for a big set-down, she thought. He's just not gonna get away with this. He might have put her on the stage, but he couldn't make her *stay* on it. Not until she was good and ready.

Ben sat in the darkness, listening to the familiar sounds of the waterfront. Idly, he held his six-gun in his hand, checked the loads, then slid it back into its holster.

He pulled his watch from his vest pocket and squinted at it in the dark. Ten P.M. An hour more. That's all he would wait. One hour.

One more hour for him to think about Dakota and what he'd done. He shook his head, remembering the look on her face as the stage pulled out of town. But, dammit, he thought. Why couldn't she see the sense of this? Didn't she realize that she wouldn't be safe until Tyson was taken care of? Didn't she understand what it had cost him to send her away? How it had torn him up to hurt her like that?

He shifted position and glanced at the Last Chance Saloon. Ellis's place seemed to be getting along fine without him. Place was packed.

Thank God he'd gotten her out of town. He cringed at the thought of Dakota anywhere near this place again. But, Lordy, how he missed her. He never would have believed it, but the day spent without hearing her voice, or seeing her smile, had been the longest one he could remember.

He could still see her face when she'd told him that she loved him. The *one* thing he'd wanted to hear, and when he finally did, there was nothing he could say in return. If he'd proclaimed his own love, Ben knew that she'd never have left town. She'd have stayed right by his side, no matter what happened. The only way to keep her safe was to get her out of town. Better she be hurt than dead.

Besides, he told himself. By this time that hard-headed hot temper of hers had probably kicked in. The rage he knew so well wouldn't allow her to nurse a hurt for long. In no time at all she'd be spittin' mad. Ben grinned. He didn't envy Tenn, having to put up with the conniption fit Dakota was likely to throw. She'd be mad enough to bite through a horseshoe.

But if something happened to him, Tenn would be able to protect his sister from Tyson. That's all that mattered.

He shook his head. And when this damn mess was over, he told himself, he'd do anything it took to make her love him again. He refused to believe that he'd lost her forever. He couldn't bear to live with this emptiness for a lifetime. After all, she was his wife now—and he'd be damned if he'd let her divorce him . . . no matter *how* mad she got.

He checked his watch again. Almost eleven. Another glance at the saloon and he smiled. The noise was at a fever pitch, and by this time of night he knew that just about everyone in the place would be good and drunk. It was time. All he had to do was get into Ellis's office and "borrow" those papers Dakota'd seen. If they were still there.

The marshal was ready to go in and search the room, but Ben was afraid that whoever had access to the office would hide the books from the law. With Ellis in jail and Tyson disappearing into thin air, who knew if there was someone else in on the shanghai business?

Still, Gordon Tyson worried him. No one had seen the man for days. Of course, it was possible that he'd simply up and left town. But even if he had, with those lists from the office, Ben and the marshal could ruin what was left of Tyson's reputation. There would be nowhere for him to run. And he would never get so close to a position of power again.

After crossing the street, Ben slipped in through the batwing doors and blended with the crowd. If the damn back door had been unlocked, he could have gone in that way. Uneasily he started for the stairs.

But it was surprisingly simple to get to the second floor. The bartenders were too busy to look up, and everyone else was too drunk to notice just another cowhand going upstairs.

He staggered slightly, giving the impression of drunkenness, in case anyone should look at him. At the head of the stairs he glanced cautiously over his shoulder at the crowd below. Still unnoticed, he went on to Ellis's office.

Almost there. A door on his right flew open, and one of the working girls stumbled out. She lurched against Ben and clamped her mouth on his. He almost gagged at the sour smell of cheap whiskey on her breath. So drunk she could hardly stand, her hand instinctively snatched at his groin. Ben set her aside, then gave her a little push back into her room and closed the door.

He moved on warily.

Finally. Ellis's office. Ben smiled when the brass knob turned easily under his hand. After stepping inside, he quietly closed the door again after him. He crossed the darkened room carefully, even though he knew the noise belowstairs would drown out any sound he might make.

At the desk Ben struck a match and touched the flame to the wick of an oil lamp sitting close by. A soft glow of light covered the messy desk. Quickly he pulled open first one drawer, then another. Searching for the documents amid the piles of crumpled and disarrayed papers was going to be a huge task. As he bent to the lowest drawer, a voice in the darkness beyond the desk stopped him.

"It's not there, Ranger."

Ben turned and reached for his gun.

"Don't do it." The clear, distinct sound of a hammer being pulled back followed the statement. "You wouldn't have a chance."

He moved his hand slowly away from his gun, then obeyed when the voice ordered him to turn up the wick in the lamp.

As the halo of light grew, Ben could just make out the figure of a man sitting in a chair not far from the desk. Ashamed of himself for not noticing him earlier, Ben cursed quietly under his breath.

Then the man stood and moved out of his shadowy concealment, and Ben's stomach dropped to his feet. Of course. It had to be. Gordon Tyson.

Tyson, not nearly as elegant as the last time Ben saw him, held a gun pointed directly at Cable's chest. A pitying smile crossed the man's face as he said, "I am disappointed, Ranger. Though I've been here every night waiting for you . . . I had almost come to the conclusion that you were too smart to show up." He came around the desk and slipped Ben's gun from its holster. Tucking it into the waistband of his pants, Tyson added, "However, I see now that my estimation of you was wrong." He backed away and motioned with his pistol. "Please, sit down."

Ben sat uneasily in the big chair behind the desk, his gaze locked on Tyson. He couldn't believe that he had been so foolish. He'd walked right into a trap. No better than some dumb kid out on his first assignment as a lawman. His only consolation in this entire mess was the fact that he had managed to get Dakota to safety.

Tyson, his gun still pointed at Ben, used his free hand to strike a match and light his cigar. He puffed at it gently for a moment, then, staring at the burning end, said softly, "I realized, of course, that Mr. Ellis would no doubt tell you everything his poor, over-taxed mind could think of to ease his own penalty. So naturally, I assumed that you would take it upon yourself to come here for my uh . . . 'papers'?"

Ben didn't reply.

"Ah, Ranger," Tyson said before drawing on his cigar again. "That wedding of yours. Very clever. I can't say that I envy you, married to that maddening female." He licked his lips and smiled. "Though I imagine she *does* have her compensations."

Ben's fingers tightened on the arms of his chair.

"You were right on one score." Tyson's tone was relaxed, cordial. "As the wife of a Texas Ranger . . . even a *former* Ranger, she is safer than before. You see, I have no wish to bring the wrath of the entire force of Rangers down on my head." Thoughtfully, he sighed. "So. It seems that I will have to content myself with you."

Ben's face was blank. Unreadable.

The older man chuckled softly. "Come, come, Ranger. Surely you can see my position. I am forced to abandon any plans of my own here in this pleasant city. Someone will have to pay for that." He rose from his chair, walked slowly around the desk, and stopped behind Ben.

Trapped neatly, there was nothing Ben could do. He hated having Tyson behind him, out of sight. But all he could do at this point was to remain calm and wait for his chance. If he got one. Ben's mind whirled with frantic, desperate plans as something struck him a sharp blow on the back of the head.

"And you, my friend, are that someone." Tyson smiled when Ben slumped over.

Twenty

DAKOTA rode into San Francisco late. She turned her tired horse toward the waterfront and Molly's place. She wasn't ready yet to confront Ben at the Fremont.

As her borrowed horse plodded slowly down the dimly lit streets, she yawned in sympathy with the exhausted animal. They'd been traveling for hours. She smiled, though, remembering the scene at the stage station.

She would never forget the looks on the stage driver's and the station hostler's faces when she'd appeared, dressed in her pants, demanding a horse. Their astonished gazes had taken in both the britches that clung to her body and the pistol strapped to her hip. Thankfully, they'd both been too surprised to offer much resistance.

With her carpetbag tied to the back of her saddle, she'd urged the poor horse into a punishing pace, determined to return to San Francisco as quickly as possible.

Now all Dakota could think about was crawling into her old bed at Molly's. She would definitely need sleep before settling with Cable. Wearily she dismounted in front of the Irish Lady and tied her horse's reins to the hitching post. Grabbing down her carpetbag, she gave the horse's neck a brief pat and walked to the restaurant door.

As she raised her hand to pound on the door, she stopped. Something was wrong. Molly was still up and sitting alone at a table in the near-dark restaurant. Dakota tried the door, and it swung open easily.

"Thank God you've come back." Molly stood up, relief shining in her eyes.

"What is it? Are the kids all right?" Dakota hurried across the room. She'd never seen the other woman so agitated. Every nerve in her body screamed out a warning as she took the chair opposite her friend. "Molly, tell me what's wrong. And how did you know I'd left town? Ben tell you?"

"The kids are fine. They're out now, though, lookin' for the marshal." Her gray hair framing her worried face like a wild, silver halo, Molly continued. "Oh, Lord, Dakota. There's big trouble. It's Ben."

"Ben?" Dakota's insides twisted.

Molly nodded. "Cable went over to the Last Chance tonight. God alone knows why. But that don't matter now. Tyson was there. Waitin' for him."

"No." Dakota slumped back against her seat. "How do you know?"

"Timmy." Molly sighed heavily. "He went to see you two today. Instead, he saw Ben put you on that stage. That's a smart boy there, Dakota. He figured you leavin' real quick like that, not even sayin' goodbye to us, meant somethin' was wrong." The old woman shook her head wearily. "Hell, you know how he feels about the both of you. And he admires Ben somethin' fierce. So, he followed Ben around town all day."

"What?"

"I know, I know. But as it turns out, it was a damn good thing he did."

"Tell me."

Molly reached for her hand. "When Ben went into Ellis's place, Timmy hid out in the alley and waited. 'Fore too long, a couple of fellas come out, carryin' Ben's body."

"His *body*!"

"Yeah. Timmy thought he was dead. Then he heard Cable moanin'. Anyhow, the boy kept his head. Followed 'em to a warehouse here on the waterfront. Looks to me like Ben Cable will be shippin' out tonight for who knows where."

"Shipping out?"

Molly sighed and nodded. "One of Tyson's 'arranged trips.' Dakota, Ben's bein' shanghaied. But we've got to have help. Like I said, the kids are out now lookin' for the marshal."

Dakota jumped to her feet, her chair clattering to the floor. "Ben . . . shanghaied?" Her mind flew in hundreds of directions at once. Ben? Just one more of the men who disappeared from the Coast? She couldn't let this happen. Would he survive? Or would Tyson change his mind and simply kill Ben? No. Not Ben. No matter what he'd done or said. She loved him. She always would.

"Come on!" she shouted. "We can't just sit here and wait for the law. God knows how long it'll take the kids to find the marshal. He could be anywhere!" Dakota paced furiously back and forth.

Suddenly she stopped and looked at her friend. "I'll just go alone."

"Dakota, don't talk foolish."

"Molly, who else is there? I can't sit here doing nothing! We don't know what they might be doing to him! And you've got to be here when the kids get back with the law."

The older woman's eyes studied her for a moment. "I guess there's nothin' I can say to stop you?"

Dakota shook her head. "Molly, earlier today I was mad enough at Ben to shoot him myself. But I'll be damned if I let *Tyson* do it!"

"All right. I don't like it, but if I was a few years younger, I'd have already gone myself." Molly sat down again and gave Dakota directions to the warehouse.

Ben's head ached. He tried to move and found that his hands and feet were bound. Dazedly he tried to clear his mind. He could feel his own breath hot on his face and knew that there was a hood of some kind over his head. He knew he was on the ground because he felt a sharp rock digging into his back. Clumsily he rolled to the side and managed to escape the stone, though his head screamed at him for the movement.

For the life of him he couldn't remember how he'd come to this. Where was he? And how long had he been there? Then the image of Tyson's face sneering at him floated to the surface of his brain. He groaned.

"Ah, finally coming around are you, Ranger?"

"Gordon Tyson," Ben breathed.

"How flattering. You remember. I'm glad I didn't hit you too hard."

"Why the concern?" The hood muffled Ben's voice. Tyson laughed. "Because my friend the captain wouldn't like it if his new shipmate should arrive, shall we say, damaged?"

"Captain?"

The scraping of boots on dirt came near, and Ben knew Tyson had squatted next to him when the man's voice sounded low in his ear.

"Yes. Captain Bigelow. Actually," he said in a pleased tone, "this is quite an occasion for both of us, Ranger. You are about to become a seaman. And I will finally meet Captain Bigelow. He was one of my best customers. For some reason, his crew members led very short lives."

Ben heard a soft chuckle close to his ear, then Tyson's fist slammed into his abdomen. Over the bound man's groan, Tyson went on. "You see, Ellis always handled the 'shipping' business. So I've never had occasion to meet my customers personally. But *you*, Ranger, put Ellis in jail. I was forced to arrange this voyage myself. I have never enjoyed anything quite as much, though, I must say. I'll be paid two thousand dollars for you, Cable."

Tyson stood up and gave his prisoner a vicious kick. He watched dispassionately as Ben's body curled up with the pain. "True, it's not much. But it will certainly see me through until I can set up shop in some other city." Suddenly he laughed. "Why, you're actually aiding and abetting a criminal. How does *that* set with a former Texas Ranger?"

Ben breathed slowly and carefully. Every bone in his body hurt like fury. He had to keep telling himself to think. As long as he was alive, he had hope. Maybe somehow he could still find a way to get out of this setup.

At least Dakota was safe. It was some consolation

that he'd managed to keep her out of this madman's reach. Soon she'd be back at Red Creek. He could see her face before him in the darkness and wished again that his last image of her didn't include the tears he'd given her.

He grunted as his captor kicked him again. Ben fought to remain silent. He had to content himself with the knowledge that Dakota was safe. That someday she would forget about him and the hurt he caused her. And, though it tore at him to think of it, find someone else.

Tyson yanked him off the floor, and Ben felt himself falling helplessly as the other man threw him against a wall. He groaned aloud. He hadn't known this much pain existed. Tyson must have been beating him since he passed out. Doggedly he struggled to remain conscious.

"How'd you get me down here, wherever this is, by yourself?" It hurt to talk. His lips were swollen, and he tasted blood.

Tyson laughed. "Ellis wasn't the only man in my employ, you know."

Ben sagged as his last forlorn hope died. There really would be no escape if the lunatic holding him wasn't alone.

"They've gone now, of course. I don't need them around to collect money." He snorted derisively. "I can certainly handle you, Ranger."

"As long as I'm hog-tied, I suppose that's true," Ben said with a painful laugh.

Tyson kicked him again. "Quiet, Ranger. I can use the money, but at this point I'd just as soon shoot you as sell you."

Ben bit his groans back and drew his knees up

to his chest. Broke some ribs that time. He couldn't keep baiting the man. Tyson just might kill him. And being alive, even aboard ship, was preferable to death. Alive, there was always the chance that he could make his way back to Dakota. He had to hang on to that notion. It was all he had left.

They slipped into an uneasy silence. Tyson ignored the occasional moan from his prisoner and stared blankly at the dancing, flickering shadows cast by a solitary oil lamp on the warped, wooden walls.

Dakota moved quietly through the alleys and the shadowed streets. Thankfully, most of the people she encountered were too drunk to notice her presence. She had to fight down her instinct to hurry. Following Molly's directions took all of her concentration, and she couldn't afford to get lost. Ben couldn't afford it.

Finally she came to what she knew must be the warehouse. Sitting directly on the docks, it was alone at the end of an unlighted dirt road. The huge building stood out vaguely against the emptiness of the night. Curls of fog wound across the bottom of the structure, and the only sounds were the creaks and groans of a short wooden pier rocking with the lapping water.

Dakota suppressed a shudder. Now she understood what Maria meant when she said that someone had walked on her grave. The icy chill that crawled up her spine paralyzed her for a moment. The task she was about to undertake would mean life or death for Ben. There was no room for mistakes.

She inhaled deeply and felt the damp ocean air go deep into her lungs. Slowly she drew her gun from its holster and mechanically checked the loads. She wouldn't take any chances with Tyson. It was up to

her alone to free Ben, and if that meant having to shoot
Gordon Tyson . . . then that's what it would be.

God, where was the marshal?

Forcing herself to go slowly, she moved down the
dirt road. A bank of clouds drifted across the moon,
shutting her into complete darkness. She stepped carefully, not wanting to alert Tyson by tripping over
something she couldn't see.

At the warehouse Dakota made her way around the
building, pressing herself tight against the wall. No
sounds. Nothing. She continued on toward the back
of the place, peering into the blackened windows as
she went. Boxes blocked most of the panes.

Finally a glimmer of light caught her eye. On her
toes, she moved closer. Through the encrusted filth on
the glass, a faint glow shone in the blackness. Hardly
daring to breathe, she held her gun tight in her fist
as she flattened herself against the building. Carefully
she leaned over just far enough to peek inside.

Tyson. He sat on a crate, his back to the door, in the
circle of light thrown by a single lamp. She craned her
neck to see more. It was no use. She didn't see Ben.

But he *had* to be there. Tyson wouldn't still be at
the warehouse if Ben were gone.

She had no choice. She moved quietly to the big
door at the side of the building. Dakota gradually
eased the wide door open just far enough to slip
through and said a silent prayer of thanks when it
made no sound.

Soundlessly, hardly daring to breathe, she slipped
through the darkness. Hiding as best she could, she
kept moving in closer to the man, going behind first
one crate, then the next. Her mouth dry, heart pounding, Dakota paused to wipe her palms on her pants

legs. The silence in the massive building screamed at her, taunted her.

"Still awake, Ranger? It shouldn't be much longer, now."

Her breath caught in her throat, and she bit down on her lip to keep from crying out in surprise. Tears pricked at Dakota's eyes as her head dropped to her chest. The relief was almost painful. Ben was alive.

She steadied herself and peeked around the edge of her hiding place. Tyson was only a few feet away. A little farther off she could just make out a dark shape on the floor. Swallowing the sharp surge of anger, Dakota moved. Slowly she crept up behind Tyson, the hairs on the back of her neck standing straight up. Then she raised her pistol and brought the barrel down in a wide arc against the back of the man's head.

Without a sound Gordon Tyson slumped over onto the floor.

One glance and Dakota knew the man would be unconscious for quite a while. She hurried to Ben and pulled the concealing hood off. Purple, swollen bruises marked his face, and blood ran down his cheeks from an open cut on his forehead. She touched his split lips gently, and he hissed in pain.

Ben's eyes opened, then quickly shut again. She knew that after the blackness of the hood, even a single lamp must seem too bright. Dakota threw a vicious glare at Tyson. For one rage-filled moment, she wished she'd shot him.

"Can you walk, Ben?" Her voice broke, and she swallowed back the tears she didn't have time for.

"Kota?" His eyes opened again. "How did you—"

"I'll tell you everything later. Right now we've got

to get out of here before he wakes up."

Ben turned his head slowly toward Tyson, and his eyes widened in surprise. Then he remembered Captain Bigelow. While Dakota untied him, he tried to explain.

She listened with only half an ear. As she worked on the ropes that bound him, hot tears choked her throat. The heavy rope had cut into his flesh, leaving raw patches around his wrists. Every time he shifted position, he bit off a groan, trying to hide the pain that she knew must be overwhelming. All she could think about was getting him to safety. To a doctor.

Finally the last of the ropes fell away. Ben cupped her cheek and gave her a soft kiss. "Ow," he mumbled and touched his puffy lips.

"Ben, don't. You're hurt."

"Was worth it," he assured her. "Kota, I've got an idea, but you're gonna have to help me." He pushed himself up but sank down again, sighing. "You'll have to do it yourself." He handed her the ropes, pointed to Tyson, and told her to tie him securely.

Dakota did it, with no questions. When she was finished, she looked up at him, and Ben said, "Find something to gag him with."

She looked around frantically for a moment, then, her eyes brightening, she pulled Tyson's own handkerchief from his pocket. Ben tossed her the hood he'd been wearing only a short time ago, and Dakota pulled it down viciously over Tyson's face.

"Bigelow is expectin' to find an unwilling seaman here tonight." Ben sighed and crossed his arms over his abdomen. "Tyson told me himself that he and Bigelow have never met, so even when the hood comes off, no one will believe Tyson's story."

Suddenly Dakota turned her head, holding up her hand for silence. Then quickly she helped Ben to his feet and almost dragged him behind a number of large crates. Once hidden, she held his weakened body against hers. Cradling him close to her heart, she listened to his slow, shallow breathing.

"Thought Bigelow was coming with us tonight," a voice said.

"It don't matter if he's here or not," another voice answered sharply. "There's the man we was supposed to pick up. I'll leave the money, you pick him up and get back to the ship."

"How come I got to carry 'em all the time?"

"Shit!" Shuffling feet and two men groaning as they lifted something heavy. "All right, let's go."

Dakota held Ben perfectly still for another few minutes in case the men came back. Finally she whispered, "It's all right now. We can go. Do you think you can walk if I help you?"

He groaned. "Yeah. I want out of here."

She stood up and gently pulled him to his feet. He swayed unsteadily and closed his eyes.

"Ben?"

"I'm all right."

"Can you make it? Should I go for help?"

"No." He shook his head and winced. "I'll make it. Let's get goin'."

Dakota took his right arm and laid it across her shoulders. She wrapped her left arm around him but dropped it when he groaned at the contact. "Ben, I have to go for help. I can't do this alone." Tears fell down her cheeks. "For heaven's sake, I can't even hold on to you without hurting you."

He gritted his teeth, then made a visible effort to

straighten up. "No. We can do this. Together." Ben forced a crooked smile. "I just want to get out of this damn place. All right?"

She nodded.

"Kota." He pointed at a box near the lamp. "See that pouch there?"

"Yes."

He chuckled and groaned. "Well, I happen to know there's two thousand dollars in there. It isn't all the money Tyson stole from you. But it *is* something."

Dakota smiled softly, then went to get the pouch. Tucking it inside her shirt, she hurried back to Ben. "Come on. We've got to get you to a doctor."

He moaned again when she touched his side, but this time they kept going.

"Well," Dakota demanded when the doctor left Ben's room. "Will he be all right? How is he feelin'?"

The middle-aged man tucked his nightshirt into his pants and yawned. Getting called out of a sound sleep every night was getting tiresome. He looked down at Dakota and managed a smile at her worried expression. "How is he feeling? Like he's been beat up by experts." He turned to Molly and sighed. "I sure could use a cup of coffee."

"Sure thing, Doc."

"Doctor," Dakota pulled at his sleeve. "How is my husband? Will he be all right?"

"Oh, yes. He'll be fine. Those ribs'll take a few weeks to mend, but he's young and strong."

"What about his head?"

"Hmmm?" He yawned again.

"The blood on his head." For heaven's sakes, where did Molly find this man?

"Oh, that. Just a few stitches. Head like a rock."

She sagged against the wall. Ben would be fine. Everything would be fine.

"He's gonna have a temper like the devil himself for a while, though. The pain he's in right now must seem like the fires of hell." The doctor smiled. "So don't pay too much attention to anything he says. He's sleeping right now. Best thing for him. Lots of rest."

She nodded as he went downstairs to the kitchen for his coffee. Quietly she opened the door of her old room and stepped inside. Sitting down in the armchair beside the bed, she watched with relief as the blankets across Ben's chest moved up and down with his steady, regular breathing.

Dakota rubbed her forehead tiredly. She'd never forget that long, terrifying walk to Molly's. Ben, half-conscious, leaning on her and trying to hide his weakness from her. And then, when he could go no farther, having to leave him there on the boardwalk while she ran the last two blocks to get help. Thank heaven she'd run into the marshal. Timmy'd found him at last, and he was on his way to help.

Between the business tonight and the killings at Kate's place, Dakota was sure that the marshal would be happy to see her and Ben leave for home. Not that he blamed them, but things did have a way of happening around them.

She reached out and laid her hand over Ben's. His fingers moved slightly as he tried, even in his sleep, to hold on to her.

"Dakota?"

"Yes, Ben. I'm here." She knelt beside him, her voice at a whisper. "You're all right. We're at Molly's." Everything's all right now, she thought. The kids are asleep, Doc and the marshal are having coffee with Molly. And Ben is alive.

"You?" His eyelids twitched with his effort to open them.

"I'm fine. It's over. It's all over." Her fingers moved lightly over his forehead, smoothing back a stray lock of hair. "But you're hurt, Ben. You have to rest."

"No. Not yet." His face turned toward her, he opened his eyes. "You're crying."

"No, I'm not," she said, wiping the tears away.

"Thought you said"—he paused and caught his breath again—"I'm gonna be fine."

"You are."

Ben lifted his hand to her face. With agonizing slowness his thumb traced the outline of her jaw. "Then no tears."

She nodded.

"Have to tell you . . ."

"Ben, please go to sleep. The doctor said—"

"Hell with him." He shook his head and groaned softly. "Have to tell you." His gaze met hers, and he licked his cracked lips before continuing. "Love you, Kota. Always did. Always will."

She grabbed his hand and held it tightly. "I love you too." Laying her head down on the mattress beside him, she said, "I was so scared, Ben."

His free hand moved over her hair, smoothing, comforting. "I know. Me, too. Thought I'd never see you again. Wanted to tell you . . ."

"What? That you loved me?"

"No." His eyes closed. "Had to tell you. No divorce." He drew a shaky breath. "Not now. Not ever."

Epilogue

One year later . . .

"WHAT do you think's takin' so damn long?"

Tenn shrugged and looked at the stairs leading to the just-finished upstairs bedrooms.

Ben walked aimlessly around the living room. Stopping at the stove, he poured himself a cup of coffee, took one drink, then set the cup down on the table. He didn't want the damn coffee. He just wanted to know what was going on. For godsake, did they have to keep everything a secret? He looked up sharply as hurried footsteps moved across the upstairs floor. A door opened and shut again. More steps. He and his brother-in-law stared at each other.

Laura hurried down the stairs and into her parlor. She passed both men as if they didn't exist. Moments later she reappeared carrying a white sheet. Mumbling to herself, the little blond woman stepped toward the stairs again.

Ben grabbed her arm. "Slow down, Laura."

She pulled his hand free. "Not now, Ben. There's no time."

Tenn grabbed her other arm. "Laura, we're goin' crazy down here. Tell us *somethin'*!"

Smiling, she looked up at her husband. "Everything's going well. Just be patient, for heaven's sake. These things take time." She nodded at Jess, sitting in the corner calmly smoking his pipe. "Why don't you relax, like Jess?"

"Huh!" Tenn snorted and glared at the foreman. "He ain't relaxed! He's lit that blasted pipe at least twenty times now."

Jess ignored him.

"Just how much time can it take!" Ben roared. "It's been hours!"

"Shh." Laura laid her hand on his chest. "Keep quiet. You don't want her to hear you, do you?"

"Why the hell not?" He tilted his head back and yelled at the ceiling, "Hurry up, Dakota! I can't take much more of this!"

"That's tellin' her." Tenn nodded encouragement.

"It won't help," Laura assured them both.

"How come there's no noise, Laura?" Tenn whispered his question. "Shouldn't she be yellin' and howlin' and such?"

She frowned at him. "For heaven's sake, Tennessee. We're not talking about a dog here. This is your own sister."

"Hell, I know that." He rubbed his hand across his stubbled jaw. "But Ben's right. It's takin' too damn long."

Laura shook her head. "Might as well get used to it." She patted her bulging stomach. "Before long you'll be waiting again."

He paled at the thought. "I don't know if I can go through this again."

"*You!*" Ben shoved his friend. "What do you mean, you? This is *my* wife. *My* baby."

"Well, yeah," Tenn conceded, "but it's my sister, you know."

Mumbling something unintelligible, Laura left the two of them to their arguing and hurried upstairs.

As soon as she was gone, the two men looked at each other and started pacing again. Occasionally one or the other of them stopped at the foot of the stairs and looked up, hoping to see *something*.

"You two simmer down," Jess advised quietly. "Runnin' all over the damn house won't hurry things up any."

"I don't know why I can't be up there." Ben looked at the older man. "Maybe I could help."

Jess shook his head. "You'd be in their way. Women never seem to want a man around when they're doin' these things. 'Sides, Doc wouldn't let you. I already asked."

Tenn's eyebrows shot up.

"Don't look so surprised, boy. I love her, too."

"We should've stayed in town, at our house," Ben said. "But no, Dakota had to be here at the ranch to have the baby."

"Hell, you'll be livin' *here*, soon as the damn town council gets around to hirin' a new sheriff."

"That's right." Tenn nodded at Jess. "The baby *should* be born here. *I* just can't understand why Laura wants to go into her pa's house to have ours!"

"No sense tryin' to understand." Ben sighed and flopped down onto a chair. A year together and Dakota still confounded him faster than anybody he ever met. However, he rubbed his tired eyes and silently acknowledged that he wouldn't change a thing.

Except maybe how long it took to have a baby!

A soft plaintive cry sounded from upstairs. Ben froze. "Did you hear that?" he whispered.

Tenn nodded.

The three of them moved to the foot of the stairs. A door opened, and Maria appeared, a wide smile on her face. Signaling to all of them, she said, "Come. Come."

Ben ran up the stairs, Tenn and Jess only a step behind him. A door at the far end of the hall stood open, and Ben started for it hesitantly. He turned and looked over his shoulder at Maria. "Dakota's all right, isn't she?"

"Sí. She did well." The older woman stepped past him and pushed the door wider. "No trouble at all."

Ben swallowed nervously. Tenn slapped him on the back. "Well, come on! This is what we've been waitin' for!"

Nodding, Ben walked into the room. His gaze went immediately to Dakota, propped up against a bank of pillows. Her hair, plaited neatly, hung over the shoulder of her plain, white cotton nightdress. Her eyelids drooped with weariness, but she smiled at him. Like a fool, he grinned back at her.

"Well, boy!" Doc Burns's gruff voice shattered the quiet. "Don't you want to get a look at your son?"

Ben could hardly get his voice to work. "A son?"

Laura came up to him and laid a blanket-wrapped bundle in his arms. As she pulled back the edge of the lacy white covering, father and son stared at each other.

Carefully Ben touched his finger to the baby's cheek and grinned when his son pulled the finger into his mouth. Looking up and laughing, Ben said, "I think he's hungry!"

Jess peeked over the younger man's shoulder at the blond-haired, blue-eyed infant, then smiled at Dakota. "You did well, Kota. He's a handsome boy."

Maria pushed Ben toward the bed, then started shooing everyone else from the room. "The baby must eat, and so must we."

"We're goin', Maria. We're goin'." Tenn looked over his shoulder at his sister. "Be back in a while. Want a good look at my nephew!"

Dakota smiled, then grinned when she heard her older brother whisper to his wife, "Ain't he a mite puny?"

"Is he?" Ben asked worriedly.

"No!" Dakota countered.

His son stirred in his blankets. Somehow Ben managed to keep from squeezing the baby in response. His jaw locked tight, a wave of raw, overpowering love filled him. The wonder of it. Because he and Dakota loved, a whole new person existed.

The baby shifted again and cried softly. Ben's body tensed. He'd done something wrong. He knew it.

"What did I do?" he whispered anxiously.

"Nothing." Dakota held out her arms. "He's hungry. Like you said."

Relieved, he handed their son to his mother and asked again, "Are you sure he's not too small?"

"I'm sure." She smiled as she bared her breast and held her son's head against it. "He'll grow."

Ben sat down beside them and watched his son hungrily nuzzle at his mother. "Eatin' like that, I expect you're right." Gently he cupped the back of the infant's head, then ran one finger lightly over his wife's swollen breast. He couldn't understand how he'd gotten so lucky.

His breath shook as he watched the baby's ferocious suckling. Ben looked again at the soft, tender expression on his wife's face and knew that without them, his life would mean nothing. The sudden dampness in his eyes surprised him.

He leaned over and kissed her. "Got a name for him yet?"

She nodded and looked up at him. "I was thinkin' about Jack."

"Jack?" He cocked his head and thought about it for a moment. "Jack Cable." He broke into a wide grin. "Sounds good. Jack number one will be pleased."

Dakota yawned.

"Are you sure you're all right?"

"Yes. Doc says I was made for havin' babies. I guess I'm just tired." She kissed Jack before she shifted him to her other breast. "I've been thinking, Ben. Next time I think we should have a girl."

"Nope."

"Why not?"

Ben changed positions, stretching out on the bed alongside his family. His arm around Dakota's shoulders, he kissed the top of her head and stifled a yawn. He was beginning to think that waiting for a baby was as hard as having one. "Because . . . I want at least five more big, strong sons first."

"What?" She turned her head to stare at him.

"Yes, ma'am. Before we have a daughter as pretty as her mother . . . I want to make sure I'll have plenty of help to keep the men away!"